'With all the twists of a double helix, *The Killing Gene* is a
voking as it is action-packed. Davey's writing is punchy, yet lyrical,
delving deep into the distant past of humankind, questioning what
makes Homo sapiens unique and what the future might hold for
the one race on earth that has inherited the killing gene.'

Matthew Harffy, author of *The Bernicia Chronicles* series

'Gripping, shocking and thought-provoking: a dispatch from the front
line where ancient history meets modern nightmares. E.M. Davey has
been to some of the wildest places on Earth, and it shows. This will
keep its hooks in you long past the final page.'

Tom Harper, author of *The Lost Temple*

'In an epic adventure stretching from the jungles of the Congo to
the valleys of Tajikistan and beyond, *The Killing Gene* blends
exceptional research and a keen observation of human nature to create
a captivating and intelligent adventure novel. Featuring a tenacious
hero who must unravel a menacing conspiracy if he is to reveal the
truth to the world, this is another stunning thriller from E. M. Davey.'

**Rob Jones, author of the international
bestselling *Joe Hawke* series**

D1079333

Also published by the author

Foretold by Thunder

The Napoleon Complex

THE
KILLING
GENE

E.M. DAVEY

DUCKWORTH

This edition first published in the United Kingdom by
Duckworth in 2019

Duckworth, an imprint of Prelude Books ltd
1 Golden Court, Richmond
TW9 1EU United Kingdom
www.preludebooks.co.uk

For bulk and special sales please contact
info@preludebooks.co.uk

Text design and typesetting by Danny Lyle - DanJLyle@gmail.com

Printed and bound in Great Britain by Clays

9780715652978

For my wonderful wife Anna

And to the memory of my grandparents

HISTORICAL NOTE

All Ice Age sculptures mentioned are exactly as described. Articles from *The Daily Telegraph, Agence France-Presse, Daily Mail* and *The New York Times* are reproduced faithfully. The scientific studies cited are genuine and all psychological research and evidence referred to is based on real experiments. Excerpts from the Old Testament, *The Epic of Gilgamesh* and Hesiod's *Theogony* are of course authentic, too.

PART ONE

Yet it might be that some very ancient language had altered little, whilst others had altered much, and given rise to many new languages and dialects.

Charles Darwin, *On the Origin of Species*

PART ONE

PROLOGUE

Mother and daughter lay motionless, furled around each other like a fox with her cub. The infant was naked, the woman wore a loincloth; a spear skewered them together. This was a murder scene, five thousand years old. The parent had gripped the spear's haft as it entered her child's potbelly, and where it exited her back it had birthed petals of ashen flesh, a lifeless rose on deadened skin.

The clearing was like a Viking longhouse, tree-trunks for columns and festooned with lianas, tapestries of the rainforest. Deep Congo, ancient jungle; one hundred tree species per hectare. To biologists, the zenith of all creation. A single note permeated the forest, a synergy of insect life just off B minor: a *suspension* of sound, given texture and depth by the hundred thousand creatures that created it.

Dr Sakiko Tsuda of the University of Bristol crouched over the pit. She'd have bad dreams that night, full of twisted bodies and frozen sneers. Tsuda was a linguist, not an archaeologist – she hadn't been on a dig for years. But she remembered from her university days how much she hated peat excavation, so often more autopsy than archaeology.

She had isolated the grave with steel panels, hermetically sealing it from the peatbog, and pumped out water until soil took to the air at the gentlest touch. Then came the brushing, the collecting, the revealing. A race before rot set in after five millennia of stasis.

Tsuda estimated the adult's standing height at 120 centimetres: these were Forest People, Pygmies, to use the nomenclature of Herodotus.

Such was the state of preservation that fingernails and eyelashes were intact, and Tsuda tried not to look at the mother's receding gums in their death snarl. A ribbon of gut dangled from the woman's back, still malleable and trembling in the heat. Tsuda was grateful for the lack of smell – that peat had going for it. The spear had snapped with the violence of the thrust, its triangle of flint removed in prehistory for re-use by the killers.

And it had to be killers plural.

Back in Bristol her husband would be collecting Aiko from primary school, and looking at the child beneath her feet a tremor went through Tsuda's lower lip. The two mothers were strikingly different expressions of the female *Homo sapiens*; yet we are all African under the skin, she reflected, with a shared ancestor not four thousand generations back. So quickly does the mischief of genetic drift do its work. And what a price we pay. Her gaze had returned to the pit. The hum of the rainforest oscillated before pulsing with new energy, momentarily piercing – as though power cells had been renewed somewhere deep below. It singed the ear, cleaved the humid air.

Four Congolese emerged from the foliage. Each of them carried an assault rifle.

"Who are you?" Tsuda stood up. *"Où est Julien?"*

"We are your replacement guides," the tallest replied in accented English.

"Replacements? What do you mean, replacements?"

"We're taking over." The second was a small man whose skin gleamed with sweat like little diamonds on the skin. "Come with us."

They walked for twenty minutes, the point man slashing through the foliage with his machete. A giant spider's web was suspended between two trees, gossamer and ethereal, in its centre an arachnid of obsidian. Its distended abdomen was graced with a snowflake of toxic yellow markings, poisonous as hell. Tsuda glanced at the Casio watch Tomas had given her while they were students.

The sun became visible through the canopy.

"We're heading north." Fear was audible in Tsuda's voice for the first time. "The camp's that way. You're taking us in the wrong direction…"

The guide turned. He was smirking now, and as all five of them stood there the rainforest seemed to ratchet up a few more decibels.

1

When Professor Randolph Harkness of the University of Bristol entered, all chattering subsided. At fifty he had achieved a certain grandeur, tall and broad with greying black hair. The stubble lent him a wolfish aspect, though it was undoubtedly a handsome face. He wore faded green corduroys and a twenty-year-old Harris tweed jacket; the shoes were old friends, too, a blatant violation of the 'Don't wear brown in town' rule. In the lined brow, in the reluctance of his movements, there was also a sadness, a gravity that drew the attention of the freshers arrayed about the lecture room.

> *prehistorian*
> *1. A student of human history in the period before recorded events, known mainly through archaeological discoveries, study, research etc.*

"Consider this." Harkness was well-spoken, with a rich timbre to his voice that recalled excellent brandy. "Recorded history is five thousand years long. Just five millennia separate us from the first writing and the earliest civilisations. Almost everything you learned of our past at school happened in those five thousand years. And yet!"

He clicked his fingers, the report echoing down the handsome oak-panelled room.

"And yet," he continued, "our species achieved modern levels of intelligence by about 70,000 BC. Reasoning and language. Problem-solving, symbolic thinking. All of it was in place. That leaves" – and here he slowed for impact – "*more than 65,000 years in which people every bit as bright as you or I wandered the earth and left barely a trace.*"

Absolute silence.

"What the devil were we doing all that time?" he cried. "It's a para-dox, the single most important question of our human story. Our job is to peer back into that great darkness."

Downstairs an urgent call was being received from Congo-Brazzaville.

"We are talking about Deep Time, ladies and gentlemen. You see, the Stone Age was *unimaginably vast.*" Harkness's upturned palms conjured an enormity of time and space. "The two most famous sets of cave paintings in France – Lascaux and Chauvet – share an identical aesthetic. And yet they were created *ten thousand years apart.* Forget about the Renaissance to the Impressionists, that takes us from the pyramids to the Mars Rover *and back.* But those elegant images of rein-deer and bison hardly changed a bit. Now, any artists here?"

A smattering of hands.

"Well, the fact that those cave-dwellers created beauty should tell you lot something, and it's this. The creatures living in those caves were *us.* They thought like us, loved like us. They were afraid of illness, too. They had big dreams for the future. They experienced an internal life every bit as meaningful as the person who sat next to you on the bus this morning. So I ask you again. *What were we doing all that time?*"

A rugby player's mouth had parted slightly and a Welsh girl twist-ed in her seat. They had never thought about this before, and it was making them uncomfortable. In Harkness's left hand – he wore only a signet ring – was a jawbone.

"Just the fourteen thousand years old." He grinned. "It belonged to a child of about ten – so a little nipper."

A scattering of chuckles.

"It's from Gough's Cave, up in Somerset. See the score marks? They're from de-fleshing."

His students absorbed the implications of this.

Looking at the jawbone, Harkness was reminded suddenly of the checkout girl in Boots earlier. Her forearms were badly scarified; things had happened in her life. Harkness had wanted to say something, but of course that would have made her feel worse.

"Oh, there was lots of bad behaviour in prehistory, I assure you," he said. "Murder, tribal warfare… and the genetic evidence points to occasional interbreeding between *Homo sapiens* and the Neanderthals. I'd say it's reasonably certain we weren't giving one another flowers and holding hands."

The millennials looked aghast.

"But it wasn't all barbarity. An elderly *Homo erectus* skeleton with no teeth has been found at Dmanisi in Georgia. It seems his family must have chewed his food for him."

A little sigh went through the room now, a flush of warmth.

"Like us," he concluded, "in the main our prehistoric ancestors were *good*. Because they must have been."

His deputy Tony Marks peered around the door. "Sorry to interrupt, but we've got an emergency."

As Harkness departed every mouth in the room was gaping.

Waiting outside his office was the vice chancellor, David Motion. Harkness let them into the comfortable little room, book-lined and cluttered with various oddments he'd found on his journeys through the strata. Roundhead musket-ball and flint arrowheads, fossilised fingertip with petrified tooth.

"Now, what the hell's going on?" said Harkness.

"It's Sakiko," said Marks.

A lurch of concern. He was fond of Sakiko, admired her spirit.

"What about her?"

"Nobody's got a sodding clue where she's gone."

2

"We last heard from her on Friday," began his deputy.

Tony Marks was a solid Yorkshireman in his forties who had once served in the army. The shorts, Tom Selleck moustache and leather Stetson hat worn as a tribute to a Texan side of the family were permanent fixtures. He looked like a man who enjoys a barbecue.

Harkness frowned. "That's barely seventy-two hours ago – the mobile network's down or something. They're in the Congo, Tony, it's hardly like phoning home from Devon."

But perhaps he could forgive the drama, Harkness reflected. Not everybody had been to the places he had.

"I've just spoken to her fixer," said Marks. "He lives a few days' drive from her camp and was due to deliver new supplies this morning. Nobody there. Bags and stuff still in the tents. The guides are missing, too."

David Motion was diminutive with a sharp, compressed face, like a hatchling bird of prey. Now his eyes darted from speaker to speaker.

"Where were they, exactly?"

"A place called Itanga," said Marks. "Middle of pisspot nowhere."

"To give you an idea of the remoteness," Harkness cut in, "it's the biggest peatbog in the world – the size of Belgium – and it was only discovered in 2014."

"The fixer says things move slowly out there," said Marks. "He reckons a donation would get a search party out faster."

Motion sighed. "Donation? Search party? Oh dear."

"I'd better call her husband," said Harkness.

"What was she doing out there?" asked Motion.

"Looking for traces of the Universal Language," replied Harkness.

"Universal Language? There's no such thing."

"Not now," said Harkness. "Of course not."

"So what are you on about?" asked Motion.

"Language as we know it developed in about 70,000 BC," said Harkness. "Something clicked in our brains – genetic, most likely – and overnight we became mentally modern. We'd been penned in Africa until that point by bigger and stronger hominids. But almost instantly the greatest migration in history got under way."

Harkness traced a line in the air, evoking this epic journey by lost pioneers.

"When those first explorers set foot in the Middle East, they would all have spoken the same language," he said. "The ancestral tongue of every language on earth. Millennia later, it's fractured and mutated into languages completely unlike each other. But some linguists think *traces* of the original mother tongue can still be found, in every language on earth."

"Call me a cynical old Yorkshireman, but I don't buy it," said Marks. "Language evolves too fast. Think about the English of Chaucer – six centuries old and already it's halfway to foreign. Spanish evolved from Latin in two millennia."

"Anyway, Sakiko's a believer," said Harkness. "Now, the Forest People of Central Africa are among the most isolated populations on earth. That means their culture's been especially well-preserved from prehistoric times. And the genetics suggest they are direct descendants of that first sweep down through Africa. We see in the Forest People a faint echo of the hunter-gatherer culture of the earliest humans."

"Then they are a window on to our most ancient past," said the vice chancellor with surprising passion.

"You need to be a bit careful about straying into stereotype with all the 'lost in history' stuff," said Harkness. "Were we to have the privilege of meeting a few, we'd no doubt find that on a personal level they express modernity every bit as much as a Wall Street banker or a tech whizz kid in Seoul. But what is undeniable is that they are living a lifestyle that dominated 135,000 years of our evolution. If traces of the universal tongue can be detected, they'll be in words used by the Forest People."

"Sakiko was out there looking for those traces," said Marks.

This had been quite an undertaking. In three years of field-work Tsuda had encountered the Kola tribe of Gabon, the Gyele of Cameroon, the Ugandan Batwa, Burundi's Twa population, plus the Mbuti and Mongo Cwa in the Democratic Republic of Congo. And finally, the Ba Aka of Congo-Brazzaville.

"Almost all the Forest People tribes speak their own language," said Harkness. "Many of them are still undocumented, so Sakiko was compiling basic dictionaries. Her idea was to compare the word lists she recorded and look for the vocabulary all Forest People tribes have in common. We can infer that these words existed in the lost ancestral tongue spoken by Forest People far off in prehistory – before their populations became fragmented, retreating into the deepest pockets of jungle. Some of those words may have been present in the Universal Language."

"All very interesting, but I'm pulling the plug," said Motion. "You must have been mad to sign the risk assessment."

"Almost anywhere can be visited safely enough with a bit of common sense," said Harkness. "When I was in—"

"Look, I really don't have time for any of your old war stories today," cut in Motion. "Call me when you hear something."

He walked out and slammed the door.

"Such generosity of spirit," said Harkness.

Marks snorted. "Well, what do you expect from a bastard economist?"

3

As Ross McCartney slapped his palm on to the keyboard his computer emitted an angry beep and the screen filled with letters and symbols, like breeding bacteria.

"Are you OK there?" Fiona Leach happened to be passing.

"I'm fine," stuttered McCartney.

He was definitely not fine.

As his colleague clicked away across the office McCartney despaired. He could no more analyse Estonia's tank defences than dance the *Rose Adagio*.

McCartney would have liked to have been a tree surgeon. Or in the army – at least that would have got him out and about. But to please his father he'd done a degree in business studies and somehow washed up at Barker and Fitch's, risk analysts of Holborn. This was a place where *Economist* articles were rewritten by people not bright enough to work for *The Economist* for clients too lazy to read it, and there was nowhere McCartney would not prefer to be. Central Mogadishu, doing a maths A Level; bring it on. He urgently needed a cigarette.

Slouched in a chair nearby was his manager, the misnamed Damien Caring. The previous day, Caring had commanded McCartney to prepare a report on how long the Baltic States could resist a determined Russian offensive and how this would affect the FTSE 100. But the sources were so conflicting he had not a hope of resolving them. He could actually *feel* his brain working at the limits of its cognition, bolts shaking and rivets fracturing under the strain. Staying late the previous evening had got him got nowhere and a Vesuvian eruption from his boss was overdue.

Six months back, McCartney would have cheerily diagnosed Caring's deficiencies as being in the bedroom department and ignored his fulminations. That was before his own medical problems, however. And now this job threatened to send him surging over the edge, like a fistful of potassium added to simmering water.

A bystander would not have suspected McCartney's ill-health. At twenty-four and six foot three, his chest and shoulders were those of an Olympian decathlete. Ginger-haired and strong-jawed, he had been compared to a better-looking, naughtier version of the young Prince Harry. But he was actually *worse* than the royal had once been at getting away with things.

"McCartney? Over here, please."

Caring, shrivelled, pockmarked and sour, resembled a lemon with a mouth cut into it. "My report on our Baltic allies?"

"Coming on," he stuttered.

"Really?"

"Well…" McCartney sighed. "No. No, it's not."

Caring's eyes worked over the younger man's face curiously.

"Let me tell you something about the way we work here," he said softly.

"What's that?"

"When a senior manager tells you to do something…"

"Yes?"

"*You fucking well do it!*"

To McCartney's astonishment, by late that afternoon he had a report. The vaunting ambitions of the Russian president had barely been factored in; neither had British commitments to the Middle East, where the push for all-out war on the Islamists who'd regrouped after the collapse of the Islamic State was building. But it was something. Maybe he could make it as a risk analyst after all. Maybe he could prosper!

Caring summoned him, lips riding up his gums in a dirty smile. "Guess what?"

"What?"

He deleted the report. "There is no client. I really don't care about Estonian military preparedness, still less the stock market. I just wanted to see you do some work for a change."

The fury soared up through McCartney, flooding his feet and hands with a fierce energy that seemed to fizz and pop in his fingers like champagne bubbles. It was time Caring heard some home truths.

"Has anyone ever told you what a horrid, snivelling little man you are?" asked McCartney reasonably.

Caring froze in his seat; the office had turned horribly quiet.

Someone dropped a stapler.

"Thought not," said McCartney.

"Has anyone ever told you that you just talked your way out of a job?" Caring spluttered. "Thought not."

"Well luckily," replied McCartney, "it just so happens I'm in a rock band. And this very morning we were offered a three-album deal with a six-figure advance. So I don't actually need to be here at all."

There was not so much a gasp as a *wobble* amongst the assembled, like panes of glass blown concave in a gale. All were aware they were witnessing an unlikely besting of tyranny by hope.

"So you can take your job and stick it right up your arse," he concluded gustily.

Caring was choking. This insolence had brought on some sort of splenetic attack, and all he could do was point at the door. The young rocker with the world at his feet marched from the room, head held high and toes flicking out before him as though he was on parade at Buckingham Palace. Three dozen gobsmacked risk analysts watched him go.

"Wow," said Fiona Leach.

There was just one problem with the record-deal story. It was a big lie. Now for Moorfields Eye Hospital: Ross McCartney's day was about to get considerably worse.

*

"I want you to open your eyes very wide," said Dr Rosenberg, a small Ohioan with darting hands and a neat brown beard. "Once your pupils are fully dilated I'll check out what's been going on."

A drop of liquid was dispensed into each pupil and McCartney's world went orange.

"Your eyesight will be blurry for the next few hours," said the doctor.

McCartney's eyesight had been blurry for the last six months, one of numerous symptoms he'd nobly ignored. Ignored the floaters; ignored the growing pressure in his temples; ignored the dark patches that sometimes bothered his peripheral vision. When it came to medical symptoms, McCartney subscribed to the 'Ignore them and hope you don't die' school of thought. But last week he'd awoken to see a ribbon of blood in his left eye that scrolled away when he looked at it. McCartney's GP noted his diabetes and a Moorfields referral was made; that this was marked *urgent* was not reassuring.

Now Dr Rosenberg shone torchlight into McCartney's pupils that burst into crystalline shards of orange inside his head, all very beautiful. The doctor's mouth opened and closed without verdict, but he noticeably stiffened. A first premonition of bad news.

"Just keep still while I finish the examination."

McCartney had the sense of some yawning pit opening beneath him. Rosenberg switched off his torch and sat down.

"I know what you want me to tell you," he said at last. "You want me to promise that you won't go blind."

Blind? *Blind?*

"I'm afraid I – I can't make that promise." Rosenberg let the apocalyptic ramifications of this statement sink in before continuing. "You have diabetic retinopathy, Ross. Your blood sugar levels are stratospheric. I'm afraid the blood vessels in the retina are already badly damaged. You must have known diabetes can cause blindness?"

"Well, yes, I suppose. I kind of… I just never…"

I never thought it could happen to me.

Rosenberg sighed. "It's a silent disease at first – by the time symptoms present, the damage is always severe. You really can't wait on it."

"Well, that's a goddamn pointless thing to tell me now, isn't it?" McCartney shouted. "Just tell me, how bad?"

"We're looking at Stage Three."

"Of how many stages?"

"Three." Rosenberg lowered his head and folded his hands, an abbot pardoning McCartney for his sins. "I'm afraid it's likely you'll lose your sight completely, Ross."

The walls had darkened. He wanted to cry. The consultation room was spinning. This was happening to someone else.

"We'll start treatment tomorrow," the doctor was saying. "So take the day off work. We'll use lasers to burn away the new blood vessels, as many of those suckers as we can. In two months you'll come back for another treatment. But – you have to know this, Ross – long term, we're looking at a downward slide. You must enjoy your eyesight while you can."

McCartney bent his fingers back to forestall tears. This was the worst thing that had ever happened to him.

"Why didn't you use your insulin?" Rosenberg was pleading.

"Stopped taking it at university," he replied thickly. "It was a party lifestyle. I missed a few injections and nothing happened. So I just – did away with them altogether."

"But it's just so..." There was despair in the doctor's voice. "So reckless."

Reckless.

McCartney's life, distilled into a single word.

He staggered from the consultation room, lurched through the hospital, somehow found his way out on to the street. Here all the sunshine turned into fractals of orange in his eyes, and as he broke into a run the tears began to fall at last.

4

As Dr Anita Johansen sprinted through the backstreets of Hackney a melange of East London flickered past. Tower blocks and Turkish mini-markets; hipsters and fried chicken shops. Her bag was heavy with books.

> philologist
>> 1. Someone who studies literary texts and written records, establishes their authenticity and their original form, and determines their meaning.

Abruptly the urban landscape changed. Now there were semi-detached houses and tree-lined streets, a preponderance of people carriers. Almost everyone was Hasidic Jewish. The women wore wigs and long black dresses and the men cylindrical *shtreimel* hats, wrapped in transparent plastic against the spitting rain. Something in her thigh gave out with a silent twang and still she loped along, gasping with every second step.

The surveillance had begun three months ago in Edinburgh, where Johansen lectured at the university. An insomniac, she'd gone for a late night stroll – to find a woman photographing her house. *Admiring the architecture* was the line. There were problems with their radio, too, an intermittent interference that had the infuriating habit of occurring whenever a long-sought remedy was divulged on *Gardeners' Question Time.*

"Electromagnetic fields?" Her husband Marcus frowned. "I think you should cut out the pot, darling. I'm worried about you."

Brighton-born, half-Jamaican and forty-five years old, Johansen wore her dreadlocks in a ponytail and had the fine-boned features of a ballerina. "Just because you're paranoid, doesn't mean they aren't out to get you."

She was paranoid. But they were definitely out to get her.

It occurred to Johansen that perhaps MI5 were attempting to infiltrate her local branch of the left-wing pressure group Momentum. A friend in Greenpeace had once dated an undercover officer in the Metropolitan Police for three years.

Next it was a break-in.

They didn't take her jewellery – nor the car keys, nor Marcus's power tools. And the old television wouldn't have fetched 50p at Cash Converters. Johansen put nothing past junkies, but she did assume they knew their business. No, the television was exactly the thing a sloppy MI5 officer would steal if simulating a break-in for acquisitive ends with another purpose entirely. And she was certain someone had touched her papers. Johansen only smoked weed once or twice a month, but she packed it in anyway. Nothing happened for a while, and she began wondering if it had been a psychosis after all. Marcus relaxed.

Then she found the tracker.

The left handlebar of her bicycle had come loose and she removed it to find a pellet of circuitry sealed inside. Johansen decided then and there to vanish. Their cleaner was visiting family in Budapest, so she bought a tin of shortbread as a gift for her parents and superglued the tracker beneath the plastic tray. When the cleaner departed, so did Johansen. She left a note for her husband explaining that she was going on the run and for the safety of them both leaving no forwarding address. She added that she loved him very dearly, which she did.

Johansen caught a train to King's Cross and a taxi to East London. She'd read enough Edward Snowden revelations to know that she could be tracked by wireless networks without logging on and eavesdropped on through television satellite boxes. So she was heading somewhere that had none of these things. But when she alighted in Hackney, it was to see *the late night photographer on the other side of the road*.

At least, it might have been her. A double-decker screened them and Johansen made a dash for it.

That was how one of Britain's leading philologists came to be fleeing through Stamford Hill with nothing but books and the clothes on her back. Then Johansen reached the River Lea and knew she was at journey's end.

Behind her was a line of grim metropolis, houses with cranes dangling over this one-time artery of commerce. But on the opposite bank marshland and fields ran away to the east, and there were cows, actual cows! It was like peering over a city boundary into an idyll of the English countryside, from Lowry to Constable in a bound. The canal boats were festooned with flowers and a swan glided past. She saw a *Sowerby Bridge*, a *Saucy Susan* – and finally, the *Tickety Boo*.

The cabin door was opened by a woman of sixty with feathery grey hair. "Anita! What are you doing here? Is it Marcus?"

"I'll tell you all about it," she said. "Can I come in?"

Later that day, after she'd recovered from the run and submitted to the fussing of her friend, Johansen unpacked her books.

Then she continued with her work.

5

Quite often in life, what *you don't want to be doing* is what you *should be doing*, reflected Randolph Harkness. So he called Tomas Nowak to tell him his wife had gone missing. As the phone rang Harkness gazed around the courtyard of his department, a handsome lodge redolent of a Tudor stately home. Tony Marks was loading a ground-scanning device into his van and he gave Harkness the thumbs up with one of those 'be strong' smiles. This was a good place; these were decent people.

"How may I be of assistance?"

Tall and pale, Tomas was fortunate to have bagged a stunner like Sakiko. But that spoke volumes about both of them. Harkness felt a huge reluctance at what he was about to do.

"It's Randolph Harkness," he began. "We met at Sakiko's book launch. When did you last hear from her?"

"Sunday, Saturday… it would be Friday morning."

Harkness closed his eyes. "Then I've bad news, I'm afraid."

"Oh?" Suspicion now, as if Harkness was trying to sell PPI claims. As if nothing bad could happen to a wife who was adventurous and sensual, or to Saturday mornings in the park with Aiko. These were the lives Harkness was about to dynamite.

"She's gone missing," he said. "Their camp's been abandoned. The authorities are trying to organise a search party, I gather."

Marks had alerted the Foreign Office and the centuries-honed consular machine was swinging into action. This was an institution of which Harkness had experience, and Nowak asked whether he would be the first point of contact.

"You've been to those kind of places, haven't you?" he said. "You understand how these things work…"

You don't know the half of it, thought Harkness.

"Certainly," he said.

Harkness got through to the Foreign Office's manager for the region. Aled Wilson was based in Kinshasa, capital of the neighbouring Democratic Republic of Congo. Straight away Harkness knew he was dealing with someone calm and capable.

"We only have a consulate in Congo-B," said Wilson. "But there's a flight leaving for Brazzaville in half an hour – I'll be on it. When I arrive I'll knock some heads together."

"Why fly?" asked Harkness. "I thought Brazzaville and Kinshasa were on opposite banks of the River Congo…"

"Yes, it's silly really," said Wilson. "But it's such a faff catching the boat what with all the bribes and such that we find it easier to hitch a lift with Air France. The Paris flight services both Congos."

A little foretaste of what lay ahead.

*

Normally, Harkness walked the two miles back to his flat. He was naturally fit, still played squash and had once been a middle-distance runner at county level. But today he just wanted to be home, so he caught the bus. Two passengers were speaking Hindi: a language fairly closely related to English, weirdly. Parts of Bristol were starting to rival London in the multiculturalism stakes nowadays. Personally, Harkness felt there was a poetry to it. That band of people who'd spread across the planet after the exodus from Africa to morph into Basques and Bolivians and Vietnamese were coming back together. It was like the reforming of a long-lost family.

"We're a multicultural society nowadays, so you might as well embrace it," he'd told a friend over a pint of bitter the previous week.

Harkness checked his smartphone. No messages, no missed calls – but on a whim he Googled Sakiko's name. The first hit was her bio on the university website, the second her Facebook profile. One of Harkness's phalanx of godchildren had set him up on the website in an attempt to bring him into the last decade.

On Thursday evening Sakiko had posted a single sentence.

When you've looked for something all your life… only to find it and wonder if you should carry on.

Harkness frowned. A little tremor of misgiving went through him. His heart pounded slow and heavy beats, like the blows of a sledgehammer.

"Sakiko…" he whispered. "What did you find?"

He composed an email to Aled Wilson.

I'm probably being daft, but in case it's of any relevance…

Harkness's finger hovered over send. Strange, this reluctance. Was he afraid of making an idiot of himself? On balance he didn't think that was it. What then? Some little intuition? Maybe best not to, he concluded. He didn't want Wilson marking him down as a conspiracy nut. Instead, he emailed the link to Marks – no such reluctance this time, he noted. But he'd accidentally opened his junk email.

A second stab of adrenaline.

Amid the adverts for penis extensions and offers of marriage from the Philippines were two emails from Sakiko. They had been sent from her personal account – peculiar in itself – and the first was already a week old.

Dear Randolph,

Unexpected turn of events here. I don't want to say more now, but I'm considering a small excavation (peat). OK to have pumps, panels etc flown from University of Cape Town? $549 USD incl cargo costs. Nearest I can find! Please bear with.

Don't want to say more? Why the hell not? And why use a personal email account? A phrase came to him then, from a different life and a different world order.

Not on these channels, Harkness.

Sakiko's second email was terse.

> *No reply re: excavation so I've gone ahead and put it on credit card. Randolph, I think I'm onto something.*

Ding!

The bell dragged Harkness back into his immediate environment. His flat was a period property in Clifton, Bristol's smartest neighbourhood. It had a bay window and the mortgage was paid off. With no children and through reasonable caution, he'd also amassed £30,000 in various savings accounts – but he gave considerable sums to charity and sponsored a child in Belize whom he'd *actually visited*. Harkness was greeted by his basset hound Percy, circling his legs and yelping for food.

A weighty envelope was on his doorstep, postmarked Brazzaville. With a final lurch of foreboding he tore it open. A ream of paper slid out.

> *Here are my word lists, for safe-keeping.*

> *S*

The research ran to hundreds of pages: previously undocumented languages Sakiko had compiled under great hardship.

Why had he been sent this?

Why not by email?

On impulse, Harkness reopened Facebook. Instant confusion. And as the implications sank in, fear at last: real fear. Her post had been deleted.

6

The Royal Automobile Club of Pall Mall is *not* to be confused with the breakdown and rescue service. You don't have to be proposed and seconded by two existing members to join the RAC. Nor is there a fourteen-month waiting list before your application is considered; nor must you go before a committee to determine if you are the *right sort*. Not as brassy as the Groucho nor as stuffy as the Garrick, its clubhouse in the West End is one of the finest buildings of the Edwardian age, built in the Beaux Arts style by the architect of the Ritz. Deep within this stronghold of luxury, two men were taking their clothes off.

"Tepidarium first?" Eric Jasper disrobed from an overcoat that would have looked *passé* when the club was founded.

A twig-like man in his early seventies with a fuzzy white beard, his bright blue gaze glittered like snow in a face that seemed permanently chafed pink by cold weather. Jasper sat on the board of Holyhead Marine, the British naval manufacturer.

"I mustn't, I'm dining with our mutual friend," replied Dennis Mirza. "Let's remove to the Turkish Bath. Business before pleasure, I say."

Mirza was plump and vain, with a glossiness to his unguent-sweetened skull. He was the proprietor of Landharbour, a Blairite lobbying firm that dabbled in political intriguing for a hefty fee. Steam erupted from the baths as they stepped inside. The benches were of marble; they might have been in ancient Rome. Now naked, each knew the other man was not bugged. And the blast of steam in the chamber was precisely the sort of white noise that frustrates microphones attuned to faint conversation.

"Now then," purred Mirza in a voice like refined oil. "You'd better bring me up to speed with our various preoccupations. What news of our philologist friend?"

He formed his words with an exacting precision, but they had a sing-song quality that lent his sentences harmony and poise.

"She's given us the slip." Jasper's accent was devoid of class or regional character, but there was something *caustic* about his voice, a sandpaper timbre that scoured the ears. "For reasons I won't bore you with, we thought she might be in Budapest. It was not so."

A snort in the gloom.

"What about the husband?"

"He's not talking," said Mirza. "A brave man, actually."

"And you've tried… coercive techniques?"

"We cut his hands off with a hacksaw," said Mirza lightly. "While he was conscious. Seared the stumps off like good steak. Not a peep on her whereabouts."

A moment as they pictured the scene.

"Gloria Hastings MP met Sir Hugh Alexander last night," said Jasper abruptly.

"*Oh*?" Mirza turned on to his back with an audible slap. "And where might this have happened?"

"Heathrow Airport, by chance, it appears – Sir Hugh is back from Paraguay after his first month at the embassy. Hastings had been on holiday."

"Anywhere nice?"

"Tenerife."

"I might have guessed it," said Mirza. "How perfectly vile. Dreadful woman. What did they discuss?"

"I don't know. Our lip readers have studied the CCTV footage without success. It looked like a polite exchange. Maybe it was by chance."

"Don't you believe it," said Mirza.

"Do you think *she* should…?"

They fell silent. A chilliness had entered the steam-room: *she* was a person who scared them both.

"No," said Mirza crisply. "We are talking about a *serving Member of Parliament*. Do you have *any idea* the scrutiny such an act would bring down upon us? Anyway, Hastings is nothing to worry about. Loose cannon doesn't come close. My influence on that side of the house isn't so great, alas – but the Prime Minister can't *stand* the woman. We need merely extract her from the Foreign Affairs Select Committee, and it shall be job done."

Mirza's swollen belly gave him the air of a fallen Buddha, addicted to luxury.

"One more thing." He had one hand over his eyes, a weary repose. "There's another fellow our mutual friend would like you to become familiar with. A Professor Randolph Harkness, at the University of Bristol. Our understanding is that he has a… hmm… an 'interesting' past."

Eric Jasper waited.

"That is all," said Mirza.

When Jasper opened the door millions of particles of water were illuminated as they shifted and rearranged themselves in a miasma of violet and turquoise.

"Good afternoon, Eric," Mirza murmured. "And… good hunting."

7

A hot-air balloon rose over the Clifton Suspension Bridge, which was slowly turning pink in the early evening sun. After a day of worry, Harkness had taken Percy for a walk along the Clifton Downs; now they overlooked Avon Gorge. As the ancient chasm opened up beneath him he remembered rock-climbing it as a young man. What year would that have been? Magically the answer came: it was 1988. Afterwards they had gone to the Coronation Tap; he remembered the day with startling clarity. That led to another memory, and Harkness twisted his signet ring hard enough to burn the skin. With practised dexterity he diverted himself from the train of thought.

His mobile began ringing: +243. *Congolese dialling code.*

The urgency in Aled Wilson's voice was made distant by the bad line. It cut into fuzz followed by an electromagnetic *ping* before gradually reforming itself.

"Sorry about that," said Wilson. "Phone lines out here are a damned nuisance. Actually, everything here's a damned nuisance – the authorities haven't even got a search party out yet. I've asked for a chopper in case she's sending up smoke signals, and if we can get permission we'll send a British search and rescue team, too. It's a bureaucratic nightmare though. I'm afraid it all comes down to bribes… but as you know, the British government just won't pay them. And that's the news from Congo-Brazzaville today."

"I'll be out there as soon as possible."

"Pardon?"

"You heard," said Harkness. "It sounds like you've got your hands full in the capital. I'll head up to Itanga myself and pull a private search party together. The emergency visa will take twenty-four hours – so all being well I'll arrive the day after tomorrow."

"You'll only complicate matters," said Wilson.

"With respect, rubbish."

"I implore you not to."

"I won't take no for an answer."

"Look, I know you've got experience of some far-out places," – a hesitation – "well, I'm *guessing* you'd have experience, in your profession. But the corruption here's out of control—"

With a click the line was gone, not to be re-established.

Harkness stared at the far side of the gorge, wild woods for the edge of a major city. So: to the Congo. If you want a job done well and all that. Besides, there was definitely something untoward going on – and he intended to find out what. Wilson had been reading up on him, that much was evident. Then there was the delivery of Sakiko's words lists, sent by post and without explanation. Why was Sakiko digging in a peat bog when she was out there to document languages? And finally there was that message's mysterious disappearance.

When you've looked for something all your life… only to find it and wonder if you should carry on.

Harkness hadn't been to equatorial Africa before, but he'd been all over Central Asia and the corruption could hardly be *worse*. And with a lifelong abhorrence of dishonesty, he had scarcely met a corrupt official he couldn't charm or browbeat into submission.

Next he called Nowak. No, he didn't have access to his wife's Facebook page – strange question – but he sounded composed and alert, and agreed to come at once. The professor left his darker suspicions for when they met in person.

Not on these channels, Harkness.

A gust of cold wind soared over from the direction of Avonmouth Docks, sending a shiver through him. The trees on the far side of the gorge were waving in slow motion, like corals flailing in the tide.

On those slopes Neanderthal Man must have walked.

With a shiver Harkness was back there. A hulking hominid, our first cousin in the human family. An elongated head with protuberant features; pale skin, eyes full of crafty acumen. Animal hides thrown roughly over him – in the Ice Age he needed all that bulk for insulation. His voice high-pitched, but possessing no language as we know it: instead his calls would have distinguished between predators as monkeys do, but lacked syntax or symbolism. As the band stalked through the trunks – listening for aurochs – Harkness was

Right. There. With. Them.

An unpleasant thought: one day, a slenderer hominid would come slinking through these forests, not 45,000 years out of Africa. *Homo sapiens*, Wise man, who spelled the doom of *neanderthalensis*. Out-foraged and out-hunted, the forests they had prowled for hundreds of thousands of years suddenly barren. Everything gobbled up.

Another gust of wind whipped Harkness's hair about his head. He was back in the third millennium and it was time to go home. He needed to find someone to look after Percy.

8

"This should be good," muttered a backbencher as Gloria Hastings MP (Conservative, Saffron Walden) took the floor to murmuring and theatrical groans.

"What I'm about to say might cheese you off a bit," she began.

> *parliamentarian*
> > *1. a member of parliament, especially a person well versed in its procedure and debates.*

The European Research Group was meeting in the famous Committee Room 17 in the Palace of Westminster, where the tiered rows of leather benches emblazoned with golden portcullises recalled the Commons in miniature. Grammar schools were an article of faith to this faction, which made the symposium more rally than debate. Yet the woman about to speak was even more right-wing than UKIP– over the hills and way off into the wilderness – and events she attended were very rarely dull.

Hastings was a superficially attractive forty-eight-year-old, though not nearly as alluring as she believed herself. Her bottle-blonde hair had a brassy sheen and there was something vulgar about her drooping lips, which were daubed a murderous crimson. She wore a pink jacket and ever-present pearls, amulets against the slings and arrows of a perpetually outraged British public.

Hastings had first entered the public consciousness amid a blaze of controversy on her *Question Time* debut by stating that the government's negotiating position with its European Union allies in the Brexit negotiations should be "Go fuck yourself". So extraordinary was this statement that the BBC ran the clip without a bleep. Hastings had recently been spotted dining with Ukip's top brass, but it was understood no defection was forthcoming: the Kippers could do without the controversy. And as a *London Evening Standard* columnist sniped, when you're too controversial for Ukip you're really in the soup. Now it was time for another humdinger.

"Grammar schools are *not* a vehicle of social mobility," she began.

Instant silence in the room at such heresy.

"OK, so the odd bloke manages to scramble up from an estate in Middlesbrough to some ghastly bungalow mansion with a big gravel drive."

Few did snobbishness like Hastings – and worse was surely to come.

"But the research shows grammar schools are dominated by the middle classes anyway!" she cried. "Working-class children just don't pass the 11-plus in any numbers. So why do I remain a champion of selective education?" Hastings' gaze swivelled malevolently across the sixty-plus MPs, and a gleeful smile spread across her face. "Because IQ is an inherited characteristic – and the middle classes got there fair and square."

"Steady on, old girl," said someone at the back.

"And like all inherited characteristics, IQ is not spread about equally," Hastings ploughed on.

"Are you seriously trying to say that middle-class children are *cleverer* than working-class kids?" snapped the Education Secretary.

"Of course they're cleverer," shot back Hastings. "How do you think they came to be middle class?"

An audible gasp. Cries of "Shame!"

"Absolute outrage!" shouted someone at the back.

"Yes, yes, I know such things are not meant to be discussed," scoffed Hastings.

"You're no Tory!" yelled a press officer.

"Before you all 'take offence' in the modern parlance, just think about it," said Hastings. "The middle classes marry amongst themselves. And clever working-class people who scrabble up add their genes to the brainy pool. It's no wonder we see a two-speed effect at the 11-plus. The middle class is like a… like a *vacuum*, sucking up clever-DNA from the estates."

"I can't listen to this," spat the new member for Witney, marching from the chamber.

When the meeting broke up, Hastings noted with a grim smile that her colleagues had been tweeting from the chamber. Her comments had been taken up with vigour by the commentariat and a *New Statesman* writer's reaction was typical: "Vile troll is vile."

This was why Gloria Hastings MP got paid twice her Westminster salary for a weekly column in a mid-market tabloid. She was box office guaranteed.

The politician stood beneath a statue of Joseph Chamberlain while she summoned a sufficiently provocative response. Then she tweeted: "If poor people were clever then they wouldn't be poor, end of. #dunce #welldurr #notfakenews."

At once hundreds of notifications flashed up on her phone. But this was no time to wallow in hysteria: she had a rather intriguing appointment to keep.

Hastings strode along the Victoria Embankment, ignoring phone calls from journalists. An elderly man was huddled against the Battle of Britain memorial with an illegible scrawl on a piece of cardboard, his faith betokened by a flowing white beard. An Afghan, probably, and he had to be eighty. Horny knuckles trembled and his cheeks were twin maws in an imploding face. Hastings glanced over her shoulder, checking for witnesses. What she was about to do was somewhat 'off-brand'. When she was certain nobody was looking, she stuffed a £20 note into his bowl.

"For Christ's sake get to a café and have a warm drink," she snapped.

The old man looked up, trying to establish his benefactor – but Hastings was already hurrying away along the Embankment.

9

Of the Regency period, the vice chancellor's office nonetheless wore the asceticism of a monk's cell. One bookcase bore economics textbooks, the other files; the only suggestion of personality was three framed photographs on the mantelpiece. Motion and Lord Mervyn King, Motion and George Osborne, Motion with two dozen worthies and the Queen. His expression was identical in each photograph: fiercely proud.

"I intend to travel to the Congo," said Harkness. "Right away."

"Randolph, it's a straight up no."

"Look, if this is about money—"

"Don't be vulgar," he interrupted. "A staff member's missing without a trace, and you expect me to send you too? Tell me, are you familiar with the old lady who swallowed a fly?"

Harkness matter-of-factly laid out all the case's peculiarities. The altered Facebook page, the curious excavation. Her treasured word lists, sent *for safe-keeping.*

The vice chancellor listened patiently.

"You're unhinged," he said.

Harkness turned puce. "How dare you?"

"You've lost the plot completely, Randolph. What are you insinuating, that the *Foreign Office* is behind all this? The *Foreign Office* is playing silly buggers with us?"

Harkness had to concede that at a remove his observations must have sounded like the sort of low-grade conspiracy theory he sometimes encountered in his local pub. He recalled the brisk intelligence in Wilson's voice, his air of integrity. And he had faith in the essential decency of the British Secret Service.

"No, I don't think so," he said. "But *something* odd's going on."

"Harkness. Your speciality is studying the bones of dead people. Correct?"

"Correct."

"Then what precisely qualifies you to make these frankly *bizarre* deductions? Tell me, are you also trained in surveillance and counter-espionage?"

The heat was still in Harkness's face. "Actually, David…"

"Yes?"

"Oh, nothing. But while we sit here on our arses, Sakiko's *out there.* Lost in the rainforest, possibly hungry or unwell."

"No. No. No."

"In that case I request two weeks' emergency leave," said Harkness.

"More than my job's worth."

"A sabbatical?"

"Denied."

"Then I resign."

*

Harkness stormed down the street with anger in each footfall, schoolchildren scattering before him like pigeons before a terrier. The *Bristol Post* had just gone on sale and Sakiko's disappearance was front-page news.

> *A leading academic from the University of Bristol is missing in the central African rainforest, the* Post *has learned.*
>
> *Historical linguist Dr Sakiko Tsuda vanished without trace in Congo-Brazzaville on Friday. Dr Tsuda lives in Clifton Village with her Polish husband and their nine-year-old daughter. He was not answering calls this afternoon. The travel guide* Lonely Planet *describes the region she was working in as "literally one of the most wild and remote regions of the planet by any scale or stretch of the imagination".*

Motion was quoted, too – no wonder he'd been so tetchy. The vice chancellor's statement finished with the blandishment, *my thoughts are with her family at this difficult time.*

Harkness walked to Tomas Nowak's house to collect his passport.

"I thought it was another reporter," said Nowak when he opened the door at last. "They've been knocking all bloody afternoon."

'Bloody' – proof of good integration, Harkness reckoned. Up there with 'not bad'. He cast about for something positive to say.

"I've found some flights," he began. "We're leaving from Gatwick the day after tomorrow—"

"I can't come," Tomas interrupted. "Aiko's seen the *Bristol Post* – like an idiot I forgot to collect it from the bloody porch. She's breaking her heart back there."

Perfect, thought Harkness. Into the Congo, on my own.

10

Gordon's Wine Bar, a sooty, candlelit cavern beneath Samuel Pepys' old townhouse in Charing Cross. Huddled at the back of the wine cellar, his pale face illuminated in the reflection of a glass, was Sir Hugh Alexander. The recently appointed ambassador to Paraguay stared at the brickwork, as if spying his own dark thoughts in its carbonised surface.

"Oh, cheer up, you!" Gloria Hastings roared by way of greeting.

"Turn off your phone," said Sir Hugh.

Contrary to Dennis Mirza's suspicions, her encounter with the new ambassador to Paraguay the previous day had indeed been by chance. They were acquainted through Hastings' position on the Foreign Affairs Select Committee; her opening gambit had been to ask why he'd been sacked from his last posting in Japan. Sir Hugh had replied that he wasn't exactly 'sacked', but he did have quite a story for her. Only he couldn't say more there.

Then that morning an underling with a raspberry-shaped birthmark by his mouth had caught a lift with Hastings in Portcullis House and flashed a palm at her. The rendezvous was written in biro. A *brush contact*, in the world of espionage; Hastings found the cloak and dagger stuff very amusing.

It hadn't taken Hastings long to realise that the Foreign Affairs Select Committee was no more than a glorified talking shop, a think tank minus the expertise. Members possessed neither power nor access to privileged information: the committee was merely a vehicle for careerists seeking a turn on the *News at Ten*. So once Hastings' politics and personality had catalysed to terminate her chance of a Cabinet seat for all time, she used her position to create havoc. The last four years had been spent vomiting out unflattering revelations about Foreign Office staff – most recently, that ambassadors' computers had been used to view pornography. She was reviled by the ministers, but civil servants passed over for promotion knew exactly where to go.

Or senior diplomats.

In that intimate setting Hastings saw how wan Sir Hugh's features were, the fretfulness of his gaze, and for the first time she felt a little afraid. She filled a glass with his claret. With two failed marriages behind her and houses but no children to show for them, she seized every opportunity for boozing with the sanction of company. She'd knocked back two gin and tonics in the Pugin Room in order to affect a nonchalance with the ERG.

"So, Paraguay," she goaded him. "It must be something juicy. An OBE, a lifetime's devotion to the diplomatic service… and a South American backwater to show for it?"

"A *landlocked* South American backwater. And my wife hates Asunción."

"Come on then, spill the beans."

"It would be a damned pleasure."

He was manlier when incensed, and Hastings briefly wondered if he was seducible.

"The trouble is, I don't know what went on myself," he said.

Hastings forced him to fill the silence.

"I was told to expect commandos," he blurted.

"At the Tokyo Embassy?"

"That's right – SBS chaps. Part of what's known as 'The Increment'. That is to say, Special Forces seconded to MI6. Some operation or other they had planned." He fiddled with a cufflink. "Only they wouldn't tell me *what*. Which is highly unusual, incidentally. As a rule, diplomats know what's afoot on their patch. My impression was an assassination."

"An *assassination*," Hastings breathed, as though the word was a painting from her attic that had been pronounced a Picasso. Such things as extra-judicial killings were impossibly glamorous – and in the land of an ally to boot.

"What happened then?" she said.

"The operation was cancelled. There was a leak, they got cold feet."

Hastings' foundation glinted with tiny particles in the candlelight, like a scattering of glass dust on her skin. "I thought you were being kept out of the loop?"

Sir Hugh looked at her askance. "It so happens that I went to school with someone who is very senior in the Prime Minister's private office. He told me there was a security breach at Number Ten – the day before my special guests cancelled. Some file or other got compromised. When I tried to find out more I was immediately bumped down to Paraguay."

Sir Hugh moved imperceptibly. He wanted to go.

"Anything else?"

"There is one little *amuse bouche*. My chum heard a codename. 'Orientalist'. Possibly it refers to the file, possibly the operation. Can't rule out that it's a person either, I suppose."

"*Orientalist*?" Hastings snorted. "Pur-lease."

"Look, there's something about spy-craft you must know," said Sir Hugh. "If you wish to mess about in FCO matters of more consequence than sleazy civil servants, that is."

Black candle smoke twirled lacily.

"It's that an awful lot of the clichés of this world are perfectly true," he finished. "And with good reason. Dabbling in Foreign Office secrets – *proper* secrets – is not a game one plays. Anyway, there it is. It'll cause a hell of a stink if it comes out."

"I should coco."

Sir Hugh was pulling on his coat. "Now, that really is all I know, and I've probably said too much as it is. Good luck – and by the Christ be careful, won't you?"

"Half a bottle, here." Hastings' lips twitched. "Shame to end the night early?"

"I'm having dinner with my wife and daughters," he snapped. "Good evening."

Eric Jasper watched them depart.

Back in mobile phone signal, Hastings was gratified to see her missive on social media had garnered 5,219 retweets. That was going some, even by her standards – champion trolling. But she'd been ordered to a meeting with the Prime Minister the following afternoon, and the Chief Whip's email ended in the foreboding line: *Surely by now you must know what is coming.*

Hastings grinned and shrugged. A spy in Number Ten? Foreign assassinations? The '*Orientalist*' for crying out loud? She clapped her hands together. Please, God, let it all be true! The Parliamentary suicide bomber had caught the scent of cordite on the wind.

11

A woman crouches before a hut of woven palm leaves, turning from the camera. Her companion clutches an object that is hard to distinguish in the sepia; she is exclaiming something, her brow defensive. A European with a W.G. Grace beard leans back in his chair, chuckling at the disagreement, and centre stage in the diorama is a little boy. Perceptive, knowing, rather sad. Harkness placed a fingertip on the child's face.

1904: A French explorer enjoying the hospitality of a village in the Congo.

The area north of the Congo River, former French Equatorial Africa, has always been mysterious and remote. Yet in spite of – or even because of – its remoteness, this 'patch of white on the map' has drawn some of the most brilliant explorers ever to visit Africa.

Harkness turned a page of the coffee-table book. To his surprise, someone else had been seeking a visa at the Congolese consulate in an office block on High Holborn: a Nigel from one of the Medway towns, heading to work on an offshore oil rig.

"The interior? You should be so lucky, mate. I've been all over Africa for work, and trust me… the Congo's the final frontier."

The *chef de mission* was a severe Congolese man in his seventies. Despite the fact that they appeared to be the only three people in the premises, Harkness had been kept waiting for two hours. Then his phone rang and he stepped into the corridor. Over the last few weeks he'd borne stoic witness to the spiral of oblivion that had engulfed his friend's only son.

"Well, how is he?" Harkness asked.

"Just about gone off the rails completely," said Allister McCartney.

"I daresay I'd go a bit feral too in his position."

A shudder in his friend's sigh.

"Has anything else happened I should know about?"

"We had a break-in," said Allister. "The only thing taken was my car keys – and they found the Volvo this morning. The joyrider had wrapped it around a lamppost and torched it. The police say he must have brought his own petrol – apparently nowadays cars don't blow up if you throw a match down the flap."

"The bastards," said Harkness.

"That's not all. Mandy went into Ross's bedroom earlier to collect his laundry – he's with us while he gets over the diagnosis. Guess what was under his bed?"

A million and one possibilities whirled through Harkness's mind, none of them good.

"Go on…"

"A jumper that absolutely *reeks* of petrol."

"Good grief," Harkness exclaimed. "You don't think that…"

"I don't think, I *know*. He must have thought it would be fun to go for a drive, and wham, bam, thank you ma'am. He's not insured either, so then he's gone and done this half-arsed cover-up."

There was nothing to say.

"I just don't know what to do," Allister despaired. "He just needs… *something*. Something to occupy himself with. Something to counterbalance that accursed reckless streak he got from I-don't-know-where."

Harkness recalled many stories, most funny, some downright alarming. Aged eight, Ross McCartney had been caught on a neighbour's roof, having clambered from a skylight and used a plank to cross the gap. At twenty, the quantity of chips he'd received in a Turkish casino for £20 was a surprise – but there was to be a reckoning. The missed decimal places in the exchange rate were discovered afterwards, a term's student loan blown on one roll of the roulette wheel (had his number come up he would have won £216,000). Yes, Ross McCartney had raised recklessness to an art form and was currently at the pinnacle of his chosen field.

A noise in the background.

"He's home," hissed Allister.

"Put him on," suggested Harkness.

"What?"

"Let me have a word with him – I've had an idea."

It had been a decade since Harkness had met Ross McCartney, and he distinctly remembered being called a 'toff'. But his friend did as he was told; Harkness heard a door opening in Maidstone; then in a voice of infinite suspicion the younger man said hello.

"Ross. Sorry to hear about your misfortunes. Listen, I've got a proposal. Don't feel you have to say yes – only I thought you could do with a distraction. You might have seen something in the papers about this academic who's missing in the Congo."

"I only really look at the back pages."

"Well, she's one of my staff. Sorry, *was* one of my staff. You know I used to work at Bristol Uni, don't you?"

"Sure!" he said, voice brightening. "Dad's always going on about all your adventures…"

"Oh, I don't know about *adventures*," said Harkness. "Just pottering about with a trowel in some out-of-the-way places, really. Anyway, the Foreign Office are being useless, so I'm going out there myself. Tomorrow, as it happens – but I could do with some help digging my vehicle out of the occasional hole. Do you fancy it?"

"Not really, if I'm honest."

"I'll cover your flights – and pay you a daily wage. £120?"

McCartney considered this. "When you say *difficult*, do you in fact mean *dangerous*?"

"Well – yes, that's exactly what I mean. But don't tell your dad."

Harkness could almost *hear* the grin spreading across McCartney's face.

"Hold on." A fumbling noise. "Heads or tails?"

"Surely you're not putting this down to a coin toss?"

"Come on, heads or tails?"

"Heads."

Forty miles away a 50p piece sung through the air, and Harkness heard the slap of skin on skin.

"Heads it is," said McCartney. "Deal me in, mofo!"

"Mofo?"

"Short for 'motherfucker'. It's affectionate…"

Harkness was far from sure they'd get on.

*

Allister's voice was querulous in the background as they raced through the logistics. Harkness would arrange a motorcycle courier for McCartney's passport and they'd rendezvous at Gatwick.

"What on *earth* was all that about?" said Allister once he'd wrested the phone back.

"Ross is coming to the Congo with me," said Harkness.

"But isn't it dangerous?"

"Dangerous? Allister, *please.* Anyway, he'll be with me."

"That's exactly what I'm worried about," he muttered darkly.

"Would you prefer him to stay here smashing up cars?"

The eminent good sense of this point struck home.

"I suppose not," sighed Allister. "But honestly, the *Congo*?"

"I may have no kids of my own," – a touch of sadness? – "but after twenty years of lecturing, what I don't know about young people could be written on the back of an illicit Rizla paper. And mark my words – the devil makes work for idle hands."

Allister surrendered. "Oh, all right then. And thank you, Randolph. But don't do anything I wouldn't do."

"That doesn't actually rule out an awful lot, old friend," chuckled Harkness.

And so it was settled. They were a team.

12

Dr Anita Johansen felt calmer somewhere off the grid, where she could shelter from helicopters and satellites and all the other enemies both real and imagined flitting about the upper atmosphere.

"Do get in touch with Marcus," implored Edith Hendry, an old comrade. "The poor man must be going out of his mind!"

But Johansen was steadfast: it was for her husband's safety. Nor would she let Hendry know what she was working on.

Good myths embody big truths.

It was this that the philologist pondered aboard the *Tickety-Boo*.

After two decades studying the coalescence of myth and truth, Dr Anita Johansen's favourite example was the Cohens. Jewish oral tradition has it that Cohens – a type of priest – are descended from Aaron of the Old Testament, the priesthood passed from father to son since Biblical times. It had always been thought that since the world's Cohens differ massively in physical appearance, this could not possibly be true. But then geneticists at the University of Arizona tested it.

They analysed the Y chromosomes of Cohens from all over the world. Like Cohen status, these genes are handed down directly from father to son, with no female DNA spliced in at conception. If the priesthood's myth was true, one would expect to discover identical mutations on the Y chromosomes of every living Cohen, a fingerprint handed down from the original copy possessed by Aaron. And astonishingly, that is *exactly what they found*.

Some forty-five per cent of Ashkenazic and seventy per cent of Sephardic Cohanim bore the identifying mutation, despite looking quite unlike each other. That not all Cohens carry it can be explained by the odd adulterous wife. Modern Cohens do possess *some* variance in their chromosomes; if you photocopy the same page repeatedly, the image mutates. And just as the deterioration of photocopies happens at a steady and predictable rate, the same is true of mutations in DNA over the generations. So to estimate the date of divergence, the University of Arizona worked backwards. They calculated that for the level of genetic difference between the world's Cohens today to have been established, some 106 generations must have lived since 'Aaron's' lifetime. This means the ancestor of all Cohens lived about 3,000 years ago.

At the start of the First Temple Period in Jewish history.

Good myths embody big truths.

Pride of place in Johansen's de facto study on the boat was given to a *Telegraph* article from 2015. Johansen looked at it now, the inspiration for the project she'd hoped might win her a Nobel Peace Prize. The project that had caused all this trouble.

*That old story... Origins of favourite fairy tales traced
back 4,000 years*

BEDTIME stories such as Beauty and the Beast *and*
Rumpelstiltskin *may first have been told thousands of
years ago in prehistoric times.*

*Both have roots in the Bronze Age, 4,000 years ago,
academics believe. The researchers, an anthropologist
and an expert in folklore, believe they have settled a
long-running cultural question. In the nineteenth century Wilhelm Grimm, one of the famous brothers, said
he believed many of the fairy stories they popularised
were part of a shared cultural history dating back to the
birth of Indo-European languages. But later thinkers
argued that some stories were much younger, and had
passed into oral tradition after being written in the
sixteenth and seventeenth centuries.*

*"We come down firmly on the side of Wilhelm
Grimm," said Dr Jamie Tehrani of Durham University.
"Some of these stories go back much further than the
earliest literary record and indeed further back than
classical mythology. Some versions appear in Greek and
Latin texts, but our findings suggest they are much older."*

Tehrani had looked for similarities in stories from different times
and places. He then traced them back to a theoretical origin in time
and space by both geography and rate of editorial change – just as
the University of Arizona worked backwards to pinpoint a long-dead
Jewish forefather. *Jack and the Beanstalk* was traced to the break-up of
the western and eastern branches of Indo-European five millennia ago.

Johansen's insight was that perhaps the earliest mythologies of man
could be traced back to a lost root, too. What if the ancestral beliefs
that informed the Bible, the *Epic of Gilgamesh* and the mythology of

ancient Greece could be reconstructed? Why, you would be looking through a telescope at the belief systems of people deep in prehistory.

If you listened to these first stories, what would you hear?

Good myths embody big truths.

Answering this question was a prospect that had filled Johansen with exuberance and hope for the species. Because by linking the earliest texts to a forgotten proto-myth, you might find evidence that the great ancient religions were once one.

Imagine the implications.

You could demonstrate irrefutably the fraternity of mankind.

But when Johansen heard those resonances of Deep Time, she was filled with horror. And then she came under surveillance.

Somebody did not want her to succeed.

13

Harkness peered through the porthole of the descending Airbus A320. Subdued early morning conversation filled the aircraft, but there was only cloud to be seen and he returned to his reading. He'd used the flight to devour every scrap of scientific literature on the Forest People obtainable at short notice. Without warning the plane banked and the curtains of moisture parted to reveal Kinshasa, a world of glinting corrugated iron squares embedded in a sea of mud. Unpaved streets spread to the horizon where the shacks fell away beyond the curvature of the earth; it was an ersatz Mexico City, thrown up in wood and tin. Approximately sixteen million people live on this plain, and Harkness felt he could account for every one of them in streets that milled and churned with stick figures, throbbed with taxis and jangled with rickshaws. He felt a first tingle of nerves. Most of the passengers disembarked in Kinshasa, then they took off again and circled the River Congo to land three miles west in Brazzaville.

When Harkness stepped from the aircraft he was assailed by the aroma of rotting vegetable matter, cheap fuel emissions and dust, edged with a hint of something burning. This is the scent of Africa. The grinding difficulty of Congolese travel was about to commence.

*

They had met at Gatwick ten hours earlier. Harkness thought McCartney looked good – bigger and stronger than he recalled, with an extra heft of jaw. His eyes were blue, sparkling and very clear: no suggestion of assault from within. As they passed security Harkness became aware how little he knew this man, how weird this all was. So, obviously, they had a pint.

"Have you been to sub-Saharan Africa before?" Harkness asked him.

"Nope. I've been to Turkey though. Expensive trip, actually."

He suppressed a smile. "The Congo might be a bit… dicier."

As they spoke Harkness audited the varied clientele of that great leveller of the classes, an airport Wetherspoons at peak hour. An olive-skinned businessman in a linen suit tried to interest himself in the *FT*, and a stag group sporting shirts with vulgar nicknames downed Sambuca. An older man with a bushy white beard nursed an orange juice. Something pious about him, Harkness thought. Probably on a pilgrimage or something. But all things considered, Harkness thought they had privacy.

A barman placed a food menu on their table, quivering in its wooden base.

"I've got something to tell you," said Harkness. "Well, two things, actually – both quite important."

"You're getting two more rounds?"

Harkness ignored this. "The first is about me – and by the way, this goes no further than us. Not even your father knows what I'm about to tell you."

Now he had McCartney's attention.

"In the eighties, I was – how can I put this? – 'loosely associated' with one of the Secret Intelligence Services. MI6, to be precise."

McCartney came alive. "No way! So you were a… *spy*?"

"Christ no! That makes it sound far too glamorous. I'm just a boring old archaeologist. But I did once specialise in an early hominid called *Homo erectus*. That was the first of our forebears to leave Africa, incidentally – a real meat-eater, big and strong but not the brightest. They wandered the planet for two million years. Most of *erectus*'s range was in Asia, and that meant I had a damned good reason to be in the USSR during the eighties, after Brezhnev and Reagan had their little fallout over the 'Evil Empire' speech. A cover story, if you like – with the advantage that every word was true."

McCartney's pint was untouched. "What did you have to do?"

"They merely asked me to note down what I saw," said Harkness. "It was never more exciting than recording any military installations I passed, military trains and tanks on the road, that sort of thing. Quite an ingenious system actually – I had a crossword book that I'd memorised the answers to, and it was capital letter for a T-64, small one for a T-72. Once they had us sitting outside some radar domes all day with a fake breakdown, looking for a particular scientist. That's about as exciting as it got. I never climbed through a window, I never recruited a double agent, and I never, *ever*, ordered a vodka Martini. I was nothing more than a glorified trainspotter, really."

"Actually, Dad always said he thought you were a spy."

"Ah."

The canny old bird. In that moment Harkness realised all his colleagues had probably suspected it too, although he had a pleasing vision of his students in the pub.

So cool. An actual spy!

"Which brings me on to the second thing," said Harkness. "You see, I still had to go through the training – counter-espionage and all that guff. So I do know a few bits and bobs about what's rather overdramatically referred to as the 'Secret World'. Hence why I wanted to tell you this in person."

Not on these channels, Harkness…

"Tell me what?"

"That every sinew of my being tells me I am under surveillance."

"But why?"

"I think my missing colleague discovered something important. And there seem to be people who really want to find out what – or are keen to keep it quiet. So you might like to pull out now, if you don't like the sniff of it. You can leave right now and I won't think any the less of you."

But McCartney was not for turning; nor did they know that the man with the bushy white beard had paid the bartender to let him place a microphone in the base of their menu.

14

Trouble began in Congo-Brazzaville before they cleared passport control. Harkness's documents were stamped without ado and he wandered into an arrivals hall stained a scabrous brown by tropical damp, but McCartney was led away. Harkness followed to find his companion detained in a side-room with a glittery picture of a Swiss chalet on the wall. His luggage had been disembowelled and a fleshy police lieutenant crackled with fury.

Harkness nodded at the painting. "The glitter's a nice touch. Now, what the heck's going on?"

"They think I'm a cop," said McCartney helplessly.

"You *are* a cop!" raged the lieutenant.

Patches of red had formed on his cheeks. "It's the shades…"

A pair of Police sunglasses lay on the desk.

"For a law enforcement officer to visit this land, especial documentation is required," said the lieutenant, slapping McCartney's passport on the table. "Please, can you tell me? Is it there? Did I miss something?"

"It's not there," replied McCartney in a tiny voice.

"But this is daft," said Harkness. "Police is a fashion brand."

"Let me show you." McCartney produced his smartphone. "You got wireless here?"

Moments later they were admiring David Beckham.

"This means nothing," growled the police officer, who was standing so that his fulsome figure filled the claustrophobic little room. "You are both refused entry. Now kindly go away."

"I apologise for my friend's conduct," said Harkness.

Irritation wrinkled McCartney's brow.

"Of course he should have the correct documentation," Harkness continued. "Perhaps I might pay his fine?"

As the corner of a hundred dollar bill emerged from his wallet, suggestive as a stockinged leg, a glint of avarice entered the lieutenant's eye. He looked away with distaste – a bishop overseeing dispensation of indulgences – and the banknote disappeared into his drawer.

McCartney tapped his iPhone. "Say cheese, dude! The camera's rolling and the footage has been uploaded to a file cloud. One click and you're on YouTube. You were about to approve our entries, right?"

"But how dare you?" asked the lieutenant in genuine wonderment.

The room had turned cold; to Harkness's horror he realised a calculation was being made. Then something seemed to give.

"Very well, you may enter." The lieutenant held a hand over his eyes to shield his disgrace.

"Aren't you forgetting something?" said McCartney. "My friend's money. Come on, chop!"

As the lieutenant handed the banknote over it trembled like a prayer flag in the wind.

"Job done," McCartney exulted as they cleared passport control. "If you want any more tips on handling bent coppers, let me know."

"You bloody idiot!" shouted Harkness. "You jumped up, arrogant little twerp!"

"What did I do wrong?"

"You nearly got us murdered, that's what. I can't believe anybody could be so stupid! Blackmailing a corrupt police officer in his own backyard like that. And then demanding the money back. The audacity!"

"You weren't getting anywhere," McCartney fired back. "All that arse-kissing made me want to puke."

The look on Harkness's face silenced him at once.

*

When they stepped into the car park it was like the breaking of a dam.

"*Taxi, Messieurs?*"

"Speak English, *Monsieur?*"

"*Donnez-moi l'largent!*"

They battled onward like rugby players through the fray, thrusting chancers back until they achieved the respite of a Bureau de Change.

"That was intense," gasped McCartney.

"Slowly you begin to understand," muttered Harkness.

Inside it was dark, a chrome fan stirring the stultifying air. A handful of businessmen in trilby hats handled foot-thick piles of Central African francs and a policeman stood guard with a double-barrelled shotgun. None of the cash machines were operational and for inexplicable reasons the cashier refused to serve them.

The sight of a hundred dollar bill outside produced uproar. Shouts and yells as the mob descended; the pulling of shirts and gripping of elbows. Then a portly Congolese man descended like the Archangel Gabriel himself and offered them a lift into town. They accepted without question. Only when they were sweeping through Brazzaville in an air-conditioned Land Cruiser did Harkness recall his training. They didn't know anything about their saviour: whether he was really called Serge, if he was taking them to their hotel at all.

The central locks clicked shut.

Serge cruised around wide boulevards laid out in Parisian style. Signs were in French and bicycles were everywhere; baguettes were on sale. The streets were oddly exploded, whole blocks given over to rubble and rampant foliage. The buildings were either wooden shacks or concrete swoops and zigzags in the Brave New World school of architecture that characterises African municipal buildings of a certain vintage. The city felt almost abandoned, and those pedestrians they did see walked with a peaceable air; they saw strutters and moseyers, lopers and swaggerers. The few cars were either rickety Peugeots or shiny Toyota four-by-fours.

And there was their hotel.

The central locks popped open.

As they explored later that day they received curious looks from the residents, many wearing Mao-style trouser suits. A refuse-strewn stream was fringed by emerald grass, a horse sipping at its milky waters. A tree had hundreds of bottle-tops nailed into it for purposes of sorcery. The post office had three mail boxes, marked France, Congo and for the rest of the world: *Etrange*. Strange. Then they emerged at that waterway that has beguiled the European imagination for three centuries: slashing Africa in two and unknowable as a python as it emanates from the continent's heart. The River Congo was a stretch of dirty brown a mile wide, people fishing with bamboo canes and laundering clothes. On the opposite bank Kinshasa was a jagged line of tower blocks cut out against sultry skies. These two cities were twin studs of civilisation in a rainforest that could swallow Western Europe with room for seconds.

A Nautical Club of Brazzaville stood on the riverbank. Spot-lit lawns beckoned and immaculate yachts were moored.

"Not what I was expecting," said Harkness. "How about a G and T?"

The travellers were shown to low wicker chairs overlooking the water. The falling sun painted the world a lurid dirty gold, the brown of the river absorbed by the sky. Two pale blue birds cruised over the water's surface, wings pulsing as one, and with a distant smile Harkness watched children diving in rapids close to shore. Then the man at the next table turned around. It was Aled Wilson, Her Majesty's Man in the Congo.

"Harkness!" spluttered Wilson. "Is that you?"

Harkness evaluated the flush of surprise on Wilson's face, his eager smile. *Almost convincing*. He was accompanied by three Europeans – same age, same sex, same colonial uniform of chinos and open-necked shirt, half-turning, half-amused. It was a scene straight from the age of Empire.

"This is the only place in town to get a decent gin and tonic," said Wilson. "Good to see you're on the same medicine. Mind if I join?"

It would have been churlish to refuse, so Harkness made the introductions. But it was only too easy for Wilson to offer his assistance – and very hard to say no.

15

Harkness set his alarm for daybreak. That kerfuffle in the airport had been laid on by Wilson, it must have been: so very British Secret Service, the staging of a polite rebuff in the guise of police corruption. This was a nudge by the brute standards of global espionage: go away, turn back, not wanted here. They were *personae non gratae* in Congo-Brazzaville. That explained why the bureau de change had refused their money. And chivalrous Serge, he of the impeccable timing and air-conditioned Land Cruiser? The man was surely of their number too, and like an interested uncle the Foreign Office had kept tabs on them ever since. Only place in Brazza to get a decent G and T? That, at least, was a possibility. But the words of his old spymaster came back to him.

We find coincidence a rather unpalatable dish, I'm afraid.

Spoken in 1988; yet Harkness saw no reason that tastes might have changed for the digital age. One thing niggled at him though. They had his file, of course they knew his background. A chance meeting was too crude, too obvious – and a double bluff would have been audacity. But lying there in Harkness's gut was something almost *chemical* that over-ruled these thoughts. The *instinct* not to trust him, the *intuition* there was something behind this freshly shaven face, too boyish for his position. It negated reason. So they would give Wilson the slip and catch the first flight to the north, regardless of cost or inglorious presence on the EU's banned airlines list. Only Wilson was waiting for them at dawn in the hotel restaurant like some infernal djinn of the United Kingdom, legs folded as he perused yesterday's *Le Figaro*, sipping a cup of tea and eating a *pain au raisin*.

"Good morning!" Wilson leapt to his feet. "My driver's waiting to take you to the ticket office, so we should be off – once you've had breakfast, that is. Where you're going there won't be any bacon to be had for hundreds of miles."

The market district of Poto simply translates as 'mud' – and soon their trousers were splattered in the stuff. Muslim traders sold football strips, brightly coloured robes and kitchenware; diphtheria-laden clouds gusted from open sewers. Towering over the thousand stalls was a hall of breezeblock, like a megalithic construction of the communist era minus plasterwork or iconography.

"Brace yourself," said Wilson.

McCartney whistled as they stepped inside. "Look at the state of that…"

The crowd funnelled down to two ticket windows, where people were pushing and pulling and shouting at high volume. But Wilson was a smooth operator, Harkness had to admit it. A delicately placed elbow here, a crisp *Excusez-moi* there; he managed their progression like a masterly draughts player, working towards the front in strategic diagonals. When they achieved a bay Harkness and McCartney held the line as insurgents cut in from both sides.

"Sold out," shouted Wilson.

Distracted by the scene of battle, Harkness had missed the exchange. "What about tomorrow?"

"For three weeks!"

"Oh, that *can't* be true," scoffed Harkness. "Look, get out of my way."

He swept Wilson aside – but the ticket-seller confirmed it with a bored *C'est impossible, Monsieur*. And a clumsy attempt at bribery got them nowhere.

"There's one more option," said Wilson. "Only… how deep are your pockets?"

Harkness thought of the ISAs and the Premium Bonds, the stocks and the shares, the Clifton flat growing steadily in value with nobody to inherit any of it save second cousins and a carefully assembled list of charities. And then of Sakiko, lost somewhere in this monster of a country.

"Deep enough," he growled. "What exactly did you have in mind?"

*

The helicopter company was housed in an old cargo crate with windows cut into it dumped in a palm glade where off-duty soldiers smoked cannabis, their Kalashnikovs set into tripods as a barbecue sizzled. The crate was furnished with armchairs and framed photographs of Soviet-era helicopters. It was staffed by an elderly *Monsieur le Gardien* plus glamorous assistant, whose dress was patterned with fluttering dollar bills. There followed a four-hour negotiation.

In flawless French and with the patience and quiet resolution of a Gandhi, Wilson whittled the fee down. As *Monsieur*'s opening gambit of $25,000 became ten and then five, McCartney paced the crate: a literal case of cabin fever. There was another sticking point at $3,000, whereupon Wilson migrated to Lingala. Hearing their own language dislodged things once more – and suddenly they had a deal.

Then the glamorous assistant dropped her bombshell.

"*Mais, nous n'avons pas de pilotes.*"

Harkness gaped at them. "Then damn well hire some!" he barked in passable French.

"*C'est impossible, Monsieur,*" she intoned.

"What is it?" asked McCartney.

"No pilots…"

"Oh. So this has all been academic then."

Despite himself Harkness guffawed with laughter.

Monsieur le Gardien was nodding gravely. "*C'est un petit problème*," he admitted.

Harkness rounded on Wilson. "What did you say to them when you switched to Lingala?"

Wilson's eyes were very round as he protested his innocence. "I said they shouldn't mess us about because I live in Kinshasa and know how things work here."

"Oh did you now?"

A moment passed in which Harkness's cynical expression was offset only by the injury forming on Wilson's face.

"Then there's nothing else for it." Harkness stood up and clapped his hands. "We'll just have to drive."

"It can't be done," said Wilson.

"Don't talk drivel, man."

"Do you have *any idea* how bad the roads are? It might take a month."

"Where there's a will, there's a way."

Wilson wearily relayed the suggestion to the staff, who hooted with laughter.

"*C'est impossible, Monsieur*," repeated the glamorous assistant.

"*C'est impossible?*" shouted McCartney. "*C'est impossible?* Everything in this whole damn country '*c'est impossible*'! It should be the national motto. Right, sod this. I'm going for a fag."

As the door closed behind him Harkness glared at Wilson. "Listen up, matey. Right now, my friend needs help. And nobody and nothing is going to stop me from providing it. Get it? Not you, not the Foreign Office, not the Congolese transport network. Not a thousand bloody miles of swamps and wild animals. I'll damn well crawl there if I have to. So if you're really so worried about road safety, why don't you earn your wages and persuade them to track down a pilot, pronto. And I'll go and find Ross – before he gets himself into trouble."

Wilson raised both hands. "I can try."

Outside the crate McCartney was smoking forcefully.

"Run," said Harkness.

"What?"

"I said, *run!*"

16

Dennis Mirza proceeded with the stately and unstoppable momentum of a cruise liner, Eric Jasper trotting alongside. Only this time both men were clothed: they were visiting London Zoo. Neither could be sure the other wasn't bugged, and thus inhibited they spoke in riddles.

"Our rapacious bookworm." Mirza ran a fat hand back over a cranium that shone like autumn sunlight on water. "Still not turned up then, has she?"

"Oughtn't to be long now," said Jasper. "We think she's with friends in London. What, er – what of her hubby?"

Mirza let his gaze slide to an enclosure that was being circum-navigated by two restless Sumatran tigers. But he didn't have eyes for the beasts. Instead he stared at the post in the middle of their domain from which hung a hunk of tattered goat, all mangled sinew and purple flesh. When Jasper understood his lips became a twisted pout of approval.

Dead meat.

A great grey owl glared at them from its aviary, its lemony eyes severe within their tree-ring surrounds. Mirza returned the stare until the bird became uncomfortable, stomping on its perch before fluttering away.

"Our wise old owl has flown the coop," he said.

Jasper blinked. "When?"

"Earlier today. And his little chickadee."

"Botheration. What now?"

Mirza waved a hand. "Life is cheap in Africa. Accidents happen. I hear the roads are particularly unsafe."

The owl had fluttered to join four others in the top corner of the aviary.

"A *parliament* of owls," Mirza observed. "That meeting you mentioned… was it of concern to us?"

"I fear it was none too *diplomatic*," replied Jasper.

Mirza sighed. "There are more diplomatic members of Combat 18 than that appalling woman."

"But you still feel Parliament has – immunity?"

"No need for drastic measures, yet. Remember, my dear, the dark arts of SW1 are my speciality…"

He pronounced the 'C' of *speciality* delicately, as though it were cut from glass. Jasper looked comforted: the lobbyist had the ear of MPs all the way from the loony left to the swivel-eyed right.

But they were here to see apes.

*

Half a continent away a pregnant woman clasped her wrists together as if bound. But she had neither hands nor feet, the wrists and ankles executed in elliptical curves. This figurine could have graced a New York modern art gallery; in fact, the Venus of Frasassi was 28,000 years old. Carved from a stalactite, the head was elongated, and a natural depression in the calcite bestowed the sinister grin of a Halloween pumpkin. Enormous breasts rode high upon her chest and the private parts were depicted gratuitously. With gloved hand, Dr Francesca Bianca of the National Archaeological Museum of the Marche Region in Ancona placed the Venus on a plinth, consulted some black-and-white photographs and began to type.

A 1994 *The New York Times* article was pinned to the noticeboard.

'Venus' Figurines From Ice Age Rediscovered in an Antique shop

WHILE strolling on the Rue Notre-Dame in Montreal, a young sculptor happened to look in the window of an antique shop and see a display of tiny statues carved in ivory and stone. It was the beginning of a rediscovery that could lead to a better understanding of a distinctive but enigmatic form of Ice Age art.

The statuettes of nude women with exaggerated breasts and buttocks were prized specimens of the first so-called Venus figurines to be excavated, in the 1880s in caves near Monaco. Other discoveries followed, opening the eyes of scholars to a shared artistic expression that seemed to unite far-flung prehistoric people from the Pyrenees to Siberia. Perhaps these were symbols of fertility rites, expressions of a common mythology or simply Ice Age pornography.

*

Mirza and his assistant had reached the gorilla house. Chattering tourists swarmed before the goldfish bowl, and a sign read: WARNING. THE ALPHA MALE IS DISPLAYING DOMINANT BEHAVIOUR.

The lesser gorillas were dotted about in the eaves, but the chief sat front of house in thoughtful repose, appraising the humans with crafty brown eyes.

"See much *Homo sapiens* in him?" asked Mirza.

"Oh, *definitely*," said Jasper.

Why, there were the furrowed eyebrows and the forehead resting upon a fist like a philosopher – the angle created by the forearm and leathery hand. But when he rose to prowl along the glass there were gasps. Something *unreal* about the size of him, those flanks like mountains.

"Our family trees converge ten million years back," said Mirza. "Not so long ago really, is it? What, 300,000 generations? That's ten Wembley Stadiums-worth of change to mould George Clooney from an ape."

The gorilla *flew* at the glass, beating it with a boom that provoked screams. The crowd leapt back, the reverberation died away; two metres now separated crowd and cordon. A toddler started crying.

Mirza's tie dangled over one shoulder. "How interesting."

"What's interesting?"

"We *knew* the glass is reinforced. We *knew* he couldn't harm us. But still we jumped back. Why?"

As they left the enclosure Jasper lowered his voice. "Talking of African excitement… is *she* going out there?"

Behind them came another boom of fists on glass, the delighted screams of the little masters.

Mirza's eyelids drooped shut, again the dark Buddha. "I rather think that she may have to, Eric."

*

The National Museum of Marche inhabits a nineteenth-century townhouse set amid chaotic cobbled streets on the Adriatic Coast. At that time of year it was still warm, and the cargo ships and oil tankers danced a slothful waltz around the isthmus. From the door of this institution slipped Dr Francesca Bianca, squat and rather plain, with roots showing in her copper hair. She crossed the piazza to an ailing Renault.

In London Mirza checked his watch.

Dr Bianca touched the door handle.

A woman parked opposite in a SEAT Ibiza clicked her Parker pen.

With an enormous explosion both car and its owner disappeared in a bolus of flame, a terrifying eruption of white that turned scarlet and then orange as black hydrocarbons went swirling up the sides. The bang was hellish in those claustrophobic streets, echoing off Renaissance walls. People came running and then stood helplessly, beaten back by heat as flames roared from the blackened hulk. But of Dr Bianca there was no trace. She had been entirely obliterated.

The woman in the car smiled and started the engine. Her phone buzzed – new instructions coming through. Then the SEAT nosed from its parking bay and *she* departed the scene.

17

Harkness and McCartney sprinted through the palm glade, dodging trees and hurdling undergrowth. Harkness's face was furious with concentration, but McCartney was in raptures.

"This is nuts!" he shouted.

As they emerged onto a boulevard that was Brazzaville's answer to the Champs-Élysée a taxi shook into view, and an hour later they had acquired a serviceable Mitsubishi Shogun at terrifying expense.

"Wilson must have told them not to supply pilots," said Harkness, "when he slipped into Lingala. Under the pretence of helping us he's closed off every fast route to the north. Very nicely done."

They withdrew two feet of local currency, acquired a hundred litres of petrol in beaten-up jerrycans and Harkness spotted two ancient tents at a market stall. Tea, sugar, tinned sardines and cigarettes for bribes made up the rest of their *materiel*; thus armed, they embarked upon one of the hardest journeys on earth.

Boulevards gave way to pitted track, stone and cement to tin and wood. The outskirts were more heavily populated and they oozed through teeming slums at walking pace, trapped behind hand-drawn carts with wheels salvaged from automobiles stacked with refrigerators or sacks of rice. At the city limits a policeman with no front teeth demanded money "for whisky", the twin pink sickles in his upper gum lending him a maniacal appearance.

"What a piss-taker," said McCartney. "He doesn't even attempt to hide it!"

"Africa might seem a bit backward sometimes," said Harkness. "But remember, for most of our history – for three million years, in fact – the opposite was true. *It was in the lead.*"

They passed a tank graveyard, the rusting machines piled on top of one another with a reddening sun briefly framed between four cannon: a vision of some science-fiction dystopia. Finally, they struck open road, heading arrow-straight through the bush. As Harkness hit sixty mph there was euphoria in the vehicle. They felt the intoxicating rush of *adventure*, of an expedition into the wild places launched with scanty equipment but plenty of guts. Harkness turned on the radio and Dire Straits' 'Money for Nothing' made the moment complete. They were absolutely certain they would make it.

*

They drove through a corridor of interlaced thorns lacking leaf or flower, like an enchanted barricade in some twisted fairy tale. The ratio of mud hut to breeze block increased; the only sign of animal life was the occasional cane rat scuttling off between the thickets. It was hot, and with a start Harkness realised they hadn't brought much water. Tarmac turned to dirt and then hardened into ridges until the car become a cacophony of bumps and bangs. Now all Harkness could do was grip the steering wheel, grimacing against the vibrations that juddered through his bones.

"Drive slower?" suggested McCartney.

"That would be most unwise," Harkness shouted. "I took the liberty of consulting the Foreign Office website before we left. You ever seen those maps they produce for dangerous countries, with the traffic light system? Red, green or yellow to show how unsafe the regions are."

"Uh-huh."

"We're deep in the scarlet, my friend."

McCartney's smile was magnificent to behold. "Yeah, baby! What's so dangerous about this place?"

"After the last civil war, some of the rebels refused to lay down arms. They're still out here, somewhere. And they call themselves – you'll like this – the Ninjas."

"Hate to worry you, but I need to piss," said McCartney.

Harkness glared at him.

"I'm serious!"

"Can you honestly not wait?" implored Harkness. "It's like looking after a child…"

"You'd prefer me to go in the car?"

"Fine, you win."

When McCartney got out it was like opening the door of a blast furnace. Only he wasn't relieving himself at all. He was taking selfies, a silly smile plastered across his face.

"I thought you needed to piss?" snapped Harkness when he got back in.

"TBH, I just wanted a photo in Ninja territory," said McCartney. "For Facebook."

From somewhere deep down in the back of his throat Harkness emitted the growl of a goaded wolf. He turned the ignition.

Nothing happened.

He tried again.

Dead.

"Oh, shit," said McCartney.

"I don't *bloody well believe it*," said Harkness. "Look what you've done!"

The world behind the thorns was remade: full of hidden enemies, yearning to maraud them. Without air-con the temperature was rising by the second and McCartney glanced at their bottle of water. It had been an hour since the last village.

"Don't you dare," said Harkness. "If we die of thirst, you die first."

They also had no phone reception.

"I'm sorry," said McCartney at last. "That was really stupid of me."

"There's an awful lot I could say to you right now," said Harkness quietly, taking a small sip of water. "But for the moment I just need to think about what we're going to do."

Because it's what one does in these situations, they opened the bonnet and stared inside. The bush was unnaturally quiet, only the engine ticking as hot metal contracted. Both men were sweating profusely.

"Wait a minute…" McCartney pointed at a loose wire. "Shouldn't that be connected to the battery?"

The excellent logic of this statement dawned on Harkness. "Looks like it got shaken loose by all the bumps…" he admitted.

There was no way of soldering it back, so McCartney clamped it to the battery by hand as Harkness turned the ignition.

They held their breath.

With a flash of sparks the Mitsubishi came back to life, engine burbling away contentedly.

"I guess this is our new way of starting the car," said McCartney.

It was an insufferably smug twenty-four-year-old who got back into the car.

18

It had been quite a week in the political life of Gloria Hastings MP, even by her own colourful standards. On the Monday she was summoned to Number Ten to have the whip withdrawn, an encounter in which the seething Prime Minister refused to utter a single word. Instead this gruesome duty was left to the Chief Whip, a supercilious twerp barely out of short trousers named Derek Riding. Hastings refused point blank to resign from Parliament, vowing to sit as an independent – and swore more vehemently still to make the government's life as difficult as possible within the bounds of the law, if not taste and decency.

On the Tuesday she received an unexpected declaration of support from her local party association, who vowed to back her for re-selection and promised the continued use of the constituency office in the meantime. This was followed by a supportive editorial in the *Saffron Walden Reporter* praising her crusade to protect local bus services. Her position looked stronger. Then on the Wednesday she was invited to table a question at Prime Minister's Questions. This was remarkable. Hastings had not been invited to contribute to this forum since her outburst on *Question Time* some years previously (random ballot her foot).

What to ask? Immigration, probably. What else? She had half an hour to retreat to her lair in Portcullis House, wallow in anger about how the country was changing beyond recognition, and rile herself up further by reading the supportive comments beneath her column.

An unmarked brown envelope had been slid beneath her door. Curious.

The envelope contained payslips from the television network RT, mouthpiece of the Russian government in Europe. They detailed payments for 'communications advice'. And the name on the payslip was Derek Riding. This was the leak to end all leaks, the scoop to end all scoops.

Revenge.

Hastings glanced at the clock. In just over an hour's time she would be addressing the House of Commons, beamed live on to the BBC News Channel with every political journalist in the country watching.

Revenge!

In her experience, a dish best served piping hot. And she could denounce the Chief Whip in perfect safety – for Parliamentary privilege provides MPs with immunity from being sued for libel while addressing the house. Hastings could say what the hell she liked in there, and contemplating this she felt a spasm of wicked glee. But diligence was required. After all, a cock-up now and her reputation would be shot for good. Lord knows, people disagreed with her – but she did pride herself on getting the facts right. Hastings immediately Googled 'Derek Riding Russia Today'. To her amazement, the first hit was a record on the Companies House website. And there was his name, emblazoned across the page: he was a director of the station's UK subsidiary. *How could he have been so stupid?*

Something else was nagging her though, some little memory. She could vaguely remember him boring Moncrieff's Bar to death about going on a jolly to Russia. Again Google provided the answer. He'd been treated to an all-expenses-paid 'fact-finding trip' to the Sochi Winter Olympics in 2014 courtesy of the Russian government. But wait… Riding had declared that in the MPs' Register of Interests, there it was in black and white. He could yet have saved himself by confessing the directorship, too, and heart palpitating, she consulted the register. But no: the idiot actually thought he could get away with it. Hastings allowed her eyelids to flicker closed as with joy in her heart she began formulating her attack line.

This would be a PMQs to remember.

*

The first question was something deathly boring about the customs union, the second a plant from Number Ten served up by a dreary careerist. God save her from lifelong politicians. The Leader of the Opposition went in on Foreign Policy; with fresh militancy springing up following the collapse of Islamic State, the US was proposing a limited ground offensive and looking to the Special Relationship for succour. But the fourth question was hers: the moment the House had been waiting for.

Hastings rose to a cacophonous roar from both sides, the din of two medieval armies facing off. She felt a frisson of nerves at the magnitude of what she was about to do. Riding was four places down from the Prime Minister and peering up at her, his baby pink cheeks full of condescension. Hastings prepared to administer a Parliamentary throttling.

"Order!" yelled the speaker. "Order. The House will listen to what the member for Saffron Walden has to say!"

She cleared her throat. For a moment there was absolute silence in the chamber. "Nobody has praised the Prime Minister for her measures to combat Russian interference in this country's affairs through cyber warfare more than I," she began.

There was a whisper of disappointment. This was not what they were expecting at all.

"I trust, therefore, that she will move with the utmost swiftness to eject from government the honourable member for Bromley and Chislehurst? For it is my duty to inform the house that this *traitor* has been acting as the clandestine mouthpiece of that hostile power."

There were several hundred grasps, the first querulous gusts of an incipient tornado. Every head turned to the Chief Whip. Then the chamber dissolved into screaming and yelling and barbarous cries. Through it all the voice of Derek Riding could be heard, strong and clear and incandescent, like the trumpet blast of a formidable infantry regiment. He stood ramrod straight, staring her in the face and slowly changing colour as he howled, "*What? What? What?*" over and over again.

It took the speaker three full minutes to calm the chamber, but he managed it in the end.

"Perhaps the honourable member for Saffron Walden will tell the House what grounds she has for such a scandalous allegation?" he said.

An unnatural hush fell as six hundred rapt MPs waited for more. But as Hastings began reading from the payslips the pandemonium was of such a tenor that for the first time in its history Prime Minister's Questions had to be concluded early.

All in all, a job well done, Hastings reflected as she returned to her office, still trembling with the adrenaline of it. In a single delicious moment she had served up the *coup de grâce* to Riding's career and one of the most iconic episodes in the history of the House of Commons. Her profile was even at that moment surging to stratospheric new heights. Re-selection was reassured. She'd demand a hefty pay rise for her column.

Something troubled her though: the beetroot quality of the Chief Whip's face as he was manhandled from the chamber, still squawking out his incorruptibility. It was the look of outraged innocence, and Hastings felt a first shadow of unease. She glanced at her phone – two hundred missed calls already, with both she and Riding trending worldwide on Twitter – and had the queer sensation that she'd *imagined* his name at Companies House. Now she quickened her pace.

Back in her office she hammered Russia Today into the website, and there was Derek Riding. Relief unbounded. Hang on a minute though… the date of birth was given as August 1961. Her Derek Riding *had* to be younger than that – he looked about twenty. Hastings' defrocking had stung that much more for being administered by a pipsqueak. She felt an alarming lurch in her gut: the sinking dread of a journalist who has published something both sensational and completely untrue. The Chief Whip's Kremlin connection was fake news. Her phone was up to three hundred missed calls, and counting.

19

Day three of the journey, and now they crossed a landscape of rolling savannah interspersed with thickets of jungle from which the screech of monkeys carried in the hot still air. This marbling of woods and grassland was punctuated by mud hut villages where each night Harkness bartered their commodities for shelter. Where rays of sunshine penetrated the clouds the grass was spotlighted in dazzling emerald, and the pockets of forest were blackened cumuli in the heat haze.

"This is just how it must have been," Harkness murmured.

"How what must have been?" said McCartney.

"The world. When our ancestors came down from the trees."

"Oh God, here we go again…"

"Aren't you interested in where we came from?"

"Go on then," sighed McCartney.

"About seven million years ago Africa began to dry," said Harkness. "And the rainforests fractured into savannah corridors just like these. So our Australopithecus ancestors took a momentous decision. They began walking on two legs."

McCartney stared out at the landscape morosely.

"They were pretty much walking chimpanzees, mind," said Harkness. "Same brain size, limited problem-solving ability. And sodding violent."

"Chimps are violent?"

"Mark my words, they are absolute wrong 'uns."

McCartney raised his eyebrows and put his headphones on.

Later that day Harkness tried again. "Did you know that sub-Saharan Africa wasn't always inhabited by people we would think of today as black Africans?"

"Huh?"

"In prehistoric times, two other races covered almost the entire continent. The Forest People held sway right across Central Africa, where we are now. Meanwhile Southern and Eastern Africa were the realm of Khoisan Bushmen – click language speakers."

"Those guys are cool," blurted out McCartney.

Harkness was encouraged. "Once upon a time click speakers roamed all the way from Somalia to South Africa," he enlarged. "Yet what remains of that mighty domain today? It's been whittled down to a patch of the Kalahari Desert. Except, that is, for one quite instructive exception. The Hadza of Tanzania speak click too – a single tribe, marooned far away on the other side of the continent. Now, what does this imply?"

"That clicking is not a great way to communicate?"

"It implies that click languages once stretched right across Africa," said Harkness. "Clicks may even have been part of the *first* language, the one *Homo sapiens* spoke as they expanded out from the cradle of mankind. Guess what the geneticists found when they analysed the Hadza genome?"

"That they like making clicking noises?"

"They found that the Hadza bear the exact same signature muta-tions on their DNA as the Khoisan. So these two populations, a continent apart, are actually closely related. The genetic and linguistic data are in total agreement. The click speakers who once roamed right across Africa were – and I choose my words carefully here – *engulfed* by black speakers of the Bantu languages predominant today. Click languages were swept away."

"Engulfed? You mean *invaded*, surely?" said McCartney.

"Out-competed would be more accurate," said Harkness. "The Forest People and the Khoisan were hunter-gatherers, but the Bantu spreading out from what's now Cameroon in about 3,000 BC – that's the last gasp of the Stone Age here in Africa – were farmers of yams and millet. So they were more successful at feeding themselves and reproducing. You can forget about armies or organised warfare in prehistoric times."

Harkness parked to let the engine cool down and they stepped into the grass, a blizzard of grasshoppers rising beneath each step. Treeline after treeline disappeared into the distance ahead of them, cresting one another like layers of cut-out scenery. The nearest was purple, farther horizons receding through shades of grey before fading away completely.

Faintly at first – no more than a murmur enfolded in the landscape – an internal combustion engine approached.

"The Forest People were replaced too," Harkness was prattling on. "They melted away into the most impenetrable rainforests, where agri-culture's impossible and they cling on today."

It was a heavy goods vehicle, still hidden by the rise but recognis-able from the clank of steel and the laboured trundle of its engine. The lorry crested the slope and started gaining speed.

"In barely a millennium, the demography of a continent was upended completely," finished Harkness. "It's one of the greatest replacements of people in human history... and most people have never heard of it."

The din of the approaching lorry had become thunder. There was a squeal of metal and the shriek of rubber as it veered off course. McCartney dived at Harkness and hurled him back as the lorry hurtled over the spot where they'd just been standing to go careering off through the grass, a fog of green threshed up in its wake.

"He did it on purpose!" shouted McCartney, who was sprawled on the ground. "He tried to kill us for sure!"

The lorry had stopped a hundred feet away. It tried to reverse, stalled and abandoned the attempt. The driver's door swung open.

"We need to go," panted Harkness.

As they sped away, neither saw that it was a woman who got out.

*

"What do you mean, missed?" said Mirza. "*She, never, misses.*"

"She just missed!" Jasper repeated down the line. "The boy pushed Harkness out of the way."

Mirza exhaled through both nostrils. "Well, let's not get hysterical. I've acquired a light helicopter from Equatorial Guinea. It ought to be at her disposal soon."

"But if they get much further north they'll be lost beneath tree-cover," said Jasper.

"Don't you believe it," Mirza replied icily. "There are two dozen rivers before Itanga – and not the sort that have bridges. By the time she's overhead they shall be high and dry."

20

That evening Harkness drove a few miles into the savannah, rounded a copse and parked beneath its canopy.

"But why would anyone want to kill us?" McCartney asked for the fifth time as they covered the Mitsubishi with branches.

"Why are the Foreign Office spying on us?" Harkness fired back. "And what happened in Stone Age Africa that's of such importance somebody's prepared to murder to keep it secret? I don't understand any of it, so please stop asking."

McCartney frowned. "Perhaps they don't want us to know something... *about ourselves*."

Harkness blinked and turned, as if glimpsing a keen intelligence for the first time.

"That's very perspicacious, Ross," he said.

"What?"

Harkness smiled. "It's a good thought."

With equatorial precision the sun hit the earth at six p.m. sharp before melting away like a sphere of scarlet wax to stain the sky around it the red of war. In the gloaming that followed the savannah came alive: kudus with bat ears and colonies of rock hyraxes like overgrown guinea pigs, flowing across the landscape. A half-moon rose, ghostly through the wash of cloud: bewitching the savannah a shimmering silver in which night animals did their solemn and lonely work. Dozens of tiny pale orbs were cast about the grass, and closer inspection revealed them to be the eyes of spiders, reflecting the moonlight like tiny crystal balls.

"What a thing to look upon," said Harkness. "Seeing it all just – I don't know – it makes me glad to be alive."

McCartney turned away, lit a cigarette and pulled on it hard, blasting smoke up at the occluded moon.

"God, sorry," said Harkness. "That was a damned inconsiderate thing to come out with."

"Don't worry about it," murmured McCartney.

Still he would not face Harkness.

"Ross..."

"What?"

So often in life what you don't want to be doing is what you should be doing.

"I should probably stop digging now," he said, "but I'm just going to bloody well say it. Even if you do lose your sight – you can still have a happy life. If you choose to."

Harkness saw the hypocrisy in his own words even as he spoke them.

"But look what I've done to myself," said McCartney.

He had no immediate reply, and a moment passed in silence.

"Sometimes I wish I'd lived a bit more impulsively," said Harkness suddenly. "Like you do. I might have had a bit more fun, not being so damn repressed. Victim of my upbringing, I suppose."

"At least you can see."

"Yes, that's true. But it's not been all sweetness and light for me either, you know. And sometimes I think that – well, my life's been a bit sad."

Uncharacteristic to emote like that, Harkness chastised himself. Very *un-British*. And was he really trying to make McCartney feel better? Or was this self-pity?

"What have *you* got to be sad about?" said McCartney.

"Oh, you know, I get a bit lonely," he replied. "There, I've said it."

"But Dad says you've got tons of friends…"

"Not the same, though, is it? Every night when I go home just me and the dog."

Just me.

Harkness's own words shivered back through him, producing a juvenile sensation of abandonment. For Christ's sake pull yourself together man, he thought. For a while there was only the sound of grasshoppers and behind them the gibbering din of monkeys indulging their nightly insanities. Then a giant eland stepped across the nearest ridge, his twin horns silhouetted against the moonlit sky. In its noble isolation, Harkness was reminded of himself.

"What about internet dating?" said McCartney.

Harkness guffawed. "I can't really see it, somehow! But thanks nonetheless. As it happens, I've had a few offers over the years."

"But you didn't meet 'The One'?"

"Er – I did, actually."

"And?"

"It's a long story. But as you say, I do have friends – one can never do with enough of those. So I apologise for my inconsiderateness." Harkness offered McCartney his hand. "How about it?"

"Go on then." They shook on it. "I will only say this once, Randolph, but you're *fairly* interesting. For an old person."

"You little charmer," said Harkness.

"I'll also try to stop acting like such a twat all the time," said McCartney.

"The hell you will."

21

The floating philologist of Hackney tapped a fountain pen against her lips as she contemplated the problem. Johansen was unsure how much she should put in writing. What she'd learned had caught the attention of – somebody. And she suspected it was meant to be silenced. So she would commit it all to paper, ready to send out at a moment's notice if she had to – although who the recipient might be, she wasn't sure. But spelling it out explicitly would be foolish. She didn't want her theories to fall into the hands of the very people pursuing her. Better to merely curate the evidence in one document, using only allusion to string each passage together. That way, with the emergency addition of a few sentences she could draw the disparate stories together. Reveal the dark foundations of our world.

Johansen had become convinced that her friend was reading her notes. It was the studied foot of space as Hendry manoeuvred around her desk with back-tilted nostrils and eyes flicking downward, as if to say *don't mind me!* And once Johansen had returned from the lavatory to find her notebook at a slightly different angle. Since then she'd kept it with her even on visits to the lavatory; at night it was stowed beneath her pillow.

Johansen smiled to hear a snatch of Yiddish outside the *Tickety-Boo*. How very apt: for her *magnum opus* had begun with the Old Testament. And as she had pulled apart that sprawling mass of stories back in Edinburgh, she'd undertaken a self-taught crash course in human origins, educating herself about times *before* the written word that had been her life's endeavour. Biology, historical linguistics, evolutionary psychology – Johansen threw herself into these disciplines like a woman possessed.

Almost immediately, she began to see it.

Much of the Old Testament was true.

"Hello there!"

Peering through the window was a man in his twenties wearing a woollen jumper and a necklace of wooden beads. His brown hair was dishevelled and he wore a goatee beard and nose ring. This was the sort of person Johansen was predisposed to like, which concerned her.

"I'm new to the mooring, thought I'd say hey." A Dutch accent. Something honest about his face. "Its Adriaen. I'm on the *Time Traveller*, two boats down."

"I'm very busy," she replied acidly.

The less people knew about her being there the better. It was bad enough having Hendry peeping over her shoulder.

"PhD or something, is it?" The newcomer took in her workspace with his decent brown eyes. "Sorry, none of my business. Come and say hey if you fancy a smoke some time. Cheers!"

When she had got rid of him Johansen opened a new notebook. Then she began transcribing from the Old Testament.

> *Genesis, 1,27 And God created man in His own image. And God said: 'Be fruitful, and multiply, and replenish the earth, and underline it; and have dominion over every living thing.*

It was Johansen's underlining.

22

The clumps of jungle had become swollen now, feeding off rising humidity, the savannah withering back in tandem as Harkness piloted them closer to the equator. Before they knew it the car was lost in pure jungle, a lonely speck navigating one bronchiole through a lung of green stretching from Lake Tanganyika to the Atlantic Ocean. Harkness was a man of mountains and deserts, those were the topographies where he'd spent the prime decades of his life in happy fieldwork, and he viewed the jungle with suspicion. The vegetation pressed in on their ribbon of ruddy earth, threatening to snip it altogether and maroon them here in the wilderness. He couldn't decide whether the jungle was one calamitous mess – trees erupting at random and bedraggled with creepers – or whether there was a beauty in its asymmetry. At least it was *alive*. Every step into the rainforest was met with scuttling and cracks, with the flight of unseen things that were plainly large.

They weren't out of the twenty-first century yet: some people wore Western clothes, though brightly coloured *pagne* fabrics or bare breasts were more common. In the villages it remained possible to buy packets of washing powder or a noggin of pastis from a roadside hut selling bottles of lurid yellow adulterated petrol: the Congo's answer to a motorway service station. Rickety bridges spanned most of the rivers; those without had a floating metal platform with an outboard motor and an attendant boatman. It was sweltering and the rainstorms were incessant.

On the fourth day, Harkness spotted a humanoid skull by the roadside. For an instant he had the vision of a *Homo erectus*, but closer inspection revealed it had belonged to a gorilla, the brow peppered with little holes.

"Shotgun blast," reflected Harkness. "For bush meat."

A boy of seven emerged from the trees behind them, very thin with frayed shorts and sandals cut from tyres. His face was painted

terracotta red and in the crook of his arms was a banana leaf full of –
something. Shyly he took Harkness's index finger.

"*Je m'appelle* Joff," he said.

"*Je m'appelle* Randolph." He gestured to the bundle. "May I see?"

Inside was the hunk of red clay with which the boy had painted his
face. As they left, Harkness extracted a 10,000 franc note from his pocket
and slipped it down one trouser leg. He refused to make beggars of children, but if the boy were to *find* the money – buy proper shoes, perhaps
– then all to the good. But the child's eyes were too quick for him.

"*Monsieur! Monsieur! Vous avez perdu de l'argent…*"

Drat, thought Harkness. Then two ideas came to him in quick
succession.

"*S'il vous plaît, pouvez-vous me vendre l'argile?*" he asked.

Please can you sell me the clay?

The child's pupils were enormous as Harkness exchanged the parcel
for an unimaginable sum.

That evening Harkness set his tent a little away from McCartney's
and sat alone on the opposite side of the canvas. The forest was illuminated a Halloween orange by the fire lit to ward off leopards, but
the space between the flickering tree trunks was black as the void.
McCartney stole towards his tent and burst around the side with a
ghoulish moan.

"Idiot," said Harkness when he'd recovered.

In his lap was a sculpture of the boy, and at his feet were
clay-encrusted banana leaves. He'd rendered only the upper torso, the
child's head turning in surprise; long eyelashes were expertly suggested
and the roundness at the back of the skull was lovely. Harkness braced
himself for derision.

But McCartney said, "I didn't know you were an artist."

"You may know less about me than you think," murmured
Harkness.

McCartney picked up the sculpture. "It's not bad. You really love
kids, right?"

"What sort of person doesn't love kids?"

Harkness's childlessness hung in the air.

"Can I ask you a personal question?" said McCartney.

"If you absolutely must."

"Why did you never marry?"

Harkness laughed. "Isn't there anything more personal you could ask? Go on, don't hold back. When was the last time I slept with someone? Did I look at pornography as a teenager? What would you *really* like to know?"

"Sorry," he said. "It's just my dad said you've never got a girlfriend…"

"I'm not gay, if that's what you're somewhat clumsily fumbling at. Actually, I was engaged once, believe it or not. 'The One' that you enquired about before. Sadly it wasn't to be."

"What happened?"

Harkness felt his consciousness rising up from that spot to high above the Congo basin. Then turning north as Europe circled clockwise away from them, its cities like golden synapses where Africa lay in near darkness. And descending once more: to England, the south west. To Bristol and the Avon Gorge, a bird's eye view of the Clifton Suspension Bridge, headlights and tail lights traversing the causeway that runs along the river beneath. Finally pivoting upward once more to a galaxy that blazed with a hundred billion pitiless stars.

"That, I'm afraid, is a story for another day," he said.

McCartney took the sculpture.

"What are you doing with him?" said Harkness.

"Just trust me, right?"

When Harkness awoke the next morning the little boy awaited by the guttering ashes of their campfire. McCartney had fired him.

23

Almost a week in the rainforest now: a week in which they'd seen nothing at a distance greater than fifty metres other than the sullen clouds that blanketed them in humidity. Their average speed was five miles an hour; the settlements grew more basic; they were no strangers to punctures, and Harkness made good on his promise that McCartney would be digging them out of the mud. A dozen blue plastic barrels abandoned by the trackside were the first manufactured objects they had seen for days, apart from motorbikes. They encountered barricades of felled trees manned by men demanding money because paperwork was "not in order"; Harkness's powers of persuasion failed him again and after bitter negotiation a sum would be agreed so they could pass. Children attempted checkpoints of their own, holding a length of string over the track in mimicry of their elders. He gave these young chancers short shrift. Then they hit a snag.

It was the fifteenth river by Harkness's reckoning, its waters deep and fast-flowing. But the metal platform that had once traversed it was submerged beneath the surface. It was noon, cloudless for once, and forty degrees centigrade. Mad dogs and Englishmen time.

"What if we take a run up?" suggested McCartney. "Hit that bad boy at speed."

"You have got to be joking."

Six huts stood downstream around a communal fire being tended in the traditional African way: a single log smouldering between two rocks with a blackened saucepan balanced on top. More timber had been stockpiled nearby and catfish were hung to dry on a frame. A fisherman hollowed a tree-trunk pirogue.

"How do we get a car across?" asked Harkness in French.

The fisherman smiled and shook his head. "*C'est impossible.*"

"Not this again," groaned McCartney. "Honestly, if I had a pound for every time I'd heard *c'est impossible* – well, I'd have four pounds."

Harkness barked with laughter.

They spread the map over the bonnet, Paris-Dakar Rally style.

"By my calculations, we're here." Harkness indicated a squiggle on the map. "Halfway to our destination. As you can see, the only other road – and I use that term loosely – that would get us even close is this one. But to join it…" He retraced their route and sighed. "The turn-off was four days ago."

"Oh man." McCartney lit a cigarette. "Then we're screwed. Aled Wilson was right. *C'est* is *impossible*."

"Don't be so defeatist," retorted Harkness. "Honestly, sometimes you millennials are truly pathetic."

McCartney's eyes blazed with rekindled fury.

"Anyway, I've had an idea," said Harkness. "Remember we passed those plastic barrels a few hours back? And in the village there were logs. As for cable, we've got the car."

Like all African off-roaders, the Mitsubishi was equipped with a coil of steel rope beneath the bumper.

"What are you burbling on about now?" said McCartney.

"We're going to make a raft."

*

Harkness collected the barrels while McCartney negotiated the purchase of logs. By the time he returned the younger man had lugged two dozen of them to the river and cut them to size. He was bare-chested and sweating.

"It's like travelling with Putin," said Harkness.

They detached the winch from the car and lashed the barrels alongside one another three by three. A carpet of logs was secured on top and within an hour the raft was built.

"Impressive," admitted Ross.

"Not just a pretty face," Harkness grinned. "Now, one of us needs to cross first."

"How come?"

"Without guide ropes we'd be washed away in an instant. Can you ask the villagers for a—?"

Sploosh! McCartney streaked across in a confident front crawl.

"There might be crocodiles, you idiot!" Harkness shouted.

But he emerged on the far side, and soon steel cable was taut across the river, their de facto ferry dancing and skipping on the rapids.

"Are you sure about this?" asked McCartney.

"Frankly, no," Harkness replied.

The raft lurched alarmingly as the front two wheels went on – but Harkness accelerated, the car zipping onto the platform before skidding to a halt. There was a series of loud reports as the steel rope skipped along the surface of the barrels until it adjusted to the load and the vessel seesawed in the water. They handed the raft out by the guide ropes, taking to the current with all the nervousness of an oversized debutante at a ball.

A speck was passing at cloud level. A Boeing 737, on its way to Windhoek.

Moments later the raft kissed the far bank and Harkness roared onto dry land, their shouts of triumph echoing through the forest.

24

Hastings' take-down had surely emanated from Number Ten. It was agent of the Prime Minister who had slid the incendiary documents beneath her door; by the PM's design had the clerk's computerised ballot had selected her to ask a question. They knew Hastings' hot-headedness, had predicted impulsive behaviour. Had she gone to the papers, the MP reflected bitterly, any half-decent reporter would have treble-checked their facts – and offered a right to reply before publishing. Thus, her appearance at Prime Minister's Questions had been confected.

Hastings' brand depended on the complete conviction of right-eousness to carry doubt before it, sweeping away compunction like an avalanche through a ski school. And now she'd been as wrong as wrong could be, making the front page of every national newspaper in the process, from the *Daily Star* right through to the *Financial Times*. But Gloria Hastings did not do apologies. Nor was she the type to take this sort of thing lying down – and she had not been idle.

Her first call was to a sympathetic SO17 police officer who checked the CCTV. The courier was revealed as a Venezuelan cleaning lady named Ximena, who recalled being asked to deliver the envelope by a white man with brown hair in a suit.

"Half of Whitehall consists of white men with brown hair in suits," Hastings protested. "Without them the business of govern-ment would instantly collapse."

It transpired Hastings' assassin had cornered the cleaner just off the main hall of Portcullis House, where white men in suits mill in their multitudes. And he had done his work well, for the exchange itself was located within the blind spot between two CCTV cameras. The chances of an identification looked slim.

Next Hastings tried a different tack. It seemed unlikely the PM's agents would have simply commanded the clerk to insert her name into the order paper against all protocol. They'd have been cuter than that: they'd have tampered with the ballot. Hastings' newspaper had recently established a data journalism unit, coder-journalists who scraped data from the web in search of stories. So she called in a favour and acquired a callow Swedish brainbox called Filip Åkesson, who in earlier life had done things of which the editorship preferred to remain in ignorance. It was easy enough to convince the clerk that her computer needed maintenance, and the program-mer went to work.

Åkesson soon established that after the order paper was gener-ated the clerk's PC had been reformatted – that is to say, the hard drive wiped – multiple times. This had been done remotely. But being offsite had prevented the person responsible from physically destroying the hard drive, and Åkesson was able to restore enough of what had been deleted to search for any files written to the machine immediately before that day's inquisition was selected.

He discovered the malware in an image file of joggers on Millbank.

This was good hacking: photographs sent from unknown sources are less likely to raise suspicion than exhortations to click a link or open a file. But even viewing them through a previewer can release the payload. The file had been sent via the professional networking website LinkedIn by someone claiming to be a civil servant at the Department for Education. LinkedIn does not require verification of employment claims, but people inexplicably tend to trust approaches through it more than via email and the clerk didn't verify his identity. This sock-puppet civil servant claimed to be organising weekly jogs around Westminster, and he had also done his research. For the clerk belonged to Putney Running Club – and she'd written for their website from her work computer, supplying the hacker with bountiful technical information. So he knew about the oldish version of Windows she was running and her outdated browser, and the malware was bespoke for her machine.

The payload was what is known as a 'reverse shell', which opened a connection back to the hacker's computer so he could install a second piece of malware in the ballot program. But in the reverse shell's metadata, Åkesson found an IP address. He now had the digital equivalent of a postcode and house number.

The computer turned out to belong to a retired cricket coach from Derbyshire. Only when the Swede telephoned in the guise of a BT engineer did it become apparent the owner's technical nous was such that he struggled placing online bets with Paddy Power. Listening in, Hastings, a connoisseur of bullshit, was convinced. So they made the drive north where the cricket coach, a Hastings fan, let them examine his computer. It transpired his PC had been taken over too: it was the hacker's first line of defence. Once more the computer had been overwritten multiple times; again Åkesson was equal to the task. But it led only to another innocent, this time the manager of a Cornish gastropub. And so it continued.

They spent the next week traversing the British Isles, rolling back concentric rings of false identities as Åkesson closed in on the user. They never got near the hacker's attack machine, the one from which he or she had taken over a host of others like a sorcerer with zombies dancing at his fingertips. But at the home of a Neighbourhood Watch warden in Ipswich they at last detected a PC their adversary had used for precisely one minute and fifty-two seconds and not bothered reformatting.

It was the chink in his armour.

And this computer – which the hacker had *actually sat down at* – was not in a private address, but an old-fashioned internet café. Gloria Hastings MP wrinkled her nose as Åkesson unveiled the birthplace of her troubles and fountainhead of her humiliation.

"The East End," she said. "Ghastly."

25

"Nothing's really impossible," crowed Harkness as they set off from the river the next morning, the afterglow of the crossing still with them. "Not when you put your mind to it. It's just some things are exceedingly hard."

McCartney rolled his eyes. "But that's not actually true, is it? You'll never get me interested in dead languages, I can tell you that now."

Harkness considered this. "Digit," he said.

"Huh?"

"Digit," he repeated. "The English word for both 'finger' and 'number'. Its double meaning is thought to have originated from the fact that we extend an index finger to indicate the number one."

"Right…"

"It comes from the Latin *digitus*. The Greek version is *datulos*, and going further back still the Sanskrit is *dis*. All three are derived from a lost Indo-European word, reconstructed as *deik*. Indo-European is the language our ancestors spoke thousands of years ago, as they spread out from northern India. It evolved into tongues as diverse as Italian and Russian and Welsh."

McCartney sighed. "Really, who gives a toss?"

"I'm not done," snapped Harkness. "In Turkey they say *tek*. But Turkish isn't an Indo-European language at all. In Nilo-Saharan, it's *tak*. Eskimo-Aleut, *tiqik*. The Sahara and Arctic Circle are not exactly next-door neighbours."

McCartney was peering at him.

"Also meaning 'finger', 'one' or 'show' – as in pointing with a finger – we have the following. Khmer, *tai*. Vietnamese, *tay*. Japanese, *te* – meaning hand. I could continue."

The atmosphere in the car had changed.

"Are you saying that *all* languages are related?" asked McCartney.

Harkness smiled. "Let's wander further afield still. The Ainu of Kamchatka, *tek*. Alaskan Yupik, *tekeq*. And dozens of tribal languages in South America say *tik*. We've voyaged around the planet in a single word."

"I like that," McCartney admitted.

"You see, if you went back far enough – to a time when the global population was numbered in the thousands – there would have been *one* language. It splintered, it evolved, and the universal language was lost. But just now, you were almost certainly hearing an echo of that first language. Their word for 'finger', to be precise, which was probably something like *tik*. This is profound, Ross." Harkness raised an index finger. "It illustrates the oneness of mankind."

McCartney's *hmmm* was audible over the banging of the car.

"By the way," said Harkness, "if all this 'we are truly one' stuff makes you feel warm and slushy inside, get ready for a corrective. Because that's exactly what Sakiko was out here trying to prove."

"What do you mean?"

"She was scouring languages spoken by Forest People right across Central Africa for whispers of our mother tongue. A crack, if you like, in that massive wall of time that separates *us* from *them*. It's my suspicion that whatever she found went right to the heart of the matter. And for some incomprehensible reason, someone doesn't like it."

McCartney had paled; suddenly the straw-coloured whiskers on his cheeks brought out the boy in him.

"So let me spell it out for you. This *is* important. Or to put it in a language even you might understand – we are playing for very high stakes indeed."

Unexpectedly, the trees had thinned, and they saw patches of grass between the trunks. It reminded Harkness of that band of sparse palm glade that often precedes a beach. Then the track turned a corner and they emerged on the shores of a vast lake, its extremities hidden far beyond sight to the east and the west. There were no platforms, no boats, not a trace of habitation. And the track ended there.

"What the hell?" said Harkness, studying the map. "This isn't marked…"

"It's here all right," said McCartney.

Wallowing offshore were the barrage-balloon forms of a pod of hippopotami, and with a jerking movement a tree trunk on the shore became a crocodile, clicking towards the water with awkward strides.

"We could make another raft?" suggested McCartney. "Punt our way over?"

Harkness placed a hand on his shoulder. "I really hate to say this to you, Ross. But *C'est impossible*."

26

"The end of the road," mused McCartney.

An hour had passed and they were sitting on the bonnet of the Mitsubishi with their backs against the windscreen. Harkness had produced the emergency bottle of Talisker and McCartney chain-smoked cigarettes; they resembled a pair of hoboes from a Steinbeck novel. Neither had admitted the inevitable, though only one course was left to them. They had to turn back.

Harkness sighed. "Sometimes, what you don't want to be doing—"

Suddenly McCartney leapt up, staring at the point where lake became horizon. "Is that a pirogue?"

Seconds later they heard it, the buzz of an outboard motor cacophonous across the still waters. Now Harkness and McCartney were both on their feet, waving their hands like castaways on a desert island. The boat changed course and met them at the bank, skippered by an elderly man with a white cape of hair and lips that puckered inward with age.

"*Je m'appelle* Kahungu," he said in a warbling voice. "*Où allez-vous?*"

Harkness showed him their destination on the map, eighty miles north as the bird flies. They were almost there.

"By car, you cannot," said Kahungu in French. "There is no track on that side, only jungle."

Without equipment or guides, hiking was a death wish.

"But I can take you," he continued. "One hundred dollars."

Harkness frowned. "But how?"

"There are rivers," he replied, tracing lines northward from the lake. "Many rivers."

A maniacal grin spread across McCartney's face. "So we're still in the game!"

Neither ingress nor egress could be discerned on the far bank, nor pathways through the foliage. This was the last frontier before total and utter wilderness, by far the most remote place Harkness had visited during a lifetime rich with adventure.

"I don't know," he murmured. "If one of us got bitten by a snake or something… we'd be really out on a limb."

Which was an understatement. As something between fear and excitement played in Harkness's stomach, the only movement was the stop–start procession of sweat down the faces of the travellers and the lazy pirouette of hippopotami offshore. Then McCartney produced a twenty pence piece, an incongruous vision in this equatorial hothouse.

"No," said Harkness. "I flat-out refuse. We are not putting this down to a bloody coin toss."

"Yolo," said McCartney.

"And what might that mean?"

"You only live once, mofo! And, honestly, do either of us have anything better to do right now?"

This was an extremely good point.

"Plus what about Sakiko?" he pressed. "She's out there, somewhere."

A moment passed. The cry of something primeval in the forest. Then Harkness shrugged.

"Oh, toss the damn coin."

The piece of metal zinged into the air and McCartney slapped it onto the back of his hand.

"Heads we continue, tails we go back. Agreed?"

The left corner of Harkness's mouth began twitching upwards. "You'd better not tell your father."

McCartney lifted his hand. And in that Jurassic setting, the image of the Queen, so redolent of red pillar boxes and tea towels, of tended lawns and *The Archers*, was the most incongruous thing of all.

"Keep calm and carry on," said Harkness.

*

Wind and water on Harkness's face, the whole planet juddering and sliding beneath him. The lift of a powerful engine and concomitant bump of gravity; air rushing in his ears. Sunlight seared through the clouds, the propeller carving the lake's surface into a green scythe as they veered towards the Western horizon.

"Wahoo!" cried McCartney, punching the air.

Beneath his knees Harkness clenched a fist in quiet exhilaration.

The abandoned car behind them was a child's toy left in the grass: their last physical connection to five thousand years of Western development. But now they could see a river issuing into the north side of the lake. Harkness also dimly registered the dot moving across the water at canopy level.

Then its significance was upon him. A helicopter. Already it was slowing. Then it changed direction. *And came straight at them.*

Kahungu seemed to know instinctively this was not good. When he gunned the engine the prow lifted clear of the water, streaking for the river and the branches interlaced over it. The helicopter was a mile away. Seconds later it was half that, losing height and gaining speed. Soon they were close enough for Harkness to see the Congolese pilot and – he registered surprise – a white woman sitting next to him. They still were fifty yards from safety, and Kahungu curved towards the ingress. But the helicopter was coming in at top speed, skimming across the water. A gullwing window opened, the woman leaned out, and Harkness knew the thing nestled in her arm must be a machine gun. Instantly the air around them was full of whistles and cracks, bullets lashing the lake around them and making it boil. They fell wildly at first, then arced towards the boat with increasing accuracy before smashing holes through the hull. A bullet glanced Kahungu's shoulder, blood tapering behind him like the tail of a kite. Still the helicopter neared, and for half a second Harkness saw the face of the woman who was trying to murder them. Suddenly the distance separating them from the helicopter was nothing and he realised it would hit –

A gale overcame them.

The noise was horrendous.

A moment of intensity, like being knocked spinning by a wave…

Then the helicopter was past, gaining height and banking. Harkness looked up from the bilges to discover they were still upright. At once Kahungu was on his feet, pulling starboard so hard that the pirogue danced upon one side, threatening to skitter over. Harkness's sculpture went spinning over the edge, lost to the deeps. Then they were in. It was dark beneath the boughs, only glimpses of sky flashing overhead. The boat slammed into the surface as Kahungu slalom-ed through twists and bends at suicidal speed. Abruptly it became mangrove swamp, branches threatening to whip their heads off as they shot past. They were following a buffalo trail, not a chink of blue visible overhead now. The helicopter was right above them, buzzing left to right. Then the zigzags grew larger until it was circling their boat in widening loops. Finally the whine of its engine faded away to the south-west.

27

"What do you mean, missed again?" spluttered Mirza.

With its tiers of neo-classical columns, the Royal Automobile Club swimming pool was the sort of place in which a Roman tyrant might have swum a few lengths before signing the morning's death warrants. Usually the lobbyist's breaststroke was serenity itself, his mouth never dipping below the surface. But now discomfort rippled from him, and bobbing alongside like a tugboat was Jasper.

"Not an easy take by the sound of things," he coughed, foam surging through his beard. "And now it's solid tree cover from there to the Cameroon."

"Try not to get your knickers in a twist," said Mirza. "We know exactly where they're going, after all. *She* can go ahead to welcome them."

"At least you put paid to Hastings," said Jasper.

A superior smile. "I daresay Lord Mandelson himself could learn a trick or two from old Dennis Mirza. Now, do you recall Dr Francesca Bianca, of the National Museum of Marche?"

When Jasper grinned his bottom teeth were like a row of pegs. "She who's currently floating about the upper atmosphere?"

"Indeed," said Mirza. "Unfortunately, it transpires she was corres-ponding with a French gentleman charged with investigating the Venus of Renancourt. Would you mind paying a visit?"

When they had changed and were ascending to the Brooklands Room for dinner, Mirza passed his man a 2014 cutting from Agence France-Presse reporting the discovery of the Venus.

> *A limestone statuette of a shapely woman some 23,000 years old has been discovered in northern France in what archaeologists described as an 'exceptional' find. Archaeologists stumbled on the Palaeolithic era sculp-ture during a dig in Amiens, the first such find in half a century.*
>
> *'The discovery of this masterpiece is exceptional and internationally significant,' said Nicole Phoyu-Yedid, head of cultural affairs in the area...*

The Venus had a bulky and elongated head, protuberant buttocks and what looked like vicious slash marks to the chest and abdomen. It also lacked hands and feet.

28

Now Harkness and McCartney were in deep, in every sense of the word. There was a silvery tint to the jungle here, a metallic sheen to the broad dark leaves bowing down to the water's edge. A pewter cast to the river too, reflecting the iron-shod skies above. New arrangements of light and shade cast webs between the foliage, and there were blossoms of scarlet and indigo on the trees. Little in the villages would have been out of place in the Bronze Age. When they couldn't buy food, Kahungu foraged for them and shot birds with a rifle that might have been used to fight the American Civil War. They had just eaten one such unfortunate when they heard drumming: wood on wood, not too far off amid the trees. Then an explosion of screeches, like the cries of some witch doctor in his madness. Kahungu gestured beneath his armpits.

Chimps.

Without warning McCartney dashed into the forest.

"Come back!" shouted Harkness.

Only the diminishing noise of McCartney trampling through the undergrowth answered him, and after a weary sigh he gave chase. Kahungu sprinted alongside, but as they caught up with McCartney an exhilaration rose in Harkness too. The apes were very close by now.

"Shall we?" hissed McCartney.

"Just this once," he whispered.

They fell into a low steal, thrilling to their pursuit. The band was on the move again and the cries receded ahead, tantalisingly beyond sight.

Darker. Denser. Quieter.

Another screech emanated from the undergrowth and they peered through the shadows, trying to make sense of the straggle of creeper and vine.

"Shall we go in?" whispered McCartney.

Kahungu took his meaning and shook his head forcefully.

Movement in the shadows.

"Something's in there," said McCartney.

The creature was definitely large, but all they could see of it was a curve, rummaging in the shadows. Harkness had the impression of the rounded back of a chimpanzee, viewed from side on. Then there was the *crack* of splitting wood and they found themselves confronted with a charging hippopotamus.

A dreamlike moment, dimly recognising this creature for what it was. The beast was monstrous, angry and coming at them fast: the most dangerous animal in all of Africa. Then a billion years of instinct kicked in hard and Harkness found himself running.

Mayhem. Blind panic. Thorns tearing at cheeks and arms, everyone for themselves. Rainforest is difficult even to walk through; at a sprint tendrils become cables of tensile strength and foliage transmogrifies into a mesh of steel. Harkness and McCartney banged foreheads and he saw stars, like they do in the cartoons. Then he burst free of the undergrowth to find himself sprinting through open space.

Too late he saw the net.

It was wide enough to span a tennis court, a dozen people holding it aloft. Harkness went into it at full pelt. He still had strength in him, but the line held easily before folding in from both sides. He heard a gunshot thirty metres away, McCartney's far-off bellow of surprise. Then beaters with clubs emerged from the undergrowth and he was unceremoniously bashed over the head. A final thought occurred to Harkness before the darkness claimed him, almost as a whimsy: that every one of the hunters was quite exceptionally short.

29

That morning brought another waspish exchange on board the *Tickety-Boo*.

"Bible studies is it now?" Hendry quipped, frying vegetarian bacon and peering at Johansen's work. "You'll be joining the DUP next."

"What do I have to do to get some privacy here?" Johansen shot back.

Hendry banged her saucepan down on the hob. "Nobody *asked* you to be here, dear. You just turned up out of the blue, remember? You might at least be civil."

Johansen grabbed her books and marched out of the cabin, scanning the sky for helicopters before stepping onto the tow-path.

"Hello neighbour!" It was Adriaen from the *Time Traveller*, wearing a Momentum badge and smoking a joint. "You want some of this badboy?"

Bringing on the fuzziness would be a respite from the thoughts of persecution that pinged around her head. And if Adriaen was for proper socialism, he couldn't be that bad. For the first time she smiled at him.

"It's Anita," she said.

*

Only when it was time for Hendry's life-drawing class did she return. Alone on the boat the philologist's nib flashed as quotations from the Old Testament filled her notebook.

> *No shrub of the field was yet in the earth, and no herb of the field had sprung up. Then the Lord God formed man and breathed into his nostrils the breath of life. Out of the ground God made grow every tree that is good for food. And the Lord God took Adam and put him in the Garden of Eden. And He took one of Adam's ribs and made a woman, and brought her unto the man. And the man called his wife Eve, because she was the mother of all living. And they were both naked, the man and his wife, and were not ashamed.*

Allegory described fact: it is common knowledge that our species once roamed the earth in a state of nature. But Adam and Eve are real too. For the genetics reveal a male who was the direct ancestor of every man in the world today *genuinely existed*. Mutations on the Y chromosome show every living male is the direct descendant of a single African who lived about 60,000 years ago. Other men were alive at the same time, of course – but their lineages all happen to have gone extinct at some point, while his continued to branch out until it was the only one left. Counter-intuitively, however, he lived thousands of years after Eve. While mitochondrial DNA – handed down directly from mother to daughter – shows all women to be descended from a single female too, 'Eve' lived ten millennia earlier than her apocryphal husband.

> *And God commanded Adam, saying: 'Of every tree thou may freely eat, but of the tree of knowledge thou shalt not.'*

> But when the woman saw that the tree made one
> wise, she took the apple and did eat, and Adam did eat.
> Unto Adam, God said: 'Because thou hast eaten of
> the tree, cursed is the ground for thy sake; in toil shalt
> thou eat all the days of thy life. And thou shalt eat the
> herb of the field. In the sweat of thy face shalt thou eat
> bread, till thou return to the ground. I will greatly multi-
> ply thy pain and travail.' Then God sent him forth from
> the Garden of Eden, to till the ground.

As an allegory for the origins of civilisation, this was spot on again.
Johansen had read that the skeletons of the first farmers were actually *less*
well-nourished than their hunter-gatherer forbears. Flesh and fruit are
a more nourishing diet than bread – while farming led to ever-denser
populations to be fed with finite supplies. So we became addicted to this
accidental invention; those pioneering agriculturalists had exchanged a
life of plenty for hardship and toil.

Good myths embody big truths.

So much for farming. What of clothes?

> The eyes of both of them were opened, and they knew
> that they were naked; and they sewed fig leaves together
> and made themselves girdles. And the Lord God made
> for Adam and his wife garments, and clothed them.

During her research Johansen had read that scientists have worked
out the actual date *Homo sapiens* first wore clothes, evidenced by the
DNA of the humble clothes louse. This species exists only on close-fitting
garments, equipped with different claws from the more common body
louse that dwells in animal fur. By the same technique with which Aaron
was linked to the First Temple Period of Jewish history, the clothes
louse's divergence from its more ancient cousin has been calculated at
70,000 BC. Ergo, that's when we must have invented the sewing needle,

something Neanderthals never achieved. It struck Johansen that rather a
lot of advanced human behaviours began in about 70,000 BC.

Next Johansen tackled the dispersal of Adam's ancestors across the
face of the planet. This was the Exodus, Out of Africa; the date was
60,000 BC.

> *Of his sons was the whole earth overspread. Of these*
> *were the isles of the nations divided in their lands, every*
> *one after his tongue. And of these were the nations divid-*
> *ed in the earth. And the whole earth was of one language*
> *and one speech.*

The Universal Language. Devastatingly accurate once again.

> *And the Lord said: 'Behold, they are one people, and*
> *they have one language. Come, let us confound their*
> *language, that they may not understand one another's*
> *speech.' And thence did the Lord scatter them abroad*
> *upon the face of the earth.*

And there's a typically human irony, Johansen reflected: the single
biggest barrier to global communication today is *language*. But the
people of the world needed to talk more than ever. She glanced at
the left of centre broadsheet Hendry had bought that morning, its
front page a symphony of violence and nativism. Syria remained a
butcher's yard; a hospital in Yemen had been hit by a Saudi airstrike;
the rivalry between Riyadh and Tehran was like two tectonic plates
grinding against each other, building towards an earthquake. On
and on it went, the geopolitical turmoil only deepening as Johansen
worked through the paper. The deranged US president wanted to "hit
reset" in the Middle East through military intervention and sought
allies; Britain's Prime Minister danced along a tightrope, committing
to nothing until their trade deal was complete. British troops were on

exercise in Estonia as a deterrent to another Russian land-grab, and by way of thanks Russian bombers had 'buzzed' British airspace again yesterday evening. Thus, were America, Britain, Russia, Saudi Arabia and Iran interlinked in a complex web of rivalry and bluff. With the exception of the US president (who hoped a limited ground campaign in Syria might improve his polling) none of the actors really *wanted* to go to war. But neither could anyone back down, and in that sense it recalled 1914. Johansen found the imbroglio as terrifying as it was depressing. Perhaps, she reflected, it would have been better had our species remained wild.

> *Because thou hast eaten of the tree, cursed is the ground*
> *for thy sake. I will greatly multiply thy pain and travail.*

The only light relief was a sidebar about that daft MP who'd smeared the Chief Whip in the Commons; Gloria Hastings had just been removed from the Foreign Affairs Select Committee for bringing it into disrepute. But Johansen paused on page nine: the misadventures of fellow academics were of intrinsic interest.

> *A DISTINGUISHED archaeologist who travelled to the Congo in search of a colleague has himself disappeared, the Foreign Office has said.*
>
> *Professor Randolph Harkness, formerly of the University of Bristol, ventured to the central African country two weeks ago to look for missing Dr Sakiko Tsuda.*
>
> *David Motion, vice chancellor of the university, said: "My thoughts are with his loved ones at this difficult time..."*

In that ghoulish habit newspapers have of curating similar traged-ies together, there was another missing persons story beneath.

MISSING EDINBURGH COUPLE 'MAY HAVE ENTERED SUICIDE PACT'

Johansen had never been one for dwelling on the tragedies of others, and she turned the page. Then it clicked. She turned back. And when she skipped down the article the page became dislocated in her vision, as though she were staring at a photograph of the newspaper and not reality. She was looking at her own name.

> *Dr Anita Johansen, 45, has not been seen at Edinburgh University for almost a week. Meanwhile her husband Marcus, 53, a property lawyer, did not turn up for work three days ago. Their car has now been found abandoned by cliffs 15 miles away at Oxroad Bay. A police source said...*

So they had him. Or they had killed him. Inconceivable that Marcus would take his own life, nor would he have run off. He was too stable, too reliable, would never dream of it. For a long time Johansen wept: hugging her own chest, rocking backward and forward, wishing she had never conceived of this accursed project. It had brought nothing but misery.

A long time later rain began drumming on the roof of the *Tickety-Boo*. But this sound of comfort brought no relief. Instead it catapulted her back into the Old Testament and the source of all her grief.

The Great Flood.

What did this represent? To answer the question, Johansen had delved even further back through the chronicles of history. For when the Old Testament was written, the flood story was not original material...

30

Harkness awoke to find himself lying on strips of beaten bark stretched across a wooden frame, head resting on a pillow of plantain leaves. He sat up and looked about. It was a small conical hut with walls of tear-drop-shaped Marantaceae leaves hung on wattle; the scratching of unseen beetles was amplified by these natural drums. A steely light shone through gaps between the leaves, and outside Harkness heard snatches of song, the *thunk thunk thunk* of something being pounded into something else. A poultice had been applied to his temple.

He was not alone.

The watcher was perhaps twenty, his eyes fixed upon Harkness in the gloom. His brows were dark and suggestive of testosterone, and the eyes beneath were quick and brown. The jawline was proud and he wore a Manchester United shirt that Harkness identified as 1993/94, the Eric Cantona year. He also carried a spear. Then the man stood and Harkness saw that he was unmistakeably of the Forest People.

Harkness was led into a clearing between several great moabi trees, their trunks rising ramrod straight for two hundred feet before exploding into mushroom clouds of branches and foliage. Three dozen of the same beehive-shaped shelters were arranged around a communal fire upon which a colobus monkey was roasting, saline bubbles foaming from one nostril. Evidently the group were nomads, for children were present and the ground hadn't been trodden into mud. The source of the thunks was a woman using an elephant tusk to hammer strips of bark into the material he'd been lying on. Most of those present wore loincloths of the same. A few T-shirts and pairs of jeans had found their way here, but Harkness saw just a handful of other manufactured objects: knives, machetes and the ubiquitous plastic bucket. When it came to weapons the spear and the bow and arrow were still king here.

It had rained and steam rose from drying huts. When a woman readjusted a Marantaceae leaf it released a cascade of cupped water, and there was a satisfying grunt of male annoyance from within. Smoke trickled from vents at the top of each hut, the surrounding leaves trembling with the rising air. Harkness was in the presence of hunter-gathering Ba Aka Forest People, the real deal, living a lifestyle mostly unchanged since the epoch he'd spent a lifetime describing. These were the last adherents to a way of life *Homo sapiens* had embraced for a thousand times longer than cities.

Squatting by the fire were McCartney and Kahungu, damp, dirty and miserable. They were surrounded by Ba Aka hunters with their dogs, absorbed in mending the net made of *kosa* vines that had ensnared Harkness. His guard hooted towards one of the huts, no larger nor more elaborate than the others, and from this emerged the tribal elder. He was about sixty, bald-headed and glowering; like all the Forest People he was impeccably clean. When the elder spoke in Be-bayaga Kahungu translated into French.

"What are you doing in our Forest?"

"Tell him we are honoured to be here," Harkness began. "We're looking for—"

A commotion was audible at the fringe of the camp, and before he could continue a teenager dashed into the clearing, babbling at the assembled. The entire band trotted to see what was happening.

"My god," said Harkness.

Two hundred feet up a great moabi tree and hysterical with fear was a five-year-old boy. The child had used the druid's beard of creepers and strangler figs to ascend in search of honey; leaf pouches dangled from his loincloth and a bees' nest was within arm's reach. He was under attack and swatted at the air, his panic rousing laughter on the ground. The Ba Aka clapped under their armpits and stamped the earth and an elderly woman grinned to reveal teeth filed into points.

"He thinks he is a Real Man," the elder explained. "But he has not killed an antelope or something bigger yet, so he is not a Real Man. If he was, he would have known to light a fire beneath to smoke out the bees."

"He's terrified," Harkness protested. "Get them to do something…"

"There is no rush," said the elder. "He must learn that the Forest is to be respected."

Before Harkness could formulate his reply McCartney began to climb.

He rose swiftly at first, but with growing care as ten feet became twenty and then fifty. At sixty he slipped, grabbing a thick creeper with both hands as his legs swung out pendulously over the void. The hunters were much amused and there was lively debate over whether he'd make it. But McCartney resumed the ascent and two minutes later he was peering down at them, scarlet-cheeked but triumphant. The child was struck into wonderment by this extraordinary new arrival. But he allowed McCartney to peel him from the trunk and place him on his shoulders. The tiny infant wrapped his arms around McCartney's head, then they descended. When they touched down on solid earth the encampment exploded into jubilation.

"They say he is a *miki nde ndura*," said Kahungu. "A Son of the Forest. Farmers or fishermen like me? We are not Real People to them. But Ross, they say he is a Real Person. They say his name is Mulefu. It is meaning, 'tall'."

The child wouldn't relinquish his saviour's hand, snot and dried tears encrusted on his face. This was nothing less than a giant, and he gazed at McCartney as if he were some preternatural being descended from Olympus.

Kahungu was giggling. "They say you are like monkey, Mulefu."

"Oh, I don't know about that," said McCartney. "It's not so difficult once you get going…"

Kahungu surrendered to hysterics. "No – it is because you have a hairy body and a white face."

"Ah. Tell them they are too kind."

Amid the fast-flowing Be-bayaga all around them the three syllables were instantly recognisable, and Harkness froze.

"…Sa-ki-ko…"

He whipped around to face the speaker. "Sakiko! Did that man just say Sakiko?"

Kahungu's translation into Be-bayaga stilled the camp. All merriment had ceased, and the elder jabbed the haft of his spear into the earth.

"Tell me what you know of Sakiko," he demanded.

"She's our friend," said Harkness.

"*Bongo yako!*" barked the elder.

"You are a liar," translated Kahungu.

When Harkness produced his smartphone a superstitious hum went through the camp. But on seeing a photograph of Sakiko the elder cried out in joy, clapping himself under the armpit.

"But she is our friend also! From the village of *Bri*-stol, where there are many hills and a bridge. And the people drink alcohol made of fruit picked from trees."

Harkness was touched by Sakiko's pride in her adopted city. "That sounds like the one…"

Now stools were brought and a girl fetched a bowl of warm water so they could wash. They were handed cups of steaming *liko*, a bitter brew of forest berries, nuts and herbs with a mildly stimulating effect.

"Sakiko arrived from the south in the company of my wife's great uncle," the elder explained. "She wanted to learn the languages of the Real People. She came with rice and beans and other things we cannot obtain easily here. She stayed with us for three months, until she knew our words and could speak to us in our own language. Then she asked us to introduce her to the Ba Aka who live far to the north-west, so they would trust her too."

"Sounds like good solid anthropology," Harkness murmured.

"All the *Miki nde ndura* in this region have encountered her," said the elder. "She wandered far and around, always in the company of the Real People. She is not herself a Real Person, like Mulefu. She would not climb the tall trees. She would not hunt or even eat meat. She did not worship the Forest – in fact she worshipped no god at all! And yet she knew the ways of the Forest well. Better than the Not Real People who came only to harm the Forest."

McCartney looked up. "Harm?"

"Who are the 'Not Real People'?" asked Harkness.

The chieftain gestured northwards with a flick of the chin, a glint of malice in his eyes.

"They arrived last month at the Great Swamp where we used to collect many frogs and *awayoto* leaves for dysentery. But none of us may go there now, and they hunt us if we do. One of my cousins is *mpenzá boweí*, that is to say completely dead. They cut down trees and dig the earth. We thought that you were Not Real People too, and that is why you yourselves were hunted."

31

Cosmo Internet Café in Bethnal Green was a little shop of many wonders. Lycamobile adverts offered cheap calls to twenty-one countries; money could be dispatched to Nigeria or Bangladesh at the touch of a button; there was photocopying, banner printing and even a small letting agency. But the owner eyed Hastings with suspicion.

"I'm a Member of Parliament," she announced, reaching for her pass.

"I know exactly who you are," he said quietly. "You're the politician who hates immigrants."

"I don't *hate* immigrants," Hastings trilled as Filip Åkesson squirmed in the background. "I just think there are far too many of them."

The shopkeeper folded his arms. "What is it that you want?"

"Two weeks ago I was hacked, disastrously. It seems the perpetrator used one of your computers and I wondered if you had CCTV."

"I don't see why I should help you."

"I'll pay."

"You think you can just buy me?"

"*Please!* Look, I got hoaxed, and—"

The shopkeeper raised a hand. "I know what happened, Ms Hastings. Us immigrants do read the papers, you know."

"I'm not a bad person! I volunteer at a horse charity!" A madness had come into her eyes. "And I know people always say this, but I genuinely *do* have lots of Muslim friends…"

The shopkeeper sighed. He was a reasonable man, and a kind one. He also sensed she was telling the truth – about the hoax and the horse charity, at least.

"Very well," he said. "But I want you to remember this favour next time you open your mouth to say something unpleasant about Muslims."

He found the recording and Åkesson supplied the timecode. But the CCTV system was a decade old, the hacker barely distinguishable through a sea of murk. Her assassin a man of shadow: the only identifiable thing was an umbrella.

"Do you recall this individual?" asked Hastings.

The shopkeeper frowned. "Actually, I do remember him. It wasn't raining, so I wondered why he had an umbrella that day. He was quite friendly. A gentleman."

"Face? Hair?"

"Long brown hair. Maybe fifty years old. And he wore a ring on his little finger."

"A signet ring," said Hastings. "Well, it's a start. Anything else?"

A light came into the shopkeeper's eyes. "Yes! I made a joke about the umbrella, and when he laughed I saw a filling in his back teeth." He indicated a molar. "But not gold. It was a diamond, I think…"

Åkesson was tapping at a machine. "Careless. He visited two other websites while he was here."

"Let me see, let me see," blurted Hastings, barging him aside.

The first webpage belonged to the Garrick Club in Covent Garden.

"There's a members' area on the website," said Hastings. "Did he log in?"

"No such luck," said Åkesson. "This is the only page he read."

As the Garrick is restricted to gentleman members only,
female members of reciprocal clubs are not permitted to
use the Club in their own right, but are most welcome
as guests, when accompanied by a male member of a
reciprocal club...

"Frightful old boors," she snorted. "And I thought the House of
Lords was bad. What was the other website?"

Åkesson brought up the homepage of Peter Harrington Rare Books
in Chelsea, where their suspect had looked at a single item.

ZURAYK, Costi K.
Provisional Readings in the Medieval History of the
Near East.
Published: Beirut American Press, 1934.
£1,250.

It was marked as no longer for sale.

"Before you ask, he didn't buy it," said Åkesson. "Not from this
computer, anyway."

"Still, we're getting somewhere." Hastings' nostrils flared. "A
member of the Garrick Club with one *very* identifying feature, and an
interest in the Orient—"

Orientalist.

The thought stopped Hastings mid-sentence. She was struck
dumb. Sir Hugh's words floated back to her, vouchsafed from a more
carefree time.

My chum heard a codename. Possibly it refers to the file, possibly the
operation. Can't rule out that it's a person either.

And more presciently:

By the Christ be careful, won't you?

Hastings had the blinding epiphany that the sensible course of
action now would be to terminate her investigations, resign from

Parliament and use her column to signal to these people that she was no longer sniffing around their business. Possibly pack in the media work altogether. Buy a place in the Cotswolds and spend her days riding horses. Go on nice holidays. But that would have meant surrender. And running up the white flag was not Gloria Hastings' style.

*

They went at once to Peter Harrington's, where the bookseller was a model of grace. But when Hastings enquired as to the buyer he sighed.

"I'm afraid we would *never* provide a customer's personal details to a third party," he said. "The best I could do is pass on a message?"

Hastings puffed up her chest. "I am a Parliamentarian. And we are dealing here with a criminal case of national importance."

"I'm well aware who you are, but I can't be of assistance alas. Just can't. Terribly sorry. Come back with the police and a court order and I'd be delighted to help…"

Åkesson had already hacked into the bookseller's system, but the buyer paid in cash.

"What now?" he asked.

"Now it's over to me, darling boy. I need to purloin an invitation to the sexist toads' club of Covent Garden, and somehow persuade every single member with a signet ring to show me his back teeth…"

32

In honour of McCartney's unveiling as a Real Person the Ba Aka prepared a feast. Two dozen fish had been caught by the 'dam and bail' method, a section of stream diked off and emptied of water to leave the unfortunate creatures high and dry. They barbecued the fish with forest herbs and prepared a delicious stew of groundnut, manioc and tiny bitter tomatoes. The bounty of the forest knew no bounds, and Harkness thought of the irony that the advent of farming had led to famines. After they had eaten, the tribe broke into song, and this was unlike any music he had heard. It had a yodelling quality, multitudinous and unearthly, skipping between the octaves in ways Europeans had never conceived of. The notes were answered by the croaking of frogs and the sonorous, plaintive call of chameleons in the trees above. The ancient Egyptians had encountered Forest People in the southern Nile region four millennia before, and were equally captivated by their song. This was music transmitted from our species' ancient past, and Harkness was greatly moved to hear it.

Later that evening he questioned the elder again.

"There was one word Sakiko was interested in more than any other," said the tribesman. "It is a bad word. Yet every camp we encountered, she asked about it first. She wanted to know more than anything where it came from."

A quiet had fallen over the camp.

"But of course, words are words." The elder laughed. "They have always been with us, we cannot know how they started."

"What word is that?" asked Harkness.

Nobody would answer.

"What word?" he repeated softly.

"*Nyónsoboma*," hissed the chieftain, and every pair of eyes went down.

Harkness consulted Sakiko's word lists on his phone. *Nyónsoboma* was spoken by the Gyele Forest People of Cameroon and the Kola of Gabon, while both the Mbuti and Mongo Cwa of the DRC said *Niosobowei*. The Twa in Burundi said *Niosobowa*, and the Batwa of Uganda had *Gbogbobowei* – presumably corrupted by a local term, but identifiable by the last two syllables. Harkness saw with rising astonishment that the word existed in recognisable form for every language Sakiko had documented. The only words with more commonality were fundamentals such as 'mother' or 'food'.

"*Nyónsoboma* must be a very ancient word indeed," said Harkness. "Almost certainly a relic of the ancestral Forest People language, possibly older still."

"What does it mean?" asked McCartney.

But when Harkness read the translation a darkness overcame him, oppressing his spirit with its echoes of an ancient crime.

"It means extermination."

*

The next morning Harkness announced his intention to continue north.

"What about the Ba Aka who got killed?" said McCartney.

"The Forest People have several categories of 'dead'," replied Harkness. "A bad fever is 'dead'. Lying in a coma is 'completely dead'. To be truly six feet under is 'dead forever'. Besides, Sakiko's dig is now under the auspices of the British Secret Service – everything speaks to their involvement. That's why Aled Wilson did all he could to push us away. I suspect Sakiko's been unlawfully detained – and the hunter who got close was roughed up a bit at worst. MI6 might be devious, but they're not evil. Not to law-abiding people, anyway."

"What about the helicopter?" said McCartney.

"Not MI6," said Harkness.

"How could you know that?"

Harkness stared at his palms, contemplating thirty-year-old vows of loyalty and secrecy.

"I haven't been completely straight with you about the nature of my relationship with MI6," he said at last. "I may have been *slightly* more involved than I let on. And I do know a fair bit about the parameters within which MI6 operates. So you can forget this Hollywood fantasy of MI6 as state-sanctioned assassins. It's just not true."

"Then who was in the chopper?"

"That I don't know."

"What if she comes after us again?"

"We're in a jungle six times the size of France. Needle in a haystack doesn't come close."

"And if it's her waiting for us up there? Along with whoever the hell she's working for?"

Harkness thought about this. "Then I'm quite sure Aled Wilson would have simply told us what's going on so we could make an informed choice not to go. They wouldn't let us wander into danger. It's not the 'house style' of the British state."

"Maybe – if you'd given him the chance. We gave him the slip, if you remember."

An interesting role reversal was going on, Harkness noted. Could it be possible that the realities of Congolese travel had instilled a soupçon of maturity into his unwilling apprentice? But there was another explanation. Already that morning the Ba Aka had taught McCartney how to carry heavy weights by the 'tump line' method, the load on his back held by a strip of bark around the forehead. And that evening they were off to hunt porcupines with dogs, a prospect McCartney proclaimed himself "stoked" about. For the first time since they'd met he seemed content, and Harkness suspected that his friend's reluctance to head north had little to do with safety considerations.

"Anyway, what will you do if you get there?" McCartney pressed him. "You can hardly go busting Sakiko out of MI6 hands…"

"I'll take photographs," said Harkness. "I'll document British involvement, this barmy anthropological cover-up they've got going on. And I'll send evidence of illegality to the papers – I've got a contact on *The Guardian* and one on *The Times*. We'll shame them into releasing Sakiko by weight of public opprobrium. And…"

He looked down.

"What is it?"

"There's something else," he said. "Something that intrigues and frightens me in equal measure."

The cries of children filled the silence, all the clatters and bangs and barks of a nomadic camp going about its business.

"I've been going through Sakiko's word lists again – and the word for 'extermination' exists in the most variety right here in northern Congo-Brazzaville. Sakiko documented a dozen Ba Aka dialects with a permutation of *Nyónsoboma*, all within a hundred miles of Itanga."

"Which is relevant – why?"

"There's a rule of thumb in evolution. Whether talking about languages, species or mutations on the genome, where you see the most diversity is where the subject originated. The longer something remains in one location, the more time it has to evolve into subspecies. For example, there are more languages in Africa than any other continent. Or closer to home, there are twenty-one languages spoken in Europe that descended from Latin, including the tiny ones like Catalan, Galician or Walloon. But in South America, there are just two – Spanish and Portuguese arrived in the fifteenth century and haven't had time to split."

McCartney was nodding.

"Another example. The grape's thought to have first been cultivated in Georgia eight thousand years ago and today more than five hundred grape varieties are found there – more than in any other country on earth. And of the five thousand varieties of potato, four thousand are found only in the Andes, where it was domesticated. Some Peruvian potatoes are as black as coal and others look like raspberries."

"That is actually pretty mind-blowing."

"Yes, it is. And it applies to humans as well. If you study the harmless mutations present in all human DNA, you'll find more diversity in African populations than anywhere else. It's a pattern mirrored in every sphere of biology and human culture."

"So you're saying the Forest People's word for extermination originated here," said McCartney slowly.

The shadows were in Harkness's eyes again. "If Sakiko's fieldwork is sound, I'd say that's a racing certainty."

"And you – you told me the Forest People were once all over Africa."

"That's right," said Harkness.

"But not anymore."

"No."

Neither man could bring himself to voice the self-evident truth. Instead it hung between them: in the moisture, in the air. High above a chameleon had begun its mournful ghostly song.

"I want to know exactly what happened in Itanga," said Harkness. "And I want to know what the Foreign Office has to hide."

"I'm coming with you."

By then Harkness knew McCartney better than to argue.

*

When they told the elder of their plans he insisted on lending them a guide.

"To walk in the Forest is to look upon God's face," he said. "Go with grace."

Harkness thought at once of something the great anthropologist Colin Turnbull had written of his own stay with the Forest People.

> Every trembling leaf, every weathered stone, every cry of an animal or chirp of a cricket tells you that the forest is alive with some presence.

The hunter who had stood guard over Harkness on that first morning was chosen to show them the hidden ways through the rainforest. His name was Batsinga and to protect himself for the journey he decorated his chest with a paste made from the heart and eye of an antelope. There was still an intensity to him, but now that they were allies a kindliness laced the habitual frown and there was respect in that frank appraising stare. Following antelope or buffalo trails they would close in on Itanga like phantoms.

Before they departed the elder made two small incisions on McCartney's collarbones, rubbing ash into the wounds so it would be absorbed beneath the skin that would become scarified. The rainforest would always be a part of him now.

"*Miki nde ndura*," said the elder.

Son of the Forest.

It was with sadness that McCartney left the camp.

33

Kahungu dropped them a day's march from Itanga. They set off through a glade of slender ironwood trees with limbs dappled yellow in the sunlight. There was something mystic about these dells, Arthurian even, and Harkness yearned to linger a while. But they continued north, drawn towards the peat.

Batsinga's camp-craft was extraordinary. At lunchtime he felled a shaft of bamboo, unfolding from it an entire dinner service and kitchen. He cut short lengths and tied vine thongs around the middle so they splayed out into three-legged stools. From another section he fashioned spoons. Then he scraped shavings from the shaft, stuffing them inside a halved section. He rubbed the other half across this at speed until the friction set them ablaze. This was a jungle matchbox, far more efficacious than the sticks Harkness had once rubbed together as a Boy Scout. He stuffed rice into a third shaft, added water and placed it on the flames. Within minutes they smelled it cooking. Venerable this lifestyle may have been; it was anything but primitive.

"I can't even cook rice at home," McCartney lamented.

Soon afterwards the jungle became near impassable, though Batsinga ghosted through the undergrowth with his high-stepping gait. He clapped to avoid startling buffalo and sang to warn off the feared leopard. The ground was soggy beneath their feet, and Harkness sniffed a pinch of coal-black earth.

He raised an eyebrow. "Peat."

Now Batsinga trod silently, scouring the forest for enemies with his bowstring taut. They encountered three wary Ba Aka, who communed with Batsinga in low voices. But when Batsinga turned to face Harkness his jaw was contorted in agony.

"Sakiko." He pointed north with trembling finger. "*Mpenzá bowei…*"

Harkness greyed. "Completely dead."

"That means she's alive," said McCartney quietly.

The rainforest here had a mutable quality, fresh arrangements of tree and creeper encountered hourly. They crept through a shifting palette of emeralds and junipers and limes. Soon their steps were taking them shin-deep into peat; the forest had become curiously quiet, even insects muting their chorus. They were miles into Itanga now. It was late afternoon, stiflingly hot. That was when they found her.

*

She was strung from the upper branches of a mahogany tree, her hands and feet severed, the stumps bound. Blood raked dark claw marks down the bark. Death had not been long. Dumped at the foot of the great tree were two Forest People. They had been machine-gunned, macabre presents beneath the Christmas tree with Sakiko at its apex. McCartney retched and bent double, but Harkness simply stood and looked as horror and grief rushed through his mind. Their journey had been in vain.

"*Libela bowei,*" muttered Batsinga.

Dead forever.

Then the hunter said a phrase that Harkness couldn't understand, yet got a sense of by the way he looked from tree to tree: by the way he peered up to the forest canopy in great reverence; how he stared at the ground beneath their feet which had given birth to it all.

It is a matter for the Forest, now.

Perhaps it was the Ba Aka's very reverence that dulled his senses for a crucial moment. But suddenly the click of metal on metal was right behind them. Harkness knew this sound of old: it was the recoil spring of Kalashnikovs, seating the bolt. Before he could react six white gunmen emerged from the undergrowth, dressed in a mishmash of combat fatigues. These were not MI6 agents, and Harkness saw for the first time his utter folly in coming here. By his adamantine willpower alone had they made it to this place, and he'd brought McCartney. Then one of the gunmen spoke, and his accent was Russian.

34

He had seen all. He possessed all knowledge. He was wise beyond measure. He had the wisdom of all things.

Dr Anita Johansen transcribed the oldest prose in existence into her notebook. Drawing on Assyrian oral tradition dating back to at least 2000 BC, the *Epic of Gilgamesh* is more ancient than the Old Testament by a millennium. And this is the earliest source of the Ark story. Climatologists speculate that both texts must draw on a folk memory of a genuine flood, caused by melting glaciers, a rising Mediterranean.

Johansen knew this was not so.

She glanced at one of her textbooks, *The Story of Assyria* by Zenaide Ragozin. All that was known of the Assyrian civilisation when Queen Victoria was crowned were a few references in the Bible. Then nineteenth-century archaeologists began digging between the Tigris and the Euphrates – and sure enough, there it all was.

Good myths embody big truths.

It was the Assyrians who created the first bureaucracies and taxation; it was the Assyrians who invented writing. *Ex oriente lux*, as the old saying goes. From the east, light.

Like the first book of the Old Testament, the *Epic of Gilgamesh* is a story about the end of innocence. But that is not the only similarity. A serpent prevents the hero Gilgamesh from obtaining a plant that will grant him eternal life, foreshadowing Eve and the Tree of Knowledge.

Gilgamesh contains an account of seven years of famine. And then there is the flood story common to both. It follows that the Bible and *Gilgamesh* are twigs growing off the same branch – like *Homo sapiens* and the Neanderthals, the English language and German.

Johansen's gaze fell on a *Telegraph* cutting from 1872, describing the first decipherment of *Gilgamesh* by a scholar at the British Museum.

> *With what a magic spell those strange broken sentences carried our minds backward! The tablets were found near the ruins of a city known to the Assyrians as Uruk. It is referred to as 'Erech' in the Bible, and the nearest town today is called 'Warka', an Arabic descendant of the original name.*

Uruk > Erech > Warka. These evolutionary relationships had come to fascinate Johansen.

Now she worked only while her host was out. She had confronted Hendry about the snooping that morning, only to be told she needed psychiatric help. When her friend suggested Marcus had merely run off with another woman the argument got fiery. It was unclear where Johansen could go next.

Half a mile away, Eric Jasper was stripping a Glock 30S pistol in a below-stairs lavatory at the canal-side Anchor and Hope pub. As the old man fed .45 rounds into the magazine he weighed one in his hand, fat as a quail's egg. These made a mess of people. The weapon had chunky dimensions to accommodate the high calibre ammunition; the polymer body gave it the look of a child's toy. He produced an Osprey 40 Suppressor, the black oblong capable of reducing the plosive discharge of the weapon to little more than a click. His hands were steady as he attached the device and a pale grey tongue protruded from one corner of his mouth. He was careful not to let his overcoat brush the grimed tiles. Then he slipped the assemblage into his inside pocket, which bulged conspicuously.

Hendry had given Johansen away. Infuriated by her erratic behaviour and convinced marital difficulties lay behind it, she'd emailed a mutual friend. That friend emailed Marcus himself, and the deceased's account was being monitored. Hendry's boat and mooring were registered with the Canal and River Trust and from there it was easy.

Oblivious to impending doom, Johansen continued transcribing from the *Epic of Gilgamesh*. First she introduced the central character of the eponymous work, an Assyrian king.

> *Gilgamesh was unsurpassed in his strength. His was a powerful force, a raging flood-wave. He was taller than all others, majestic and fearsome. Mountain passes did he open and he dug wells on the slopes. The city of Uruk did he build. He had the wisdom of all things. He knew of the Secret and of the Mystery. He knew of the time before the Great Flood.*

Johansen too knew of the time before the Great Flood. It was a heavy cross to bear. From the east, *darkness*.

Now the supporting character of Enkidu.

> *Hair covered Enkidu's entire body. Naked was Enkidu. He knew not people or homestead. He quenched his thirst at waterholes with the beasts. Then one day, a hunter came face to face with Enkidu at the waterhole. The hunter was filled with terror. And the hunter told his father, "I have beheld a wild man come down from the hills. His strength is the greatest in all the land. His power is mighty. He has filled in the pits I dug with my own hands. And he has torn asunder the traps which I set."*
>
> *Thus the hunter said unto Gilgamesh: "There is a mighty wild man come down out of the mountains. I am afraid and dare not approach him."*

If Gilgamesh symbolised civilisation, then Enkidu was the Other.

> *Then Enkidu said, "I will challenge Gilgamesh, for my strength is great. I shall alter destiny. He who was begotten in the wilderness possesses the greatest strength. Look upon me and despair."*
>
> *Enkidu journeyed unto Uruk, whereupon the multitudes thronged around him. "How like Gilgamesh he is," they said. "Though shorter in height, he is more stalwart in appearance."*
>
> *Then did Gilgamesh and Enkidu grapple, one against the other. Their anger was inflamed. Neither would yield. In fierce combat did they struggle, and they raged and snorted like wild bulls. Then Gilgamesh overcame Enkidu and placed his knee on the fallen wild man. Thus was Enkidu vanquished.*

Ought she to say plainly what this fight represented? Or hint at the reality behind the metaphor?

A *clunk* in the stern of the boat, which shifted in the water with the addition of a male body. Johansen leapt to her feet: ready to scream, ready for combat, ready to dive into the canal.

Adriaen.

"Didn't mean to scare you," he said. "I heard you and Edith arguing again earlier. Why don't you stay on mine for a bit? Just until things have calmed down, like…"

Deliverance? Or deceit? Johansen chiselled through that open steady gaze in search of a motive, but saw only decency.

"Thank you," she said. "That would be nice."

"It's no biggie. Let's go for a cruise."

They loaded her possessions onto the *Time Traveller*. A powerful shudder went through Johansen then, a swirling recognition of all that she had lost. She was homeless, a hermit, and her husband was dead. The pressure on her larynx became instantly immense; her cheek muscles were cords of steel, drawing the corners of her mouth irresistibly downwards.

"Hey, you…" said Adriaen gently, diagnosing the imminent as he eased into the waterway. "Let's find another mooring and get you sorted out."

Eric Jasper rounded the corner of the nearest boat. One hand was inside his coat. But the *Tickety-Boo* was deserted; the vessel next to it had vanished. His quarry had escaped, heading very slowly to the east.

35

"There's a woman who wants to meet you." The nearest gunman made a scissor action at his wrist. "Come with us."

Harkness and McCartney were led to a freshly cut clearing the size of a football pitch. Prefabricated buildings were linked by log paths across the peat; there was a canteen and barracks with washhouse, and scientists percolated through three white tents.

Also pits. Hundreds of pits.

The clearing was defended by gunmen displaying all the swagger and menace of the 'irregular combatants' who retook the Crimea for Russia in 2014. A heavy machine gun emplaced at the perimeter was fearsome to behold, and a transport helicopter rested on a timber helipad. This Harkness recognised as a Mil Mi-26, workhorse of the Soviet armed forces for three decades. It bore the red star of the modern Russian Air Force, and Wilson was exonerated. It had been *Moscow* keeping them at bay, *Moscow* behind each little inconvenience. The terror of an old fear was reborn in Harkness now, like a cancer returned after years in remission.

As Harkness neared the first pit he knew what he would find.

It was a hunter-gatherer of the Forest People, head staved in like a crushed grapefruit. Harkness did not need to see the lithic weaponry to know the murder scene was prehistoric: the body was two metres down in the peat. Next they passed three teenagers, tongues lolling and legs akimbo. A disembowelled man, sinews still wiry in muscular shoulders. This was a mass grave. A genocide had taken place here, lost in prehistory. Harkness noticed the industrial freezers adjoining the tents.

"*Nyónsoboma*," breathed McCartney.

She awaited them.

Her features were bulbous with protuberant eyelids and rounded lips. The complexion was anaemic, yet it would still have been a kindly face were it not for the stillness with which she watched them approach. That and the citrine pupils that yet seemed strangely colourless. Instinctively Harkness knew this was a killer.

She spoke to them in an accent Harkness put at Caucasus-Russian: "You should know that the area we've cleared is the tip of the iceberg. Our preliminary investigations suggest the mass grave stretches for at least four kilometres."

Harkness recalled a study undertaken in 2009 by the evolutionary biologist Etienne Patin that he had read on the plane. After examining the genetic variety in Forest People populations today, Patin calculated that a *genetic bottleneck* had occurred at the end of the Late African Stone Age, circa 3,000 BC. Their populations had plummeted by ninety-five per cent. Again the darkness. Harkness's gaze had returned to the pits.

She clicked her fingers and a gunman produced a syringe; they were restrained and then injected. As the chemicals hit Harkness's bloodstream he felt dazzlingly alert, and he wondered if this was what ecstasy felt like.

"It's a mix of amphetamine and phenmetrazine," she said. "You will now stay awake, almost no matter what we do to you."

Then Harkness saw the box: a suburban vision for this nightmarish world. It was a Bosch PST 500 watt jigsaw. He had one in his shed.

"Now, are you left-handed or right-handed?" she asked McCartney.

A brief hesitation. "Left-handed."

"Hold out your right hand, then."

"No," he cried, "I'm a right-hander really…"

"And a *very* bad liar."

It took four men to brace McCartney as she picked up the power tool.

"We'll sear the stumps so that you don't pass out from the bleeding," she reassured him. "Unless you prefer cooperation."

"What the hell are you jabbering about?" shouted Harkness. "We came here to find our friend."

She smiled primly, blood evacuating lips that turned as white as her skin.

"There are a few elements of Dr Tsuda's work we would like you to explicate," she said. "I understand that she was searching for traces of a far *older* tongue than that of prehistoric pygmies. The first language spoken by humankind, no less. Tell me what she found. I want to hear the Universal Language from which all others are descended. I want to know what it *tells us* of those times."

"But she was nowhere near that sort of breakthrough." Harkness was grimacing, arms pinned behind his back. "Nobody is. It probably can't be done."

"You must consider the ramifications of your lies to me," she hissed.

"Think about it!" he shouted. "A thousand years after two languages split, they share seventy per cent of the same words. After three millennia, that drops to forty per cent. Now, the ancestral tongue broke up *twenty times* longer ago than that. Do the maths. Virtually every one of these words is lost, vanished beyond reconstruction. Still less could the diction tell us anything meaningful about prehistory itself."

Her thumb caressed the power switch of the jigsaw. "Well. Let's lop a hand off your protégé and see if that helps."

She traced a line on McCartney's wrist with the tip of her finger. Then she hit the power and a high-pitched buzz picked up, the twin blades jiggling back and forth like the mandibles of a bull ant, ready to tear and rip and chew.

*

Harkness stared at the fighter opposite him. Six foot six with a huge blond grinning head; mismatched shoelaces and a tattoo of the Spetsnaz, Russia's Special Forces. The man glanced at Harkness, fleetingly unsure of himself: as if remembering that this was not a normal situation, or thinking of someone back home.

Then something extraordinary happened.

With an audible *plop*, an arrow planted itself in the fighter's cheek. He seemed perplexed and attempted to speak, but the shaft was inhibiting his tongue. Before anyone could respond a wave of arrows fell, darkening the sky like pumice from a volcano. Quills juddered from backs, stomachs, calves, eyes. The fighter holding McCartney was nicked in the carotid artery and scarlet fountained skyward, his roar ebbing swiftly to a gurgle. Then the Ba Aka were spotted. Dozens of them were ensconced in treetops to the north of the clearing, and at once the air around Harkness exploded with the discharge of assault rifles. When the machine gun opened up too the primordial rainforest began disintegrating. Branches snapped in half and trees were felled; sawdust and leaf-mulch clouded the air. Archers were blown from their perches and fell spinning to the forest floor, their bodies garlanded with settling leaves. The rest withdrew, and though the woman screamed at them to hold position a dozen Spetsnaz gave chase.

Seconds into the jungle the point man tripped a vine. A spear hafted in a heavy log came whistling down upon him. The spear-fall trap is designed for slaying elephant or buffalo, and it pinned a human being to the peat like a butterfly on felt. Another trip, another twang, a second whistling descent. The spearhead entered a fighter's body through the base of the neck and snagged on his colon before exiting through the belly, three feet of intestine streaking out in its wake like line through a fishing reel. A cruel rush of arrows whistled in on the surviving band of Spetsnaz from all sides. They had thought this would be easy. They had thought it would be fun! But there was little fun as hunters darted forward to stab and slash until nothingness replaced the agonies.

Back in the clearing Harkness glimpsed dozens more Ba Aka amongst the trees, bare chests and spears massing in the shadows. It dawned on the defenders that they were surrounded, and he had the premonition of a wave of retribution about to be unleashed from these sacred woodlands. For the casual slaying of their warriors and the destruction of the Forest; for what had gone before. Again the clearing roared and blazed with gunfire: cordite stung the eyes and percussion pained the ears. All around Harkness red faces jiggled with the recoil of powerful weapons. More Ba Aka fell, but the rest withdrew again. It was as if the trees themselves were drawing their breath: preparing to unleash waves of *Miki nde ndura* from the jungle's dells and dark places.

"Hold back!" she screamed. "Form a line along the south!"

The heavy machine gun was being repositioned when the real assault came from the north.

Not dozens but *hundreds*, their chests daubed with the black juice of the gardenia fruit and spears gripped murderously overhead, skimming across the open space with that high-stepping run. The response of the Spetsnaz was terrible. For the first time the defenders found themselves confronting a foe in open ground, and a dozen Ba Aka dropped to that first ferocious fusillade. But even as they fell another wave disgorged from the treeline to the south, and archers fired down from the treetops on both sides. The charge of the Ba Aka had come at a terrible price, but in their hubris the Russians had not cut a wide enough kill-zone between their defences and the trees. Now it was hand-to-hand combat. The helicopter's rotors began to turn.

The Russians had physicality on their side in these close encounters, but they were not ready for the quickness of men who'd spent a lifetime hunting wild animals. Throat slashed, belly pierced, spear through the heart. As a fighting retreat to the helicopter began a drumbeat took up from the forest.

One two three, *One* two three, *One* two three…

The woman who could not be named was last into the helicopter, screaming in frustration as the huge machine heaved off the ground. Arrows pattered harmlessly on the hull as it circled once around the clearing, seemingly unable to comprehend the spectacle beneath. The hunter-gatherers waving spears in the air; abandoned Spetsnaz being speared and clubbed. The hundreds of graves, the canteen going up in flames. And in the middle of all the mayhem, Randolph Harkness and Ross McCartney, lying on the ground with their hands over their heads. The helicopter banked hard before powering away westwards. The Battle of Itanga was over.

36

Harkness and McCartney surveyed the humble spectacle of the Forest People filling in the graves of their ancestors, newly dead buried alongside the old. Harkness grieved for Sakiko, for the death all around him – and for what had transpired in this place before. But McCartney was silent, numbed by death and violence.

"Nothing except a battle lost can be half so melancholy as a battle won," said Harkness quietly. "The Duke of Wellington. Battle of Waterloo."

"I don't understand," whispered McCartney. "Why? Why all the killing? Why must this be kept secret? What is it all for?"

Harkness stood up. "Let's go and find out."

Two dozen medical trestles were arranged in the tents, which had been industrially chilled with fans. Several ancient cadavers had been opened at the cranium, exposing various lobes of the neocortex. Ba Aka were collecting the corpses and returning them to the peatbog for burial where the long-dead hunters – preserved for so long by lack of oxygen – were swiftly beginning to rot. Harkness found this painful to watch. The acidic soil of equatorial rainforest eats through bones, and

Neolithic Central Africa is almost unknown to palaeontology. But here each body was a cornucopia of information about diet, ethnography and the human story. This was one of the most important prehistoric discoveries ever made, clearly. But Harkness didn't try to stop the hunters: the profundity of their connection with their ancestors was clear. How would he have felt watching the Ba Aka exhume war graves in Normandy? He was forced to re-evaluate treasured beliefs.

On the far side of the tents was a cabin where they found paperwork.

"Extraordinary," Harkness muttered.

McCartney peered at pages of unfathomable diagnostics. "What is?"

"Isotope readings, taken from their bones and teeth."

"I didn't pay much attention in GCSE chemistry."

"You surprise me," said Harkness. "An isotope is a slightly different form of any given chemical element. For example, carbon is found as C12, C13, C14 and so on, depending on the number of neutrons. We absorb carbon from the water we drink, and it's stored in our bones. So by testing the carbon isotope in a particular skeleton, you can see whether someone lived in an area with C12 ground water present, C13 groundwater and so on. That means you can take an educated guess where they lived."

"Got it."

"The stupefying thing is that these bodies seem to have come from right across Central Africa. This poor bloke they seem to have traced all the way to Uganda."

Again the darkness, bleeding out from across the millennia.

"They were *brought here*," said McCartney.

Both men fell silent. This did not feel like dispassionate academic enquiry – it was too close, like stumbling upon fresh tragedy.

"But didn't you say there was no organised warfare in prehistory?" McCartney continued.

"That's the belief of every authority on the subject," said Harkness. "But sometimes the received wisdoms are – well, wrong."

Pinned to a noticeboard was the helicopter schedule. Frozen specimens had been assigned serial numbers and flown to the ageing aircraft carrier *Admiral Kuznetsov*, which lay in the Gulf of Guinea with a tugboat in case of breakdowns. But one row of the chart was in a different format, and Harkness thumped the table.

"The vicious bastards!"

"What is it?" asked McCartney. "I don't know Russian. Wait – you speak Russian too?"

"Live cargo," he translated. "Male adult, age approximately sixty, high intelligence. Male adult, thirty, average intelligence. Female adult, twenty-two, high intelligence. Male child, ten, low intelligence."

As Harkness thought of the trestle tables he felt sick. Then he found a list of IQ assessments carried out on both Forest People and Bantu-speaking farmers in the region. They found no variance in average or median IQ and no difference in the proportion judged 'highly intelligent'. And the Ba Aka and Bantu subjects with the highest IQ had been scored within two points of each other.

"This is just absolutely horrendous," said Harkness.

The computers were password protected, but in the barracks they did find a curiosity. The billets were divided into military and civilian sections – easy to tell apart – and in the scientists' half they found objects connected to Poland. Polish cigarettes by one bunk, Polish vodka under the next; the business card of a Warsaw hotel, postcards of the Masurian Lake District in what was once Prussia. And on an unlocked laptop, photographs of a bison reservation in Bialowieza taken on a scientist's day off.

"These guys are working in Poland too," said Harkness.

37

The Forest People took down Sakiko and bore her to the clearing with great gentleness. Batsinga had reappeared bearing pink orchids from the jungle that they laid upon her chest, and for lack of better ideas Harkness recited the Lord's Prayer. Then they gave her to the Forest.

"What now?" asked McCartney.

"Now?" said Harkness grimly. "Now we find a way out of this bloody jungle. Then I'm going to Poland. Sakiko's killers have a secret, that much is clear. It *must* go beyond what happened here. And it strikes me that the key to it lies in Poland. The best way I could avenge her death is by discovering it and shouting it from the sodding roof-tops. I've got no dependants and I'm damned angry, so the hell with it."

McCartney was nodding along.

"I've also got a rather long history of – how you youngsters say – *trolling* our friends in Moscow," Harkness continued. "It's high time I came out of retirement. And I also confess a small professional interest. My list of achievements in my field is rather humble, really – a paper here, an obscure book there. I'd rather like to be the one who reveals whatever it is these guys were on to. Taken all in all, and with nothing waiting for me back home, it's worth risking my life for."

"I've always wanted to go to Poland," said McCartney.

"Ha!" Harkness folded his arms. "Sorry, not a chance. I made a promise to your father – which I've already broken many times over."

"So you're allowed to risk your life, but I'm not? That's hardly fair."

"Imagine if something happened to you," he said. "How could I face him? My past and his are already intertwined in ways that are… complicated."

McCartney frowned, but he let it go.

"I'm going blind," he said simply. "And I know lots of blind people jump out of planes and have great lives or whatever, but the reality is I've only got one chance to do something like this. Besides, you're not exactly young anymore. You could do with a wingman in case things get lively."

"Ouch. Be careful, Ross. You may find there's fire in the old belly yet. The answer's still no, by the way. My foot's down. You're going back to Maidstone."

"You can't actually stop me," replied McCartney craftily. "I'm a grown man. I could join the army if I wanted, fight a war."

Harkness had to admit he had a point.

"So I'm going to Poland," he continued. "Either we're together or we're rivals. Your call."

Harkness pinched the bridge of his nose between thumb and index finger and exhaled slowly.

"Jesus wept," he said at last. "Fine. You win. But when we make it back into civilisation, you'll need to square it with your old man. And you'd better make it damned bloody clear I didn't put you up to it."

*

The Ba Aka led them north. A day's hike would bring them into contact with farming populations, and from there they could go up the Ubangi River by boat to the Central African Republic. There were regular flights servicing Europe from its capital Bangui, on the southern border. The language-communication paradox being as it is, of course, neither actually knew this was the plan. They just followed the Sons of the Forest.

After four hours' hike they ascended a lion-headed mountain – it was rare for the Forest People to have the chance to perceive distance, and they wanted to see the horizon. Scarlet flies swirled around the summit; Harkness pointed out oxbow lakes and in the distance a volcano. To the south they could see for fifty miles before the millpond-flat jungle became haze: an anarchic struggle of treetops, nature at its most outrageous. This was the landscape they had navigated, and the magnitude of their achievement struck both men simultaneously. As they turned to look at each other there was nothing that needed to be said. Harkness merely rested an arm on McCartney's shoulder and together they looked back at the way they had come.

Harkness saw it first: almost like a Concorde, sweeping in from the west at ten thousand feet. Then McCartney spotted it too, though his eyelids trembled with the difficulty of focusing.

"It's a Tupolev Tu-160," said Harkness.

"What's that?"

Before he could reply the answer presented itself in the shape of a cigar-shaped object unfolding itself silently from the aircraft. This was an ATBIP, known in military circles as the Father of all Bombs. With a payload equivalent to forty-four tons of TNT, it is the most powerful non-nuclear device devised by man, four times more devastating than the American equivalent. A parachute stabilised the weapon, then it descended plumb-line straight on the clearing.

They saw the explosion before they heard it, a carpet of orange the height of a five-storey building that rumbled horizontally across the jungle for the equivalent of ten city blocks. The extremities of the explosion were bulbous, a convex wave annihilating everything in its path. Light was followed by noise, a cacophonous crash that sounded quite unreal in its enormity at such a distance. Thousands of birds took to the air and the landscape came alive with the screeches of outraged simians and the honks of creatures unknown. Vibrations came rushing through them next and beetles scurried past Harkness's feet. Finally a rush of displaced hot air arrived, singeing cheeks and stirring hair.

"What the hell is really going on here?" murmured Harkness, almost to himself.

"I don't know," replied McCartney. "But we're going to find out."

PART TWO

All that is really known of the ancient state is contained in a few pages. We can know no more than what old writers have told us.

Dr Samuel Johnson, quoted by
James Boswell in *The Life of Dr. Johnson*

38

Professor Vincent Fournier was one of the foremost experts in Europe on the Ice Age Venuses, so it was the most exquisite moment of his life when the first of these enigmatic objects to be unearthed in fifty years was discovered on his patch. That the Venus of Renancourt was found in the *quartier* of Amiens where he'd lived all his life – and promptly made his responsibility – felt a fitting finale to an entire career spent contemplating the mysteries of these most perplexing examples of Ice Age art. This was a devotion to which he ascribed a lifelong bachelorhood. Professor Fournier had been on the brink of retirement when the discovery was made, but it was agreed he would continue at the Musée de Picardie, dispensing with all other responsibilities to spend a civilised three hours working on the Venus each morning.

As the Itanga mass grave was wiped clean by fire, Fournier was paying his daily visit to Amiens Cathedral, the largest Gothic church in France. He was a short man with spectacles and downy black hair that lent him the air of an ageing mole, which was only accentuated by his habitual black mackintosh. He prayed to the Virgin Mary for half an hour (bad thoughts plagued him these days) then set off for his lunch. As he left the cathedral he had the peculiar thought that the left-hand tower – it was slightly taller than the right – would have been an excellent spot for a sniper in 1914. He then had a frighteningly clear vision of a body sprawled beneath it, blood pooling down the steps where at that moment a school trip was filling out worksheets.

He chastised himself for having such a thought – and at a place of the divine! – and hurried on.

Such visions had come to him frequently since Dr Francesca Bianca of the National Archaeological Museum of the Marche Region had contacted him the previous month. In truth, Fournier had entertained little hope of throwing new light on his Venus, or any other for that matter. Their purpose, in currency right across Ice Age Europe and western Russia, has eluded scholars for two centuries. At first he considered Dr Bianca's theory outlandish; then he gave it some serious consideration. Now he was convinced.

By sheer good fortune she'd first called him from a hotel room, and his subsequent notes remained offline. This was the reason he was still alive. But since the tragedy of her murder at the hands of Italian far right lunatics (in her spare time Dr Bianca was a left-wing activist) Fournier considered himself the keeper of the flame. That was why he had emailed a colleague in Romania the previous week and written to another in Portugal that morning.

The medieval St-Leu district was an industrial town in the Middle Ages, its tiny hunchbacked houses home to tanners and weavers. The network of canals make it one of numerous locations dubbed 'The Venice of the North'. Fournier crossed such a canal and took a table outside the Bistro Ad'Hoc. From there he had a view of the cathedral, its mismatched towers dominating the tiny medieval conurbation. He opened his laptop and ordered a ham omelette.

From around the corner came a little old man with a white beard who pulled out a pistol with silencer and shot him twice in each lung.

Fournier flew back off his chair and banged his head on the cobbles. He felt his lungs filling up with blood. He spluttered as his body tried in vain to evacuate it. He was drowning.

It is common for the last thought of a dying man to be abstract or nonsensical, and so it was with Professor Fournier. He wondered whether this might be something to do with the Ice Age Venuses. Then he ran out of oxygen and lost consciousness.

*

Eric Jasper took two steps backward, blinking fast, mouth opening and closing mechanically, still high on the intensity of the act. Tourists were screaming and the waiter cowered beneath a table; a mother snatched up her toddler and dashed for cover. They probably thought he was a jihadi convert. He hesitated before grabbing Fournier's laptop, then walked briskly from the scene.

39

The Palace of Culture and Science is known in Warsaw as Stalin's Syringe. The dictator's gift to the Polish people, it resembles a squat Empire State Building with a 140 foot spire protruding from the top. Peering from the observation terrace were Harkness and McCartney. Ninety per cent of Warsaw was destroyed in the war and the city centre laid out before them was a mess of dreary 1960s tower blocks. There was a jarring dissonance between the Soviet-era architecture and the modern glass skyscrapers now leaping up over it.

"Ah, Warsaw," sighed McCartney.

Harkness frowned. "I thought you'd never been to Poland?"

"I just thought it would sound worldly."

Harkness's laugh died away as he looked east.

"Ironic coincidence, wouldn't you say?" he muttered. "We're investigating an ancient genocide... and of all the places in the world, it leads us here."

Even McCartney knew of the events that had transpired in this part of the world. But before he could reply the lift opened.

"As I live and breathe!" Tony Marks stepped onto the terrace. "Good to see you, lads. I like the beards! You must be this Ross rascal I've been hearing about?"

He dispensed a pair of bone-crushing handshakes, and as Harkness took in the Stetson hat and shorts he felt a rush of warmth for his old deputy.

Harkness had called Marks from Bangui, hoping he might use his contacts to enquire whether any prehistoric sites had recently been discovered in eastern Poland.

"I can go one better than that," said Marks. "I'll chuffing well come out and help you look."

Harkness's next call had been to Tomas Nowak. The new widower wept silently down the phone, and Harkness heard himself utter the cliché that *I can't imagine what you must be going through*, though that was entirely untrue. There were no words to address the ruin of a man's life.

Marks was once in the Territorial Army and had been part of Operation Granby in the first Gulf War. Harkness's acceptance of his offer to join them was on grounds of security as much as archaeology. The sight of Marks' brawny forearm on the railing reassured him now.

"Any closer to finding this dig of yours?" asked Marks.

"We don't even know what we're looking for," sighed McCartney.

Marks rolled his eyes. "You're a right barmy pair, you two. D'you not realise how massive the Masuria region is? There are two thousand lakes out there. What were you planning on doing, just driving around till you find it, like?"

"I do have one iron in the fire," said Harkness.

"What's that?"

Harkness cleared his throat. "There's something I need to tell you, Tony. In the eighties, I was – now, how can I put this?"

*

Old Praga is one of the few neighbourhoods in Warsaw that survived the war more or less intact. The dilapidated tenements remained pockmarked with bullet holes and shrapnel scars that recalled a crumbling farmhouse cheddar. Many buildings were left with three walls standing; the Poles simply rebuilt the fourth and returned them to use, dubbing them *plomba* – after the Polish for dental filling. For most of the post-war period, Old Praga was home to the poor. Now, of course, the artists are moving in, bringing coffee shops and galleries in their wake. But the gentrification is a crust. Delve deeper in and one still finds some of the bleakest poverty in Europe.

Harkness led them through a passageway into a rubble-strewn courtyard. A brick wall separated them from an adjoining yard, but residents had knocked a gap through to pass between the tenements. The endemic graffiti made it a fallen Secret Garden. Harkness led them through the portal, then a second and a third. The effect was of a little labyrinth, and soon McCartney had lost all sense of direction.

"Been here before, haven't you?" Marks had been wide-eyed ever since Harkness confessed his former life. "Talk about a dark horse…"

Harkness stopped at a grisly eight-storey block and pressed an enamel bell that was by far the building's most attractive feature. An elderly hunchback hobbled down the corridor to meet them. Artur Wójcik was an octogenarian with two wings of white hair jutting straight up from the back of his head, as if he'd inserted his fingers into an electric socket. He wore chipped half-moon glasses, an old checked shirt with the sleeves rolled up and pinstriped trousers held up with red braces.

"Randy! Randy! Long time is this!" As they embraced, Wójcik patted Harkness on the back. "I thinking I never see you again, my friend. A happy day! Please, let us drink vodka together, why not? You are in Poland now."

The lift clanked and rattled up to the fifth floor and Wójcik ushered them into his flat. It was furnished with cheap Soviet-era furniture, the chairs as light as balsa wood and upholstery threadbare. Books and yellowing newspapers were stacked in towers and from his balcony came the cooing of pigeons.

"Still a fancier, then?" said Harkness.

"Oh-ho, you bet!" cried Wójcik. "In Istanbul last week, someone selling one for 100,000 euros. Can you imagine this?"

Harkness smiled and turned to his companions. "Before the Berlin Wall came down, Artur maintained surveillance equipment for the MSW – the Polish KGB. Only he also worked for our side. And when you *really* need a message to get through… accept no substitutes."

Cooing emanated from the balcony.

"You weren't really an archaeologist at all, were you?" said McCartney in fresh awe.

"Oh yes he bloody well was," said Marks. "I can vouch for it."

"I don't want to get into all this again," said Harkness. "Let's just say it's my belief that when your country comes asking for help, you should offer it. Gladly."

40

Good as his word, Wójcik filled three tumblers with vodka. They chinked glasses and McCartney necked his at a gulp.

"We've got a live one here, Randolph," said Marks.

The others had merely sipped.

"How was I supposed to know we weren't meant to down them?" McCartney protested.

Harkness disregarded the ignoble spectacle. "Are you still in touch with your old colleagues, Artur?"

"Certainly I am," muttered Wójcik. "Several are still in the business."

It was Harkness's hope that Russian activity in the lakes region – archaeological or otherwise – might have caught the attention of what was now the Agencja Wywiadu.

The elderly man cast an abashed look at the peeling wallpaper, the acrylic carpet. "I shall ask them, yes. But perhaps you can making me a small consideration for my services? As you see, things are not too good here now."

As Harkness reached for his wallet Wójcik's cheeks were endowed with a new warmth to match that of the vodka.

"You go to Masuria this afternoon, yes?" said Wójcik. "Warsaw is still city of ears and eyes. And this request may taking me few days. Is safer for you hiding in the woods there, I think."

"But how will you let us know?" asked McCartney.

The old man held one hand to his ear with a crafty smile. "Coo-coo, coo-coo…"

Harkness took his fingers and clasped them. "May you never change, Artur."

"There is a lake," said Wójcik. "Name is Jezioro Kruklin. A quiet place, not too many noseys snooping about. You will wait each night. One of my birdies, he knows the way. If no bird coming one week, I not knowing. But I try for you."

"Thank you, Artur."

When Harkness began putting on his coat Wójcik wagged a finger.

"You getting sloppy, eh?" he cackled. "Perhaps British training is not what it was, yes? Maybe these Muslamic types giving you the run-around in England these days are not quite at KGB levels, no?"

"What is he on about?" said Marks.

Wójcik opened a sideboard wherein a tiny black-and-white television flickered. Harkness recognised the courtyard outside.

"I must to be careful, even these days," said Wójcik sadly. "Many scores still not settled for old times. No rest for me, until I am in my grave."

He clicked a button and the image changed.

"The passageway we just came through," said McCartney. "So what?"

A man moved into shot and lingered before stepping back.

"Holy shit," whispered McCartney.

Now Wójcik selected a third camera. "And here, also."

A trimmer figure leaned against a wall. His posture was languid, the shot down from the eaves silhouetting his face.

"They following you all the way here," Wójcik finished.

"Who are they?" exclaimed Marks. "What the heck are we going to do now, Randolph?"

"The FSB?" suggested Harkness.

"We're not dead," said McCartney shrewdly. "So that should tell you something."

"What do you think, Artur?" said Harkness.

The old man leaned inward and squinted. "Is difficult to say. Russian? I think maybe no. But I have plan just for in case of this happens."

A roguish grin was back on the old spy's face as he held out his hand, and Harkness reached for his wallet for the second time.

*

Down the rubbish chute they went, spinning through fifty feet of tenement before crashing into a six-foot pile of stinking black bags. The stench was eye-watering. Harkness clambered from the refuse sacks and prised the door open a crack. The slimmer man was twenty feet away now, still leaning on the wall with his back to them.

Wójcik's voice crackled through a vintage earpiece. "Wait…"

Harkness did as he was told.

"Wait…"

Only the sound of something clawing its way into rubbish deep beneath them broke the silence.

"OK – now – go!"

Harkness opened the steel door with a horrendous screech, but their watcher had turned the corner. They fled across the courtyard and ducked into another Secret Garden.

"Wait…"

Harkness brought them juddering to a halt.

"Hide, quickly hide."

They cowered behind a shed as a man passed the gateway.

"OK – now – go!"

Again they sprinted through open space, scrambling through another gap. The watcher had rounded another corner, and the three men dashed across a second courtyard as *Run! Fast! Go!* exploded in Harkness's ear. Down an alleyway. A final courtyard. No looking back now. Feet hurtling over needles and used condoms, dodging weeds that sought to snare and trip them in their flight. Marks stumbled on a patch of rubble and almost lost it, arms windmilling forward and cheeks bulging as he regained his equilibrium. There was one more hole in the wall to climb through, then blessedly they were on the Vistula, a skiff upturned on the riverbank.

Wójcik's skiff.

Two minutes later they were buzzing across the water. But now there was no jubilation, no smiles or laughter or jocularity. Their expressions were grim and pinched and frightened. It had been a very scary moment.

41

To Gordon's Wine Bar again: Sir Hugh Alexander was back in town. Another brush contact – same raspberry birthmark, the flash of a civil servant's palm – and a second evening rendezvous, though the weather was getting colder. Only this time their demeanours were reversed. Now it was Hastings glancing at strangers, Hastings who insisted that they turn off their phones. She had acquired a nascent fear of the Secret World and learned that – real or not – practitioners of its trickery are best respected. Just as any sensible West African respects voodoo. Meanwhile Sir Hugh was excitable, swallowing a blended Oloroso sherry in a gulp.

"I have news," he began.

She studied him with ringed eyes. "Shoot."

"You'll recall my source at Number Ten?" Sir Hugh's pupils gleamed treacherously in the candlelight.

"I do. And?"

Hastings was no longer interested in the antics in Tokyo: her priority was pinning the Russia Today hoax on the Prime Minister. This SBS stuff might damage Number Ten, but it was a distraction she could do without.

"A Russian cell is operating in and around Westminster," he said coldly. "MI5 found out about its existence and reckoned the Tokyo job was blown. That's why they got cold feet. Tokyo was a staging post. It's not to do with Japan at all; it's to do with *Russia*. They wanted to do a Litvinenko, over there."

Bombshell. Bloody hell.

"But *The Sun* would pay a hundred grand for that story!" she hissed.

"And the change."

"Any idea who the Russians have got in Westminster?" Abruptly Hastings soured. "Wait a minute… if you're referring to the whole Chief Whip thing, the joke is in very bad taste."

"Do I look as if I'm joking?" She thought he looked unhinged. "MI5 don't yet know who's in the cell, or obviously they'd have been arrested. But if the Russian penetration isn't at Cabinet level, it's near as damn it. I'm told at least one member is a high-profile figure in politics."

"An MP?"

Sir Hugh shook his head.

"A Lord? A SpAd?"

"Some sort of leading donor or politico seems to be the best guest. But that's not all. Remember this 'Orientalist' you were so scornful of? Not a thing, not an operation – but a *he*. Orientalist is their leader."

Provisional Readings in the Medieval History of the Near East. Published: Beirut American Press, 1934.

A physical sensation went through Hastings as she saw that the two sides of the thing might fit together, a wobble that began at her diaphragm before spreading down through her abdomen and up into her throat. She felt a little sick and pushed her glass across the table.

An awful lot of the clichés of this world are perfectly true. Dabbling in Foreign Office secrets – proper secrets – is not a game one plays.

Oh lordy, thought Hastings. What would my old dad make of what I've got myself into this time?

"One more thing." Sir Hugh polished off his sherry. "That file I mentioned, the one that got compromised before Tokyo got called off."

"You know what was in it?"

"No."

"You have a filename?"

"Er – no."

"Then with all due respect – what do you have?"

Sir Hugh looked peevish. "Just the tip-off that Number Ten is still in a heck of a flap about it. My source reckons whatever was in that file holds the key. Get the file, you get to the bottom of this thing. The assassination, the Russian cell. Orientalist."

And whoever stitched me up, thought Hastings.

Get the file.

"A toast then!" Sir Hugh seemed genuinely euphoric. "To both of us getting our careers back."

They chinked glasses.

"Incidentally," she murmured, "I don't suppose you know anyone with membership of the Garrick Club?"

The diplomat frowned. "As a matter of fact, I'm a member myself. Why do you ask?"

42

Once Warsaw was behind them Poland became lovely, an undulating tapestry of fields and woods dotted with cheery red roofs and the odd medieval barn. The landscape's piebald quality almost recalled the savannah corridors – but mellowed, made tranquil by centuries of pastoralism and hard labour. Tolkien's Shire sprang to mind, Devon too, and Harkness felt elation that such places still existed. He had a sudden, painful longing for England, a rare emotion for this wanderer.

But he kept this to himself. Marks would only start banging on about Yorkshire, while McCartney's generation lived in a world made boundless by the digital revolution.

Harkness didn't much care for BMWs, but with security and long distances to consider he'd argued for a Seven Series, which they sat in now. As they drove he reflected upon himself: in charge again. Marks was no longer his deputy, yet Harkness's authority was unquestioned. Why? Was he bossy? He hoped not. He was popular, and that the diagnosis had against it. All those Christmas cards and godchildren were the testament. But did this instinctive taking of command forestall any deeper connection? Was it responsible for those decades watching *Blackadder* or *Twin Peaks* with only successive hounds for company? No. The explanation was that other thing. Harkness was suddenly aware of the wheels spinning beneath his feet, of the trees flashing past and the white lines zipping by his wing mirror like laser beams, and he lessened his speed. Then they encountered lakes.

The *Rough Guide* informed them these were formed in the Pleistocene Ice Age, and Harkness felt a leap of adrenaline at the disclosure. Some were small, others gigantic; the forests surrounding them grew denser and more ancient as they headed east, with trees both coniferous and broadleaved. Boar and wolves still roamed through these woodlands; they were entering the Wild East of Europe. Finally they arrived at Jezioro Kruklin, a jagged body of water lined with pine and bulrushes. They pitched tents and waited until midnight.

The messenger did not come.

Nor did it on the second night, nor the third. As they waited, Harkness, Marks and McCartney gave themselves over to a bucolic existence. Their days were spent fishing and walking, or gathering firewood to warm themselves against the bitter Eurasian cold encroaching from the east.

That angst was still with Harkness.

When you've looked for something all your life… only to find it and wonder if you should carry on.

And also – deep down, but still there – a whisper of ambition.

*

On the fourth day Marks and McCartney walked three miles to the village of Kruklin. They returned with bread, ham – and strong Polish beer. The sunset that evening was achingly beautiful, the lake a mirror in which the infinitesimal shift through red and yellow to darkest navy was doubled, like the wings of a butterfly. One litre of beer became three and then four; it occurred to Harkness that they were going to get pissed.

Harkness knew from bitter experience that Marks could put away fifteen pints without discernible effect – yet the Yorkshireman turned in early, leaving him and McCartney by the guttering fire. Last time they had kept to the flames it was for safety from carnivores, like the humans of old. Now both were changed men, albeit slightly.

"OK then," said McCartney, "it's time. Why didn't you marry?"

Harkness appreciated that he was drunk, but he no longer cared. In fact, he *wanted* to tell McCartney. Alcohol: truth drug *par excellence*. As spies and journalists know, if you want to get the facts out of someone, accept no substitutes.

"I'd better fetch the whisky," sighed Harkness.

43

"Her name was Elizabeth. We met at university in Bristol. Witty, beautiful, daring, offensive. I would say it was love at about third sight." Harkness stared into the embers of his past. "I was twenty-one when we got engaged, which was normal in those days. On her birthday that year, which is to say the evening of the fifth of December, 1987, I called on her house. She was living in St Paul's at the time – not a bad place nowadays, but then it was wall-to-wall crack houses and prostitutes. She lived in typical student digs, you know the type. Sublet, damp, walls made of chipboard. I managed to get in – I wanted to surprise her. I had flowers plus what passed as a decent bottle of wine in eighties Britain. I was about to knock on her door when I heard her speaking. 'But I don't love him, I love *you*. You're such a sexy man.' Those were the exact words, 'sexy man'. They're seared into my memory."

"Sorry, mate," said McCartney.

Harkness refilled his glass – a double. He was a moderate consumer of alcohol, but this one went down in a gulp.

"I haven't finished. I waited outside until her visitor had gone, then I confronted her. She claimed he was 'just a friend'. The cover story was that he was about to be in a play – I remember the name to this day. *In Felicity We Trust*. And she was, get this, *helping him rehearse his lines*. Supposedly, that's what I'd overheard."

"That's a good one," said McCartney.

"Suffice to say I didn't believe her. In those days, I remind you, there were no mobile phones or internet – so it wasn't like I could verify her story there and then. We had a blazing row and she accused me of not trusting her. She questioned, rightly, whether this was a basis for marriage. Then she stormed out and naturally I went to the pub."

"What a bitch," said McCartney.

"I *haven't finished*, Ross."

It was only the second time McCartney had seen Harkness's temper rise.

"Sorry, mate," he said again.

Harkness refilled his glass. Braced himself. Knocked half of it back. This story circled his own mind endlessly, but it had been a few years since he'd told it.

"The police woke me with a knock on the door in the middle of the night. Lizzy had gone to the pub too, with a friend of hers – denouncing me, I don't doubt. She had this red MGB convertible, nice little car. Idiotically she drove home. Three times over the limit."

"Oh God."

"Have you ever been to Bristol?"

"Never."

"Well, a causeway runs along the River Avon, underneath Brunel's suspension bridge. It's the only place in the centre of town you can get up some speed. Hell, I've done it myself. There's a short tunnel built into the cliff-edge to protect from falling rocks. She wrapped the MG around a pillar at fifty. It was more or less the same crash that did for Princess Di. In a '72 sports car? She never stood a chance."

McCartney touched the corner of his left eye with a little finger. Things like this affected him.

"So horrible," he managed.

"I was in mourning, obviously," said Harkness. "And it was all the worse – and more confusing – that she'd betrayed me."

"Total and utter mindfuck," said McCartney.

"Guess what happened next?"

"What?"

"Posters went up at the student union for a new play."

"No…" whispered McCartney.

"*In Felicity We Trust*. Ironic title, don't you think?"

He was speechless.

"I killed her." Harkness tossed the rest of his whisky into the fire where it burst into flame. "I bloody killed her, Ross. So I've never forgiven myself. And nor will I. There are other things I've done in my life that I'm not proud of either, and that, seeing as you are so determined to know, is why I'm a bachelor. I feel that I don't deserve… it."

"You *didn't* kill her." McCartney grabbed him by the wrist. "It was a misunderstanding, that's all! A terrible misunderstanding…"

"I wish I was convinced." He sighed. "Or more importantly, I wish that I at your age was convinced. My life would have been – better."

McCartney was thinking about a boy in the Congo formed from clay.

"Anyway, we are where we are," said Harkness hoarsely. "Can't complain. It's been a good life, on the whole. By the way, after Lizzy died I tracked down the actor and went to see him. I thought it might help me. That was your father."

McCartney's mouth fell open.

"So every cloud has a silver lining. It's been a lifelong friendship." Harkness blinked: he was welling up, too. "That's partly why I thought I'd take you off his hands. Deep are the roots, et cetera. Well, there it all is." He cleared his throat. "Terrible, eh?"

Something popped in the fire.

"Enough of this stuff for tonight, I think," said Harkness.

"Next time you meet someone…"

Harkness had been examining the legs running down his glass, but now he looked up.

"Take a chance," said McCartney.

The younger man's face was a mask of inexperience, flickering in the flames. Harkness envied him then, all of it still to come. Behold, the invincible naivety of the young man. Then he remembered. McCartney was going blind.

"I think not," he said.

In the stillness of the night, only the lapping of gentle wavelets to disturb it, the noise that interrupted them was very clear as it carried from the woods. It was the cooing of a bird. When Harkness held out his hand, a Noah for the modern age, a carrier pigeon fluttered from the darkness. Upon its ankle was a message.

Deliverance.

44

Barclays, Citibank and HSBC were glowing monoliths that might have been implanted on the Isle of Dogs by creatures from outer space. Canary Wharf peered over them like the pyramid of Freemasonry, the beacon at its apex an all-seeing pupil. These monuments to the earth-shaping potency of money were the logical conclusion of the mercantilism that had come alive at the time when the *Epic of Gilgamesh* was first written, Johansen reflected. She smirked as the thought came to her: she was hiding from the System in its very eye.

The *Time Traveller* was moored at Poplar Dock Marina, and it was early evening. Alone in its cabin, Johansen transcribed the account of Gilgamesh's meeting with an old man named Utanapishtim into her notebook. He was instantly recognisable as Noah; for this was the Flood Story, Version 1.0.

> *Gilgamesh journeyed over a far distance to meet Utanapishtim, who had survived the Great Flood.*
>
> *Gilgamesh said, "I gaze upon you, old man. You are Utanapishtim, the Distant One. I have journeyed far to seek you. I am resolved to learn your secret."*
>
> *And Utanapishtim replied, "I will tell you, O Gilgamesh, the whole hidden story. To you I will reveal the Secret and the Mystery. In bygone days, the multitudes teemed upon the face of the earth and the unending clamour and wickedness of the people aroused the wrath of the Gods."*

Johansen looked back to the skyscrapers, where in twelve hours' time a babel of tongues would once more be unleashed, where fingertips would jab and click with greed. Why did languages mutate and split with such speed? Given the constant warfare in prehistory, words and dialect were the key to identifying outsiders before they could cause harm. It was a dark and dangerous world in which other human groups posed the deadliest threat; the mutability of language had evolved as a defence mechanism.

> *"And so the Great Gods purposed a mighty flood to wipe out mankind. The Great Gods swore a vow of secrecy. Enlil, God of Storms, swore the oath. Also did Ninurta, God of War, swear it. Ea, the cunning God of Wisdom, also swore the oath not to reveal the secret to any man. But Ea was crafty. He spoke the secret unto the reed fence of my house, and by chance I overheard his words.*

> *"'Tear down your house and fashion a boat from it. Aboard this vessel, take the seed of every creature. Abandon all possessions, and save your life.'"*

So it was Wisdom that warned Utanapishtim of the coming flood. It was wisdom that saved mankind.

> *"The launch was arduous," said Utanapishtim. "All that I possessed I placed aboard the vessel. And then I embarked onto the boat all my kindred and family. Then Shamash, the Sun God, decreed that the hour of the Great Flood had arrived. I beheld the storm, and it was fearsome in aspect."*

A flood: but not of water. A deluge: but not of rain.

> *"With the first light of dawn, a darkling cloud rose upon the horizon. Rushing before this cloud were Shullat, God of Despoilment, and Hanish, God of Destruction, heralds of Doom over the mountains and plains. Ninurta, God of War, unleashed mayhem upon the realm."*

Johansen sighed, her gaze returning to the Isle of Dogs. Smashed to pieces by the Junkers and Heinkels of the German Luftwaffe; blown up again by the IRA. War was truly the natural state of mankind. And what of the 'noble savage' myth? A study of hunter-gatherer tribes today gives the lie to the fantasy that they live in peace. With no courts or organised system of arbitration, disputes are typically settled by violence – and conflict with neighbouring bands is ceaseless. She had read that among the Yanomamo of northern Brazil, thirty per cent of adult male deaths are due to violence while fifty-seven per cent of people over forty have had two or more close relatives murdered. This is the reality, Johansen mused: the prehistoric world would have been a bad one.

"And the assembly of Great Gods scorched the land with their flames. Like a mighty invading army, the Great Flood overwhelmed the people. And lo, all of humanity was returned unto dust."

Now Johansen transcribed the Old Testament's account of the same. It was no more sanguine.

God said unto Noah, "The end of all flesh is come before Me; for the earth is filled with violence; and, behold, I will destroy them with the earth. And I do bring the flood of waters upon the earth, to destroy all flesh; everything that is in the earth will perish."

And every man in the dry land in whose nostrils was the spirit of life died.

Johansen closed the *Epic of Gilgamesh*. Closed the Old Testament. Closed her notebook and shut her eyes, exhaling as she imagined it.

Ever more frenetic attempts to find her were underway.

45

When Harkness awoke it was with a sense of dislocation. Canvas above him and a visceral headache; the distinct sensation of poisoning. The pressing question, *where am I?* Slowly the dimensions of the tent took shape around him, and he followed the chain of events that had led him there. This was precisely why Harkness did not drink to excess. McCartney and Marks were murmuring to each other and cooking breakfast; the temperature had fallen again and a mist hung over the lake as if it were hiding an Excalibur.

Wójcik's message had been written on a specialist typewriter in Point 1 size – even in daylight deciphering it hurt the eyes. But the Agencja

Wywiadu, now a modern Western-style intelligence service rather than a brutal secret police, had no new excavations on their radar. Why would they? Harkness could well-imagine the amusement at Agencja GCHQ, the implication that Wójcik had lost his marbles at last.

A coda intrigued him, however. There was one outfit the Polish spooks had never liked the smell of: a team of archaeologists from Moscow who exhumed the remains of Red Army soldiers killed in the Great Patriotic War for a fitting burial. They'd been operating since the late nineties, but in case it was of interest, the group was currently digging at Wolfschanze. The Wolf's Lair.

"What's the Wolf's Lair?" asked McCartney.

"The sprawling compound of fortified bunkers in eastern Poland from which Hitler commanded Operation Barbarossa," said Harkness. "The invasion of the USSR."

"But when Germany was retreating, Wolf's Lair was abandoned before the Red Army got there," said Marks. "The Nazis tried to dyna-mite the place, only the bunkers were so ginormous not even placed explosives could destroy them. You wouldn't find dead Russians at Wolfschanze… not unless there was some kind of military accident or something else we don't know about. The bunkers are all still there, incidentally, being slowly reclaimed by the forest. I've always wanted to see the place."

"That's fortunate," said Harkness. "Because I rather think we should pay Wolfschanze a visit."

*

It was dusk when they arrived, the mist drifting through the pine and birch lending the scene a spectral aspect. There was something of the twilight too about the chilliness and the silence of the place. A feeling of catastrophe, sunk into the forest floor like cold dew. Of bad memories absorbed and taken up into the trees around them. They approached from the south, and the first sign they were nearing Wolfschanze was

Harkness's foot catching on a rail track half-buried beneath the pine needles. Then the bunker of Hitler's architect Albert Speer loomed from the mist. The fleeing Wehrmacht had placed explosives in a central reinforced corridor that had concertinaed outward without collapsing. Harkness had a vision of it in 1942, alive with voices and energy, as yet convinced they would prevail. Field Marshal Keitel's residence was next, this one reduced to a slab of bracken-covered concrete balanced on a chunk of masonry. Now bunkers started emerging from the trees all around them: hunks of reinforced concrete the size of barns, fissured but not obliterated. They were bearded with moss and the rusted steel cables bristling from broken concrete were like the fur on some Leviathan bear. Trees sprouted around and through them, found their way into the cracks and prised them apart, nature's patient erosion gradually achieving what high explosives could not. At this hour the site was inhabited only by ghosts, by the reverberation of evil decisions taken here. And by the memory of lost victories and cataclysmic defeat.

Harkness indicated an unprepossessing pile of rubble. "All that remains of the conference room where they tried to take Hitler out with a bomb in 1944..."

"I've seen the movie," murmured McCartney.

They crept the length of a mess hall, where stalactites of leached minerals dangled from the ceiling. Ahead of them was the largest fortification of all.

"The Führerbunker," whispered Harkness.

This was a slab of reinforced concrete the height and length of a terrace of houses, spindly trees perched on the summit. The explosives had lifted the top of the bunker clear before it came crashing back down, a two-hundred-tonne hat at a rakish angle.

"Someone there," hissed McCartney.

To the left of the bunker stood a solitary figure, breath steaming the air. They retreated and used the ruins of Alfred Jodl's headquarters to edge the length of the Führerbunker in cover before creeping forward once more.

At the far end of the fortification stood a second man.

"Don't look like no sightseers to me," murmured Marks.

Now they circumnavigated the gigantic construction, taking advantage of a series of outbuildings. The tearoom where Hitler once pontificated to a captive audience; the remains of his personal cinema; the bunker of Hermann Göring, obese as the man himself. Finally they rounded the Führerbunker, and through the billowing fog Harkness glimpsed two white tents: another phantasmal vision in the gathering night.

A man stood outside each.

"They're sentries," murmured Marks.

"Agreed," said Harkness.

"Look there," whispered McCartney.

In the centre of the Führerbunker an almighty detonation had sheared off an entire plane of concrete. The exposed cliff of masonry was blackened with age and overhanging, like a mountain on a Chinese vase right down to the trees clinging to the upper reaches.

There was a fissure in the rock big enough to wriggle through.

46

They darted from tree to tree and flattened themselves into the dead space of the Führerbunker wall. Then one by one they eased themselves into the cleft.

"Flipping 'eck," wheezed Marks. "This is a bit of a tight squeeze."

"Then wait here," whispered Harkness.

"Not a chance."

The fissure opened out into a corridor set at a drunken slant, as if the Führerbunker was a ship capsizing to starboard. Once this space would have been a hubbub of messengers pacing, of officers clicking back and forth with the self-importance of men who know eighty million Germans and the industrial might of the Ruhr are behind them. Now only the paint remained, a single Gothic letter glistening in the torchlight. At the end of the corridor was a spiral staircase, partially blocked with rubble. As they squeezed through the gaps Harkness felt the sickly claustrophobia of the trapped miner; but up they went. They emerged onto the roof of the Führerbunker, brushing high-up branches with their fingers. The moss bed here was thick as a palace carpet. A wall of light beamed upward from the north end of the construction like a rising force field, turning the fog into a vaporous milk. They peered over.

A digger had clawed ten feet through the topsoil, revealing a crevasse through the bedrock beneath. Six archaeologists were inside the chasm, removing dirt and scree with painstaking care.

"If them lot are looking for Red Army soldiers my name's Aunt Fanny," whispered Marks.

They watched and waited, Harkness straining his ears for snatches of Russian.

"…nothing here… five hundred roubles says it."

"…wasting our lives in this shithole…"

Bitter laughs emanated out of the earth. And one entire phrase, which Harkness heard very clearly.

Don't grumble too much, or they'll send us back to Saimaluu Tash.

He frowned. That name was familiar.

"Back down?" mouthed Marks.

It was dark and the temperature had fallen to zero; they risked hypothermia. "Let's get out of here," whispered Harkness.

Back into the manhole. Down the staircase. A retreat through the entrails of the bunker, evil still seeping from the very concrete. Was it down this corridor that Stalingrad was birthed? Had Treblinka been rubber stamped in this chamber? Was it here that Hitler signed off on Kursk, the greatest tank battle in history? Harkness's stomach churned to think about it.

Like boarders sneaking from a dorm they issued from the bunker. Vapour swirled around them, wraithlike in the evanescence of a rising half-moon. Each tree seemed to be a warrior, striding through the mist.

Gunshots rent the night.

The bangs echoed off concrete walls all around; hard to tell if they had come from the same place. Marks' moustache and nose were twitching, his eyes as bright as a rabbit's, and McCartney turned to Harkness. A moment of complete indecision. East to Göring's bunker and then loop around? Or back the way they'd come?

Two more gunshots rang out, the officer's mess flickering yellow in the muzzle flashes.

"Just get down," hissed Marks.

Torchlight scythed through the mist. Someone was sprinting northwards from the canteen. Three more gunshots, three more snaps of yellow. A single guttural howl.

Something was coming towards them now.

Something fast, approaching across the leaf bed.

Pad pad pad...

Harkness could distinguish nothing in the dark but the sentinel tree trunks and the silvery humps of bunkers beyond. But still the noise approached, panting, twigs snapping. He lay as still as possible. It was a moment from a child's nightmare.

Pad pad pad...

A wolf materialised from the night and fled right past them, ears flattened to her skull. So much bigger and stronger than a dog; here was a beast.

"This is absolutely nuts!" McCartney whispered.

He and Marks were both grinning. God help me, thought Harkness. I've entered a warzone with two madmen for company.

"I think she's got the right idea," whispered Marks.

At that they were up and sprinting, out in a long eastward arc and around until they reached the car.

*

"Well, that were a pointless and dangerous endeavour," said Marks once they were huddled around their campfire at Jezioro Kruklin.

"Bollocks," interjected McCartney. "We've learned loads of stuff. First of all, these 'Red Army' archaeologists aren't looking for the bodies of fallen heroes at all. Second, whatever they are after, they haven't found it. And third, other people are involved too. They weren't shooting at us."

Marks had impaled chicken on sharpened sticks for their supper and he adjusted them over the flames.

"And we can make another deduction," said Harkness. "This project began in the nineties – so presumably a first discovery was made then. Something of such importance that they've been out here ever since, searching for more."

Marks looked up from his cooking. "That's a good thought."

"So we need to know where ground zero was," said McCartney.

A gentle cooing came from the trees, where they had tethered their messenger in case of further need.

"Time to set our feathered friend loose again," said Harkness.

47

"A tree! A fucking tree!" Sergeant Ainsley Jones shook his head. "Oh, they are really taking the piss with this one."

"Just be grateful it's not August." Sergeant Gary Rees was a former PE teacher from Southampton who'd joined the SBS because school life was dull.

The four Increment commandos had jogged to the peak of Pen y Fan, the highest point in the Brecon Beacons. Beasting season was summer – that was when new recruits died of heatstroke on these mountains with shameful regularity. But now there were just the four of them, staring at the carcass of a huge oak tree dumped incongruously on the mountaintop.

"How'd they even get it here?" Jones was incredulous.

Born not far away in Merthyr Tydfil, he had black curly hair and a boxer's brow and nose. A former member of the Royal Marines' mountain warfare cadre, he'd just scraped the height requirement.

"Chinook helicopter, I guess," said Rees.

"Never mind how they bloody got it here," said Captain Woody Donaldson – tall, posh and grizzled, he spoke with a lisp. "Our job's to get it down again."

"Easy!" Andrew Jackson slapped his hands together. "Piece of piss, Staff."

Jackson, a Nigerian-born NCO, was the second most decorated living serviceman in the British military. His Victoria Cross had been awarded in secrecy for deeds carried out in Libya involving hostages, a petroleum refinery and a very high chance of being killed. What had not been mentioned at Buckingham Palace was his extreme lethalness. Jackson's confirmed kills gave him joint fourth position in the British Armed Forces' all-time table. He was tall, handsome and smiley.

"It's probably not as heavy as you expect," said Captain Donaldson, knocking on the trunk. "Look, it's been dead for ages. All the moisture's evaporated."

"It's actually illegal to cut down live oak trees," piped up the Welshman.

"Thanks for that, Jonesey," said Donaldson.

They all chuckled.

"Watch this!" cried Gary Rees, heaving up the root end by himself until the tree was an inch off the ground.

Everybody cheered. 'Watch this' was their catchphrase, a nod to the daft and improbable things they found themselves doing on a daily basis. Rees was the most physical of the men, stocky and muscular with thinning black hair. But when NCO Jackson grabbed hold of the oak he groaned. His hand was in fungus.

"I don't know what you're grumbling about, Jacko," said Jones. "This trunk must remind you of your wife's thighs, I'd have thought."

As they laughed again Jackson's frown segued into a smile. "Damn good to see you again, boys."

Two months previously the squad had been waiting at Helsinki-Vantaa Airport for a British Airways business class connection to Tokyo when the plug was pulled on their mission – whatever that was. The hop back to London was boozy and uproarious.

"Looks like we're having another run at it then, Staff?" grunted Jackson as they manoeuvred their burden down the ridge.

"Seems that way," said Donaldson.

They were making for the Afon Cynrig that sparkled far below them. In the dell one click east nestled Cwmcynwyn Farm, the light in its kitchen windows evoking distant memories of comfort.

"Any idea of the target yet?" asked Rees.

Since their selection that spring they'd trained remorselessly with no inkling of the purpose.

"Honestly, Gary, I'm as much in the dark as you are."

"I still think the whole thing's some glorified training exercise," said Jackson.

"Don't you believe it," growled Donaldson. "Business class flights? What army have you been serving in?"

"Perhaps Japan's after nukes?" offered Jones. "And they've got a facility by the sea somewhere that needs taking out. Heavy water… that's a thing, isn't it?"

Coasts, mountains, compounds. Coasts, mountains, compounds. The training had been cyclical. They'd done lochs in Scotland and fjords in Norway; the previous month they'd bouldered their way along the Icelandic coast for twenty miles in dry suits as Arctic waves tried to smash them from the rocks.

Captain Donaldson sighed. "Don't you think the Japs have had enough of nuclear power, Jonesey?"

Guffaws at that.

"You soft-headed bastard," said Rees.

"If I was a betting man," said Donaldson reflectively, "I'd say Japan is just the stop-off point. It's North Korea, I reckon. Search and destroy. Which'll put us in the history books, lads."

When they had descended from Pen y Fan they upped to a canter, crossing open ground with their tree at the speed of a fast jogger. Thirty minutes later they stood at Llangorse Lake, the largest in Wales. In the frail October light its waters looked black and cold as the abyss.

"Yes, Staff, got it," Donaldson sighed into his radio. "Right, lads, let's see what boxer shorts we've all got on today. They want this tree swum over the lake. And then carried up that mountain there."

Another round of groans.

"I might've known it," said Rees.

"Someone up there's got a *seriously* sick sense of humour," said Jones.

48

Hastings was determined to hate the Garrick. She was no feminist, but to paraphrase her idol Elizabeth I, she *thought foul scorn* that there were places where she still had to be chaperoned by a man. Moreover, the members club was a bastion of the Establishment that she and fellow travellers on the alt-right railed against (while simultaneously claiming to defend). But here's the thing: she really rather liked it.

There was something so civilised about the cloakroom corridor, the old boys' hats and coats all hung on their own numbered pegs. Under the grand staircase was a little den where she spied two aged lords tucking into single malt, and every inch of wall was hung with paintings of dead thespians in a miracle of tessellation. But this was no time for art appreciation: they had a job to do. Long brown hair, signet ring – and that diamond tooth cap that would leave it beyond doubt. Oh yes, Orientalist would be there tonight. *She sensed it.*

Sir Hugh recommended the dining room as the place to scope out the most members at once, and there indeed were the old buffers in all their glory. Many were blue-blooded, some stockbrokery; most were of legal stock these days, the Groucho having replaced the Garrick as the actors' lair of choice. In one corner she spotted a Supreme Court judge, and the burble of conversation was straight from the Square Mile.

"…what do you think of Sumption?"

"Very bright man…"

But the atmosphere was rather fun, and Hastings realised she was going to enjoy herself. There was only one problem: every blighter in the room wore a signet ring. A long thin table bisected the hall, club-bable men in double-breasted suits tucking into plates of steak and pie along the length of it. The scene reminded her of—

"School dinners!" Sir Hugh smiled. "Just glorified school dinners, really. Very nice all the same. Anyone you like the look of?"

Indeed there was. At the end of the long table sat a mountainous fellow with wavy brown hair, gold glinting on his little finger as he demolished a plate of salmon.

Hastings marched up and extended a hand. "I haven't had the pleasure."

The diner peered up at her as if through opera glasses. "This one of yours, Hugo?"

If the diplomat was embarrassed to introduce the most controversial politician in Britain as his dinner date, he didn't show it. "May I present Gloria Hastings MP?"

"Then perhaps you might tell her that in this club, members prefer *not* to shake hands."

Faux pas number one. But she had seen right inside his mouth during the outburst – and this was not Orientalist.

Another suspect sat further along the table. The place next to him was vacant so Hastings plonked herself down.

"My goodness!" he cried. "Is nothing sacred?"

"I'm sorry, Gloria, I should have told you," said Sir Hugh. "The central table is strictly for gentlemen only. Ladies are asked to dine at the side."

Women in pearls were being entertained on circular tables along both walls, and Hastings' eyes glittered. But again she'd been able to see right back into his mouth. Not Orientalist.

An older man wearing a tweed suit with a pocket watch and boot polish brown hair sat in a far corner.

"That's Jim Goad," said the diplomat. "You'll like him. High Tory of the old school… and a very naughty boy. But don't get him too excited, he's recovering from a heart attack."

It didn't take Goad long to get on to the topic of his ill-health.

"I'm overdue an appointment with the grim reaper," he roared. "Tried to jump my place in the queue!"

Not Orientalist.

The man who caught her eye next looked out of place. He wore an avant-garde jacket in sky blue and a shirt with a mandarin collar. The flowing brown hair was expensively coiffured – like that ridiculous celebrity hairdresser on the telly – and according to Sir Hugh he produced television drama for the BBC. Hastings' dislike increased. A luvvie, a wet; a fully paid up, card-carrying member of the hated London liberal elite. Hastings prayed to her dark gods that this was Orientalist: everything about him was begging to be brought down a peg.

"His last series was *Romanus*, a sword and sandals thing," Sir Hugh confided. "Absolute flop."

Hastings affixed her most luminous smile and waded in.

"*Huge* admirer of your work," she purred. "I'm—"

"I know who you are," he drawled, refusing to look her in the eye. "You're Mrs Nasty from the H.O.C. What is it the *Mirror* called you again? Gloria Hating?"

She forced a laugh. "Would you mind if we joined you? I've *so* many questions I barely know where to begin."

The flattery bought her time. "If you *absolutely* must."

But damn it, nothing she could say would make him open his mouth properly. She tried humour and then provocation, utilising the full gamut of her powers of outrage. But he merely *endured*, the distaste on his features akin to a man sampling cat vomit.

Finally he said, "Look, whatever you're selling, I don't want any. Kindly leave me in peace."

Sir Hugh stamped a chair leg on the man's toe and he yowled in fury. Not Orientalist.

"Terribly sorry, Oscar," said Sir Hugh. "I'll see to it that your dinner is on my account."

No more longhairs were dining, so they scouted various bars without success. They'd been at it two hours now and Hastings was beginning to feel squiffy.

"Let's leave it a week and try again," said Sir Hugh.

It was as they collected their coats that she saw him.

Six foot four, wearing a dinner jacket and white bow tie; he had a graciousness to his movements, courtly manners with the attendant. The mane was side and back-swept, brown and well-nourished. But the umbrella grabbed her attention most of all. It wasn't raining.

"Who he, who he?" squeaked Hastings.

"You've got the wrong end of the stick this time," chuckled Sir Hugh. "That's Lord Richard Wakeford, a veritable pillar of the establishment. He established a youth charity with the Prince of Wales, for goodness' sake."

"What does he do?"

"Made his fortune in property, big Labour donor." This gave Sir Hugh pause for thought. "Oh, and out of passion more than anything he owns a—"

He stopped dead.

"Owns a what?" said Hastings.

"He owns *an antiquarian bookshop on the Charing Cross Road*."

Like footpads they tracked Wakeford through the club. Up the staircase again and past the dining hall, from which sounds of good living still emanated; finally to the Irving Room, where Wakeford took a red leather chair and a Carlos I brandy.

The diplomat struck. "Richard, do you mind? May I introduce my guest for the night?"

There was a languor in Wakeford's pose, copy of the *FT* unfolded over crossed legs. But when he saw her he responded. It wasn't so much a flinch as an *anti-flinch*, a momentary but conscious deadening in his movements.

"Enchanted," he said, gesturing to two empty armchairs. "Always a pleasure to meet an – independently – minded lady."

Hastings laughed at the little witticism. Here I am, she thought, face to face with the man who in all probability brought about my downfall.

They discussed Parliamentary mischief, the Americans' chances of knocking out the Syrian Islamist groups in one ferocious invasion (high) and of winning the peace (non-existent). Next they tackled what British boots on the ground would mean for multi-ethnic harmony at home. Nigel Farage was milk to Hastings' brandy on this topic, yet still she could not enrage him. Lord Wakeford was sublime. Finally she tried President Putin's manoeuvring in Estonia, where the Russian minority had just demanded a plebiscite on re-joining the Motherland. But Wakeford remained inscrutable, and presently he rose.

"I hope you'll excuse me," he said, reaching for his briefcase. "The reason for the penguin suit is I've a ticket for the opera."

Hastings yawned, a real ripper.

Scientists have sought in vain to discover why yawns are contagious. The best guess is that it is some primeval bonding mechanism, being part of the band essential to survival. But right away the ripples began beneath Wakeford's chin. Hastings saw the yawn rise up his throat like a wave, building unstoppable momentum; his eyes shut involuntarily. Then he yawned too, his entire head rotating and the mouth cavernous. One hand held his drink, the other his briefcase, and in his back left molar a diamond glittered and shone.

"I beg your pardon," he said. "How rude of me."

Hastings did not shake his hand.

49

Artur Wójcik's second missive was concise.

> *Проектное возвращение домой – Project Homecoming.*
> *Began 11 March 1998. Farmer found mass grave of Red*
> *Army soldiers executed by Nazis near Szestno, Masuria.*
> *Site excavated later filled in create memorial lake. Yeltsin*
> *inaugurate state visit to open November 1998.*

A

"It must have been one of Yeltsin's last acts as Russian president," said Harkness. "I do hope the vodka was to his taste."

The pigeon had taken thirty-six hours to return, and Marks was frying eggs and bacon on the fire as they digested the correspondence. The day had dawned bright and sunny, though there was a crystalline snap to the air. They could not camp out much longer.

"They made a memorial lake," muttered Marks, "in a region with more than two thousand lakes? Memorial my arse."

Harkness was thinking of the Father of All Bombs.

"So we find the farmer," said McCartney.

"Good idea, Ross," said Harkness.

"But how?" said Marks. "It were more than twenty year ago."

"A public library would be a good place to start," said Harkness.

*

The town of Giżycko was an exemplar of bleak communist planning. Cheerless housing blocks ran on uninterrupted and the city library resembled a provincial prison right down to the bars over the windows. But the librarian was flattered by the intrusion of foreign visitors into her quiet little world, and she hurried to fetch yellowing mounds of the *Gazeta Giżycka*.

The papers were a portal into late nineties Poland, a lost world of tractors, mullets and ill-fitting leather jackets. Marks and McCartney were limited to scouring the pile for place names and pictures. But Harkness's Russian – a millennium of divergence from Polish, thirty-eight per cent overlap – meant he could make sense of the articles. After an hour, McCartney went for a smoke.

"We should send him home," said Marks.

"What?"

"Ross. He shouldn't be here."

Harkness bristled. "Why? He's coming out with some good stuff."

"Too impetuous," said Marks. "He puts us both at risk."

"Listen, Tony, Ross and I have been through the fire together. And he's maturing, almost by the day. I—"

McCartney's return interrupted them.

Five minutes later Marks brandished a newspaper. "How's about this, then?"

An elderly couple shook hands with a Russian general on the yellowing front page. The woman wore a headscarf, her husband leaned on a garden fork and the peak of the general's hat soared above them both.

Harkness frowned. "Bolek and Anastazja Pawlak sell their land in… something–something… commemoration of the Great Patriotic War," he read. "Something–something, something else… *jezioro*. That must mean lake, we're staying at a jezioro. Like the Russian '*ozero*', see the relationship?"

"Do you know, I think we've found it," said Marks.

*

"What do you think it is that they discovered?" asked Marks.

They were speeding towards the hamlet of Szestno, where according to the telephone directory the Pawlaks still lived.

"Another mass grave," said Harkness. "Probably Neolithic. Something along the lines of Schöneck-Kilianstädten."

"What's that?" asked McCartney.

Marks uploaded a 2015 *Daily Mail* article on his phone.

> *Scientists say they have found rare evidence of a prehistoric massacre in Europe after discovering a 7,000-year-old mass grave with skeletal remains from some of the continent's first farmers bearing terrible wounds.*
>
> *Archaeologists painstakingly examined the bones of 26 men, women and children buried in the Stone Age grave site at Schöneck-Kilianstädten, near Frankfurt. They found blunt force marks to the head, arrow wounds and deliberate efforts to smash at least half the victim's shins to stop them running away.*

Harkness shivered as he recalled the slaughterhouse at Itanga, and his own words taunted him.

Oh, there was lots of bad behaviour in prehistory. But in the main, I'm convinced our prehistoric ancestors were good. Because they must have been.

His lecture might have been given in a different epoch – yet still he clung to the belief. The steady rolling back of prehistory would show the atrocities of Itanga or Schöneck to be the exception and not the rule. These were glaring abominations amid millennia of decency.

Because of course they were.

50

With its crumbling farmhouses and cottage gardens filled with turnips and potatoes, Szestno was typical of the region. On the outskirts stood a modern abode, however, covered in satellite dishes and by far the ugliest. And sure enough, when Harkness enquired about the Pawlaks that is where they were sent.

The door was opened by a middle-aged man with sunken eyes and a sallow look.

"Yes?" – intuitively he knew they were English-speakers.

"I'm hoping to speak to Bolek or Anastazja Pawlak," said Harkness.

"Bolek was my father," he replied. "He is dead now, but my mother is here. Please, what is this about? Are you journalists?"

"Archaeologists, actually," said Marks. "We want to talk about the lake."

"As you like…"

The house was quiet and dark, with lace curtains and china ornaments. Through a closed door they heard a television game show.

"She can barely see the screen," whispered the son. "She is more than a hundred years old now. But her ears and mind are good. You will see."

He led them into the sitting room and there was the woman from the local newspaper, still recognisable and shawl still wrapped around her head. Now she was well and truly a babushka. The skin on her face was rumpled and folded like cooled lava; parted lips lent her a look of slight confusion.

"Ask her whatever you like," said the man. "I will ask her for you."

"I have just one question," said Harkness.

The babushka blinked and nodded.

"Was it really soldiers that you found, where they put the lake? Or something else?"

Anastazja Pawlak was completely still as her son translated into Polish. Then she replied in a voice as high and shrill as a greenfinch.

"I always knew someone would come knocking on my door to ask about this one day," she said. "The Russians gave us money not to speak to anyone, you understand. That is how we built this house. My husband was able to purchase a good herd of cows and we have finished our days as wealthy people. It was a strange blessing." She clapped her hands together producing a dry noise before continuing.

"But I am old now, and soon I will be dead. So I don't care. I would like to tell somebody what we found."

Her son frowned and said in Polish, "Mama, are you sure?"

"What can they do to us now?" she scolded him. "Poland is a member of the European Union these days. The era of Russia doing what she likes is over. Besides…"

She pulled down her sleeve and showed Harkness the web of scar tissue down her forearm.

"My back, it is the same," she said. "In 1939 the Red Army set fire to our house with us inside it. In that fire…" Her eyes became glassier. "Never mind. I never wanted to take their money though. But my husband insisted. He said it would make things better for us. He was right, my husband, always right."

"Tell us about the day you made the discovery," Harkness urged her.

"We had only twenty acres then," she said. "One day the ground collapsed in the east paddock, where the lake is now. The canyon was deep enough to swallow a horse up to its ears. Inside there was a cave and there my husband found bones. Many, many bones."

"Have you got photographs?" asked Marks.

The elderly woman looked surprised. "Yes!"

Her son fetched a shoebox full of prints from upstairs and they gathered around her chair.

"This is my husband, Bolek," she said, holding the first photograph to her nose for inspection. "A strong man."

She produced another photograph and instantly Harkness felt a frisson of excitement. It was the entrance to the cave; the crest and ischium of a pelvis protruded from the mud.

Marks had turned hoarse. "Not a chance in hell is that *Homo sapiens*. Way too robust."

When Pawlak showed them the next photograph a jolt went through Harkness, an electrical, *physical* reaction unlike anything he'd experienced in his career. It was the skull that left no doubt. By the size of it; by the huge eye-sockets that loured at them from the print; in the gargantuan brow ridge, evolved to absorb blows and maximise the appearance of aggression. He was looking at the complete skeleton of a Neanderthal man.

"That's got to be the most perfect one ever found," breathed Harkness.

"Just wow…" whispered Marks. "What a beauty."

Only the hands and feet were missing.

*

"A caveman, right?" said McCartney.

"Literally, in this case," said Marks. "Let me give you a massively simplified explanation of the human family tree. Australopithecus was the first to come down from the branches…"

"When the jungle broke up into savannah corridors," interjected McCartney.

Harkness glanced up at him from the photo.

"Exactly," said Marks. "Lucy, the famous 'missing link'. From there we get to *Homo erectus* – bigger, smarter, may have had fire. Erectus was the first to leave our home continent and colonise Asia."

"Out of Africa, Part One," said Harkness.

"Then in about 600,000 BC, Homo heidelbergensis turns up," said Marks. "Smarter again – something was definitely afoot now. We were well on the way to what you might call human. And from heidelbergensis came these guys." The photograph trembled in Marks' hand. "Almost human. Massive, aggressive, cunning – and built for the Ice Age. Jeez, they were machines. They should have been masters of the planet."

"Only back in Africa, something else was stirring," said Harkness. "Something a bit more… enigmatic in its nature. Anatomically modern *Homo sapiens* comes on the scene about 300,000 BC, also evolved directly from heidelbergensis. The point here is that Neanderthals are our cousins, rather than a direct ancestor in the human lineage. We didn't evolve from them. In fact, they kept us pinned in our home continent for another 240,000 years."

"Europe and the Middle East were Neanderthal country." Marks adjusted his Stetson like a cowboy on the lookout for Apaches. "In the Ice Age we couldn't compete."

"Until our full faculties arrived circa 70,000 BC, that is," said Harkness. "We created harpoons and throwing spears. We see the beginning of cave painting and complex symbolism. We could out-hunt, out-forage and out-breed them at last. Within fifty thousand years Neanderthals had disappeared for good. And—"

As Pawlak held up another photograph the words caught in Harkness's throat. He was blindsided, rendered temporarily unable to speak.

Marks managed it first. "It's a hoax. Got to be…"

A dozen Neanderthal skeletons were heaped down the cave. Maybe more. Given that mankind's knowledge of its own past is based on the fragmentary remains of a few thousand individuals – you could dispose of the lot in a skip – they were looking at unquestionably the most astonishing discovery in the history of palaeontology.

Harkness was shaking violently. "This is huge. Lucy times ten. Tutankhamun times fifty."

"I'm not having it," said Marks. "Don't believe your eyes."

"But the set-up's too perfect to be contrived," said Harkness. "The lake, the newspaper, her story. The levels of secrecy we've been forced to broach. And look at them, Tony. Just look at them."

The patina of the bones, the shapes and the contours. They just *felt* real, and the first flush of belief came into Marks' cheeks, too.

"How many?" rasped Harkness as he raced through the photographs. "How many were in there in total?"

Pawlak produced a high-pitched clucking noise. "About thirty, something like this."

"*Thirty?*"

Then Harkness clocked the little detail that had first eluded him: every single skeleton lacked hands or feet. Something troubled him about this.

"And sculptures," the old woman was saying. "All of them the same."

Harkness's vision seemed to sharpen with new acuity. "Did you say sculptures?"

"Many sculptures," said Pawlak. "They took them back to Russia, but my husband kept one."

She rummaged in the box and produced an *entirely unknown Ice Age Venus.*

"You have got to be shitting me," said Marks.

Like most Ice Age Venuses, the sculpture lacked hands or feet. Harkness looked to the photograph. Back to the Venus. Photograph. Venus. And suddenly he knew what the Venuses were, what they meant. The greatest mystery of Ice Age art was solved at a stroke. And he knew why Neanderthals are no longer with us, why the branch of the human family tree that leads to *Homo sapiens* is artificially straight, as though all offshoot species had been snipped away. He also knew that a lifetime's belief in the goodness of prehistoric man was built on a lie. The Venuses were tokens, handed along the trade networks of early modern humans across the breadth of Europe and Siberia. No, *instructions* – that described it better. A message that united far-flung peoples, communicated over vast distances long before the written word. And that message was: exterminate. For wars of genocide were nothing new. Early humans had contrived and brought about the organised extinction of their nearest surviving member of the family.

Nyónsoboma…

The babushka handed over the Venus.

"A gift for you," she said.

51

The philologist was woken at four a.m. by her feet kicking out beneath the duvet. She sat up in bed and blinked. She knew exactly what she needed to do. An urgent 'if anything happens to me' letter was required, which she could send to a person of responsibility – Marcus's partner at his firm would suffice. She would detail her suspicions of MI5 surveillance and include every scrap of research (with explainers). In the event of her death, he'd be directed to send it to the twenty most prominent philologists in the country along with *Newsnight*, *Panorama*, Channel 4's *Dispatches* and all the nationals. Perhaps one of them would take it seriously. And she would do it right now to make the first post.

Adriaen's snores radiated from the bow of the *Time Traveller*. Did he want to sleep with her? He was fifteen years her junior and Johansen didn't even know his surname, but she reasoned probably yes. She wouldn't let him, of course. Marcus remained missing, presumed dead, and she was in mourning. At least Adriaen wasn't interested in her work, and for that reason she trusted him. Maybe she was mentally ill, maybe not; but events thus far were proof she wasn't completely mad. The things that had happened to her were corporeal, evidential, fact. With a vindictive little smile, she wondered whether MI5 had got on with her cleaner's aged parents in Budapest. But that brought back thoughts of Marcus, and of her old existence that she hadn't realised was perfect until it crumbled away.

Johansen made herself a cup of tea and turned on a desk lamp at the galley table. All the wealth and power of Canary Wharf glittered in the surface of the marina outside, those hundred thousand lights diffuse in slicks of boat oil.

It was time to join the dots.

> And God said replenish the earth, and <u>subdue it</u>; and
> have <u>dominion</u> over every living thing.

This was a trace in mankind's cultural memory of the holocaust he had brought down upon the only other hominid left standing by the end of the Ice Age.

Hair covered Enkidu's entire body. Naked was Enkidu.
And the hunter told his father, "I have beheld a wild man
come down from the hills. His strength is the greatest in
all the land. His power is mighty. He has filled in the pits
I dug with my own hands. And he has torn asunder the
traps which I set."

Enkidu was, of course, an allegory for Neanderthal man. And the hunter's exasperation summed up well the contest for resources during the long struggle with the Neanderthals for Europe and the Middle East. This was a story that was told and evolved for many millennia before writing, and had slipped into metaphor by the beginning of Assyrian civilisation. Meanwhile, Gilgamesh – founder of settlements, sinker of wells, clearer of the high mountain passes – symbolised man.

Then did Gilgamesh and Enkidu grapple, one against
the other. Their anger was inflamed. Neither would
yield. In fierce combat did they struggle, and they raged
and snorted like wild bulls. Then Gilgamesh overcame
Enkidu and placed his knee on the fallen wild man. Thus
was Enkidu vanquished.

What of the Great Flood? Ancient Greek writings tell of a vast migration in about 1200 BC, by a population known, enigmatically, as the Sea People. The turmoil was such that it caused the fall of the Minoan kings and brought about the first Greek Dark Age. It was a cultural memory of these fallen Greek kingdoms – an age of heroes – that Homer drew on in the *Iliad*. No philologist disagrees with that.

But Johansen posited another movement of people, far older and much greater in its sweep and consequence. A flood, if you will. Hordes of Neanderthals, driven south by the expanding polar deserts as the last Ice Age reached its peak in 23,000 BC. They would have come up against biologically modern *Homo sapiens*, newly armed and dangerous. An ancient Armageddon was born.

> *In bygone days, the multitudes teemed upon the face of the earth and the unending clamour and wickedness of the people aroused the wrath of the Gods. And so the Great Gods purposed a mighty flood to wipe out mankind. With the first light of dawn, a darkling cloud rose upon the horizon.*

A flood: but not of water. A deluge: but not of rain.

> *Rushing before this cloud were Shullat, God of Despoilment, and Hanish, God of Destruction, heralds of Doom over the mountains and plains. Ninurta, God of War, unleashed mayhem upon the realm. And the assembly of Great Gods scorched the land with their flames. Like a mighty invading army, the Great Flood overwhelmed the people. And lo, all of humanity was returned unto dust.*

Or in the Old Testament:

> *The end of all flesh is come; the earth is filled with violence; and, behold, I will destroy the earth. And I, behold, I do bring the flood of waters upon the earth, to destroy all flesh; everything that is in the earth will perish.*

Gilgamesh and the Old Testament, two twigs on the same branch. *Homo sapiens* was almost overwhelmed in this conflict, yet we prevailed. What gave our species the edge in this titanic conflict? She went back to *Gilgamesh*.

*Ea, the cunning God of Wisdom, also swore the oath not
to reveal the secret to any man. But Ea was crafty. He
spoke the secret unto the reed fence of my house, and by
chance I overheard his words.*

Sharper. Faster. Equipped with that mental *je ne sais quoi* that
defines our species, the blossoms of which appear in the archaeological
record almost overnight from 70,000 BC. Quite a date in the story of
humanity. So *Homo sapiens* was victorious in its first struggle, but had
also perpetrated its first crime. Truly the end of innocence.

*And the Lord God said: "Behold, the man is become as
one of us, to know good and evil." Therefore God sent
him forth from the Garden of Eden.*

There. She had pulled the disparate strings together. Johansen put
down her pen and stood up. Dawn was breaking, strips of lilac forming
over the Thames Estuary to the east, and she stepped out onto the stern
to take the crisp dawn air. A pair of Canada geese flew overhead; she
could see office lights turning on automatically in the towers of capital-
ism to the south, entire floors coming alive and specks moving about
on them. Johansen held her notebook close to her chest, this work of
scholarship she had lost everything for.

"Give it to me."

Johansen wheeled around. Adriaen wore a dressing gown that
he hadn't bothered to tie and his manhood dangled grotesquely. He
pointed an automatic pistol at her.

"Honey, give it to me," he said more reasonably.

Johansen dived headfirst into the water, hitting it with a *crack* that
startled the seagulls who patrolled the marina into flight. Already she
was kicking: down, deep, deeper into the murk, opening the pages
so the fountain pen ink bled from the paper. She surfaced in a front
crawl, notebook clasped between her teeth and head twisting from

side to side. Adriaen fired at her, missed, fired again, missed a second time. She duck-dived back down, bullets corkscrewing through water on either side. She resurfaced at the entrance to a canal lined with new-build houses and powered around the corner, out of his line of sight. Adriaen sprinted along the marina to the entrance – but it was gated access, he couldn't get in. He rushed back to the marina and dived into the water. But when he made it into the canal she had vanished.

52

In an age of Starbucks and Subway, of globalisation and homogenisation, the Charing Cross Road retains an essence of early twentieth-century London. The northern end is lined with antiquarian bookshops where one still has a sense that a valuable folio may be discovered for a song. At first glance R. Wakeford Rare Booksellers was much like the rest: the tomes piled high and in apparent disarray. The right side of the window display was given over to Dickens and the left to the owner's speciality: for Lord Wakeford was much interested in the Near East. He had a mint 1926 copy of *Kings of the Hittites* by David Hogarth and a first edition of Henry Layard's ripping travelogue *Early Adventures in Persia, Susiana and Babylonia*. But pride of place was given to a new acquisition: *Provisional Readings in the Medieval History of the Near East* by Costi Zurayk at the princely sum of £1,450.

Were a visitor to descend to the basement there, however, he or she would find something unique amongst the row of booksellers. In place of a book-filled stockroom or grubby kitchenette was a lead-lined chamber, the door activated by thumb print and two keys. Inside were a table, chairs, a device that interrupted electrical circuits and a red light that flashed should Wakeford need interrupting. Within this secure zone (less chance of being spotted on arrival than at the Russian Embassy) a crisis meeting was taking place.

"Twenty years," began the man codenamed Orientalist by British intelligence. "For twenty years, this little band of unreconstructed Trots have kept our ears to the ground. In all that time, precisely nothing happened. Then suddenly – poof! – something happened. And things are already in danger of running away with us, are they not?"

Wakeford ran a hand back through that luxuriant hair. He wore burgundy corduroys and a navy blue blazer with a pocket square; though his deportment was relaxed there was a wince of stress at his crow's feet.

"You'll find no excuses at my end," said Jasper gruffly.

"You did a solid job in Amiens," said Wakeford. "If only we'd known of Professor Fournier earlier we could have prevented this situation entirely. We've examined his laptop and on the morning of your intervention – the very morning, damn it! – he emailed an acquaintance about Dr Bianca's work. And we found the draft of a letter he presumably did send to another expert in Lisbon. We have a hydra on our hands, my dears. Cut one head off and two more replace it. The danger now is that two becomes four."

"So we burn the stumps off," said Jasper, opening and closing his fists. "I have a meeting at British Marine to attend later today, then I shall be right down to business."

"Knew you'd say yes. And Dennis, I do give you credit for discrediting Hastings. On face value, the plan was masterful. She's broken as a political force and will never again wield even a tatter of credibility."

Orientalist flashed Mirza that smile that made the recipient feel the centre of all warmth and affability in the universe, and the lobbyist bowed his head.

"However, last night I actually met her."

"*No!*" gasped Mirza, with a hand to his clavicle. "But where?"

"She was a guest at my club."

"By chance?"

"She was there with Sir Hugh Alexander."

Mirza crossed himself. He had been born in a Christian enclave of Lahore; though a lapsed Catholic, tension brought out old habits.

"Kill her," he said. "Kill them both."

"Yes," said Wakeford, "I rather think we might have to now. But you saw the fuss that got made over Litvinenko – and crikey, he was a minor dissident. The feeling from above is that if we were implicated in the death of a sitting MP there might be an actual war. The desire is to keep the diplomatic powder dry for now. So wiser heads than ours are working on a plan to resolve the situation with the necessary subtlety."

Jasper was shaking his head. "But how did they get on to us? I just can't fathom it."

"I take complete responsibility." Mirza was suitably funereal. "I was a proponent of the light touch. That was wrong."

Wakeford sighed, another spasm of tension manifesting itself at his crow's feet. "I suspect that my technical skills are not what I thought they were. My foray into computer science has been useful and rewarding these last few years, but perhaps I should have left it to the geniuses at the FSB this time. Pride comes before a fall, as they say. So we are all of us fallible, gentlemen."

"What of Harkness et al.?" enquired Mirza.

"That side of the case is under central control now," said Wakeford. "To put it bluntly, they're on the kill-list. No warning, no interrogation, no survivors. We're coming up against a little third-party turbulence out there, so Moscow's taking no chances. That leaves Johansen for you, Dennis."

Mirza smeared his hair back against his pate and nodded.

"And given 'Hastings-gate', I must tell you that they upstairs are very unhappy with how things are proceeding. She *needs to be found*." Wakeford emphasised the last four syllables with a swish of his pen, eyeing both men in turn. "But if we all do our jobs, we can still keep a lid on this."

The red light began flashing.

"Wait here," he said.

When the lord returned his satisfaction was palpable.

"It appears one neck of our hydra is to be imminently cauterised," he said.

"Oh?" said Mirza.

"I've just been told that our friends' rustication at the Masurian Lakes is about to come to a rather abrupt halt."

53

In Szestno the mood was sombre.

"You can't say there's no supporting evidence," Marks was saying. "Christ alive, the bodies are buried all over Europe! You've got the Neanderthal found at the Saint-Cesairé cave in France with a blade injury to the skull. In Les Rois, the bones of a Neanderthal child who was de-fleshed by human beings. In Shanidar, Iraq, Neanderthal remains show a fatal missile wound to the chest – and we know that only *Homo sapiens* possessed throwing weapons. Then in the El Sidrón cave of north-west Spain, what was it – six adult Neanderthals, three adolescents, two juveniles and an infant? All of them massacred by early modern humans, their bones showing marks of cutting and percussion. Not very nice."

"Plus there's the 'arms race' of spear tip length and design that occurred during the human–Neanderthal overlap," said Harkness. "And to crown it all, 144 Ice Age Venuses – sorry, 145 – virtually all of them missing hands and feet. Just do the Google image search…"

"Face facts, Randolph, our discipline has dropped the ball badly on this one," said Marks. "The truth's been staring us in the face. The only missing piece of the jigsaw is why Moscow is hell bent on keeping it secret."

"That's why I need to go to Central Asia," said Harkness quietly.

"What?" said Marks. "How come?"

"When we were in Wolf's Lair we overheard the archaeologists mention somewhere called Saimaluu Tash. It's a mountain in

Kyrgyzstan – I've actually been there. I knew it rang a bell. Back in the eighties I went on an expedition to that part of the world, while it was still part of the USSR. Part digging, part 'extra-curricular activities'. Officially we were looking for remains of *Homo erectus*. Saimaluu Tash was considered a sacred mountain for most of the historical era, but it's home to some petroglyphs much older than that."

"Petroglyphs?" said McCartney.

"Rock carvings – from the Greek '*petros*', stone, and '*glyphein*', to carve. There are supposed to be thousands of them up there."

"Supposed to be?" said Marks. "You didn't see for yourself?"

"I didn't make it to the top."

"You big jessie."

"I'll have you know that most attempts on Saimaluu Tash fail," said Harkness. "It's very remote, ten thousand feet above sea level, and we got beaten by the weather. As a matter of fact, a few months later a young French archaeologist died up there. Or she went missing and they never found the body, or something. It was quite big news in the world of palaeontology – perhaps you remember it, Tony? Her name was Olivié-something, if memory serves."

"You've got a bloody good memory," said Marks. "How the hell do you remember a detail like that?"

"Ah, one of my goddaughters is called Olivia and I got asked to be her godfather at more or less the same time. These things stick with you, for some reason."

"But why go to Saimaluu Tash at all?" asked McCartney. "We already know what happened in Poland and the Congo."

"Because apart from one Ice Age Venus our evidence consists entirely of photographs," said Harkness, "which are extremely easy to fake. And experts on human origins are on permanent high alert for swindlers – the Piltdown Man hoax still sends a shiver down the spine of palaeontologists after a hundred years. No, what we need are some *bones*. Plus we still don't know why this is being covered up. I mean, there must be a reason for it, mustn't there?"

"They ain't doing this for their academic enlightenment," said Marks.

"I'm not ready for Maidstone yet," McCartney grinned. "I say we go."

"Me too," said Marks.

"You have a wife and young child," Harkness replied. "I'm on a mission now, and Ross, well, he's a mad bugger. But you have responsibilities."

Marks looked out of the window. He flinched.

"Actually, I don't think we're going anywhere," he said.

Two Mercedes Benz saloons had been parked across the lane leading to Pawlak's house. Several vans were lining up behind them and gunmen were fanning out across the fields. Marks dashed upstairs and returned a few seconds later.

"They're all around us!" he shouted.

"Well, we've got a big car," said McCartney.

"So what?" said Marks.

"So let's drive it straight at them."

*

When they emerged from the farmhouse there was a stir of activity at the barricade.

"Duck down beneath the bonnet," shouted Harkness as they dived into the BMW.

Immediately they came under fire: the windscreen blown out and tufts of foam from the headrests filling the car. Harkness hit the accelerator and six seconds later they were doing sixty. One bullet smashed right through the engine block and out of the radio, showering them with splinters of plastic and microchip. Neither Mercedes had moved; instead the gunmen sheltered behind them, firing into the fast-approaching object as if it were a charging elephant. At the last instant Harkness swerved left and the car lurched from the lane. It smashed through a wooden fence and into a field, bouncing across half-frozen furrows.

High-velocity rounds tore through the side-panels like tinfoil, but they were travelling at such speed that only a handful of rounds entered the vehicle.

"Anybody hit?" shouted Harkness.

"A few cuts back here, but we're fine," said Marks.

The BMW battered its way back through the fence half a mile past the roadblock. But for bullet holes, an irregular ticking sound and one thin coil of smoke spiralling from the bonnet the car seemed unscathed, and Harkness swore he would never denigrate the output of Munich again.

As they accelerated south nobody saw the Russian team coming under fire.

That their vehicle now resembled a mobile colander *sans* windscreen raised eyebrows as they rolled into Warsaw. But onlookers assumed it must be a publicity stunt – a new computer game, perhaps? – and they dumped the car without harassment from the *Policja*. An hour later they were at Chopin Airport and by that evening they were in Istanbul waiting for an onward flight to Bishkek. Harkness would deal with Hertz back in Bristol. If he obtained proof of his thesis in Kyrgyzstan he could buy an entire fleet of Beamers with the book royalties.

54

Gloria Hastings was now certain that she had been set up by Russian spies and that Lord Wakeford was an FSB agent. A patriot, she was tempted to go at once to MI5. But once the Secret Services got involved, Wakeford's misdeeds might be airbrushed from existence. He could cut a deal in return for immunity, possibly even be recruited as a double agent. Clearing her name would hardly top the establishment's list of priorities, given how difficult she'd made the lives of Foreign Office ministers over the years and ergo their spooks. Plus there was the small matter of *revenge*. It all pointed to the file.

But now Åkesson became frustrated in his sleuthing. He hacked Wakeford's home computer and smartphone to find both without a blemish, and a desktop at R. Wakeford Rare Booksellers was only used by staff. There *had* to be another machine. But where? The lord's Hampstead pile had a single CCTV camera in the eaves, whereas the security measures at R. Wakeford were excessive. Several cameras had been installed front and back, the door was hewn of plate steel and the shop window measured a centimetre thick, probably bulletproof. It had to be the shop. Somewhere within these defences lay Wakeford's personal computer – most likely protected by an air gap, connected to neither internet nor a network, his files passed to a handler on an encrypted pen drive.

Once again, Hastings enlisted the help of her newspaper. An editorial meeting was attended by the editor-in-chief, the head of investigations, Åkesson and Hastings herself. The journalists concurred that this was dynamite but they lacked evidence. All were in agreement that the authorities did not need to be involved – only terror offences compel journalists to contact the police. Instead they deployed a practitioner of newsroom black magic: someone who could hack the human.

Milo Fallon, proprietor of the sinisterly named Corporate Solutions Ltd, was a slight Dundonian whose talents were mostly employed by City firms wishing to test their own security systems. Typically they would challenge him to retrieve a certain document from their own offices; Fallon claimed never to have failed to gain entry to a site. Very occasionally, however, he took on hot work for newspapers – and a 'Crown Jewels' raid on the premises of a suspected Russian spy was as hot as it got. The agreed fee was £20,000.

Fallon began with a week-long surveillance of the bookshop, which gave him time to grow a beard. This was useful, because the ruse he'd settled on was a Health and Safety Executive snap assessment. Was it a cliché that such an inspector would be hirsute? Undoubtedly, but this stereotype was also likely to be shared by the staff of R. Wakeford. A freshly scuffed luminous jacket with the HSE's logo, a forged identity card, an ill-fitting suit and a clipboard completed his disguise. The HSE obligingly publishes all its inspection forms online.

This was a cunning cover story. Not only is it the *job* of HSE inspectors to make surprise checks on businesses, but they have the legal right to demand entry and visit all areas. They may also insist on managers not being present so staff can speak freely; the risk of lifting injuries made a bookshop inspection plausible.

Fallon launched his attack on a Wednesday morning. From his reconnaissance he knew Wakeford tended to visit in late afternoon – and the cleaner came that day. Fallon had calculated Wakeford would have a private office his staff were banned from entering, but a man of the ermine was surely too grand to do his own vacuuming. The newspaper laid on six security guards, three of them ex-Special Forces. All looked unremarkable: the best private security resembles normal people. Two would peruse the shelves of R. Wakeford with the others on standby in Caffè Vergnano three doors down in case of emergencies. When he got deeper in, Fallon was to text every five minutes confirming he was safe. If he didn't the security would call the police and go in after him, so it was impressed on Fallon not to forget.

R. Wakeford was supervised that morning by a short, friendly woman from East Finchley named Alexandra Beeson. During his recces Fallon had assessed her as an *amiable* character type, but by the stylish bouclé jacket he also diagnosed *expressive* tendencies. The respective Achilles heels of these two traits – eager to please and impulsive – would inform his management of her.

And so it began.

Fallon established common ground by claiming to have a son about to study English literature at Sheffield, as she once had. Soon Beeson was prattling away merrily about it all. Getting people to talk about something familiar is a good way to make them relax – and Fallon forced himself to *genuinely like her*, which would be communicated to her subconscious automatically. Beeson responded, as he knew she would. She seemed surprised that the HSE would bother themselves with such a small shop, but their website bore out Fallon's story. He busied himself with fire alarms and fuse boxes for half an hour until the cleaner turned up. Wakeford did indeed have a private office.

"Goodness knows what he gets up to in there," chuckled Beeson.

But she did not give in easily to Fallon's demand for access. Lord Wakeford was a kind employer and his staff were loyal; he had also been clear that they must under no circumstances venture within his sanctuary from the world. Fallon reminded Beeson that the maximum sentence for obstructing an HSE inspection is six months in prison, whereupon she told the cleaner to open it. She also telephoned Wakeford. Fallon refused to speak to the irate lord, calculating that he now had ten minutes before his victim, the Metropolitan Police, the FSB, or all three at once put in an appearance. At least the Russian Embassy was on the other side of Hyde Park.

The office door was titanium, and Fallon heard the whirr of expensive servos as the cleaner placed her thumb on a fingerprint reader. He prayed he wouldn't have to crack a safe. The door slid open and the cleaner left him and Beeson to it.

The office was furnished in olde worlde style.

The pelt of a tiger snarled up at him from the floor.

A laptop was on the writing desk.

Now Fallon felt suddenly faint and collapsed onto the red leather sofa. Beeson's belief in his identity remained absolute and as she rushed for a glass of water Fallon switched Wakeford's laptop for one of several dummies in his backpack. The glass of water had a marvellously restorative effect on the HSE inspector, whose assessment was complete.

"Don't you want to see downstairs?" said Beeson. "We've got a stockroom where most of the lifting is done. And Richard has a private gym – I've always wanted to peep in there."

But the HSE inspector had a busy morning and could not be diverted. As he departed, so did the two customers who'd been browsing the Near Eastern collection for half an hour. Alexandra Beeson had the first inkling she'd been stitched up.

*

Åkesson got to work on Wakeford's computer right away. This was a challenge: not only had it been protected by the FSB, but Wakeford, an enthusiastic learner of new skills, had been schooled by them in cyberwarfare for ten years. The device was laced with his own traps and pitfalls. It was late afternoon by the time Åkesson got access and just before midnight that he found the file.

It was an MI6 report with a covering letter from the Chief. With a stomach-churning spasm of excitement, Åkesson saw the recipients were listed as the Prime Minister and the Foreign Secretary. At a stroke they had penetrated both the FSB's London bureau and the innermost circle of the British state. But when Åkesson began reading he frowned. This couldn't be right; it was either an extremely elaborate hoax or a very silly joke.

The report was all about chimpanzees.

55

Bishkek hadn't changed much since Harkness's previous visit during the denouement of the Cold War. Cubist architecture was overlooked by snow-capped mountains and they passed row upon row of appalling Soviet housing projects, dreadful to behold. There was something mesmerising about these, about the tessellations and repetitions – the sheer unrelenting awfulness of them. Statues of Lenin jostled for position with mythic Kyrgyz warriors, and Stalin beamed down on them from a municipal building in icon form. The train station still bore a hammer and sickle and a mural projected the old USSR at the centre of a vanished world order.

The Kyrgyz had an Asiatic look, their elders still walking with hands clasped behind their backs just as Harkness remembered. The luxuriant goatee beards and extraordinarily tall *kalpak* hats of embroidered white felt remained in fashion, too. Those Russians still in residence were red-faced from sun and altitude, and there were a host of other ethnicities: ethnicities – Uzbeks, Kazaks, Turkmen and Afghans – each with a distinct look but faces united in hardship. This was the farthest nation from the sea on earth, a crossroads of the ages slap bang in the middle of the Eurasian landmass.

They dined on a curious orangey pork served with rice that smelled like potpourri at a restaurant that reminded Harkness of a North Korean propaganda video. The centre of Bishkek was full of eight-lane boulevards and neoclassical government buildings, but the dusty back streets were more appealing, leafy with wooden shacks. Here they acquired a 1995 Audi RS2 estate bearing Dutch plates for a thousand dollars; Harkness had the zeal of the fresh convert when it came to German engineering. As the crow flies, it was the same distance from Bishkek to Saimaluu Tash as they had travelled in the Congo. Instead of three weeks, however, Google reckoned on seven hours. They set off straight away.

Outside Bishkek heavy industry sprawled. Some factories still belched out coal smoke, turning the vast brown valley into a haze; most had fallen into rust and decay. But the grimness had a weird science-fiction beauty of its own, set against the snow-capped Tian-Shan Mountains. The mountain range resembled a squatting stegosaurus: dun foothills for legs and hillocks the flanks, the peaks its armour-plated spine. All of it was fleeced by a maelstrom of cloud. Finally they left the heavy industry behind. Horses and yurts were dotted across the steppe and the odd abandoned train carriage had been converted into a home, smoke puffing gaily from stationary chimneys. They spotted relics of the old Silk Road, ruined forts and ancient tombs.

"What's so sacred about this mountain of yours then?" asked McCartney.

"In the nineteenth century Saka priests still made sacrifices at the peak," said Harkness. "It was 'found' in 1902 by a Russian cartographer who'd heard shepherds' tales of stones with pictures on them. In Kyrgyz, Saimaluu Tash means 'place of embroidered stone'."

"Ah, that's pretty," said Marks.

"Most of the petroglyphs date from 3,000 BC to 1,000 AD," Harkness continued. "We can expect ibex, lions, wolves – and hunters. But the Saka tribes worshipped the sun, mountains and the galaxy… so expect some pretty far-out cosmology, too."

"Hang on a sec," said McCartney. "Didn't the Neanderthals disappear in, like, twenty-something BC?"

"Yes, but there are *ten thousand* petroglyphs up there. The remoteness and sheer number means most are still undocumented. There could well be prehistoric rock art too."

"How can you tell the age?" asked McCartney.

"It's notoriously difficult," said Harkness. "I could take an educated guess based on style, but erosion's the big clue. These carvings are on basalt, which is a hard rock and wears down at a steady rate. Anything less than a few thousand years old should still be well-defined. Stuff from the Ice Age? Not so much."

"Will you cop an eyeful of that," Marks interrupted.

Lake Issyk-Kul was a blaze of azure, starkly beautiful against the barrenness of the steppe and the cragged Tian-Shan.

"It's the seventh deepest lake in the world," said Harkness. "Almost a kilometre to the bottom."

"Who's up for a swim?" said McCartney.

"I wouldn't, if I were you," he replied.

"Too cold?"

"Nope. It's highly radioactive. The Soviets used Kyrgyzstan as their nuclear playground. The water table's still contaminated – and will be for several thousand years to come."

*

As they headed south the valleys became softer, with a touch of Provence or the Languedoc about them. They passed meadows filled with flowers and orchards of apricots or tiny pink apples that were sweet as candy. Cannabis grew wild. Horses drew carts and the odd bleak factory was plonked down amid the vales, a reminder of Moscow's once-mighty reach across its lost empire. In the villages the men leaned on one another in twos and threes clutching bottles of vodka. It was mid-afternoon. Empty vodka bottles were another constant; like scales, they glittered across the country.

"A poisoned land," murmured Marks.

It was another bitter legacy left behind by the departed power.

That evening they arrived at the wretched mining town of Kazarman, where nine thousand people housed in concrete apartment blocks eked out a living on seams of gold. Their hotel corridor was lit by a naked bulb attached to a car battery and internet access was a far-off dream. But a local predicted good weather the next day. The assault on Saimaluu Tash was go.

56

Johansen darted across the A1261, dodging four lanes of commuter traffic thundering into the capital from Essex, white vans beeping and HVGs blaring, headlights turned to lens flare in her vision. Where to hide on the Isle of Dogs at dawn when you're soaked, on the run from MI5 and the one guy you had trusted pulls a gun on you? The answer presented itself in the form of Leamouth Peninsula, a teardrop-shaped bar of land in the River Lea left to go wild. She could pitch a tent amid the bushes and live in perfect solitude. But even as Johansen considered it the plan unravelled. She had no tent, no means of access; there was no clean water or sanitation. It was a dream.

Her next ploy was to break into a vacant yuppie flat. Thousands of units lie empty in that part of London, bought off-plan from Shanghai or Singapore. But the cheap towers of breeze block and coloured Perspex are guarded by expensive alarm systems and dogs, and even as she scoped them a private security car rolled past. Finally she saw the answer.

She was into Tower Hamlets proper now, a borough bedevilled by poverty and corruption. But if its disgraced ex-mayor had done one thing right, it was homebuilding. Thousands of council houses were coming online, a glut of social housing to mirror the yuppie flat explosion to the south. And there before her, plastered with 'condemned' signs, was a post-war project due to make way.

Robin Hood Gardens was not so much a tower as a *hulk*: a leviathan of crumbling cement whose lower section resembled blast walls and upper third a sixties polytechnic. It was the sort of building that makes one wonder how anybody in any time or any place could have thought it looked good. Most of the flats were boarded up, although a few families had refused to leave; the corridors glinted with human excrement and used hypodermic needles. In a hallway she encountered two Bangladeshi children playing cricket – it was as if civilisation had fallen while they fiddled amidst the ruins. Johansen had travelled much of the developing world and seen nothing worse than this; it enraged her that such things could be within eyesight of Canary Wharf. If she got through this she would devote herself to her causes with fresh fury. Vehemently she swore it.

She picked an abandoned top floor flat, using a plank to smash a window and let herself in. Three bedrooms with embossed and peeling wallpaper and yellow grease stains on the kitchen ceiling; a sorry detritus of rejected possessions. Wearily Johansen took in the broken rice cooker and yellowed telephone, the child's mattress from which Tigger grinned up at her. She realised she was shivering and stripped before towelling herself with a polyester curtain. In a cupboard she found a pair of men's suit trousers and an old shirt, which she slipped into gratefully. The water was still connected and when it was dark she could sneak out to a late night minimarket. Well, then: this was home.

*

By night Johansen heard the feral cry of drug addicts and the occasional thud or crash of glass. This place was scarier than a prison and she barricaded the door against the terrors. But by day it was largely peaceful, and she risked a visit to Cubitt Town Library to get some books. She still had work to do. And now everywhere she looked she found ancient half-memories of what had gone before.

The oldest surviving source for the creation myth of the ancient Greeks is Hesiod, a contemporary of Homer. Written circa 700 BC, his *Theogony* describes a war between Zeus and his Olympian host versus the Titans, godlike figures used interchangeably with giants in Greek legend.

> *If anyone holds sorrow from fresh grief, the singer hymns the deeds of the men of the past and right away he forgets his troubles. By hymning of men and powerful Giants, they delight the mind of Zeus within Olympus.*
>
> *The Titans stretched with great recklessness to accomplish a huge deed, and for it retribution shall be laid up for the future.*
>
> *Night bore hateful death and black doom.*
>
> *Then destructive night bore retribution, a bane for mortal men.*
>
> *Zeus summoned all to lofty Olympus and said whoever fought the Titans on his side would have honour.*

The Titans were Neanderthals. And here was Hesiod's description of the conflict:

> *They settled themselves against the Titans in the dire fray, holding huge rocks in their sturdy hands.*
>
> *From the other side the Titans strengthened their ranks, and the boundless sea resounded dreadfully.*

How reminiscent of the Flood of Gilgamesh, mulled Johansen. *Like a mighty invading army did the Great Flood overwhelm the people...*

And here Hesiod described the Titans' rout:

> *The heavy pounding of their feet reached murky Hell, as did the shrill screams of the terrible pursuit and powerful missiles. They clashed with a great war cry. No longer did Zeus restrain his might, but straightaway he showed all his force. Although the Titans were stalwart, the work of power was revealed. They cast shadows over the Titans with missiles. They sent them beneath broad-wayed earth and bound them in painful bonds, having conquered them by hands.*

Johansen recalled the many other Indo-European cultures to have spawned giant myths. Celtic, Hindu, Norse and Basque, they spanned a continent. And they were always presented as primeval creatures, associated with chaos and the wild. A fight had broken out between two resident alcoholics outside; Johansen double-checked her barricade and began to weep.

57

Harkness, Marks and McCartney stood before a wooden farmstead in the dell of a deep valley, contemplating what lay ahead. At dawn the only sign of life in the smallholding was a family of chicks who had made their home in one of the reclaimed car doors that comprised its fence. Saimaluu Tash bulged out copiously before them, its gargantuan midriff blocking their sight of the upper reaches. But the sky was blue and the air clear, the morning sun already warm on the cheeks.

"We've been lucky with the weather," said Harkness. "But let's not get complacent. Things change quickly at altitude."

They followed the grassy valley floor along a river of gushing snow-melt from the upper reaches. Soon the stream turned into a grubby ribbon of glacier, fastened to the mountain at a forty-five degree angle. The valley enclosed it on both sides and they heard rushing water beneath the ice.

"Up the glacier?" said McCartney.

"A bloody death trap is that," said Marks. "Fall through and you're getting swept through an ice cave underwater. And that is not a place you want to be."

Instead they attempted to work up the left side of the valley, grabbing tufts of grass for handholds on scree that became ever steeper. They were thirty feet above the ice and the slope was near vertical.

"This is a really bad idea," growled Harkness.

McCartney was about to say something cocky when he slipped. He went hurtling down the scree, scrabbling for purchase and grinding to a halt just above the ice.

"Which way did you try last time?" Marks asked Harkness when they had descended.

"I don't know, it was thirty years ago!"

So they chose the ice, clawing hands and feet into the snowier extremities and hacking their way upwards. After an hour all three were pouring with sweat. When they turned to look back they could see *over* the mountain behind them to glimpse a vista of still higher peaks, recessing away towards the horizon. The glacier descended for hundreds of feet in a wicked death slide. Then they encountered the ice bridge.

It was five feet wide and fifteen long with a ten-foot drop into rapids beneath. The water was cobalt blue with the freshness of the snowmelt and it swept into the entrance of the ice cave, a black throat in the glacier.

McCartney walked across.

"An absolute maniac is that lad!" shouted Marks.

Harkness crossed, too. "Try being reckless for a change, Tony."

"I've got a wife and children. Plus I'm four stone heavier than you…"

"Man up and get over here!" shouted McCartney.

Marks walked across, too.

"That was probably the most stupid thing I've ever done," he said as the applause died away.

After another hour altitude sickness hit like an express train, thieving lungs and enfeebling limbs. But they struggled on, emerging at last onto a moraine where the slope was gentler. Tough grass fought through the basalt rocks strewn ahead; the temperature had dropped again and clouds came tumbling in. Then the first bullets of ice-cold rain began to fall.

*

"Do we go on?" roared McCartney.

A cigarette was plucked from his fingers and whistled away across Kyrgyzstan. They were sheltering from the gale in the lee of a boulder and steadily turning blue.

"We can't continue!" Harkness shouted into the wind. "Utter madness…"

"We can't go down either," said Marks grimly, ice speckling his moustache. "Just imagine trying to manoeuvre on the glacier in this."

"If we stay here we freeze to death," said McCartney.

"So we continue," said Harkness.

58

Hastings settled herself down in the comfortable sitting room of what her newspaper would have designated a '£2 million, four-bedroom country house outside Saffron Walden'. It was one a.m. UK time and her lapdog Lucy hopped up onto the sofa, curious that her mistress was still awake. Hastings placed a mug of hot chocolate on the coffee table and began to read.

Dr Andrew Starling, Chief of MI6
85 Albert Embankment
London
SE1 7PT
2 September

Rt. Hon. Patricia Morrell
Prime Minister
10 Downing Street
London
SW1A 2AA

Dear Patricia,

I enclose the Secret Intelligence Service's report on the activities of Dr Agneta Christodoulou. It covers our work between 12 January this year, when we became aware of Dr Christodoulou's research, and 31 August. Officers met 28 times during the reporting period. Oral, written and covertly recorded material was considered. I look forward to meeting you shortly to discuss in detail.

Yours,

Andrew

INTRODUCTION

1. *This report pertains to research carried out by Dr Agneta Christodoulou BRFAA of the University of Athens (D.O.B. 20-10-75).*
2. *Dr Christodoulou was a primatologist and began her study of bonobo populations in the Iyondji Reserve,*

northern Democratic Republic of Congo, in October 2017.

3. The bonobo is an endangered great ape closely related to the chimpanzee. Although 99.6 per cent genetically identical, it has been recognised as a separate species since 1928. The bonobo is now found only in the Democratic Republic of Congo, where an estimated 30,000–50,000 individuals remain. They are separated from Western chimpanzee populations by the River Congo, the natural barrier that caused their speciation.

4. Dr Christodoulou came to the attention of the Secret Intelligence Service following the announcement of a lecture at the National and Kapodistrian University of Athens entitled, 'Why don't bonobos kill each other?'

5. In March, Dr Christodoulou was diagnosed with lung cancer. She died from this illness in May. A report prepared by Athens-Limestone Hospital confirmed the presence of Non-Small Cell Lung Cancer in the upper lobe of Dr Christodoulou's left lung.

6. As part of our investigation into Dr Christodoulou's work, we:
    *   intercepted telephone calls and emails;
    *   obtained the working manuscript of her thesis, length 21,412 words at time of death;
    *   inserted a PhD zoology student into her department who was subsequently seconded to Dr Christodoulou's team in the Democratic Republic of Congo.

ABSTRACT

1. *Chimpanzee and bonobo societies are fundamentally different in character. Chimpanzees are highly aggressive and territorial whereas bonobos are conciliatory.*

2. *Chimpanzee males band together to defend areas rich in fruit trees for their females to feed in. The desire to secure such forests explains their inherently aggressive nature. They frequently attack the territory of neighbouring bands to secure new feeding grounds.*

3. *Chimpanzee territorialism closely resembles that of human beings. They are frequently observed to exterminate rival bands of chimpanzees completely, apparently possessing the intelligence to foresee that survivors might carry out a revenge attack.*

4. *Humans and chimpanzees are the only species known to display such behaviour.*

5. *Within individual bands of chimpanzees, dynastic wars take place to establish a single animal as the dominant male.*

6. *Brothers, allies and (especially) mothers of aspiring alpha males will facilitate a bid for power. They actively recruit others to their clique.*

7. *This behaviour is likely to have a genetic basis. In one chimpanzee band numbering 120 individuals, the alpha male accounted for 36 per cent off all conceptions. Family members who assisted his bid for power share much of his DNA and therefore benefited from a genetic 'umbrella effect': large chunks of DNA identical to their own were passed on to the new generation. High-ranking, non-familial males*

allied to the alpha male achieved an above-average conception rate.

8. *Rival coalitions have been observed to overthrow alpha males after diplomacy and pre-planning. An overthrow would typically involve several chimpanzees pinning the victim to the ground while the incumbent hits him on the head with a rock until he is dead.*

9. *All chimpanzee communities habitually use tools to gather food, typically using sticks to obtain honey or stones as hammers to open nuts. Western chimpanzees use pointed sticks to impale bush babies and extract them from tree boles for protein.*

10. *Not a single case of habitual tool use has ever been discovered amongst bonobos.*

11. *Bonobos from neighbouring tribes have been observed interacting peacefully. Such behaviour is entirely unknown in either Western or Eastern chimpanzee populations.*

12. *Genetic evidence suggests chimpanzees and bonobos diverged two million years ago. Dr Christodoulou asserted that chimpanzees must have acquired a <u>genetic propensity</u> for tool use that bonobos lack.*

13. *Dr Christodoulou asserts that this problem-solving ability was bestowed following a mutation on the FOXP2 gene.*

14. *In human beings, FOXP2 regulates development of the Broca's Area of the neocortex. (The Broca's Area is a frontal lobe of the human brain linked to speech.)*

15. *Dr Christodoulou argues that this genetic change means that chimpanzees possess a <u>fundamentally different system of thinking</u> to bonobos, which means they are capable of some degree of higher reasoning.*

16. *Dr Christodoulou termed the chimpanzee's supplementary enhanced mental operating system as 'Mode II' as opposed to the bonobo 'Mode I'.*

17. *Dr Christodoulou claimed it was 'Mode II' that enables chimpanzees to identify the elimination of all rivals as a bountiful reproductive stratagem.*

18. *Bonobos do not pursue warfare against neighbouring tribes. Neither do they assassinate political rivals within their own band in the manner of chimpanzees and humans. Dr Christodoulou asserted that this is due to the lesser capacity for planning and deduction inherent in 'Mode I'.*

19. *Dr Christodoulou speculated that were it not for the natural barrier of the River Congo, Western chimpanzees would have long ago forced bonobos into extinction and assumed their territory.*

20. *This is highly likely.*

OTHER TASKS RELATING TO THE ACTIONS OR INTENTIONS OF PERSON(S) DESCRIBED

1. *Under a voluntary agreement, Google has agreed to a Foreign Office request for removal of content related to Dr Christodoulou's work from its web-cache.*

CLASS SEVEN ACTIVITY UNDERTAKEN UNDER THE INTELLIGENCE SERVICES ACT 1994

1. *A sum of euros 350,000 (£296,100) was paid to Professor Mikhail Hatzidakis, rector of the University of Athens. Professor Hatzidakis:*

- *prevented Dr Christodoulou's lecture from taking place;*
- *obstructed publication of her thesis;*
- *denied subsequent requests from the Department of Biology to pursue related research.*

2. *A sum of £1.35m has been paid to Mr David Motion, vice chancellor of the University of Bristol, for suppression of research in a related field.*

Gloria Hastings MP finished reading and addressed a question to the dog. "What the flying fuck is all that about?"

59

Like Shackleton and his men crossing the Antarctic they battled on, three fighting figures consumed by raging curtains of rain and snow. Boulders stung to the touch with cold and McCartney's face was burned a livid scarlet. Then, as abruptly as it had begun, the wind dropped. The clouds parted and as the Central Asian sun hit them steam began to rise.

"Back down," panted Harkness. "While we still can. Another storm will finish us."

"Eat something first," grunted Marks. "Need the energy."

All they had been able to obtain was horse sausage and bread – yet it was surprisingly delicious, and life returned to enervated limbs. The moraine had flattened out, like a cushion enthroned by the mountains that rose vertiginously on three sides. No white tents could be seen, but the snowy peaks were blinding in the sunlight. Lying on the tufted grass with tiny purple flowers and wild herbs it was suddenly idyllic.

"Definitely got the sacred mountain vibe going on," McCartney murmured.

Marks plucked something from the ground and took a bit. "Wild spring onion! Want one?"

A coin was in McCartney's fingers. "Do we press on?"

"Not this again," said Harkness.

Marks froze mid-bite of onion. He wasn't looking at McCartney, but *beyond* him.

"What is it?"

"There, by your elbow…"

An ibex sporting oversized horns had been carved into the boulder McCartney was leaning on.

"We made it to the petroglyph field!" yelled Harkness.

Then all three men were jumping up and down and yelling in triumph, their voices echoing across the moraine. There could be no question of turning back now, so they pressed on up the slope. And soon every rock was enchanted with images. They spotted snakes and horses, bizarre long-necked figures, geometric patterns and the Wheel of the Dharma.

"These all look recent to my eye," said Harkness. "See how clearly defined the designs are in the basalt?"

"How about this?" said McCartney, and they both turned round.

He had found a swastika.

"The swastika was a religious symbol in Asia for thousands of years before the Nazis so rudely appropriated it," said Harkness. "I don't think this is relevant – despite the connotations."

The surface of one boulder had been chiselled away completely.

"Maybe we came too late," ruminated Harkness.

"Maybe not," said Marks. "By your feet, Randolph…"

The carving was timeworn almost to invisibility, but with its scimitar of a horn and shaggy coat the animal was unmistakeable.

"A woolly rhinoceros," breathed Harkness. "They went extinct ten millennia ago."

"Then there *are* prehistoric carvings here," said McCartney.

Now they redoubled their search. And it wasn't long before McCartney found an image that made Harkness shudder, a single word returning to him from the steaming rainforests of Central Africa. Two oversized figures were carved into the rock, surrounded by stick men armed with spears. It was clear who had the upper hand.

Marks traced the near-vanished carving with the tip of a finger. "Deeply ancient, is that."

But there was more.

Giant figures being corralled into some kind of pen; giant figures with what looked like flames licking beneath their feet; giant figures with rocks raining down on them. An instruction? Or commemoration? Harkness was reminded of Assyrian reliefs at the British Museum celebrating the enslavement of Jews at Lachish. The other source for this event was the Old Testament. *Good myths, big truths.*

"But these might not be Neanderthals at all, right?" said McCartney. "This might be completely coincidental…"

Harkness glanced at him with approval. Then they saw the hands, five pairs of them chiselled neatly across the surface of the rock – as if keeping score. Harkness thought of the famous 32,000-year-old hand print in the Chauvet-Pont-d'Arc Cave of France, how that had always spoken to him of human innocence (*I was here…*). Part of him didn't want to reveal what they'd discovered.

"Just think what this tells us," he managed, "about ourselves."

Marks looked at his watch. "We've not got much time. It's three p.m. – and I really don't want to be halfway down when we lose the light."

McCartney opened a packet of cigarettes, but the plastic wrapper was snatched by the wind and went whistling across the moraine to the eastern valley wall. He dashed after it – this was a place to be kept pristine – and found it wedged beneath a boulder that had toppled in some ancient tectonic movement. There were carvings on the underside.

"Come and look at this," he shouted.

Six hulking figures were depicted laid out horizontally, stick men standing over them in the process of lopping limbs.

"It might as well be a production line," said Marks.

The figures were framed by two zigzags that converged on the rock. A mass of upturned triangles had been etched either side, with a single oval. The effect was undeniable. It looked like –

"A map!" exclaimed Marks. "The confluence of two rivers in the mountains and a lake. This is a *place*."

"But it can't be," said Harkness.

"Why not? There's precedent. That map of valleys and walking routes found at Pavlov in the Czech Republic has been dated to 25,000 BC. And the ability to think symbolically goes even farther back in time. Think about the Blombos Cave in South Africa – they found bone plaques carved with crosshatchings dating from 70,000 BC that clearly *meant something* to their creators. Pierced tick shells were used for necklaces and red ochre for body painting. It all speaks to the modern mind existing fifty thousand years earlier. Why shouldn't the people here have thought of describing their surroundings pictographically?"

The wind whistled across the moraine, blades of grass fidgeting in the earth.

"We really do need to get down," said Harkness.

They photographed the boulder before heaving it upside down so the image would be concealed. For the first time during this insane journey Harkness felt they were in the lead.

"Eagle!" cried McCartney.

The bird's wingspan was almost eight feet. It surfed and eddied upon the air-currents, taking in these intruders on its domain. The moment was truly majestic, and Harkness leaned on McCartney's shoulder to admire it, as he'd done on their escape from Itanga. He realised there were tears in his friend's eyes.

"What's wrong?" he gasped.

"No, it's OK, it's fine." McCartney wiped his eyes with a sleeve and summoned a grin. "I'm glad I came, that's all."

You must enjoy your eyesight while you can...

"Then I've achieved everything I hoped for," said Harkness.

They watched the eagle circle three times before it beat away across the mountaintops on powerful wings. McCartney's eyelids trembled as he watched it go.

"Destination unknown," murmured Marks.

"People," said Harkness.

Three specks were discernible on the summit over which the bird had flown. A tell-tale wink of sunlight on glass, and then the figures withdrew.

"We're being watched," said Marks.

60

The last time Harkness had spread his map across a car bonnet they were halfway up the Congo. Now he did so again beneath a sacred mountain.

"Perhaps they were goatherds?" suggested Marks.

"What, with binoculars?"

"Remember what happened at the Wolf's Lair," said McCartney. "It's almost like they are *protecting* us."

"I hope we're not somebody's cut-out," said Harkness.

"What's a cut-out?" asked McCartney.

"It's an MI6 term. If you don't have the skills or contacts to perform a task but those who do won't help, you trick them into doing it unwittingly. That person is what we – sorry, they – would call a cut-out."

"Well, no one's cutting me out." Marks flattened out the map. "So, a convergence of two rivers with steep ranges on both sides and a lake."

They began at Saimaluu Tash, working outward from the epicentre. But nowhere looked quite right.

"How far away do you think it could be?" asked McCartney.

"Potentially, off the map completely," said Harkness. "In the British Museum they've got a prehistoric hand axe made from jade that was found near Canterbury. The nearest place it could have been made is the Italian Alps. People underestimate the length of prehistoric trade routes; just think how far the…"

"The what?" said Marks.

"I was going to say think how far the Ice Age Venuses travelled."

"The borders in this part of the world are crazy," said McCartney, studying the chart.

Uzbekistan, Kyrgyzstan and Tajikistan were like octopuses tied in knots.

"You can thank Stalin for that," said Harkness. "He wanted to mix up all the Kyrgyz, Tajiks, Uzbeks, Turkmen and what have you, so they lost their cultural identity and became good Soviet workers. Call it a communist take on multiculturalism."

"He were a bad bastard," said Marks.

"Mind you, we Brits are hardly blameless on this count," said Harkness. "Look at the Wakhan Corridor here…"

He indicated a dogleg of Afghanistan sandwiched between Pakistan and Tajikistan. Crushed between the twin anvils of the High Pamir Mountains and the formidable Hindu Kush, the sliver of territory was two hundred miles long by just ten wide. It followed the River Wakhan before meeting the misnamed Little Pamir Valley, high altitude lakes dotted along the corridor.

"Drawn up as part of the Great Game of course," Harkness continued. "A buffer zone, meant to keep the Russian Empire and British Raj apart. Is there a more ludicrous bit of cartography anywhere in the world?"

Neither Marks nor McCartney were listening. Instead they stared at the map, and the older man whistled through his teeth.

A confluence of two rivers in the mountains with a lake.

Then Harkness saw it too and went as white as the snow above them.

*

They set off on the two hundred mile journey south to the Tajik border. Mountains, yurts, more domesticated railway carriage hovels marooned upon the steppe, wild horses and traffic jams of sheep clogging clifftop passes. Rickety telegraph lines straggled gallantly over the massifs like polar explorers tethered together, and pre-Islamic burial mounds were pimples upon the foothills. Finally the Audi burst free of the mountains to enter a long, broad plain dusted with Kyrgyz villages. Rearing up on the far side of the steppe was the frozen wall of the High Pamirs and Tajikistan, the forest of white spires like the encampment of some medieval king. Two radar domes were far to the east, and Harkness stared at them from the passenger seat; a distant look had come into his eyes.

"What is it?" asked McCartney.

"Do you remember me telling you about staging a breakdown outside a pair of radar domes to observe a particular scientist? Well, there they are." Then more to himself: "I never thought I would see this place again…"

It had been bittersweet for Harkness to return to Kyrgyzstan at all, but revisiting this spot disarmed him especially. The last time he'd been here was April 1988, four months after the road accident that had become the defining event of his life, as much a part of him now as pubs and dogs and digs in strange places. He supposed they'd call it depression nowadays, but back then it was just plain *grief*. That day in '88, spent at the wheel of a ZiL van, he'd been thinking about the future. About what the coming decades held for him, this new not-quite widower. Seeing it again, Harkness had the eerie sensation that he was in *direct contact* with his old self, the less grey and grizzled version of the man who now stared back at him in the rear-view mirror. He wished he could beam advice back through that tunnel of time.

The nineties was coming, hopeful decade for the world. *Live it.*

Curious, too, to think that his future self might be watching him in this place once again, through memories. What might he say to a Harkness with white hair instead of grey?

"Looks like they've seen better days," said McCartney as the domes slid past.

One radar dome was grey and the other white, with panels missing from both to reveal the black hollow within. They were like a pair of gigantic golf balls in a state of dilapidation, discarded here by a race of giants.

"Every bloody inch paid for with the sweat of Russian peasantry," said Marks.

A nomad had tethered his flock in the shadow of one of the domes where a washing line was now suspended from one of the missing panels.

"We won," said Harkness, and there was no triumph in his voice.

*

After the plain came the foothills of the High Pamirs, the bedrock turning to red and grasses withering back. At the border four Kyrgyz guards waved them into no man's land – but the reception committee was less benign. At the centre of a long wide table squatted a pockmarked army major with a Pashtun beard. By his right hand, a corpulent police chief wore shades and black leather gloves; to his left sat an imam in flowing white robes. This trio were flanked by a bandolier-draped army sergeant and a muscular police officer with a milky eye. By chance the tallest actor in this tableau was the major, heights diminishing on either side. It was Leonardo's *The Last Supper* with guns and bad intentions.

"I'll handle this." Harkness glared at McCartney meaningfully. "You, stay there."

He collected their passports and sauntered over with every scintilla of height he possessed.

"Border closed," said the major.

It was the code for battle to commence.

With the flattery, dissembling and flowery evasion that characterises a successful *baksheesh*, Harkness fought them down to $1,000 for the paperwork. He returned to the car and counted out ten pristine $100 bills from their dwindling supply.

"Years of practice," he told McCartney.

The major placed them in his wallet and nodded – whereupon the police officer with the milky eye leaned forward to inform Harkness that if he did not immediately return to Kyrgyzstan they would all be arrested for bribery. The beneficent smile of the imam had remained in place throughout.

"What happened?" asked Marks when he got back in the car.

"They're not letting us in," said Harkness, shamefaced.

"Yeah, we got that," said McCartney.

"Well for god's sake don't try that little stunt you pulled in Brazzaville," snapped Harkness. "It's a much more dangerous situation – that lot will put us in the earth without hesitation."

Too angry for eye contact with the officials, Marks made a jerky three-point turn. As they departed the imam raised a hand in farewell.

"Seventy miles to the next border point," said McCartney, map crinkling on his knees.

"We might as well save ourselves the petrol," said Harkness. "We won't be let in there either. I think whoever was peering at us from the mountaintops yesterday has called in a favour. Our friends back there just saw an opportunity for a bit of graft on the side."

"But we can't give up now," said McCartney. "Think how far we've come."

"Actually, I do have one last card to play." A wry smile was on Harkness's face.

"How do you mean?" said Marks.

"As I may have previously hinted," Harkness replied, "my last spell in Central Asia did involve a few more – ahem – *swashbuckling* activities than mere trainspotting."

*

Harkness swore them both to secrecy and then laid it all out. In 1988 he'd been tasked with recruiting and running a network of saboteurs from amongst disaffected Kyrgyz nomads. His band had carried out small-scale but expensive sabotage against an ailing USSR that could no longer afford an increasingly technological arms race. Those radar domes had been taken offline for several weeks with the plastic explosive he'd supplied. They'd blown up a launch pad and hijacked a lorry load of plutonium, which was then buried twenty miles away from where they were now and covered in cement with advice from the United Kingdom Atomic Energy Authority. It was almost certainly still there. Other things had happened that Harkness preferred not to think about; but the salient point was that his nomads would know their way over the High Pamirs. They just had to find one of them.

61

A very enjoyable date, reflected Dr Maria Daescu of Transilvania University of Brașov as she strolled back through the medieval hill-town of Sighișoara. Her suitor that evening had been a banker and she was expecting brash, but the man was charm and self-deprecation personified. He had definite potential.

The town was built by Saxons in the twelfth century, and from its promontory nine defensive towers overlooked glowering forest in every direction. Descended from those Germanic settlers, Daescu, tall and blonde, looked more surf model than palaeontologist. It was just past ten p.m., the cobbled alleyways emptying. But this was a safe part of the world and she felt no fear. She was happy and tipsy on Romanian pinot noir.

Daescu passed through the gate of the old clock tower, an array of murder holes looming high above her. There was something vampiric about these portals, with their sinister caped design; so too the tower's spires, five fangs whose forms were mirrored by distant pines. Vlad the Impaler was born in Sighişoara, but Daescu had never found Transylvanian myth unsettling as many did, nor its forests with their packs of wolves and itinerant bears. Until a few days ago, that is. Now she thought anew of what must have transpired within those silent ranks of trees in the time before written records.

The earliest *Homo sapiens* to be discovered in Europe were found in Romania: the 40,000-year-old Oase specimens, who were part of the first wave of hunter-gatherers radiating out from the Middle East. One of the individuals had ten per cent Neanderthal DNA, representing a single union with the cousin species six generations previously. This finding had always reminded Daescu of the unpleasant fact that the male-inherited Y chromosome in Iceland comes from Scandinavia, while the female line traces back almost exclusively to Scotland and Ireland. She fancied that neither circumstance was a case of arranged marriage. Looking at the needles of pine beyond the city walls she thought again of the lives that the Oase people must have led there, and a little of the evening's good cheer left her. The email from Professor Vincent Fournier and his murder. They changed it all. She increased her pace now, feet pattering down a deserted twelfth-century flight of steps that curled towards her tiny hunchbacked house. Light pooled on cobbles, reflected yellow and blue in their surfaces.

Click, pffft… Click, pffft.

Two plumes of moisture erupted from her chest. Both her lungs collapsed and she sank to her knees. It felt as if she'd been kicked in the back by a rearing horse. This was followed by an awful feeling of strangulation from within, and Daescu realised she'd been shot.

Click. Click. Click.

An old man was standing over her, fiddling with a jammed pistol and silencer. Daescu keeled onto her back. Gurgling. Fighting for breath. The old man's face appeared above her, his bristling white beard. He seemed to be assessing her chances of survival.

"Blast it," he said, opening the type of tiny silver penknife only gentlemen of a certain age and upbringing carry.

Daescu felt the blade slip between two vertebrae in her neck with an audible *tick* and the state of emergency in her chest was overwhelmed by a still more pressing disaster. Blood gushed up the man's bony knuckles and then she was gone.

*

"I am pleased to report some *good news*," said Lord Wakeford, clapping his hands together. "Text message from Eric in the Balkans. Simply reads, 'A sweet goodnight.'"

Orientalist and Dennis Mirza had been summoned to the Russian Embassy for a dressing down.

"That's something, I suppose," said their handler, Sergey Osintsev.

He was an FSB inquisitor of the old school: red-rimmed eyes and a florid complexion, aviator-style wire-framed glasses from the first time around. He placed a battered attaché case on the table.

"You will give this to *her*, when she arrives tomorrow. Inside she will find something experimental for this bothersome Member of Parliament. From Russia with love, by diplomatic post. It's a type of gun – dispenses a short-range microwave at 300 GHz. Fired into the back at point-blank range, there is a blooming effect. And so the microwaves disperse. Liver, kidneys, stomach, pancreas, lungs, spleen. The human chromosome is badly damaged – we typically see one or two carcinomas within a couple of months, metastasising and cascading on to other organs. It really is a very nasty device. You'll remember the quick illness of Dr Agneta Christodoulou?"

"Yes, I do," said Wakeford.

"Mark my words, in six months' time Hastings' friends will be doing fun-runs for Cancer Research. Not our normal style, I grant you – in Russia we like to make more of an example of disobedient politicians."

Wakeford and Mirza chuckled politely.

"But we cannot risk an autopsy finding unlawful killing – and by the time of death any external burns will be healed. Frankly I don't care how you finish off Anita Johansen. Hang her from Nelson's Column and blast her with shotguns if you wish. Just find her."

"It might be prudent for us to know the identity of the other interested party," said Wakeford. "Are you chaps any closer?"

"The chatter in Moscow is the Saudis. Riyadh will insist spreading a message around the world that is not exactly *helpful* to wider society. As *she* knows only too well."

She had learned to hunt and kill men in the academy of death that was the Second Chechen War.

"Incidentally," said Osintsev, "Mr Harkness and friends attempted to enter Tajikistan yesterday. They were rebuffed, but the expectation is that they will now attempt to cross the High Pamirs. President Ibragimov is a friend, of course. While he would not have his soldiers detain them in international territory, he has permitted that we insert kill teams into their side of the range."

"Oh, fab," said Wakeford. "I wish them well..."

62

Thirteen names. Thirteen old comrades who were aged between nineteen and sixty-four when Harkness had last seen them. The majority would still be alive, and they drove from village to village asking after them. This proved easier than he had feared: the Kyrgyz steppe is one of the most sparsely populated geographies on earth, its people acquainted over huge distances. Trade and intermarriage had knitted far-flung communities together in this region since the age of the Silk Road – and nowadays they have mobiles. So it was that in the dust-blown market village of Sary-Tash on the northern edge of the plain they got lucky. Watermelons and cheap plastic toys were laid out on blankets; old women with gold teeth clucked and gobbled; an old man wearing an embroidered waistcoat and one of those remarkable *kalpak* hats shielded his face against the dust coming off the plain. The first few names drew a blank, but when Harkness mentioned Aibek Abdulov the old man's eyes came alive.

"I know this person! He came here three weeks ago with livestock. A good man, and his father was a good man, too."

Aibek. It had to be Aibek.

Harkness had always assumed he'd never see Abdulov again, although he'd thought of him often over the past three decades. His youngest cold warrior was practically a boy back then, his family forced to work in a collective farm before resuming their ancient lifestyle. This gentle teenager had shown a steely desire to grieve the Soviet overlord. Harkness recalled an uneven fringe and gap-toothed smile. He was alive, and that gladdened him.

The elder directed them twenty miles west to the village of Kabyk, where he was informed Abdulov and family (*a family!*) had been seen two days previously. They were thought to be pasturing their flock a few miles away, in a valley at the foot of the Alay Mountains with no phone reception. So they drove up the wide, grand vale, grass giving way to rock and scree above them on either side; the dark sheep dotted up distant slopes were like black onion seeds scattered across the landscape. Then Harkness saw two yurts and a horse. He parked and got out.

A man wearing a woollen jumper, beanie hat and red Wellington boots was foddering his animals. He peered at them, one hand on his back. Then the confusion on his brow resolved itself and Aibek Abdulov raised a hand in stunned greeting. He cried out, staggering closer before breaking into a run. Harkness was sprinting, too, and they threw their arms around each other.

"My friend, my friend," cried Abdulov, and Harkness thought that perhaps the moisture in the corners of his old comrade's eyes was from the cold dry air whipping up the valley. Eurasian winds and sunlight had carved deep creases across his forehead and ravines by his eyes. But it was still a boyish face, full of vivacity and warmth. Abdulov drew his head back again to study Harkness as if satisfying himself this was no illusion, then he burst into laughter.

"You are old! You are an old man now, Randolph Harkness! Come, let me introduce you to my family. And we can take tea!"

*

It was warm inside the yurt. The walls were spun from felt, the ground carpeted with hand-woven rugs, all red for good luck. Cushions were thrown about and a small brassiere burned brightly with horse's dung. This was *hygge*, Kyrgyz style. A rickety chimney poked through the apex of the structure, which was a hoop of wood braced by sticks that Harkness recognised from the Kyrgyz flag. He also recalled the huts of the Ba Aka.

Abdulov's wife was younger than him, graceful but somehow garrulous with it, and they had an elfin daughter of six whose steppe-whipped cheeks were like ripe pomegranates. She possessed her father's smile – boyish, bold and then shy – and looking at her Harkness felt his heart bowing under a familiar happy-sadness. Then Abdulov's wife slid an ornate hand-carved cradle from beneath a dresser and the travellers gasped. The baby within was a wriggling gremlin just a fortnight old, born right here in the wilderness.

"And you?" Abdulov could not hide a glance down to Harkness's hand. "Wife and children, no?"

Harkness shook his head. "Afraid not, my friend. It wasn't to be."

Abdulov's 'tea' consisted of a lamb stew, fried potatoes with cabbage and onion, skewers of grilled yak and a feisty natural yoghurt. He refilled their glasses with cleansing black tea and produced a watermelon that he seemed to unzip with his knife. In seconds the fruit was splayed out symmetrically across a board, and Harkness was reminded of Batsinga conjuring a dinner service from bamboo. McCartney had one hand on his collarbone.

Life was still hard here: foreign mining companies were all over Kyrgyzstan now, with a ravening need for water to cool machine parts. This was draining the aquifers deep beneath the steppe and leading to desertification. The pastures shrank each year; an ancient lifestyle was becoming untenable. Then Abdulov's wife knocked the brazier and the whole chimney came tumbling down in segments.

"Ook-a-chook!" she trilled.

Only when she'd rebuilt it did Harkness mention his reason for coming.

"I was hoping you could guide us across the High Pamir," he said. "But I can't ask for that now. We are being hunted – and look what you have here."

Abdulov and his wife spoke animatedly in Kyrgyz, and then he smiled.

"She says that you are an old friend, and I must assist you. She reminds me that it was with money from Britain that I was able to buy my first flock and become a man of substance here. And she says that while your friend Ross is a very big man, he also looks still like a boy, so I must look after him."

Harkness and Marks hooted with laughter.

"Yes, I know a way across," said Abdulov. "It is difficult, especially for people who are not from the mountains. But you will be able to do it, Randolph."

"Thank you." Harkness raised a tea glass. "To friendship."

Another round of clinks rang out inside the yurt.

63

That afternoon Gloria Hastings posted one of the most highly classified reports possessed by MI6 on Twitter.

The MP had just finished her surgery at the Old Armoury in Saffron Walden; constituency work was a pleasure, for there was nothing she enjoyed more than giving some footling local planning officer both barrels in the name of righteousness. But thoughts of personal safety kept distracting her – publication by social media was her solution. After taking this step, neither MI6 nor the FSB would dare assassinate her because scrutiny would fall immediately upon the report. That was her reasoning, anyway.

Hastings tweeted: "Why would #MI6 produce a top secret report for the Prime Minister into the behaviour of chimpanzees and bonobos?" #bananas

She attached screenshots of the document, her missive retweeted straight away by Julian Assange and WikiLeaks. Within five minutes Gloria Hastings was trending worldwide *yet again*, and the constituency phones began ringing. Twitter diagnostics would later inform her the tweet garnered sixteen million impressions in a hundred countries.

Hastings left the growing shitstorm for her long-suffering staff to handle. She firmly intended to break her 'don't drink at home alone' rule and Waitrose had a good Chablis on offer.

*

Lurking outside the Old Armoury as Dr Agneta Christodoulou became famous on social media was the woman responsible for her decease. The experimental weapon (it resembled a small hairdryer) was already primed as Hastings emerged. *She* got out of her Ford Focus – dressed in a hijab, her weapon concealed within its folds – and Hastings was oblivious to the demure figure closing in as she set off past seventeenth-century cottages and fancy boutiques. But it was not the place to strike: there were both too many pedestrians and too few. She needed to be alone or in a crowd.

The assassin tracked Hastings to the main road, past Specsavers, the Co-Op and Laura Ashley. It was busier here, and she closed the gap again. Every few paces Hastings stopped to greet a constituent; the assassin bided her time. Outside Waitrose a mix of affluent forty-somethings, students, anarchists and women wearing headscarves was milling about for no obvious reason. *She* blended with them as Hastings stepped into the shop. Through the plate glass window the politician could be observed paying for a bottle of wine and a piece of salmon. Laughing with the cashier, tossing shiny hair about her shoulders.

The weapon vibrated in her grip.

*

Waitrose was always calming with its faint aroma of bread and expensive foods, and as she paid for the goods Hastings enjoyed a moment of contentment. When she emerged the street exploded with rage.

"Islamaphobe!"

"Facist!"

"Tory scum!"

From nowhere, banners had appeared – a Marxist newspaper, an anti-war group with questionable alliances – and Hastings was assailed from all sides. A pretty seventeen-year-old girl in Harry Potter spectacles screamed that she was a *fucking bitch* as mobile phones captured the scene for posterity. Someone spat at her.

"Brutes!" cried a local councillor who happened to be passing. "Brutes!" he cried again, thrusting them back.

"Oh, fuck off, grandad."

Amidst the mayhem Hastings did not notice the hijab-wearing woman melt away from the cameras and remove herself from the scene.

Later that evening, shaken but resolute, the MP surveyed the pandemonium caused by her tweet. Security pundits were unanimous that she had fallen victim to another hoax; her reputation had been downgraded to junk status. But she felt safer. And this was now about survival.

64

They issued from the valley on horseback to traverse the plain for a final time. A dawn mist was pooled on the steppe; Abdulov was a ghost rider at their head, slipping into invisibility so only the clop of hooves on stone led them on. Out there, somewhere, were Harkness's radar domes. They began the ascent into the High Pamirs through a thin gulley between two brutal slabs of mountain. This was a land of snow, not grass, and as they rose the temperature plummeted to minus ten.

After an hour they popped up onto a snowfield, five thousand metres above sea level. Mount Lenin was visible to the west, sails of white clinging to its side before tapering into the heavens in a fine powder. An armada of fluffy white clouds sailed along merrily at eye level; between north and south Harkness could see for eighty miles. The border was unmarked: there were no checkpoints here, no sentries subjected to this world of wind and ice. Nature was the wall. Tajikistan fell away precipitously beneath their feet, and Kyrgyzstan seemed a land of pastures compared to the altitudinous death-scape that lay ahead. This was a Martian world lacking shrub or tree, only salt to mottle the arid red land. They followed a sweeping stony valley that curled downwards from the ridge.

The Spetsnaz awaited; each pass had been garrisoned. They hid in crevices and behind boulders. Their snipers scrutinised the valley ahead. There was no way past.

When they were halfway down the ridge Abdulov dismounted from his horse. Light flickered from a crevasse in the rock, and he led them in. Huddled over a fire was an elderly Kyrgyz nomad whose many jumpers and jackets gave him the look of some kind of vagrant bear. Snuffling in the gloom behind him were four yaks.

"This my uncle," said Abdulov. "From here, he will take you. There are soldiers in these valleys. You ride underneath."

"We ride *underneath?*" said McCartney.

Abdulov pointed to the nearest yak, its coat shaggy in the dirt.

"Underneath."

Harkness had to smile. It was by this ruse that Odysseus and his men escaped the Cyclopes.

*

Abdulov and aged uncle bound them beneath the yaks, running ropes under the fur and re-arranging the animals' coats to obscure any sight of underslung passengers. It reeked beneath the belly of the beast, but at least it was warm, and Harkness relaxed against the cords that bound him. A hand protruded through the fur. Harkness clasped it for a moment and then his friend was gone. The last he ever heard of Aibek Abdulov was the *trudge–trudge–trudge* of boots over ice and rock.

The little caravan departed down the valley. The only sound was the jingling of the yaks' bells, the heavy clomp of their hooves, the whining heave of huge lungs and the meandering song of their driver. Harkness glimpsed a red rock-scape through the ruddy-black hair; the animal ejected a stream of steaming excreta from which he cowered in his bonds.

He sensed the Russian checkpoint by the cessation of the old man's singing and a change in the yak's gait as it spotted a curiosity up ahead. Then he heard Russian voices, bored and at ease.

"*Zdravstvuyte!*" one called out.

"*Zdravstvuyte,*" replied the driver dutifully.

They passed so close Harkness could smell tobacco and hear soldiers stamping their feet. Then he spotted a toecap and cringed into the animal's abdomen, lice pinging against his cheeks. This was considerably madder than anything he'd pulled in the eighties. But the animals kept trudging, the bells kept clanking and the Russian voices receded into the background. They were going to make it.

"*Vernis'!*"

Harkness went rigid.

Come back.

He sensed the yaks being tethered and listened to the yak-herd's weary tread back towards the soldiery.

"*Vy videli kakikh-nibud' angliyskikh turistov?*"

Have you seen any English hikers?

"The nearest thing to an Englishman I have seen… are my yaks."

A pithy reply, and beneath his animal Harkness was grinning. When the guffaws had died out the yak-driver begged a cigarette, and then they were on their way. Relief coursed through Harkness, warm and magnificent, and even the stench of the yak seemed more bearable. He had no idea of the landscape now: only that it was flatter, the air still thin. But his body ached from the unnatural position and the ropes were like piano wire throttling his limbs.

After two hours the old man whistled. The yaks clattered to a halt and after an eternity he untied them. The travellers took their first steps in Tajikistan – blinking in the sunlight, stretching out tingling legs and grinning at one another. The rocky red sky-desert ran for miles in each direction, hemmed in on all sides by mountains of blinding white. There was something pristine about it, utterly still: a perfect, sterile world formed for the appreciation of gods. A young shepherd awaited them, wearing goggles and a facemask against the bitter air, and he thumped his chest in welcome like some alien bandit on a desolate world. Besides the yaks and sheep the only living things were the pebble-shaped leaves struggling through the stone, waxen against the aridity and high altitude. They had penetrated Tajikistan. *They were in.*

As they began to walk, Tony Marks turned back. He stared at the mountaintops, as if spotting someone there. But he said nothing, and the three travellers continued on their journey.

PART THREE

I am constantly amazed by man's inhumanity to man.

Primo Levi, *If This is a Man*

65

Lights were on inside the seven forts as the sentries admired the growing pinkness of dawn away to the east. The fortifications resembled Tripods from *The War of the Worlds*: boxes of rusted steel, each perched above the sea on a trio of concrete legs, all linked up by walkways. The fourth most deadly sniper in the history of the British Army bobbed up beneath the southernmost tower. As Andrew Jackson wriggled from his oxygen tank he was joined by Captain Woody Donaldson; seconds later Sergeants Gary Rees and Ainsley Jones appeared to the far side of the complex.

"Not the nicest spot…" Donaldson's RP accent and lisp were somehow incongruous amidst the lapping murk. "You ready?"

Jackson nodded. They wore dry suits but his lips had turned purplish in the icy waves. Captain Donaldson raised five fingers aloft and counted down to one.

"Watch this!" shouted Jackson.

All four men fired grappling hooks, the rubber-coated claws finding purchase on beams and girders with a *clunk*. Then came the *hiss* of firing gas cylinders as the grappling hooks reeled in the cord at thirty feet per second. The SBS squad were whipped up into the air like kingfishers bursting from water and seconds later they were scrambling onto gantries. Donaldson was point man and kicked his way into the first fort, releasing two short bursts with his cocoon-like FN P90 submachine gun. Two men fell without protest. Jackson circled the outer walkway, firing liberally at the inner forts. From the north side of the fortifications came more machine-pistol fire as Rees and Jones gave battle, too.

Then through the gunshots, through the crash of waves on concrete and the squall of startled gulls, the dreaded cry: "Man down, man down!"

Donaldson grimaced as he raced across a walkway and barged into the second fortress. Two more bursts, two more victims. Behind him Jackson was spraying gunfire in all directions, and Donaldson felt safer knowing it was him. Huddled on the floor was a man in handcuffs.

"You, on your feet, now!" Donaldson used bolt-cutters to free him. "We're going to jump into the sea in" – he checked his watch – "one minute and thirty seconds exactly."

The firefight was intensifying to the north.

"Miniature submarines are surfacing to take us off. They're essentially underwater motorbikes, so jump on one and ride pillion. You'll see an oxygen mask protruding from the rider's headrest. And hold on bloody tight. Got all that?"

"Got it."

"Sergeant Rees down, Sergeant Rees down," screamed Jackson.

"Fuck's sake!" shouted Donaldson.

He and the prisoner burst from the fort, a crackle of muzzle-flashes illuminating the strongholds opposite. Then they jumped: down, down, down, hitting the water with a *crack* that rent the dawn air.

*

"Well, that was an effing disaster now, wasn't it?" said Sergeant Jones, frustration bringing out the Welsh accent. "I'm dead, he's dead, you're nearly dead… I just hope this hostage is worth it."

Rees flexed muscular forearms. "Not fucking good enough, boys."

Showered but with hair still drying and now nursing mugs of tea, the squad had reassembled inside a cabin in the Royal Navy's anchorage at Nore. This was the meeting point between the Thames Estuary and the North Sea, the World War Two era Redsand Forts five miles offshore; a total of 102 blanks had been fired during the exercise.

"Well, you'll have plenty more opportunity to improve your bullet-dodging skills." Major Harold Larmour, their commanding officer, had availed himself of the naval right to grow a beard. "I'm told to drill you on nothing but hostage rescue for the next three weeks. Make of that what you will…"

66

Crossing the High Pamir by foot took three days. They trudged across an endless landscape of barren pink rock from which the white-capped mountains rose like the fangs of a wolf; behind the beards their faces were chafed pink, too, and their clothes turned rancid. By night they stayed in yurts, many of Abdulov's kin having been dumped in the wrong 'Stan by the whims of Stalinist cartography. The Tajik goatherds they saw had an Iranian look, and Harkness heard traces of Persian Dari as they chivvied along their animals. He marvelled again at the language tree, radiating out incessantly from its source. Something of these lone wanderers reminded Harkness of himself, once the shell of friends and colleagues had been stripped away to reveal his essential oneness in life's journey. He recalled the giant eland in the Congolese savannah, twin horns silhouetted against a moonlit sky. Marks seemed moody, too, dwelling on his own thoughts; only McCartney's joshing interrupted the solipsism of the journey.

On the fourth morning they descended from the plateau, rewarded with a first sight of Afghanistan. The Hindu Kush was revealed as a triangle of white heading off the valley like a handkerchief in the breast pocket of some indomitable god. They followed a stream, its mossy banks turning to mud as they lost altitude, the rising heat bringing rivulets of water down from the upper glaciers to trickle through the blades of grass. The final approach to the Wakhan Valley was pure slog, squelch after wearisome squelch.

Then something totally unexpected happened.

Harkness heard the approach before he saw it: the slithering of rubber in glutinous sludge. A European woman in her forties was approaching by bicycle, three inches of mud forming a protective outer tyre on each wheel. Her woollen hat gave her the appearance of a mountain pixie, an impression accentuated by her tiny size, red nose and bright brown eyes.

Tony Marks barked with laughter. "She'll be coming round the mountain when she comes…"

"*Bonjour, mes amis*," she said.

Hit by the absurdity of the moment and splendour and brilliance of the mountains, Harkness heard himself reply, "How the devil are we?"

She laughed. "English, then? I might have guessed it."

"Guilty as charged," said Harkness.

"But surely you are all needing the tweed jackets, no? To complete the *ensemble*…"

"Whisper it quietly, but the damned things aren't actually much good," said Harkness. "Too cold for the mountains and too hot in the sun. Tweed has the most infuriating thermal qualities."

She laughed. "Well, enjoy the *campagne*. We do not often see travellers here."

Before he could reply her pedals whirred and the bicycle went slithering away towards Afghanistan.

"By the way, it's Randolph!" he shouted.

Without turning back she raised a hand. "Natalie. *Enchantée!*"

"Randolph!" exclaimed McCartney as she receded into the distance. "Was that you *flirting*?"

"Never thought I'd see the day," said Marks.

"Don't be idiotic," replied Harkness. "Just being friendly, that's all. Besides – I couldn't flirt if my life depended on it."

"No kidding," said McCartney. "That was a rookie error. Always leave them wanting more…"

*

Soon they were in the Wakhan Valley itself. The river lay two full kilo-metres below both the Pamir plateau and the Hindu Kush opposite, bestowing an entirely different microclimate and ecosystem. Harkness found it heavenly to be somewhere verdant again, where water ran and there were trees and leaves, and wildflowers about which insects bumbled. Tajik women in colourful dresses were harvesting chickpeas and potatoes while others scythed grass, tying it into bundles with string. The old men in their impeccable waistcoats and flat caps might have been transported from 1917 Leningrad; their mud brick huts were of biblical Bethlehem. Each one of these abodes was topped with a Marco Polo sheep horn – a pre-Islamic symbol of purity – and the clear mountain streams that irrigated the fields were cleverly diverted for domestic use, too. After the days of cold and aridity Harkness had the sensation of stepping into a paradise.

McCartney lobbed a rock over the gushing fluorescent waters of the River Wakhan.

"*Literally* a stone's throw from Afghanistan," he grinned.

He did not know that they were within walkie-talkie distance of Taliban commanders in the hinterland. But the Wakhan Valley had been spared Islamist militancy by the vagaries of a colonialist's pen; it remained a sanctuary of Sufi mysticism throughout even the bloodiest days of the last war. That night they bartered for shelter in a farmer's hovel, succumbing to exhaustion under the gaze of seven children.

Four thousand miles to the west new orders were being issued. The travellers had been picked up by a spy-plane crossing the Pamir – but Moscow was now curious about what they were on to. And the other group of watchers had tracked them all the way from Saimaluu Tash. There would be many eyes on them the next morning.

67

East London was Hastings' least favourite part of the country, to her mind a symbol of the dagger Britain had thrust into its own heart. And now this ghastly affair had necessitated a second visit. But when she saw Robin Hood Gardens it was worse than she could possibly have imagined. Hastings thought of Saffron Walden and prayed all England would not go this way.

Amidst the usual abuse following her publication of the Christodoulou report, there had been one intriguing response. A Dr Anita Johansen (whom Hastings noted with distaste was a member of Momentum) tweeted: "Please follow me back so I can direct message you. V important."

Hastings did as asked and a few hours later Johansen messaged her.

"I know why PM interested in chimps/extermination. Meet?"

Half-suspecting another left-wing ambush, she agreed.

"Like a fortress or something, isn't it?" said Peter De Vries as they pulled up. "From the *Alien* movies?"

Her newly acquired close protection officer parked his bullet-proof Lexus and opened the passenger door. She had been disappointed by his size, five foot five tall and slim. But something about his greying crew cut, quick movements and dark shrew eyes told her this was a hard man. He'd been procured from the UK's most exclusive firm of bodyguards and usually protected the Duke of Westminster.

An elderly Bangladeshi man wearing a skull cap and sensible Clark's shoes – one of the demolition refuseniks – was weeding his vegetable patch. He waved as they passed and Hastings thawed. She could appreciate someone making the best of their lot. But once inside the housing block her horror grew afresh. She took in the torn bin bags, the dead cat, the junkie vomit and abandoned pogo stick, most haunting of all. She bashed on Johansen's door and a barricade was scraped back; then they confronted each other.

Hastings offered her a hand, but Johansen hesitated. To her this woman was the Great Satan, up there with Trump and Maggie Thatcher.

"You're not one of *those* people, are you?" said Hastings.

"Sorry, that was rude." With a metaphorical holding of the nose Johansen did what needed to be done. "I've had a rough few weeks. Welcome to my humble abode."

She'd made the flat as habitable as late night shopping runs enabled. Once Johansen had made tea on a camping stove and they were perched on opposite ends of a bed, the academic said, "You're being followed, I take it?"

Hastings stiffened. "How do you know?"

"Because I am, too. And I have a feeling we've been investigating two sides of the same coin."

"What is that that you do, exactly?" said Hastings.

"I'm a philologist."

"Which is?"

"I study the origin and meaning of ancient texts." Johansen passed her a document. "This morning, for example, I've been looking at *The Bibliotheca*. It was written by the Greek poet Apollodorus in 150 BC."

> *Earth, vexed, brought forth the giants, matchless in the bulk of their bodies and invincible in their might; terrible of aspect did they appear, with long locks dropping from their head and chin. An oracle had said that no giants could be killed by the gods, but that with the help of mortals they could be made an end of. In the battle, Porphyrion was shot dead with an arrow, Ephialtes was shot with an arrow in his left eye, Eurytis was killed with a staff, and Clytius by torches. The other giants Zeus smote…*

"It's my belief that ancient texts like this let us glimpse at the *proto-myth* on which they were based," said Johansen. "Mythology often draws on a seed of truth. I was making progress. But I came under surveillance. And since then…" She sighed and looked around the flat. "My life's fallen apart. And my husband is missing, probably dead."

"I'm sorry." Hastings handed back the page. "They're ruthless bastards. But what could this possibly have to do with bonobos?"

Johansen looked out of the window and wiped her eyes. "Two themes occur again and again in the texts of the ancient Mediterranean," she said. "In Graeco-Roman mythology, we see repeated reference to a war involving a race of Titans or Giants. And in the Middle Eastern corpus there's this idea of a great flood almost destroying mankind. I think they are the *same thing*."

Like a mighty invading army did the Great Flood overwhelm the people.

As Johansen explained her research, Hastings flinched. This resonated with her: its shades of the migration crisis. This battle for survival, as she saw it, of European culture.

"And the link to Christodoulou and her primates is?"

"Don't you see?" said Johansen. "She was writing about organised genocide, too. How the chimpanzees are… *bright enough* to wipe one another out. Though I realise that's an oxymoron."

"Let's say you're correct," said Hastings. "Why is this a matter of national security?"

"I don't know," she admitted. "But it is. We both came under surveillance at the same time and the only link is genocide. There *must* be a logical answer."

Hastings lapsed into silence, and for a few moments they watched De Vries checking lines of sight down into the estate.

"It's just possible you may be right," she said at last.

"So let's work together. I won't pretend you're my favourite person in the world – but we can help each other. You have access to Parliament and the Foreign Office." She sighed. "And I need all the allies I can get."

As they shook hands again Hastings snorted with laughter. "Oh crumbs…"

"What is it?"

"An unholy alliance is this!"

68

"Just take it all in, gents," said Tony Marks with a sweep of the hand.

They were scaling the Tajik side of the Wakhan Valley, a forty-five degree shelf of rock that was partially buried under boulders and scree. On the Afghan side boiling black rock erupted almost vertically upwards; it was craggy and evil looking, a Mordor. But where streams from the high places had cut tributary valleys through the massif silt fanned out across the River Wakhan in raised mounds. This rich alluvial soil had been cultivated into fields, so it was as if a series of giant lily pads had been placed along the river. Away to their right the Wakhan was joined by the equally cavernous Little Pamir Valley to create a vastness of negative space. To their left and glinting in the morning sunshine like a silvered tongue was the Kul-e Chaqmaqtin. Harkness looked from a photograph of the petroglyph to the lake and then the confluence of the valleys. The resemblance was undeniable.

They spent the morning scouring the exposed rock face for petroglyphs. Marks climbed high out of sight seeking caves and Harkness quizzed curious village children without success; in their schoolroom Russian the youngsters voiced bafflement at the idea of pictures on rock.

"We're being watched again," said Marks.

The Frenchwoman from the previous day was picking her way down the mountainside to meet them.

"What are you doing here?" she asked brightly.

"Might ask you the same question," said Marks.

"I live in the valley!" replied Natalie, as though this were perfectly obvious. "And you?"

"We're looking for rock carvings," said Harkness. "We're archaeologists."

Hello, he thought: *I don't know quite whether to look you in the eye or not.* It had been many years since Harkness had experienced that.

"But what makes you think there may be rock carvings here?" she asked.

"Call it a hunch," said Marks.

She shrugged. "Well, I have lived here for thirty years, and I have never seen these things."

Thirty years...

A memory tugged at Harkness.

"What brought you here in the first place?" he asked.

"I will tell you all about it this evening." She smiled sweetly. "When you come to eat something at my house."

She pointed out a mud brick hut beside the village's tiny white-washed mosque. Hibiscus flowers had been planted around a vegetable garden and a hulking ginger cat cleaned its paws on her doorstep.

"It is rare that I have the chance to speak to Europeans," she explained. "I'd like to know what is happening out there in the world. And I promise I am a good cook."

"We'd love to," said Marks, before Harkness could interject.

"Well then!" She smiled again and set off. "See you later."

"What's the matter?" said Marks, noticing the troubled look on Harkness's face. "French cooking served up by a beautiful woman? Yes bloody please."

"We don't know the first thing about her, that's what," said Harkness. "Is she who she says she is? Attractive and apparently unattached woman wandering alone in the High Pamir? Come on. The honey-trap's the oldest trick in the FSB playbook. MI6 and the CIA don't go there, but pretty much every other intelligence agency does."

"Didn't think of that," admitted Marks.

And yet, at the end of a fruitless day's scrambling about the valley, it was noted that Harkness did not take much persuasion to accept.

*

It was dark when they knocked, the Milky Way traversing the valley like the smear of some celestial snail as the mountains bookended outer space. The cracks around Natalie's door flickered bright orange, and when she opened it they stepped into the warmth of a log fire. Carpets and cushions were festooned around a single low table; her kitchen was an ancient dresser with mismatched crockery and a gas hob on which lamb stew bubbled. Harkness cast a critical eye over the signs of inhabitation: Kodak family photographs of relations, a chipped bowl for the cat. It looked organic, authentically aged, and he struggled to see how the dust could have been laid down at short notice. The only sign of recent disturbance was the bookcase, where several volumes appeared to have been removed. Books on history and Islam leaned against each other in a tent shape where the dust-line came to an end.

They satisfied her yearning for knowledge of world affairs, describing the new US president to her horror; she was astonished and intrigued to learn of Britain's exit from the European Union. But when they described the Baltic crisis, she sighed.

"This is exactly why I came here," she whispered.

"How about a tot of this then?" Marks produced a bottle of Scotch. "All the way from the other side of the planet."

Natalie smiled. "I don't drink actually, I'm a Sufi. But please, I don't mind – *santé*."

Marks was turning the lid when Harkness said, "Maybe not, eh, Tony? It's a tad disrespectful."

It came out sterner than Harkness had intended, too much the white knight, but she smiled at him and again he felt that flutter of some ancient instinct. This was followed instantly by memories of his fiancée. A guilt that had been the loyalty of his life.

Natalie told them how she'd been a charity worker in Afghanistan during the eighties before discovering religion. She recounted her discovery of the Wakhan, falling in love with both the valley and its inhabitants. And she described the flowers that grew in spring; the freeze each winter when the valley became as deadly and beautiful as the moon; the flows of Marco Polo sheep that came skipping and bounding down the rocks in summer and the autumn that she had seen a snow leopard. As she spoke Harkness saw that she was indeed beautiful: talking of this place brought out the brightness in her eyes. But even as he detected attraction in himself he knew it could not be. This was a schoolboy's daftness, and he mocked himself for it bitterly – and reminded himself there was every indication this woman was an intelligence officer.

There was also that other thing: a sense of something evil in this valley they had come to uncover. And the secondary feeling of connected things acting upon one another out there, of a malignance on the stride in the world beyond these mountains. But despite everything, Harkness continued telling his best anecdotes – and he couldn't help but notice that she laughed at every one.

69

The next morning they split up to continue the search. McCartney traversed the lower slopes while Marks circumnavigated the Kul; meanwhile Harkness climbed to the Yamchun Fort, an eagle's nest of craggy black masonry that had controlled this leg of the Silk Road in Hellenic times. He was skirting the ruined citadel when he saw Natalie further down the slope, foraging into a satchel. So naturally Harkness did what any conflicted Englishman would in that position and pretended not to notice her.

When he glanced up again she was walking towards him, and as she waved he felt an awkward kick in his ribcage. Natalie was panting by the time she reached the fort, and there was a freshness to her breaths that stirred something in him.

"Mushrooms, and wild herbs." She tilted the bag for him to inspect. "With fish from the river, it's *very* good. And how is your own hunt?"

"I ought to have my head examined for bringing us here," he admitted. "I don't even know what we're looking for. What was I thinking? Look at the size of this place."

"To discover something Upper Palaeolithic, it is not a chance afforded to everybody," she said.

Harkness was sure he hadn't used that terminology over dinner. He recalled the bookshelf in her home: dust delineating the removed volumes like chalk lines at a murder scene. Harkness thought again about 1988, the missing archaeologist Olivié something – namesake of his goddaughter. For the life of him he couldn't remember her face, only the glaring fact of the tragedy so close to his own ascent of Saimaluu Tash.

"Your charity," he asked. "Was it an... *archaeological* organisation?"

"But why do you ask?"

"Your use of 'Upper Palaeolithic'. It was very precise."

A Gallic shrug. "I come from the Ardèche; we have many prehistoric sites there. We are almost all of us enthusiasts."

"I know the Ardèche well – most beautiful bit of France."

Harkness realised he was standing too close and stepped back. Again the old guilt, rising like fog from the ocean. And also a suspicion.

We find coincidence a rather unpalatable dish, I'm afraid.

Natalie cast a proprietorial look down the valley. "Describe to me your own home."

Another red flag. Then again, any spook worth sixpence could find his home address.

"I live in Bristol. I have a flat – it's Georgian, and I'm fond of it – just off an exceedingly steep street called Blackboy Hill. The slave trade's a part of our civic heritage, I'm afraid. I also confess to being a rosarian. I grow roses," he added, seeing her confusion.

She said nothing, forcing him to paint the personalities into this domestic still life.

"And I have a basset hound called Percy," he added. "He's a miserable bugger, but we muddle along OK."

"I think you are the most English man I have met."

"I fear that's what one might call a back-handed compliment."

She laughed. "Let me show you something."

As Harkness was led up the hillside excitement did battle with unease and desire with intrigue. She led him into a gully where he was astonished to see steam billowing through the curtains of rock, swirling and opaque. Scalding water gushed from a fissure, collecting in a rock-pool before spilling down the valley.

"A secret within a secret," she said. "It's very nice for bathing – nobody has hot water in the valley."

Alarm versus longing, guilt against the searing actuality and possibility of the present.

"Just don't expect me to bathe too!" she said before departing.

*

But there was to be another encounter that day. At sunset Harkness and McCartney wandered into the village for food.

"You might as well ask if there's any way of contacting her," McCartney was saying. "In years to come you might feel differently."

Harkness glared at him. "Look, shut up. I don't 'feel' anything – and even if I did, I've told you my reasons for not taking a partner, which are very personal. So I'd appreciate it if you'd respect them."

"Sometimes you've got to take a chance!" insisted McCartney. "Like me coming to the Congo—"

The conversation was interrupted at the sight of Natalie fishing for her supper. When the waistcoated old men passed in their ones and twos she conversed with them easily in Tajik; if this was a plant from Moscow, the setup and roleplaying were exquisite.

"*Salam alaikum,*" she called. "Come join!"

McCartney took the fishing rod and to everybody's annoyance caught a trout right away. The sun fell away and one by one the stars emerged, followed by an Islamic crescent moon.

"Olivié?" Harkness asked pleasantly.

"Yes?"

In a thunderous instant everyone realised the import of what had happened. Without further comment Olivié Lefebvre snatched the trout and ran, and as Harkness watched her flee towards her hut a single thought hammered through his head.

What have I done?

70

Wakeford was a finer figure than Jasper or Mirza, almost an Atlas in his late middle age. He swept damp hair back over his head and exhaled contentedly in the steam. They were in the Turkish bath at the Royal Automobile Club, where Wakeford was a guest; it was a return fixture for hospitality received at the Garrick.

"Allow me to bring you up to speed on the Venus situation," said Wakeford.

Jasper leaned closer, trapping the spymaster in his gaze. Wakeford felt uncomfortable in his presence.

"It appears she didn't contact any more of her peers – which means only Lisbon left."

Jasper's fingers were like little pink worms squirming around one another. "I'll be there tonight."

"Excellent," said Wakeford. "But I do have one more disclosure… it appears Anita Johansen contacted Hastings after she so unwisely published the Christodoulou report."

"Whatever next," Mirza hissed.

"I don't need to tell you what a catastrophe it would be if all these people get to know one another," Wakeford continued. "And I'm afraid the accursed Hastings dodged the bullet at her monthly surgery. Something about a left-wing demonstration? Anyway, she seems to have gone to ground since then. Not at her home address, nor her constituency office. Now she and Johansen are corresponding we really do have no choice. You won't like this, Dennis, but we'll have to nab her in the Commons."

"*In* the Commons?" gasped Mirza. "You're right, I don't like it. The last person to try a Parliamentary assassination was Guy Fawkes – and I seem to recall that didn't end well."

"Those are the orders," said Wakeford. "I gather Hastings has acquired personal protection as well – so you will need to do as exactly as *she* instructs you."

"Not only that," Mirza pressed, "Hastings hasn't had the whip returned yet. So we can't actually guarantee her presence in the Commons at all."

"She won't be able to resist the Middle East debate," said Wakeford. "Any excuse for a bit of blood and thunder. And the chamber will be heaving; the melee as they leave will be the moment. You're about to join a very exclusive club, Dennis. Not many people can say they've murdered a Member of Parliament."

71

The next morning Harkness went looking for Olivié Lefebvre. As he walked towards her home he had the feeling of the earth turning beneath his feet, rumbling to meet him from the east with each stride. He found her digging up beetroot in her garden and wordlessly kneeled to help. She glared at him but did not protest; they worked in silence; the beetroot pile grew.

Finally she turned to face him. "So, now you know."

"I wasn't trying to catch you out... Natalie."

She threw down a beetroot. "Is that so?"

"I had my suspicions. But the names got mixed up in my head."

Was that true? On balance Harkness thought so. But so rich and full of trickery is the human mind that he couldn't be sure. Perhaps his subconscious had placed the name in his mouth deliberately; perhaps some part of him wanted to bring things to a head.

"What I'm trying to say is that I'm sorry," he finished. "Everyone should have the right to put an old life behind them, if they want to."

The truth in his own words hammered through him.

Olivié was looking at her hands. "It's funny how deeply a name can be stored in you. Like it is in the bones. Nobody has called me by that name for twenty years."

"Why did you come here?"

"Why did *you*?"

Harkness considered this. "The truth is that we think this valley holds a secret. Something bad. I didn't want to tell you before because... because this place is special to you."

"You are a gentleman," she said quietly.

"I don't really know how to respond to that."

Two yellow wagtails went spinning and chirruping over the garden, chasing each other.

"Why is it just you living there in Bristol?" she asked. "You and your 'miserable bugger' dog?"

He sighed. "I consider myself a widower."

She abandoned an attempt to disentangle mud from a beetroot tendril and tossed it into her basket. "How long?"

"Oh, about thirty years."

"Thirty *years?*"

Olivié unearthed another beetroot and stared at him. This close he could see flecks of honey in her caramel brown eyes. She leaned across and kissed him on the cheek.

Harkness flinched.

"So that you know, because I am religious, it does not mean I am forbidden from falling in love with someone I have just met," she said quietly. "And neither is this something I do very often. You can be assured of that."

Harkness had to consider the possibility he was falling in love with her, too – and at breakneck speed. This was not something he thought could happen. Guilt and excitement chased each other's tails, and his reasoning mind screamed a warning.

"But I have to stay here," she continued. "This valley is my home. It is where I have chosen to spend my days. And you, Randolph, are a man of the world. I know this. You could never be happy, living here in the mountains."

Harkness bowed his head in recognition of the fact.

"I think you must do what you have to do," she finished. "But the world beyond the valley, it is not for me."

Harkness felt a great weight inside himself. But the gravity of the past was counterbalanced by the hollow pull of the future, drawing him into its vacuum – away from this place and this woman. Awkwardly, he offered her his hand, and she shook it and laughed; then tears were in her eyes.

"So be it," she said.

"I'm terribly sorry."

"I am 'terribly sorry' too." Olivié plucked a spade from the earth. "Now, come with me."

"Where are we going?"

"I know why it is that you came here. I'm going to show you what you are looking for."

*

Olivié led Harkness back up the valley. For the first time since their meeting there was no bounce in her step, no *joie de vivre* in her conversation, and he recognised in the sorrow of her movements a little of himself. They rendezvoused with Marks and McCartney half a mile up the slope. From up here they could see silt disgorging from each tributary of the Hindu Kush into the River Wakhan, like a series of pale starfish stirring in the turquoise waters.

Olivié struck her spade into the scree with a satisfying *smunch*. "Help me dig."

They worked until all four were red-faced and sweating, McCartney with the spade, the others using their hands. After half an hour they'd removed two feet of stones and gravel, and the metal hit the bedrock.

"Petroglyphs," breathed Marks.

They fell upon the rock face, brushing away pebbles and dust with their fingers until the forms revealed themselves. The same gigantic figures, hands and feet removed; all around them danced the persecutors with their spears and clubs. By both the style and erosion Harkness deduced extreme antiquity.

"They are *Homo neanderthalensis*," she said.

"We know," said McCartney.

"You also found the inscription on Saimaluu Tash?"

Harkness nodded.

"There are many rock carvings like this in the valley," she said. "When I understood what they meant, I was so upset. The Cold War was not yet over. I was certain that this" – she indicated the carvings – "would happen again. I no longer wanted to live among people who could do such things to one another. My parents died when I was in my early twenties and I am an only child. I had no reason to return to France. So I stayed here, where people are peaceful and kind. I learned Sufism. That is how I became the person that I am. And I also asked the villagers to help me cover up the carvings. They seemed to me a thing of sadness."

"But how did you work out what the petroglyphs mean?" asked Marks. "Bit of a leap, isn't it?"

"Because that is not all I found."

She led them higher still, to a fifty-foot nape of vertical rock that bisected the valley. A slab of rock leaned against the cliff face, boulders and stones piled up against the sides.

"Can you move this?" she asked.

The slab toppled with a boom that echoed across the Wakhan Valley to reveal the entrance to a narrow cave. They ventured into the darkness. The crack opened out into a small chamber, where McCartney struck his lighter. Harkness spotted the ceiling of another branch leading deeper into the hillside and he realised that the cave system was huge. His heart was pounding.

Then he saw the thigh bone.

It protruded from the earth thick as a rolling pin with a socket like a cricket ball.

"If that's *Homo sapiens* I'll eat my hat," said Marks.

Other bones were littered about the surface; McCartney examined a scored rib and a fragment of crushed brow-ridge.

"This is violence," he said.

At the back of the cave was a shinbone, sheared at the ankle.

"Did you excavate farther down?" Harkness asked.

"A little. Enough to know that the pictures on the rock, the chopping of hands... they actually did it."

Shades of Rwanda.

"At Saimaluu Tash I found another grave," she continued. "This was an ancient Holocaust – that is how I see it. And so I know that we humans are built to kill one another. I hope you can use this knowledge to bring some goodness into the world, somehow. Now I must go. Goodbye, Randolph Harkness."

When they shook hands again Olivié's fingers lingered on his infinitesimally. Harkness watched her all the way down to the village.

72

Tony Marks placed a hand on Harkness's shoulder. "*C'est la vie*, pal. You'll get over it."

With a supersonic crack something slammed into Marks' chest. He staggered backwards into the cave. A patch of scarlet was forming on his shirt, spreading outward at speed. When he coughed blood erupted from his mouth, beads of red catching on his moustache. Another bullet smashed into the rock beside them and a chip of stone tore McCartney's cheek.

"Sniper!" screamed Harkness, thrusting him back.

Marks' Stetson had been sent flying to reveal a balding head, and there was something pathetic about the comb-over dangling down one side of his face. The noise he made as he tried to breathe was the worst of it: a harsh inward rasp like the ripping of a membrane. Harkness couldn't triangulate where the shooter was. Then a dozen men with Kalashnikov assault rifles came scrambling towards them from the western valley. They were pinned by the sniper as the kill-squad neared. Then all twelve gunmen fell. *They were under fire, too.*

Marks leaned against the rock, eyes bulging as he tried to speak. He coughed out a mouthful of blood that splattered grotesquely against the rock.

"Help me," he uttered into the cuff of his shirt. "Get me out…"

"He's speaking to someone!" McCartney grabbed Marks' head and shook it until his eyes opened. "Who were you talking to?"

"Who's on the other end of the line, Tony?" said Harkness.

Marks' eyes focused and refocused with difficulty. "'When your country comes asking for help, you should offer it. Gladly.' Just doing my duty, Randy, like you said."

"What country?" Harkness shouted. "Britain? Russia? The USA?"

But Marks only smiled. His entire shirt glistened crimson now, the blood pulsing over the fabric like a stream over pebbles.

"Open my top left pocket," he whispered.

Inside was a photograph of his wife and daughter.

"On my knee please, if you'd be so kind."

Harkness placed the photograph where Marks could see it and the dying man's eyes brimmed with tears.

"I'm sorry, Randolph," said Marks. "You're a good fella. So's Ross. Look after him. He will need you."

Marks' gaze returned to his young family and he mouthed his daughter's name. Thirty seconds later he was gone.

When McCartney peered from the cave another bullet slammed into the rock. "Jesus *Christ*!"

More gunmen were emerging from a ruined compound of mud huts at the foot of the valley, struggling up the slope towards them. But these were different figures: they wore desert combat fatigues and bore French FAMAS assault rifles. One of them was shot in the head, the second in the neck.

It was happening again.

Harkness heard the *bloop* of grenade launchers, saw six spirals of vapour as six canisters went spinning through the air to land amongst the assault team. With a *poof* the smoke grenades exploded, and the soldiers' approach was lost amid acrid yellow dye. Now battle commenced in earnest. A heavy machine gun raked through the sulphurous clouds, and this Harkness saw by the muzzle-flashes on the Afghan side of the valley. Even at a mile's distance the rip and bark of its discharge distressed the ears. Harkness heard the howl and scream of the assault team, fingered beneath the smokescreen by weight of lead. Sparks flew on rock as the machine-gunner came under fire himself; the first straggles of yellow were tapering past the cave. Another six *bloops*, another six *poofs*, and now the valley was full of yellow smoke. Dimly Harkness saw figures running into it, like First World War soldiers going over the top. He heard the discharge of small-arms fire within the melee, screams and wails. All planning had gone out of the window. This was the fog of war.

"This is our chance," hissed Harkness. "Let's try for the river. Keep low and go from boulder to boulder."

Harkness seized both thigh bone and brow fragment and they ventured into the billowing mustard air, arcing out to avoid the assault team. He grasped McCartney's shirt tail to stop them becoming separated: the blind leading the blind. Bullets whipped past at random and once a wounded Russian commando stumbled right into them. Harkness smashed him over the head with the thigh bone and they continued. The river opened up before them majestically, a floor of molten glass for that jaundiced world. The icy rapids swept straggles of dye from its surface; half a tree trunk lay on the river bank.

"That's how we get out," said Harkness. "Grab hold and try not to freeze or drown…"

They pitched the tree trunk into the water and dived in after it. The blast of cold was electrocution and suffocation simultaneously – it beat the air from Harkness's lungs and sent his nervous system into panic. The log was racing downstream as he grasped it with hands that were already cramping. McCartney grabbed his boot and the awkward assemblage was swept clear of the smoke clouds. There was gunfire and the occasional flash of white within the palls of yellow behind them; it was a scene from the last Afghanistan War. They rushed past the village – Harkness caught a last glimpse of the mosque's crescent moon – then rode another set of rapids, clinging grimly to the timber. By the time they had stabilised she was lost to him.

73

Barely a glimpse of green was visible on the benches in the Commons and the atmosphere was raucous even by the standards of that hooligan corner of SW1. The title of the debate was studiously neutral – *Proposed military intervention in the Middle East* – but for most present it was a 'here we go again' moment. The Opposition, still haunted by the ghost of Blair, tore into the prospect of a new entanglement in the Middle East with a zeal and anger that would have put the fear of god into the Islamists themselves. But the government benches had largely yielded to that natural geopolitical gravity which aligns London with Washington in peace or war.

"The place of the United Kingdom," as one impeccably mannered High Tory opined, "will always be alongside the United States of America – and that is especially true of an America governed by the Grand Old Party. I daresay the current president's personal etiquette may strike members as distasteful. But that is by the by. Should Russian tanks roll from Kaliningrad I have no doubt Britain and America will stand together to defend the sovereign and independent Baltic nations. It is beholden upon us to do our duty for the oppressed of the Middle East, too."

A Scottish National Party politician retorted with such fury that his pupils seemed to flicker red. "The president's former adviser, a fundamentalist Christian, is on record as saying at a rally he wants a 'new Thirty Years War' to 'press reboot' in the Middle East. The Thirty Years War, may I remind the House, was among the bloodiest and most destructive episodes in European history. Is the right honourable member *seriously suggesting* that we trigger a twenty-first-century equivalent? It's hardly as if our previous attempts to remake the Islamic world in the Western democratic image have been covered in glory. If Iran and Saudi Arabia want to duke it out in Yemen or Syria, I say: let them. This is not our fight."

The hawks had not been helped by the US president's tweet the previous evening: "Cheese-eating EU surrender monkeys won't help US fix Syria once and for all. Sad!"

"Yes, the opinion polls are shifting in favour of yet another war," the SNP politician continued. "But that should not concern us one iota. I remind honourable members that we are representatives of our constituents not their advocates. Should this matter eventually come to a division I trust each and every one of us will vote with our consciences."

The Prime Minister had given a typically non-committal perform-ance, speaking for ten minutes while saying nothing. Everyone knew though that if push came to shove she would be for invasion and her MPs would back her. As with Cameron and Blair before him, peace or war came down to the decision of a single individual. Then the attempt to swing public support behind it would begin in earnest.

Peter De Vries skulked in the Members' Lobby behind a bronze of Lloyd George with his back to the main chamber. From here he would be well placed to observe Hastings as she departed. Even on the parliamentary estate Hastings felt unsafe; she trusted nobody and had signed in her close protection officer as a 'consultant'. De Vries was unarmed, of course, but this was not a man who needed weapons to injure or protect. Every now and then a roar escaped the chamber, and a statue of Thatcher pointed into the furore.

When Hastings rose to speak six hundred voices thundered. Half the house considered her a laughing stock; the other half thought she was mentally unwell and ought to be in a home. She had not one supporter left in the entire Palace of Westminster.

"In the aftermath of 9/11," Hastings began, "the Bush administration threatened to bomb Pakistan back to the *Stone Age* if it refused to cooperate with the war on terror." Now Hastings stared into BBC Parliament's camera: as if addressing someone directly. "I personally believe that if we choose the path of conflict again, a *powerful force* will be set in motion, a *raging flood-wave*."

"She's finally cracked," murmured the Chief Whip.

But Hastings had not cracked. She was sending a message to them.

"The earth will be *filled with violence, humanity returned unto dust*." There was a murmur of confused recognition at words from the Old Testament. Next Hesiod rang out across the despatch box: "*Retribution shall be laid up for the future. Hateful death and painful woe.*"

All across London journalists were hitting Google. A *Telegraph* correspondent got there first and tweeted: "Gloria Hastings MP quoting the Bible, Epic of Gilgamesh and ancient Greek poetry at a bewildered Commons."

Others were listening, too. Richard Wakeford and his handler; the Russian president; other watchers in Europe and in Asia. Hastings was addressing them all, and her message was this:

We are on to you.

Leave me alone.

When the debate finished the MPs surged for the exit. Hastings was caught in the tide and propelled into the Members' Lobby. De Vries was behind Hastings, drifting innocently between his client and unknown bodies.

"What on earth was that about, old girl?" guffawed a backbencher.

She emerged. From downtown Grozny to the Palace of Westminster, it had been quite a journey. Fifteen political assassinations in eleven countries; now for the mother of parliaments. The woman too feared to name looked every inch the parliamentary researcher in her knee-length dress and Jarvis Cocker glasses. She carried a stack of files in which nestled her device, humming with potential energy. De Vries clocked the pale-skinned woman advancing through the crush of MPs and swivelled elegantly around his client. Which was when Mirza tripped over the foot of a junior minister and sent five mugs of scalding liquid cascading over De Vries. The bodyguard yelled in pain; several MPs cried out, too; Hastings was buffeted backwards by the politicians. She felt a scorching sensation behind her left kidney, somewhere between a pulled muscle and heartburn. It seemed to rise up right through her and briefly Hastings thought she was having a heart attack. Amid the hoo-hah nobody noticed the parliamentary researcher with the bulbous features retreat.

"I'm so sorry," gushed Mirza. "How can I make it up to you?"

De Vries glared at him then turned to Hastings. "You all right?"

"Fine," she said. "Just had a bit of a hot flush, that's all."

But that evening's events were not over. As they queued for the Cromwell Green exit, Hastings spotted the Foreign Office emissary whose missive had brought all this down upon her. Was Sir Hugh in the country? It seemed unlikely. He had a diplomatic mission to run and the Argentinians were going through one of their bolshie patches. Written on the civil servant's palm in black felt tip were five words.

Durbar Court. Clive of India. With that he was away.

"It's in the Foreign Office," said Hastings.

Her pass still worked and the security guard eyed her with weary recognition. She led De Vries through the old India Office to an Italianate piazza with red granite columns. Once exposed to the elements, an iron and glass roof now covers Durbar Court; with flag-stones of white marble, it is the only place in the Foreign Office with a red wine ban. Around this courtyard whirled all the business of the

British Empire during the Victorian age; that night it was deserted and Hastings made for Clive of India. A man who had snaffled a subcontinent extended a marble foot, as if taking the first step of a complicated dance. A piece of paper was folded between the statue's knuckles.

74

The primary sensation of being in London after the solitude of the High Pamir was one of bewilderment. Four lanes of Tottenham Court Road traffic blared past Harkness and office workers roamed with eyes on phones; even the KFC sign seemed alien, a marker from a different life. The pedestrians walked eight abreast and as Harkness struggled through them he had another flashback of that giant eland stepping into an African night. This brought on thoughts of Olivié – and the suspicion that he had made the third great mistake of his life. Their whole affair felt not quite real, a sensation heightened by the dreamlike quality of the Wakhan. Perhaps he should have listened to Ross.

They had hitchhiked to the regional capital of Khorog and caught a taxi on to Dushanbe. Harkness needed to transfer money for the aeroplane tickets, but they were unmolested at the airport. The thigh bone elicited lively discussion amongst security – yet it was evidently too big for a human being and his University of Bristol identity card persuaded them. Now they were back in London. That morning McCartney had attended Moorfields Eye Hospital for another round of lasers, emerging grim-faced but stoic.

"It's fine," was all he would disclose.

Looking at the hundred nationalities pouring from the London Underground, Harkness thought of the closeness of the human family. There is more genetic difference between western and eastern chimpanzee populations than any two ethnicities on earth: "Bad news for racists," as Tony Marks had once commented to him cheerfully. Yet this was a family with a secret.

In the main, I'm certain our prehistoric ancestors were good. Because they must have been.

The beliefs of a lifetime were built on a lie.

They walked to the Institute of Archaeology at University College London. The sixties block had been constructed on a bombsite, an abomination amidst the Georgian terraces of Bloomsbury; students strolled past with bicycles and a bandana-clad Italian sold complicated coffees from his tuk-tuk. This was a carefree scene, one that reminded Harkness of his old life, and he wondered if he would ever return to academia. He took full advantage of the surveillance traps – the shopfronts had reflective surfaces and he chose a cut-through that would have forced a follower to expose himself in the dead ground. But Harkness's tradecraft was not good enough to spot the grey men – or perhaps they were too grey – and the individual who called himself Adriaen was not the only tail he missed.

The laboratory was on the fourth floor of the institute.

"Blimey, look at that," exclaimed a technician when Harkness produced the thigh bone. "What a beaut!"

The scientist removed a speck of calcium for carbon dating and Harkness placed both thigh bone and brow-ridge into a cabinet where lasers would scan their dimensions. He began fiddling with the dials.

"Out of interest," muttered McCartney as he peered at an electro-spin resonance machine, "what A Levels would you need to study here?"

The question stopped Harkness dead.

"You don't have to pretend to be interested on my account, you know," he said, staring straight ahead. "Each to their own – I'm big and ugly enough to take it."

"I got a B in maths plus Cs and Ds. But I never did biology. Would that be a problem?"

Harkness felt a sudden warmth in his eyeballs. "I reckon we could probably wangle you on to a course," he said thickly.

"The last few weeks have opened my eyes," said McCartney.

Whether the turn of phrase was deliberate, Harkness did not know. But he was in danger of becoming emotional and swiftly changed the subject.

"What you're about to see is a magical process," he said. "Right now the computer's comparing the dimensions of our two bones against every other hominid specimen on the database. That's thousands of fossils, representing species from *Australopithecus* to modern man and everything in between. It uses this library of anatomical data to 'import' the missing bones – essentially, borrowing them from the fossils closest to it anatomically. Filling in the blanks."

"Nice."

"So we're about to reconstruct this chap's skull using a 3D printer."

The stereolithographic device was a transparent box containing a metal platform on which to shape the object about to be printed. Beneath that was a resin tank that Harkness filled to the line. When he hit start ultraviolet lasers began flickering inside the box, and they heard the click and groan of data feeding through cables. The platform lowered and raised, busy as a worker ant, as liquid plastic hardened before their eyes. Almost at once a jaw bone began to form, which sprouted a chin and teeth. It was ghostly to behold, as mysterious as the workings of DNA itself.

"Something's not right," said Harkness.

McCartney looked up sharply. "What is it?"

"The chin's more rounded than I'd expect. It's too small for the thigh bone."

The teeth were overlarge, too, lending the impression of imbecility. And as the cheeks flickered into existence Harkness saw the head was short and round. It was a deeply archaic skull.

"This isn't a Neanderthal at all," he whispered.

The gigantic eye sockets emerged next, like the headlights of a vintage automobile – and the creature's brows were huge. This was a forehead that could have absorbed the kick of a reindeer. Finally the skull case began to form, and as the cranial capacity became clear there was no doubt.

"He's a *Homo erectus*," said Harkness.

The laboratory door burst open and the technician brandished a printout. "Carbon dating results in. Twenty thousand years? You were way out! Try doubling that…"

"The Venus of Hohle Fens is that age," whispered Harkness. "It's the earliest yet discovered…"

"Missing hands and feet?" asked McCartney.

Harkness nodded and their gaze returned to the *erectus*. "Do you know what this means? Do you understand the significance?"

The only noise was the ticking of the laser as the final layers were lacquered on to the skull.

"I understand," said McCartney. "It means our ancestors wiped out *Homo erectus*, too."

75

An unimaginable gulf of time separated them from this individual and the world in which he had lived and died. Lakes had formed and vanished, the Sahara greened and dried; the polar ice cap had grown and shrunk and Britain had become an island. As the weather changed around them the hunters of Eurasia switched from reindeer to mammoth, then ibex and red deer, then back to reindeer. Dogs had been domesticated and the first great works of art conceived in the caves of France. History had begun and man had split the atom.

"The mountains of Central Asia must have been *erectus*'s last redoubt," said Harkness. "This guy belonged to the very last chapter of a two-million-year existence. An entire geological age of survival, and we brought it to an end."

Harkness pictured the human line of descent. It was more a family *bush* than a tree – a maze of offshoots and dead ends as nature in all its randomness tried new things. But the branch leading to *Homo sapiens* was unnaturally straight, as if all cousin species had been pruned away.

"For most of my career there were only two things one could say with certainty about our status as lone survivors," said Harkness. "First, that we are here and our rivals are not. And, second, that they disappeared suspiciously close to the time that we got smart. I've spent thirty years arguing we merely out-competed them. It appears that I was wrong."

Harkness was staring at his hands, down through the skin and on to molecular level. Our past is carried within us – and he knew that it was a wicked past, tainted from the exodus, as the ancient books said. First *Homo erectus*, then *neanderthalensis*: we had killed off our closest relatives. But the long lamentable story of human genocide was just getting started. The Forest People had been decimated; Khoisan click speakers were all but swept from the African continent; the population of South America declined by a ratio of fifty-eight to one after the arrival of the Spanish. Australian aborigines were almost obliterated and so were Native Americans. Then came the modern era, which put these exterminations in the shade. For bleak though the first chapters in human becoming were, they were nothing to Adolf Hitler. Harkness saw then how genocide was the story of our species. It was intrinsic to us, like laughter or song and dance. We were *built for it*. And the industrial revolution only raised this capacity for killing to new levels, barbarous pinnacles of achievement. How inappropriate, Harkness reflected, that such crimes were called *inhuman*. And what a paradox: with our higher reasoning skills were inner demons unleashed.

Harkness saw it all now. Massacre upon massacre, genocide upon genocide; indeed even as they spoke the last tribes of orangutans were clinging to survival in the depths of Indonesia. And behind all this wickedness? *Homo sapiens*. Wise man.

"I always ask my new students one question," said Harkness. "Human beings achieved modern intelligence in about 70,000 BC. Civilization began in 3,000 BC. That leaves 67,000 years in which people are bright as you or I roamed the planet and left barely a trace.

What were we doing all that time? It's called the Sapient Paradox. But now I know. We were just doing what we always do."

"We were killing one another," said McCartney.

With the very minimum of fuss, Harkness began to weep.

76

At eighty-nine years of age, Dr Duarte Freire of the University of Lisbon still walked the streets of the Alfama district of Lisbon where he had lived his whole life. Bowed, pinstriped and liver-spotted, he hobbled up the Rua São Tomé, which was cobblestoned and steep as a breaking wave. At the top stood his blue-tiled house wherein his wife had prepared venison for supper. After they had eaten Freire made a *bica* and sat with his papers, the aroma of strong coffee wafting through their high ceilings. His wife left him to it: Duarte hadn't been this vital for years, and she was reminded of him as a young man. She wanted him to enjoy this last burst of life-force.

After the letter from Professor Fournier had arrived, a lifetime's work needed to be reassessed. Freire was too old for digital – like scholars of the early twentieth century, he worked in only analogue – so he had spent the last fortnight reading, leafing, ordering. And now he was convinced. That the Ice Age Venuses were not a thing of beauty pained him; but truth trumps sentiment. Or it ought to.

It was one a.m. when a bearded figure stopped outside the blue-tiled house. A dim light emanated from an upstairs window, but the building spoke of slumber and the street was deserted. He began pouring petrol through the letter box. The cobbles were illuminated and a rattling came up the hill; Jasper paused until an antiquated tram clattered past, its cyclopean headlight carving a beam through the night. Shift-workers stared glumly at this unremarkable figure through windows misted with condensation. When the vehicle had passed Jasper tipped the final contents of his jerrycan through the letter box, lit a match and posted that after it. With a *whoomph* the frosted glass door-panes turned orange and several of them cracked.

Jasper hurried off down the road and caught a taxi to Portela Airport, where a private jet registered to a Russian businessman awaited. There was paperwork he needed to attend to for a Holyhead Marine board meeting the next afternoon, but his work would be interrupted frequently by sinful thoughts. For Jasper had come to take a dirty enjoyment in the work of killing. And he itched to be the one who shot Randolph Harkness in the head.

Back at the blue-tiled house the elderly scholar was dozing. He sat at his desk with chin dangling, flinching when something occurred to him in his night-imaginings.

He had the feeling of something closing in.

Freire awoke to find flames all around him. They leapt up the curtains and devoured the parquet floor. The hallway was a wall of heat and light, and boughs of black smoke writhed across the ceiling. His first thought was that his wife was a heavy sleeper and vainly he screamed for her. But the old man's voice was drowned out by the roar of the flames, by the crack and pop of splitting timbers. Already the air had been stripped of oxygen and suddenly the room began to swirl around him. Dr Duarte Freire was unconscious before his head hit the table.

Smoke crept beneath the bedroom door, runnels of black sand flowing upward. Mrs Freire was dreaming of the village of her birth in the Dão Valley. The main square was as it had been on the day of her marriage in 1947; tables had been set up with flowers on them. The faces of her childhood were there and everyone was smiling. She coughed in her sleep, and then she drifted away to meet her husband.

*

Harkness saw the breaking news pop up on the BBC News Channel at ten a.m. the next morning. He and McCartney were staying in vacant rooms at a Bloomsbury hall of residence where the warden was a friend, drinking instant coffee and wondering what to do next.

Breaking news: fourth European academic 'murdered'.

Harkness rushed to turn up the volume.

"…it follows the shooting of both Professor Vincent Fournier in France and Dr Maria Daescu in Romania," the anchor was saying, "while a car bomb killed Dr Francesca Bianca last month in Italy. All four victims specialised in human origins. It's thought someone with mental health problems might be behind the spate of killings. Europol have issued the following image of the suspect."

An identikit image of Eric Jasper was on the screen.

"I knew Vincent Fournier," said Harkness. "I met Maria Daescu at a conference, too. And Freire was a living legend." He clenched a fist. "One by one they're killing every leading prehistorian in the world."

"What do you make of this?" said McCartney, showing him a broadsheet media blog.

> *Gloria Hastings' newspaper has terminated her column following the hoax MI6 report debacle, this newspaper understands.*
>
> *The controversial MP's judgement has been under even more scrutiny than usual since she tweeted screenshots of a document purporting to be authored by MI6 on the penchant of chimpanzees for wiping one another out. Security sources have confirmed the document was bogus.*
>
> *Editors at the newspaper acted as the furore over her previous allegations…*

As Harkness read the report he paled.

> *Dr Christodoulou claimed it was 'Mode II' that enables chimpanzees to identify the elimination of all rivals as a bountiful reproductive stratagem…*

"I think we need to ask this Gloria Hastings some questions," he said. "Don't you?"

77

Two figures waited at the bandstand in Regent's Park. It was a wet Tuesday morning and billionaire's row was shrouded in mist; the BT Tower emerged and disappeared through the fog, like a high-tech sentinel pulsing over Fitzrovia. A few dog-walkers braved the bad weather, but the two men on the bandstand cut lonely figures. The bandstand itself was slightly sad, suggestive of Edwardian seaside resorts that had fallen out of fashion.

Three people emerged from the Avenue Gardens, past dahlias and fuchsias that seemed muted in the grey light. A man held back as two women joined the pair on the bandstand. So that made four of them: four disparate people from four different worlds. All had been thrown together by the Sapient Paradox.

"You must be Randolph Harkness," said Hastings. "I've read up on you, sunshine."

Harkness shook her hand. He had heard much of this woman and most of it appalling; but he also believed in taking people as they came.

"I'm Dr Anita Johansen," said her companion. "Philologist, Edinburgh Uni."

"And I'm Ross. A… a student of his."

Hastings' eyes gleamed. "A politician, a palaeontologist, a philologist and a Prince Harry lookalike meet in a park. What's the punchline?"

Another sheet of rain swept across the boating lake where three swans were huddled together; the roof of the bandstand thundered like timpani before the charge. One by one each described their own journey to that rendezvous, Hastings trilling with pride as she explained how she'd tracked down Orientalist.

"It all fits together," said McCartney.

"But there's one thing we remain in total ignorance of," said Harkness. "Why would anyone need to suppress crimes that occurred in prehistory? How is it of any bearing to the modern world? That's what stops us going public with this thing, from getting our old lives back. Just imagine calling in this story to the *Times* newsdesk without a motive. We'd be a damned laughing stock."

"Thinking it through…" muttered McCartney.

They all turned to him.

"*We* might not know the answer – but the Russians do. They must, or none of this would have happened."

"Baker Street's that way, Sherlock," said Hastings.

"No, wait, there might be something in this," said Harkness. "If *we* don't know the answer, we need to *find out from them*."

It all led back to Orientalist.

"What are we going to do," scoffed Hastings, "lock him in a room and threaten to duff him up?"

McCartney was flexing his fingers, but Harkness cut in, "No, we won't be doing that."

"Ask him very nicely?" suggested Hastings.

"We can be cleverer than that," said Harkness. "Just think what an insight into human psychology this group possesses. You're a politician, Gloria, I should have thought you know a little about manipulation. Anita, you've had a ringside seat at the very formation of human intellect. Ross definitely thinks outside the box. And I've got the odd trick up my sleeve, too."

"Such as?" said Hastings.

"First up, if you want someone to tell you something, they're likelier to trust you if you're in their building, past the barriers. They assume you're one of them."

"Not particularly helpful," said Hastings. "What are you suggesting, one of us masquerades as a bookseller on the Charing Cross Road?"

"I was thinking about the Russian Embassy, actually. Second, people are much more likely to divulge a secret that they *think you are already in on.*"

"Interesting thought," said Johansen. "But we're known to Wakeford. We'd never make it into the Embassy, let alone strike up conversation with him."

"Agreed," said Harkness. "We need a clean skin, someone to go in for us. Anyone got any bright ideas?"

"Actually, I do know someone suitable," said Hastings. "Horrible little man named Milo Fallon, but good at this sort of thing. He's the guy who did Lord Wakeford over last time. Perhaps he's got someone else on his books. He's expensive though – and I no longer have a newspaper to cover my bills."

"I do have some savings left," sighed Harkness.

"There's also this," said Hastings.

She handed him Sir Hugh Alexander's communiqué. The printed sheet of A4 bore nothing put images.

"I've checked and he's in Paraguay," she said. "Evidently he wanted to tell me something but didn't feel able to in words or by email. So he's gone and done it in pictures."

Harkness studied the images. "Not bad spy-craft, actually. If this was picked up by a passer-by it would mean nothing."

1. SAS commandos smashing their way into the Iranian Embassy. A green tick.

2. The Good Friday Agreement being signed. Didier Deschamps lifting the World Cup for France. Bill Clinton denying he had sexual relations with that woman.

3. The Kremlin. Maddie McCann. Sigmund Freud. Prison bars. The Kamchatka peninsula.

4. The Thunderbirds. Sigmund Freud again. And a calendar, that week circled in red.

"I've already worked out number one," said Hastings. "The cancelled Special Forces raid that dragged me into this horror show in the first place. It's back on. They're going for it."

"Number two's easy too," said Harkness. "It's a year – 1998. Who could forget Beckham getting sent off against Argentina?"

"So something happened in 1998," said Johansen. "Something pertinent to this SBS raid."

"The Kremlin abducted Maddie McCann?" quipped McCartney.

"Don't be vulgar," said Hastings.

"You can talk," McCartney shot back.

"Wait, I think he's got something," said Johansen. "Could Sir Hugh be saying the *Russians* abducted someone in 1998?"

"Sigmund Freud?" suggested McCartney.

"Freud died eighty years ago, numbnuts," said Hastings.

Johansen frowned. "So they kidnapped… a *psychologist?*"

"That's it!" said Harkness. "Prison bars, Kamchatka. That's where they've been holding him… for more than thirty-five years."

"Then it's not an assassination at all," said Hastings. "It's a rescue attempt – hence Tokyo. Japan's the nearest friendly country. That's where they'll launch it from."

They turned to number four. Thunderbirds International Rescue; Sigmund Freud; that very week.

"Things are coming to a head," murmured Harkness.

78

Captain Donaldson and his men sat in a waiting room at the British Embassy in Tokyo like a band of truants summoned to see the headmaster. The japery had died away after they transferred through Helsinki – catching the onward flight to the Far East felt symbolic, a point of no return. They had been put up in the Four Seasons Hotel until their body clocks were reset, spending four days in the gym while dining on Wagu beef courtesy of the HM Treasury.

"Six hundred dollars a night and this steak cost more than my monthly mortgage!" Jones had crowed at dinner. "Thank you very much, Your Majesty."

"Yes, and that should worry you," Captain Donaldson countered in his cynical drawl. "They aren't doing this for our enjoyment and relaxation, you know."

On the fifth day they were moved to quarters at the British Embassy. Built in the style of a Georgian stately home, it inhabited 35,000 square metres of parkland, separated by a moat from the Imperial Palace. In a city where a broom cupboard costs a lifetime's labour, this statement of British influence was not lost on the soldiery.

"Shit just got real," said Jackson.

Now they were about to find out what they'd been training for. They were led into a secure speech room, where Major Harold Larmour awaited. On a table stood a model volcano surrounded by snowy mountains.

"I flipping told you it was Japan, didn't I, lads?" said Jones.

At the foot of the volcano was a circular lake – the flooded crater of a far older eruption – and on its shore was a compound comprising a single cube-shaped building with a watch tower surrounded by two concentric fences. It resembled the fortress in Abbottabad where Osama bin Laden had been found, and outside the fences was a small barracks. The diorama had been modelled and painted with exquisite care; flocking was used for grass and tiny men patrolled the compound.

"It's not Japan, actually," said the man sitting at the back of the room, youngish with flushed cheeks. "It's the Karymsky volcano in Kamchatka."

"This gentleman is from the Secret Service," said Major Larmour.

"You don't say," quipped Jones with immaculate Welsh sarcasm.

"Behave yourself," said Donaldson.

"Now, as you may have twigged, this is a search and rescue operation," said Larmour. "You're looking for a man named Brian Finer, who the FSB snatched back in the nineties. Jones, you're deploying right away. We'll drop you offshore by submarine, and it's a good job you like a yomp because its twenty clicks inland to the compound. This is an active volcano, so you'll certainly see smoke and possibly a bit of orange. But don't worry, nothing's due. Which is for the best, as I want you to take a heavy machine gun and a rocket launcher and climb it."

"Terrific, that's absolutely terrific," said Jones.

"See here." Major Larmour indicated a rocky outcrop halfway up. "These boulders form a natural firing point. Get yourself comfortable and wait. We're inserting the others by helicopter just before dawn on Friday and when we do it's your job to make one-man war on the north side of the compound. Captain Donaldson, we'll drop you and the others on the roof – you'll have to blast your way in. Our intelligence is that it's essentially a luxury villa, but heavily fortified. Jones will be unleashing hell, so, it is hoped, the defenders will be in a state of complete confusion. But you'll have to fight your way out overland."

"What?" exclaimed Rees. The muscle-bound ex-PE teacher had been silent until then. "What the heck's wrong with the chopper?"

On his laptop Larmour summoned a map of the Kamchatka Peninsula, a two-hundred-mile lion tail dangling from eastern Russia. He indicated a spot in the middle of the tassel.

"Sharomy Air Base – it's a small interceptor base fifteen clicks from Karymsky."

"When you guys rescue Finer it's going to stir the hornet's nest to levels we've never seen before," said the spook. "They won't hesitate to shoot her down."

"And we're inserting you by Sea King, not Osprey," said Larmour. "An Osprey would be too easy to trace back to us, not deniable enough. Whereas Sea Kings are everywhere nowadays. Unfortunately, the speeds they go at we don't think it's at all likely the chopper will make it back to the coast. We've put as much armour on as we can without changing the profile."

"So you're going to sacrifice a pilot, too?" said Donaldson. "What the hell is all this?"

"Of course not," said Larmour. "He'll bail out ten clicks into the home run and there's a separate extraction plan. The chopper will keep on heading east under autopilot until it's shot down. The hope is that gets them off your trail a bit."

"Then what?" said Jackson. "There's nothing but mountains for twenty clicks. We'll be sitting ducks – and with a civilian in tow to boot."

"We think the prisoner's in good health." The intelligence office pointed to the compound. "See this? An outdoor gym built especially for Finer's use. Our satellites have seen him out there training."

Jackson was staring at the major. "You haven't answered my question, Staff. How do we get out?"

Larmour grinned. "In his old life, our man used to be a scuba diver – so he's comfortable in the water too. And that got us thinking." He tapped the lake.

"We got a diver in a couple of months ago to do some exploring. There's a cave network off the east side, some of it above the water table. The idea, and I think it's a good one, is that during all the mayhem you scuba down to the cave, find the air pocket, and then hide and wait until they think you've got away. They'd never dream you could be so close. Then when things have calmed down you'll hike to another RV where an Osprey will exfiltrate you. You'll take a mask, oxygen tank and dry suit for Finer."

Donaldson was incredulous. "Food? Warmth? Toilet facilities?"

"Our man's done a few legs back and forth to the chamber already – rations, spare oxygen tanks and some blankets are in there now. We'll give you purification tablets for water and you can shit in an adjoining chamber. You'll get to know each other pretty well though, I daresay."

"Wait a minute, how do I get out?" said Jones.

"You're going to summit Karymsky," said Larmour. "Then you're going in."

"*In?* I am going *into* a live volcano?"

"That's it," said Larmour.

"You lot have gone absolutely crackers now," said Jones. "This has got to be a wind-up."

"It's hot in there but not lethal," said Larmour. "And you'll have a mask against the fumes. The point is that your body heat will be covered up if they're using infra-red cameras. Nobody would think you'll be mad enough to enter a live volcano, that's the genius of it. There's food and water in there now too and a rim to shelter under. You won't need blankets."

"I don't like it," said Jackson. "Far too complex."

"It's as simple as we could make it," said Larmour. "Besides, we're the SBS. Thinking outside the box is what we do, remember? By Strength and Guile."

Donaldson turned to his men. "Well, this is it lads, the sharp end. This is what we've trained for, all our lives. And we'll do it well."

"Just to be clear, you are shooting to kill," said Larmour.

Donaldson eyed the spook. "If we're identified, we're looking at war, aren't we?"

"There won't be a war," said the spy. "Not on your account, anyway. The Russians will be far too embarrassed at having Finer whisked from under their noses. They're a macho bunch, Moscow, much concerned with losing face."

"Madness it is, absolute madness," muttered Jones.

"He's important to us," said the spy. "We realise we're asking a lot of you chaps, by the way. So by way of danger money we'll be doubling your pension pots – I've got the paperwork here for you to sign."

They all sat up straighter.

"Well that's a bit of all right then, isn't it?" piped Jones. "Double bubble!"

"And if we get caught?" asked Donaldson. "What then? Are you coming in for us? Or are we deniable along with the chopper?"

There was a long silence.

"Don't get caught," said the spy.

79

"Don't get caught," said Harkness.

"Don't worry, I won't," replied his passenger.

They were parked outside a stuccoed Georgian terrace a stone's throw from the Russian Embassy at 5 Kensington Palace Gardens. In the vehicle were Harkness, McCartney, Hastings and the operative supplied by Milo Fallon of Corporate Solutions Ltd. Jason Moss looked impressively Russian – tall, blond and pallid with deep-set eyes – but his accent was as estuary as they come. Then he had slipped into pitch-perfect Russian. The company's fee was another £20,000, which Harkness and Hastings went fifty–fifty on; he had blown most of his savings.

They checked and double-checked the secret camera that would film what transpired within the embassy. Shooting through a hole in the third button of Moss's shirt, the recorder itself had shrunk markedly since Harkness's time with the service. Nowadays it was the breadth and thickness of a hotel matchbox and sown into Moss's shirt. McCartney had been unable to find the recorder even during a pat-down. In addition to recording on a micro SD card, the device relayed the footage live to Harkness's smartphone using an app called PV Cam Finder. To set up the sting, Filip Åkesson had discovered the format of FSB email addresses and established a new one in the name of a fictitious agent. He then informed Richard Wakeford that his handler had suffered a stroke and summoned him to a meeting with his new spymaster. That the suggested location was in the embassy had been sufficient to satisfy him.

Fallon had recced the embassy personally, a grand mansion on the Bayswater Road where security was lax. A single elderly security guard was charged with searching bags in the courtyard, thus frequently distracted. Oddly, although the upper ground floor windows were barred, the lower ones were not. And as many staff wore identity badges it was a simple matter to photograph one from a distance and concoct a replica.

"*Srazhat sya,*" murmured Jason Moss once the camera was transmitting.

Into battle.

Then he set off down the road.

Harkness parked in a bay opposite the embassy and consulted his smartphone. The images were blotchy but clear as a kindly Nepalese security guard checked Moss's bag; Fallon, next in line, caused a scene. Moss used the distraction to hop into the light-well, landing on all fours and trying a lower ground floor window. It didn't open. He tried the next one. Fastened shut. The security guard was ten feet away, his back to the intruder as Fallon shrieked in protest. Moss tried the final window. Also locked. Without hesitation their man stepped out of the light-well and walked smartly around the building.

"Good, isn't he?" said Harkness.

Moss paced down a side alley, London brick flowing past on both sides of Harkness's screen. This was tunnel vision. He emerged into a large garden. A back door was open with three people smoking outside, but nobody objected as Moss stepped into the building. He was in. Now Moss needed to commandeer a vacant room; assuming Wakeford was on time, he was four minutes away. This was the diciest part of a very dicey plan. Moss tried a door.

"What is it?" cried the inhabitant in Russian. "Can't you see I'm busy?"

Moss tried another door and got a still more unfriendly reception. It was like a high-stakes gameshow where the price of failure was a diplomatic incident. But the third meeting room was vacant, and the watchers in the car sighed with relief. A watercooler; whiteboards; a portrait of the president; through the window Harkness saw the guard checking another bag. Moss affixed an 'in use' sign to the door and headed for reception.

Harkness looked up to see Lord Wakeford walk *right past them*. Tweeds, umbrella and a copy of *The Guardian*, he looked every inch the liberal English gentleman. It was a rush to be so close to him: Harkness could see the whorls on the back of Wakeford's neck and an errant piece of cotton on his elbow.

In 5 Kensington Palace Gardens Moss had emerged into the reception on the right side of security. Embassies are big and busy places where new faces from the mother country pass through each day, and nobody questioned his presence there. Wakeford walked through the front door and now Harkness saw Orientalist's face. They were doing him over in 360 degrees. The Orientalist knew exactly what boxes to fill as he signed himself in – he had done this before – and Moss introduced himself. They shook hands, and then he led Wakeford into the bowels of the building. When they were in the meeting room he closed the door.

"Lord Wakeford," he began. "Thank you so much for coming."

80

On the other side of the planet it was an hour before dawn. A cable-laying boat flying the Filipino ensign loitered in international waters, just east of the Kuril Trench in the north Pacific; an old Westland Sea King was warming up on the vessel's helipad. The three commandos stood on deck facing east, the approach of dawn visible over the grandness of the Pacific.

"Cheer up, you'll see another one," said Rees, slapping Jackson on the back.

When they were airborne and in a losing race with the approach of daylight they did a final kit-check. Each man wore black combat fatigues without insignia and no one carried identification. They were under no illusions as to what this meant in the event of their capture – the fate of a spy – and privately each man had considered putting a bullet in his own head in this eventuality. They had the Special Forces privilege of choosing their own weapons; Donaldson and Rees carried the French FAMAS assault rifle while Jackson bore a Beretta ARX 160, more accurate at range. Each man also carried a Glock pistol and commando knife. Thirty feet below the aircraft the Pacific was a slick of gleaming black speeding along beneath them, moonlight glinting on its surface.

"What do you make of all the killing people, Staff?" Rees shouted over the engine noise.

Donaldson's mouth was loose and one eyebrow raised; for a moment his expression remained immobile.

Then he said, "I don't particularly like it. Why?"

"It's just that – well, I've shot quite a few people, but the Taliban were all mad fucks. These will just be normal lads, right?"

"Look, now is not the time for a fucking Socratic dialogue," said Donaldson.

Before Rees could answer his water bottle toppled over backwards; the engine whine had changed and the craft tilted up. Through the cockpit Kamchatka rushed to meet them. Surf broke white across the shore and a whale skeleton was cast up on the sands, its ribcage ghostly in the moonlight. They crossed a broad stony riverbed where a group of bears scattered before the aircraft, lolloping away in twos and threes; then the helicopter followed the path of a valley, and their stomachs heaved as it dipped and swerved expertly around the hillsides.

Then the dreaded announcement crackled through the intercom: "Karymsky two minutes, Karymsky two minutes."

Donaldson made out the giant cone of the volcano ahead, like a Japanese screen painting as vapour issued from the summit.

"This is it," said Jackson. "Good luck, everybody."

All three men lowered ultraviolet goggles and masks and attached themselves to the line.

On the ground Jones had heard the approach. He primed his rocket launcher and aimed for the guard tower, the weapon emitting a plangent electronic drone as it locked onto the target. On the pink and violet screen he could see two soldiers leaning against the gantry and smoking.

"Sorry, guys," he mouthed.

Sentries patrolled the northern perimeter and three men were already doing press-ups outside. Jones's machine gun was set up in the crook of two boulders nearby, with an extended muzzle to disguise the flashes. One of the men in the guard tower stiffened and cocked his head, as if hearing something in the distance.

"Watch this," murmured Jones as his finger tensed on the trigger.

With a *fizz* and a *whoosh* the missile streaked down the volcano, a vision of Guy Fawkes Night as it traced a wavering line of sparks through the night. Two seconds later it hit the guardhouse and detonated in a ferocious *kaboom*, phosphorus and flame turning night into day. At that exact moment the Sea King popped up over the ridge to the east and came skimming down the mountainside. Jones opened up with the machine gun, raking across the sentries and scything through the group taking exercise. Other men came running and Jones took no pleasure in cutting them down. *Just get it over with.* The flesh on his cheeks jiggled and the heat of the weapon seared his face. This is what it must have been like on Omaha Beach, he reflected as the figures skittled over. As a defender.

The helicopter was no more than a flea as it circled the plain to approach from the south. Then it was over the lake, coming in directly so Jones saw the machine in full frontal. The Welshman's second rocket blew the main entrance sky-high, and as chunks of debris somersaulted through the air an obscure memory popped into his mind: of setting fire to a bench in his local park as a fourteen-year-old. He'd matured into a decent man, he reckoned. Half-naked men stumbled from their huts and those closest to the entrance were on fire; with another splurge of angry spinning lead Jones put them out of their torture. Then the helicopter crossed the southern perimeter and sprayed sidewinders down into the compound, the eight smoke trails making a spider of the aircraft as they descended symmetrically from a central point. This was the otherworldly beauty warfare sometimes conjures: like napalm over Vietnam or parachutes above Normandy all drifting in formation. Works of art for warriors with the world as their canvas. Then the sidewinders delivered their payload and the compound was lost within a cloak of dye.

Small-arms fire rattled the helicopter's armour and it pitched and rolled as the pilot sought the building's roof. The blast door slid open and there it was just below them, a model made real as the rotors blasted smoke clear.

"Watch this!" yelled Jackson.

And all three soldiers dived out of the aircraft.

81

"How's Osintsev bearing up?" Wakeford enquired with trademark graciousness.

"Not so good," replied Moss. "Out of his coma, but still can't speak."

Harkness felt powerless to watch. He had subcontracted his future to this man at ruinous expense.

"We go back a long way, you know," Wakeford was saying. "It was Osintsev who recruited me actually, when I first alerted them to these matters back in 1997."

Harkness felt a burst of adrenaline hit his stomach. So Wakeford had been involved from the beginning. What a break! But would Moss seize the opportunity?

"Did Osintsev believe you, then? When you first told him?"

Excellent question.

"No, I think he thought I was rather mad," said Wakeford. "Until he saw that it worked, of course. And the rest his history. I'm still awaiting my Hero of the Russian Federation Award, by the way."

"I'm sure it is..." Moss's pause was an exquisitely Russian mannerism. "In the post. And to think it all stemmed from a single psychologist. What a difference he has made to our national story."

Moss was winging it blatantly now and Harkness gripped the car door.

"He brought back self-respect to the Russian people," said Wakeford. "He was and is a genius, an Einstein of the human mind. It seems harsh that he has spent the last few decades locked up. In another life he'd have a Nobel Prize."

"Quite right," said Moss.

"I still watch the debriefing video myself sometimes," Wakeford murmured. "His insights remain quite revolutionary. And I... I find it guides me today, in my own work here."

"You still have a copy of the tape?" Moss had spotted the opportunity.

"In my safe, yes," said Wakeford. "That was agreed with your predecessor a long time ago."

"Unfortunately that is *not* a state of affairs that can continue," said Moss. "All copies must now be with us – especially after recent untoward events at your premises. It can no longer be considered a safe environment for classified material. Surely you understand this?"

Harkness was hunched forward in his seat now, staring at the phone.

"The raid was organised at the highest echelons of MI6 with the help of that creature Hastings," said Wakeford. "Must have been. As you know, she won't be with us much longer."

"Remind me when you mean to attend to her?" said Moss.

He had erred and the Orientalist frowned, studying the imposter's face. Harkness could make out individual pores on Wakeford's nose.

"But we already have acted," he replied after an eternity. "We got her in Parliament the other day. You know this. Three to four months."

In the backseat of the car Hastings was examining her cuticles.

"I had not been brought up to speed with that detail yet," said Moss.

Wakeford removed the piece of cotton from his elbow. "Should I destroy the tape?"

"No," said Moss. "I must account for it physically. Go back to your shop. We will send a courier to collect it later today – he'll tell you that he's there to collect a mint copy of *Kings of the Hittites* by David Hogarth."

This knowledge of his own shop seemed to comfort Wakeford.

"Have you thought any more about the child?" he asked.

"The *child?*" mouthed Harkness.

"A little," Moss blustered. "How have your own views developed?"

Wakeford sighed. "Gosport's a tough nut to crack, but I still think you should get him out."

In the car Harkness's eyes were wide. Gosport was an MI6 base mainly used for training; he'd been there himself.

"We are considering this carefully," said Moss.

The interview was concluded; Moss departed through the smokers' exit. And in the car Harkness wondered how to break it to Hastings that she'd possibly been poisoned.

*

Regular customers at R. Wakeford Rare Booksellers were surprised to find the lord himself manning the till that afternoon, a rare occurrence indeed. Before long a car parked on Charing Cross Road – the hastily fabricated diplomatic number plate was a further reassurance – and to underline the point the Corporate Solutions operative flagrantly parked in a bus lane. The ticket could be added to Harkness's bill. Wakeford passed over a padded envelope and half an hour later it was in the Bloomsbury halls of residence. Harkness wrote Fallon a cheque and tore it open; a VHS tape with a yellowing label slid into his hands. It simply had a date: *17 апреля 1998 г.* Lord Richard Wakeford had been engineered into handing over the direst secret of kleptocratic Russia. Milo Fallon had delivered the goods once more.

"Can I hold on to the camera and shirt for a few days?" asked Harkness.

"Do you have any idea how much they are worth?" said Fallon.

"We've just given you twenty grand."

The Dundonian sighed. "Let me draw up a contract…"

82

Rope whistled through Donaldson's carabiner as he fast-roped onto the roof, its high-pitched whine competing with the howl of the rotors and the blasts of assault rifles being discharged beneath him in all directions. To the north he heard the far-off rip of Jones's machine gun and all around the compound were shouts of panic. Donaldson landed on the roof first, followed by the others; at once the chopper banked away, sparks dancing on its underbelly. They were committed now, marooned in Russian territory: only surprise and martial excellence could get them out. Jackson and Rees fired downwards from the roof; men were scattered across the ground like dolls cast aside by some malevolent child. In that instant Donaldson appreciated the merciless-ness of his colleagues for the first time, and he realised that he was merciless, too. Then he leapt over the side of the building, landing on a balcony with a jolt that hurt his diaphragm. Rees was with him too as Jackson provided cover. There was a lull in the firefight; they had killed everyone in the vicinity.

Crack!

Donaldson felt heat and air rush past him as Rees detonated a limpet mine, blowing the reinforced shutters open. They stepped into a darkened room: huge flatscreen television, snooker table, minibar. A guard dashed in and opened fire with a pistol, but the smoke and chemicals had blinded him and Rees put three bullets in his chest. They stepped into the corridor and immediately heard a voice. "I'm in here…"

Another reinforced steel door.

"Stand well back and protect your face and eyes," shouted Rees. "If you have a mattress, put it up against the wall and stand behind it."

"OK."

Crack!

The cell door was blown open and the mattress flopped to the floor. Behind it was the man they had come to find. Brian Finer was balding, pallid and quaking with fear. Donaldson outlined the plan, handing him an oxygen tank and mask.

"Your plan is completely insane," said Finer, a wet patch spreading across his tracksuit bottoms.

"That's as maybe," said Donaldson. "But we're doing it anyway. And so are you. Do you remember how to use the equipment?"

"I think so."

"Then let's go."

They fought their way to ground level and burst from the front door. Up above them Jackson had assumed a position of complete domination, but on seeing their emergence he attached a rope and leapt from the roof, abseiling down to his colleagues. A black-brown blur came barrelling across the ground towards them, a beast of many heads. The three Dobermans leapt through space and affixed themselves to Jackson's throat, cutting off his scream. Jackson was sent skittling across the ground and began thrashing about. Glimpses of fang and flapping ears; slobber and blood catapulted from the fracas. Rees took careful aim and shot one of the dogs. Steadied himself. Shot another. Then he was shot in the back and sank to his knees. Jackson stuck the remaining Doberman in the ribcage with his knife and swiftly cut its throat, then he and Donaldson dragged Rees against the side of the building.

"Lung collapsed..." gasped Rees.

"You'll be fine," said Donaldson.

But Rees would not be fine, and they all knew this simple fact. This was not the Afghanistan War; no medivac helicopter was airborne; he would not be on a Camp Bastion operating table in thirty minutes' time. Instead their only sanctuary was the lake, where ice-cold water would fill his chest cavity. Rees pulled out a Glock and shot himself through the temple, turning cross-eyed as the bullet pulverised his brains. The smokescreen was thinning by the second.

"We've got to keep moving," said Jackson.

Donaldson grabbed Finer by the arm and they darted to the southern perimeter. They blasted their way through the first fence, and then through the second. But no onslaught came: behind them was a hiatus in the fighting while to the north the battle sounded frenzied. Men were trying to run from the barracks to the compound but Jones kept cutting them down. He had the entire base in a stranglehold and for the first time Donaldson began to consider the prospect that they might make it. He let off another smoke bomb to cover their retreat, and then they were out and sprinting across tufted grass and dewy earth, ditching packs and assault rifles in their flight. And even as dawn spread beyond the mountains they saw the lake right up ahead, its waters dull and dark as pig lead. Masks on. Oxygen connected. Shouts behind them in the mist now, but getting closer. No more noises of battle to the north: Jones was running or dead. They plunged beneath the surface, seeking the safety of murk and of depth. Finer clung to Donaldson's belt, but he was kicking too, kept kicking. He wanted to survive this, to get out. They had seconds to find the cave or Donaldson knew the cold and pressure would claim him and all those men would have died for nothing, including his friend.

83

Harkness was back in Tottenham Court Road to source a VHS player when he thought he saw her. The back of an elfin head, that diminutive frame; her walk away from him with typical purpose and energy. His response was physiological, a sway of the stomach and a *bang* in the chest, and he found himself crossing the road to overtake. But it wasn't her.

It was all very odd. The melancholy he had lived with for thirty years was like a single low cello note, always running through him. Yet on spotting Olivié's lookalike he'd heard the crash of cymbals and the singing of flutes. Come to think of it, he hadn't thought of Elizabeth all day either. Normally memories of her would come to him by eleven a.m. at the latest before recurring sporadically throughout each day. *Face facts, Harkness,* he reflected: *you've been thunder-bolted, you've fallen head over heels in love.* Not for the first time he cursed his own absurdity.

When he returned to the halls of residence, McCartney, Hastings and Johansen squashed into a tiny bedroom to view the footage. Harkness weighed the cassette tape in his hands before inserting it. They had traversed three continents for this object, negotiated some of the remotest and most dangerous environments in the world; they'd fought jungles and rivers, and battled across mountains and plains. Now they were going to find out what it had all been about.

The tape began with VHS fuzz before forming itself into an interrogation room, grey and spare with feeble strip lighting. The middle-aged prisoner was ashen and bruised, his features washed out further by the poor quality of the video. He was tall and balding with a scathing quality to his grey eyes. Beads of static pulsed across the screen: this video had been watched many times.

"Then you understand," said a voice off-camera. "You are staying here for the rest of your days. That is already decided."

A tremble went through the man.

"The first question, then, is about the nature of your life with us. The type of food that you eat, whether you get books and television and exercise. Cigarettes and alcohol. Even prostitutes and illegal drugs, if that's your thing. Or whether you are tortured and kept awake and made to do hard labour and sleep in a cold room. The second question is about your wife and young daughter – whether they are killed, or provided for. If you choose to cooperate, we propose a monthly stipend of £10,000 to be paid into your wife's account."

For five seconds the man looked directly into the camera with such loathing that his eyelids flickered. Then some inner resolve seemed to break.

"You win," he said.

"Then please, tell us about your work. From the beginning."

"Can I have something to eat first, please?"

When the tape restarted Finer was leaning towards his interrogator.

"Prepare to be amazed," he said.

*

"The human mind has two systems, two modes of operation," Finer began. "The first, which I call Old Brain, is what you use for every snap judgement, movement, perception and quick decision. How far away is that wall? Is crossing this road dangerous? What direction is a sound coming from? Does this person look happy? What does the sentence, 'I like dogs' mean? Is there anger in someone's voice? What's two plus two? The answer to all these questions is computed automatically and instantly by Old Brain. It's the basic operating system that tells you what's going on, and it makes simple decisions effortlessly."

"OK…"

"All sentient animals have Old Brain. When a domestic cat evaluates whether it can jump across a gap, it's making an automatic mental calculation using Old Brain. It has no voluntary control over Old Brain and cannot turn it off. You could never train a cat – nor indeed, a human – to simply ignore a charging buffalo, for example. Old Brain takes over and makes survival a total priority. It is the operating system used for ninety-eight per cent of human decision-making. It's also very good at what it does, as you would expect of a processor that evolved over billions of years. Now, work out fourteen times twenty-three in your head."

After a lengthy pause the interrogator said, "It's three hundred and twenty-two."

"Correct. But you couldn't come up with that answer off the top of your head, instantly and automatically. You probably multiplied the twenty-three by ten, and had to hold that answer in your memory while you worked out four times twenty-three before adding them together. This calculation is too complex for Old Brain to handle – it goes far beyond Old Brain's capability for mental load. To do it you had to engage something else. That was what I call New Brain, the higher cognitive powers that our species – and only our species – is in possession of."

"Mode I versus Mode II," whispered Harkness.

Dr Christodoulou claimed it was 'Mode II' that enables chimpanzees to identify the elimination of all rivals as a bountiful reproductive stratagem.

"But New Brain is not just for doing arithmetic," Finer continued. "All advanced reasoning, problem-solving, symbolic thinking and analytical decision-making is done there. As an aside, try asking someone what fourteen times twenty-three is when you are walking alongside them. Almost certainly they'll stop dead to work it out. Unfortunately, New Brain can only undertake a limited workload. Push it too hard and it overloads. You have to assign additional energy and concentration to use it for difficult questions, hence why a walker asked to do long multiplication jerks to a halt. Try it on a friend! So in answer to your question, my work is about Old Brain and New Brain, the frailties of both systems and how they can be tricked. Because Old Brain often *gets it wrong*."

"What do you mean?" asked the interrogator.

"It has biases, blind spots. Predictable Achilles heels. And if people can be manipulated into using Old Brain when making a decision, they can be engineered into coming up with an incorrect answer. This has implications for politics and democracy. If you can stop people from applying New Brain, you can influence their judgement. You can *make them do what you want.* People can be blind to the obvious – and they are blind to their own blindness."

84

"Tell me more about New Brain," said the Russian.

"Well, if Old Brain is constantly generating thoughts, judgements and feelings, one of New Brain's jobs is to scrutinise those judgements and either approve them – whereupon they become beliefs – or reject them. Imagine, if you will, a good-looking and charismatic politician. Old Brain is preconditioned to notice the strong jawline and symmetry in the face. It registers the confident speaking. It will automatically make sense of his or her words and be preconditioned to give them credence. That's why the uglier candidate rarely becomes Prime Minister."

Harkness struggled to think of an example to disprove this.

"Now, imagine I'm calling a press briefing on domestic politics," said Finer. "And you're in the audience. 'It's time that we cracked down hard on those Belfast communities still harbouring terrorists.' Old Brain processed the meaning of that sentence automatically – you couldn't *not* understand it. New Brain's job is to apply higher reasoning and judgement to the claim and reject or accept it. If you engaged New Brain to analyse the implications of a campaign against Catholic communities in Northern Ireland – and looked at the empirical success rate of such approaches around the world – you might deduce it would merely push more young people into the arms of the IRA. New Brain is capable of assessing the statistics for the number of young males whose behaviour becomes more violent if subjected to draconian measures. But a lazy thinker rarely uses their New Brain – because cognitive heavy lifting is hard work. For most people, it's not an intrinsically pleasurable sensation trying to calculate fourteen times twenty-three or making sense of disparate pieces of statistical evidence. And it uses up a lot of energy, which once upon a time was at a premium. So a lazy thinker will surf through life using Old Brain whenever possible, relying on the evolutionary, calorie-preserving impulse to use the least effort possible. A lazy-thinking population will not apply New Brain to the decisions and policies of its rulers."

"Fascinating," said the interrogator.

"Do you have the internet in this building?"

"Da."

"Great. Please print out something called the Müller-Lyer illusion. I'll need a ruler, too."

The recording stopped and started again; now Finer held a diagram in his hand. "Which is the longest line?"

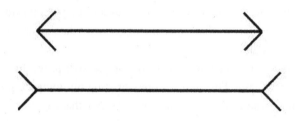

"The bottom one."

"Measure them."

A moment's pause, then: "Ha! They're the same length."

"Old Brain got it wrong. And now – even though your New Brain *knows* they are the same length – the bottom line still looks longer! As I say, you cannot turn Old Brain off. But Old Brain doesn't only fall for visual illusions. There are also such things as *illusions of thought*. And just like with visual illusions, Old Brain's cognitive illusions cannot be turned off at will either."

"Give me an example."

Finer wrote on a piece of paper:

A pencil and sharpener are £1.10 in total.
The pencil is a pound more expensive than the sharpener.
What's the price of the sharpener?

He handed the paper and pen to the interrogator and there was a pause as he wrote down his answer.

Finer smiled.

"Are you sure about that?"

"Sure I'm sure."

"Almost everyone says 10p, too. But that's Old Brain's reply. It *feels* right. Now try engaging New Brain. Actually do the maths. If the sharpener cost 10p, then the total cost would be £1.20: 10p for the sharpener, £1.10 for the pencil. If you'd applied the New Brain to check the intuitive answer – if you'd used reasoning, not a snap judgement – you'd have found the correct answer is 5p. You *knew* I was testing your New Brain, and yet you *still* let Old Brain blurt out the wrong answer. Now, imagine propagandising directly to people's Old Brain, lulling them into making the decisions you prefer…"

Finer wrote on the piece of paper again.

Pizza Sick

"Something amazing happened when you saw those words," he said. "Your mind automatically generated some loose scenario linking pizza to throwing up. Old Brain instantly came to a judgement on how likely this was and the danger presented to you. There were minor physiological changes too, though you wouldn't have noticed them. Your heart rate slightly increased and the hair on your arms rose imperceptibly, all thanks to Old Brain. The main part of Old Brain's job is to *make sense of the world*, and it does that by constantly seeking causal relationships, looking for coherence. It's a *machine for jumping to conclusions*. These two words have now primed you at a subconscious level with a very slight reluctance to eat pizza. If we were to show them to a hundred of your staff and subsequently offer pizza or burgers for lunch in the canteen, we'd see a slight statistical drop in the number of people choosing pizza – even though New Brain knows these are just words. That's the power of Old Brain. That's its capacity for manipulation."

"This is incredible," said McCartney.

"It's almost time for lunch," Finer was saying somewhere in Russia in 1998.

He wrote on a piece of paper:

$S O \_ P$

"Now, what's the missing letter? What's the word?"

"U," said the interrogator. "The word is soup."

"Indeed. Statistically, if food's just been mentioned, people are much more likely to say 'Soup'. But my experiments show that if I'd primed you by mentioning washing and laundry instead, you'd probably have said 'Soap'. Primed with thoughts of lunch, however, all sorts of food-associated ideas are rippling through your subconscious courtesy of Old Brain." Finer smiled. "Despite what you thought you knew, your knowing mind, your New Brain, is not actually in the driving seat at all. And the effects are very powerful. People who have been primed with the idea of money – even, for example, by a mere Monopoly set left on the table – were more likely to act selfishly in my tests. Interestingly, they also show a greater preference to be alone. Priming people with the idea of death, meanwhile, makes them more aware of their mortality and they become more receptive to authoritarian policies. Again, the implications for politics are self-evident. If I wanted you to fear a nuclear war between our countries, I would run an advert for mushroom soup before the headlines. It would prime your subconscious with thoughts of a nuclear explosion – and make you more receptive to my message. Sounds absurd. But it works."

"That can't be true," muttered Johansen in the twenty-first century.

"Your incredulity is understandable," said Finer, as if reading her mind. "All your life you thought New Brain made the decisions, not that you knew it by that term. But it's built on and controlled by Old Brain – the stranger within you. By the way, the findings of my experiments are not a statistical fluke. *You too* would be more likely to agree with an authoritarian argument if you'd been primed with thoughts of your own mortality."

"Maybe..." said the interviewer.

"You would. And let me tell you about another peculiarity. When a problem is simple or you are well-practised at it, you experience a pleasurable feeling of *cognitive ease* – just as relaxing on a sofa is more enjoyable than running up a hill. The brain is an incredibly thirsty organ, you see. That's the reason it took hominids five million years to grow such big brains, which use up valuable proteins and carbohydrates that could otherwise be used for muscle and power. Brawn counts for a lot in the animal kingdom."

High alert in the Bloomsbury halls of residence as Finer veered toward human origins.

"One thing that generates cognitive ease is *familiarity*," he said. "The more familiar you are with something, the more you're likely to trust it. That makes perfect evolutionary sense too, of course. An animal that isn't suspicious of novelty will probably not be about very long. To prove it, I took out a small page-three advert in the London *Evening Standard*. For three months, my ad contained one of the following Turkish-sounding words: kadigra, saricik, nansoma and iktitaf. They mean nothing, by the way. One of the words I ran only once, two of them fairly often, one of them lots. Then I questioned a large sample of *Standard* readers as to whether the words meant something good or something bad. The words I showed most were viewed far more favourably than those I did rarely. Yet none of the readers recalled even seeing the mysterious adverts. I repeated this experiment many times – with faces, shapes, symbols and so on.

Always, the result was the same. I call this the *mere exposure effect*. Simply being exposed to something repeatedly makes you trust it. Old Brain mistakes *familiarity* for *truth*. Out of laziness, it is *answering the wrong question*. The mind doesn't ask, 'Is this a good thing?' but 'How familiar am I with it?' And the lazy mind – that almost all of us possess – does not call in New Brain to check. This has relevance to political messaging. Our new Prime Minister Mr Blair, for example, plans to increase spending on public services. Now, if I were to place repeated messages in newspapers referring to national debt, then subconsciously readers would begin to believe *this* was the pressing public concern – as opposed to, for the sake of argument, the natural state of our national finances since the Napoleonic Wars. Conversely, if I were Mr Blair, I'd constantly refer to it as 'investing' not 'spending' until familiarity had bred a subconscious acceptance of the fact that people's taxes had somehow not really been 'spent' at all but were still there somewhere, accruing interest."

"That's neat," said the Russian.

"Or let's say Mr Blair wanted to declare war on Iran – not that he'd be so daft, he seems a fairly sensible chap. If I was his press secretary, I'd prime people with messages about long-range missile attacks, nuclear testing, that sort of thing. Then the public's Old Brain would be more receptive to a push for war. Not everyone would be swayed by priming, of course, perhaps as little as three or four per cent. But three to four per cent is more than enough to swing an election—"

Harkness hit pause, the pallid psychologist frozen in time. Everyone in the room looked shocked; Johansen was shaking her head.

"I think," said Harkness slowly, "that we may have stumbled on the scandal of the century."

85

"And now, it's time for *PM*."

In the studio the presenter was experiencing the surreal comprehension that his microphone had just been connected to a million cars and kitchens full of real sentient people.

"This afternoon, the speculation is over," he began, pushing the thought aside. "The United Kingdom *will* be alongside the United States of America when it puts boots on the ground in the Middle East – *if* Parliament approves of it. A date for the vote has been set for just three weeks' time."

As they played a clip of the Prime Minister outside Number Ten the presenter made eye contact with his producer in the gallery. And their expressions were grim.

"Britain has *never* ducked its responsibilities on the world stage," said the premier, "nor can it now. As only too many attacks on the streets of our country have shown in recent years, we are *all* put in mortal danger by the extremists."

In the studio the presenter pressed the cough button to cut the microphone and cleared his throat. They were in the old wing of Broadcasting House where the studios were gloriously art deco, and the cloth-covered walls made it pleasantly warm.

"As two polls show growing support for military action," he continued, "we'll ask: what's behind the swell of public support for a ground invasion in the face of past disasters?"

Next came the ageing leader of the opposition, apoplectic with fury as a crowd of young supporters cheered. "How many bodies must there be, how much blood, how much folly, before the West finally learns the idiocy of trying to meddle in the Middle East?"

"And in a dramatic day of developments on the world stage, we've got a breaking news story from Latvia – where armed pro-Russian demonstrators have seized one wing of the Parliament building in Riga to demand re-unification. Spontaneous celebrations have broken out in Moscow and St Petersburg. We'll be asking, will the Baltic States go the way of Crimea? And what, if anything, is the West going to actually do about it? With the BBC News headlines now, we join…"

86

"I'm not convinced," said the interrogator.

So Finer wrote down another sentence.

> *After he'd spent all day visiting tourist sights with the London crowds, Alex discovered his wallet was missing.*

"What happened here?" asked Finer.

"He got pickpocketed."

"Old Brain strikes again! As I say, a machine for jumping to conclusions. Statistically speaking, people are far more likely to mislay a wallet than have it stolen – even in London. When I showed this sentence to a hundred people and later asked them to recall words in it, more people remembered the word 'pickpocket' than 'sights' – even though 'pickpocket' isn't in the sentence."

A gruff laugh off camera.

"Old Brain automatically seeks *coherence* and pulls together a plausible plot to satisfy that. Your subconscious mind is bent on identifying traits, motives, plots. It's another evolutionary hangover from prehistoric days, when Old Brain was constantly on guard for betrayal by other hunter-gatherers in your band. Once you know this, it's possible to speak directly to Old Brain with clever language, bespoke propaganda. You need to engage New Brain to give the lie to it. But most people don't bother to apply New Brain. Most people don't ask, 'Is this really important?'"

"Give me a real-world example of that," said the interrogator.

"Sure thing. Throughout the entirety of the Troubles, the IRA killed about 1,700 people. Yet during the 1980s there were more than 5,000 deaths on British roads *every year*. Now, which issue do you think resonated more in the public subconscious that decade? What will my daughter most associate with the eighties when she's grown up? Road safety, or Irish Republican terrorism? Old Brain makes the judgement. Most of us assess the danger of terrorism not by the statistical chance of actually being killed – which would be a New Brain judgement – but by its emotive power and thus by the *ease with which examples come to mind*. Again, lazy Old Brain answers an easier question. Not 'What's more dangerous to me, terrorism or traffic?' but 'How easily can I think of an example?'"

An appreciative laugh off-camera.

"Now, during the Troubles, terrorist events got huge amounts of news coverage," said Finer. "Old Brain effortlessly conjures up numerous examples of terrorist attacks – whereas most people struggle to think of more than one or two road accidents that have affected people they know. The fluency with which Old Brain does so makes it seem like terrorism is a real and present danger. Whereas of course it is actually extremely rare, and the vast majority will never see a terror attack nor know anybody who has. So New Brain's take should be that terrorism is not actually a big threat at all – and never has been. Stories get massive news coverage because of emotional intensity, and that same emotional intensity distorts our views as to how common they are. Because the world conjured up by Old Brain is not an exact replica of the world as it really is. Old Brain is prone to cognitive illusions, and these can be exploited to make the public back the policies you want them to."

"How might you go about doing this? Practically speaking."

"Let's just say Blair goes ahead with this fictitious invasion of Iran. If I was in charge of gaining support for it, I'd come up with a simple, emotive message – for instance, we believe Iran means to bomb a jumbo jet – and repeat it endlessly. We've seen the intelligence, we know it's going to happen unless we take on the Mad Mullahs, that kind of thing. The images of broken bodies and debris fields being invoked are exactly the sort of visual, visceral thought that speaks straight to our Old Brain. Familiarity breeds acceptance and trust at a subconscious level. It would permeate the national Old Brain. Certainly it would shift polling. And polling shifts MPs, when it comes to a vote in the House of Commons. Now, let's say the worst happened and a plane *was* actually taken down by Iranian-backed terrorists – another Lockerbie – and five hundred people were killed. But in 1996, there were *137 million* air journeys in or out of UK airports. That's a one in 274,000 chance of becoming a victim, *if* you are a passenger and *if* such a bombing occurred. Not really worth turning the Middle East into a warzone for when you put it like that, is it? New Brain gives us alone the ability to do complex statistical reasoning. But most people just don't bother."

"It's clever," said the interrogator.

"It's more than clever. The average voter is guided by emotion and not, as they believe, by reason. They are certainly not sensitive to differences between high and low probabilities. Understand this, and you can control the news cycle. Sometimes, a story about a particular danger grabs the public's attention. They become concerned and worried. This prompts additional coverage in the media, which produces yet more concern. Journalists compete to grab the headlines with ever-more extreme and unrepresentative examples – although the actual frequency of this bad thing happening is tiny, and it's really not important."

"Do you have a good example of that in action?"

"Certainly. A British schoolgirl named Leah Betts died after taking ecstasy a couple of years back. Ecstasy users are less likely to die from their hobby than horse riders, but nonetheless, we soon had a media feedback loop. There was mass coverage of the perils of doing E. That prompted growing concern, prompting further hysteria, prompting further coverage. It's a cascade, speaking directly to Old Brain, and it affects public policy. Yet the base rate risk – utterly tiny – is ignored by almost everyone. This is how you distract the public from things you don't want them to apply their higher intelligence to. What else happened that year? Race riots, millions unemployed, genocide in the Balkans that we were too slow to respond to."

"I see."

"Old Brain has a basic limitation when it comes to risk. We either ignore small risks completely or give them far too much attention, with no shades of grey in between. People will *almost always* ignore the base rate of actual risk when a specific tragedy comes easily to mind, the harrowing image of a dying teenage girl, say. A willingness to entertain the notion of extremely rare events happening – and let that emotion cloud one's judgement – is a classic Old Brain Achilles heel. Politicians can speak to this, if they know how. Do you have teenage children, by any chance?"

"As a matter of fact, yes."

"Have any of them ever come late back from a party?"

"Of course."

"And what came to mind?"

"All sorts of horrible imaginings," said the interrogator.

"Out of all proportion to the actual risk that something bad had happened?"

"Ha. Yes."

"Here's another thing about Old Brain. *Negativity dominates*. An angry face stands out in a happy crowd, not vice versa. The brains of humans are designed to give priority to bad news – this reflects our evolutionary history, too. By shaving time off the detection of a predator, our odds of survival and hence passing on our genes were enhanced. In a political context, bad words – *war*, *crime* – have been shown in the lab to attract our attention faster than good words, *peace*, *love*. Old Brain has an intense capacity for fear."

As Harkness listened, he realised this described almost every successful election campaign in his lifetime – and also the appeals to war. When it comes to messaging, *bad is stronger than good*. The Iraq War, which had a majority backing in opinion polls. The Scottish Independence Referendum. The 2015 election. Trump. This is how all of them were won.

87

"You've just been diagnosed with cancer," said Finer, scribbling on his paper again. "There are two possible operations you can have. Choose."

1. *Ninety per cent of patients survive at least a month.*
2. *Ten per cent of patients die in the first month.*

"I prefer the first operation," said the Russian.

Finer grinned. "So does almost everyone, using Old Brain to make a decision. But as your New Brain may have noticed, the odds of survival are actually exactly the same. They are just *framed* differently, the first in a way designed to appeal to Old Brain. Old Brain cannot ignore emotion. Mortality equals bad, survival equals good. Old Brain's snap judgement is that ninety per cent survival sounds encouraging, and a ten per cent chance of death is very frightening. You see how a canny politician can manipulate Old Brain by *framing* things right?"

"It's powerful," said the interrogator.

"Let me give you another example."

He wrote again:

A rare disease is expected to kill six hundred children. Two medical programmes are being considered. Choose which to employ.

1. *Programme A is guaranteed to save two hundred children.*

2. *Programme B has a one-third chance of saving all six hundred people, but a two-thirds chance of saving no children at all.*

"I choose Programme A," said the Russian.

"Again, you are in good company. Almost all subjects I surveyed preferred the certainty of saving some lives to the gamble. Although a bookmaker would see that both options do of course have identical value. But let's reframe it."

1. *Programme A will lead to four hundred deaths.*
2. *Programme B will lead to the one-third probability that no children will die, and a two-thirds probability that all six hundred will die.*

"Now which do you prefer?"

A dry chuckle. "Programme B looks more tempting now. But they are the same."

"I reframed it, and your Old Brain now thinks something different." Triumph gleamed in Finer's eyes. "An illusion of thought. To understand the difference between Old Brain and New Brain is to control public opinion. To brainwash people, putting it crudely. When you craft speeches and propaganda informed by this polemic, take it from me: it's the crack cocaine of political messaging. It works."

The interrogator considered this.

"It's a bit of an irony, I suppose," mused Finer. "By manipulating human intelligence you can lead people like sheep… in their millions. They have merely the illusion of choice. This is how governments can get their populations to go along with whatever they want. I daresay whoever follows President Yeltsin into the Kremlin could do with such assistance."

"I daresay."

"I want £50,000 per month for my wife and daughter and a £2 million down payment right away. I want them to know that I'm safe.

I want regular visits from them. And I want serious luxury. Then I will obtain popularity ratings for your next leader that Yeltsin could only dream of. I guarantee Russia will be behind him in his every endeavour."

A low laugh from the inquisitor. "These are discussions to be had in the fullness of time, once we have done a few tests of our own, to assure ourselves of your brilliance. But tell me, how did you come up with this... this wonder?"

"It was 1978 and I had just been awarded my first seat, at Cambridge. I was helping my daughter with her homework."

"Oh?"

"She was doing a school project on Neanderthals. Cavemen, to put it simply."

McCartney gripped Harkness's arm.

"I got interested myself. My expertise is in human psychology, of course – but then I began to wonder how the Neanderthals *thought*, and whether there was any difference between our fundamental modes of mental operation. When I saw a Neanderthal endocast – that's a mould of the inside of a skull – I got *really* interested. Because their brain capacity was actually *bigger* than that of our species, despite having a provably lower intellectual wattage. Only the Neanderthal's neocortex was much smaller than ours – eighty-five per cent of the human brain is neocortex. It's the home of human language and reasoning facilities, and it lights up like a Christmas tree when a subject uses New Brain in a CT scan. In particular, the Broca's Area was tiny in our Neanderthal cousins. This is a part of the left frontal lobe that underpins higher reasoning, and it's closely linked to speech and symbolism. You can't carry out analytical work unless you can think symbolically. How could I have thought of Old Brain and New Brain without the words to describe these concepts, in my head? The skull of Turkana Boy – he's the most famous *erectus* skeleton, found in Kenya – showed a smaller Broca's Area still. So I got thinking about how this would have affected them, too. It was my first dabbling in what's known as *cognitive archaeology*, a new field."

"Cognitive archaeology?"

"The archaeology of the mind. I learned that although scores of Neanderthal sites have been found, not one has been discovered with artefacts showing evidence of symbolic thinking, reasoning or higher thought processes. Of a New Brain. Neanderthal had a highly sophisticated Old Brain, yes, and it used intuitive processes for simple problem-solving – just as a dog, chimp or parrot does. But New Brain is indeed unique to late *Homo sapiens*, developing after what's known as the *cognitive revolution* of 70,000 BC. That's when we start seeing sudden evidence of symbolic thinking in Southern Africa, in the form of, for example, pierced shells that were obviously part of necklaces, red ochre used for body paint and so on."

"So something was astir," muttered Finer's interlocutor. "Something had definitely kicked into life."

"Indeed it had. The famous cave paintings in Europe come soon after, and we see the transition into the far more sophisticated tools of the Upper Palaeolithic – harpoons, needles for sowing and what have you. Thus, I realised how it was the development of New Brain that allowed us to replace the Neanderthals. We were using an entirely revolutionary symbolic system to process information, enabling New Brain thinking. For tens of thousands of years *Homo sapiens* had been trying to break into the Middle East and Fortress Europe from our cradle in Africa. But against these hulking Ice Age hunters? We had no chance. One genetic mutation is all it took to give us our souped-up Broca's Area – and with it speech and symbolism. New Brain. Without this new capacity for language, our thought processes would have remained forever like those of the Neanderthals, entirely intuitive and non-declarative. But inherent in New Brain and dependent upon it came our predilection and aptitude for mass murder. Our understanding, based on logic and analysis, that the world was not big enough for our two species. This is another paradox. Our neocortex, our Broca's Area, our New Brain, led the species from darkness into light and from light into darkness. Though of course Old Brain is still very much with us now, trying to leap to conclusions. Waiting to be spoken to. It underpins everything."

Twenty years in the future the profundity of these thoughts had stilled the room. Hastings was wondering how many of her prejudices stemmed from the ancient part of her brain.

"New Brain gave us both the cognisance that it would be benefi-cial to get rid of other hominids and the ability to carry the project through," said Finer. "And Eurasia was the prize. Sniff about the Neanderthal extinction long enough, and you'll hit upon the concept of New Brain – whatever you might call it by."

"How do you know that?"

"Because two other experts looking at the Neanderthal disap-pearance have already arrived at the very same conclusion, an anthropologist at the University of Nottingham and an evolu-tionary psychologist from the States. Like myself, both were paid handsomely to can their research by London and Washington respectively. We shared all this with the Americans, naturally."

"What if the academics had refused to keep quiet?"

"I'd rather not know. Anyway, the lack of New Brain in the Neanderthal mind – or in *erectus*, or in *Homo heidelbergensis* or *Homo habilis* or any of the other hominids you care to name – is why we are still here and they are gone. You can tell how violent our early ancestors were by the thickness of the skull, which has become ever more gracile up to the modern day. Less need to resist blows. But the intelligence to take killing to another level? That took sapience. So there's another paradox for you. The very thing that makes us human also made us monsters. An understanding of the Neanderthal extinction would lead to an understanding of Old Brain and New Brain. And this would bring an end to the government's powers of mind control. For mark my words, that is what it is. It's why you will find the British Secret Service is much interested in suppressing research into the disappearance of *Homo neanderthalensis*."

While Harkness and McCartney had been at the Russian Embassy, the man known to Johansen as Adriaen had got into the halls of residence and planted monitoring devices in that very room. So the very same British Secret Service were listening to every word.

88

There weren't many advantages to living in Paraguay, but proximity to the Iguazu Falls was one of them. Sir Hugh Alexander had just returned from Miami, where he'd spent two pleasant days in the company of a fellow Old Harrovian, the Prime Minister's private secretary. His mole had more news; Sir Hugh had sent this not to Hastings but via human courier to his family solicitor in Worcester. He was scared and wanted an insurance policy. Then he had returned to Asunción and driven to Iguazu. Something of the power and rage of the waterfalls spoke to him. He wanted to see them once more, to order his thoughts in the presence of such elemental nature and violence. Sir Hugh had crossed to the Argentinian bank from where he stared at the falls now: they were the jaws of a god, foaming and steaming with wrath.

A woman stood by the barrier, briefly meeting his gaze with leopardine eyes. There was something of the leopard about her stillness, too, and *she* leaned on the barrier as though it were a bough on the savannah. Sir Hugh nodded at her and peered back into the raging white below. She unsettled him.

He was grabbed by the ankles and pitched head first over the barrier.

He fell, writhing and rotating in the air like a spinning top, and in the seconds before he was devoured he knew for certain that he'd been killed for his involvement in the Wakeford affair. Then he hit the water with a body-numbing crack. He was conscious of being driven far beneath the surface, his body pummelled from all sides as if on an anvil. Then the pain and pressure were too much and that was it.

*

Gloria Hastings received the phone call at six p.m. UK time. She and De Vries set off for Worcester right away, and three hours later they were sitting in the home of Sir Hugh's family solicitor. The lawyer explained how only that morning he'd been given a dossier by one of the diplomat's civil servants to be passed to Hastings in the event of his death. Hastings, a dead woman walking for whom the coming months would be full of oncologists and blood tests and scans, took the manila folder and headed back to London. It was midnight when she got into Paddington and at once she made for the Bloomsbury bolthole.

Harkness and McCartney were consulting Blair's House of Commons speech in 2003 urging the invasion of Iraq.

> When the inspectors left in 1998, they left unaccounted for: 10,000 litres of anthrax; a far reaching VX nerve agent programme; up to 6,500 chemical munitions; at least 80 tonnes of mustard gas, possibly more than ten times that amount; unquantifiable amounts of sarin, botulinum toxin and a host of other biological poisons; an entire Scud missile programme.

"Well and truly primed," said McCartney.

"And there was the frequency of the dodgy dossier claim that Saddam could deploy biological weapons within forty-five minutes," said Harkness. "It's straight out of the Finer playbook. Familiarity breeds belief and ease of retrieval leads to a conviction that something is important. It's why successful political parties hammer the same simple message again and again."

"'Strong and stable leadership'," said McCartney. "'Long-term economic plan'. 'Take back control'."

"So you do listen to the news!" said Harkness. "Of course, this is all entirely speculative. We don't have a shred of hard evidence that Finer's insights went into Blair's speech."

But every British and American tract they found urging war – George Bush Senior in 1990, Thatcher in 1982, LBJ on Vietnam – used priming and direct appeals to Old Brain. So did the Kremlin's every pronouncement since Finer's forcible relocation. What other evidence did they have? This too ranged from the incomplete to the circumstantial. Johansen's studies of myth; Hastings' SIS report; photographs from the three mass graves they'd found and three actual bones. There was the new Ice Age Venus, which tied in with the recent killings. And finally both the footage recorded in the Russian Embassy and the video of Finer. Enough to prove incontrovertibly decades of covert psychological propaganda? Not when the allegations were so enormous.

"Why did Russia cover up what happened to the Forest People?" asked McCartney.

Harkness recalled the IQ assessments, comparing Forest People and Bantu-speaking farmers in the region. No variance in average, median or high intelligence and the brightest Ba Aka and Bantu within two IQ points of each other.

"My guess is that with outdated assessments of their so-called 'primitive' lifestyle, they thought the hunter-gatherers lacked such a developed New Brain. Whereas we've seen the intelligence of the Ba Aka for ourselves..."

Memories of an entire dinner set unfolding itself from lengths of bamboo before their eyes. McCartney touched his tribal marking.

"And they feared Sakiko might have found traces of a more ancient Armageddon in her search for the Universal Language," said Harkness. "They couldn't risk it leading to an understanding of New Brain, or it might – how can I put this – *inoculate* their people to the president's message. Anyway, for Neanderthals and *erectus*, the evidence is clear. They *didn't* have a New Brain. This *did* lead to their eradication. A study of the Neanderthal extinction *would* lead eventually to an understanding of our two modes of thinking. And if that was exposed, it could no longer be manipulated. The Russians

– and possibly the Brits and Americans too – would lose their most powerful propaganda tool. A proven way of making people do what they want."

The ticker on the BBC News Channel was rolling breaking news.

UK ambassador to Paraguay 'commits suicide' in Iguazu Falls jump.

"That's Hastings' source!" shouted Harkness.

He turned up the volume, but details were sketchy and they soon cut to a story about a decorated SBS soldier who had died during a training accident. A knock on the door interrupted them and Hastings breathlessly brought them up to speed. Sir Hugh's final dispatch contained three revelations. First, that the SBS raid had been success-ful; Finer was being debriefed at MI6's training centre, in a Victorian coastal stronghold called Fort Monckton.

"It's at Gosport, opposite Portsmouth Harbour on the South Coast," she said.

"Gosport!" said Harkness. "Remember that weird line from the Russian Embassy?"

Gosport's a tough nut to crack. But I think you should get him out.

"Second," said Hastings, "they're keeping a little boy there. For tests."

"That's sick," said McCartney.

Again they thought of Itanga.

Live cargo. Male child, 10, low intelligence.

"And third—"

The door was kicked down and a dozen commandos with machine pistols rushed in.

"*Down on the floor! Down on the floor! Hands on heads!*"

De Vries and McCartney put up some resistance and in the scuf-fle Harkness managed to post his mobile phone through the grate of the fireplace. But the only means of escape was via the fourth-floor window with an associated drop, so they were arrested under the Official Secrets Act and detained at Her Majesty's Pleasure.

The funny thing is that this merely got them where they wanted to be. For they were hooded and handcuffed and driven south, to a little known government property overlooking the Solent.

Three miles away in the Russian Embassy another conversation was taking place about Fort Monckton. All interested persons were descending on that place.

89

Somewhere between funeral cortège and royal cavalcade, the three blacked-out saloon cars swept through the streets of Gosport with their police outriders and a helicopter overhead, mandatory for Category A prisoners in transit. Past the ranks of Lego houses built for servicemen; past the military compounds with their long redbrick walls and barracks; past Haslar Marina with its forest of masts and bow-legged leisure sailors swabbing decks. This last glimpse of freedom was denied to Harkness, still hooded and handcuffed in the middle vehicle. The World War Two submarine HMS *Alliance* loomed like a man-made mountain behind the cheery flotilla, and as if to underscore the military tradition of this place a Spitfire on a heritage flight crossed overhead. Harkness instantly recognised the earthy drone of its Rolls-Royce Merlin V12.

"Supermarine Spitfire," he said to no one in particular. "Am I right?"

"Impressive," replied a male voice in the driver's seat.

"The sound of liberty," said Harkness. "If you'll permit a condemned man his moment of indulgence. Plus courage, principle and pluck – everything, in other words, you lot have betrayed."

"Yeah, yeah," said the driver. "And hedgerows and pipe smoke with father in his tweeds, while Hawker Hurricanes paint pretty ribbons of smoke in the skies. A single tear rolls down my cheek."

"I don't think the Poet Laureate will be looking over her shoulder any time soon," said a female voice.

"I can smell the sea," said Harkness. "Gosport?"

"Clever little sod, isn't he?" said the woman.

The cars emerged onto Gosport and Stokes Bay Golf Course, its greens and ponds tame before the churning grey Solent beyond. Fort Monckton itself was encircled by two razor wire fences and a dry moat. The earthworks and masonry rose for thirty feet, laid out in zigzags by their Victorian engineers to create kill-zones should an attack come from inland. A few cannon remained in situ, but the large modern office block on top of the citadel might have been inhabited by a firm of actuaries. Peeping over Fort Monckton's fences were pods of CCTV cameras, like hammer-headed sharks as they swivelled to spy upon the golfers. The razor wire fences protruded thirty feet out into the waves on either side of the stronghold and the Isle of Wight ferry ploughed past a string of World War One forts out to sea. For some reason a local rumour had it that this place processed asylum-seekers, but the golfers knew the signs:

MINISTRY OF DEFENCE

KEEP OUT

This is a prohibited place within the meaning of the Official Secrets Act. Unauthorized persons entering this area may be arrested and prosecuted.

And:

MINISTRY OF DEFENCE

DANGER

Blasting/Live firing is taking place when red flags are flying.

Not a place to trespass in.

The cars slowed at the entrance while steel doors slid open, and they crossed a drawbridge over the moat before driving through the gatehouse into the fortress itself.

Watching the cavalcade enter from a terrace were Andrew Jackson, Ainsley Jones and Woody Donaldson, at Fort Monckton for debriefing.

"Bloody royalty visiting, is it?" Jones' arm was in a sling and he had burns on his face. "Come to offer their sincere gratitude, have they?"

"Can it, Jones," said Donaldson.

They did not comment on the bearded old man and the wearer of red corduroys strolling down the golf course with his umbrella to take the sea air.

A man was sitting at another table on the terrace with his briefcase open, chain-smoking as he consulting a textbook. He was tremulous, sweating and pale.

"Where can I get a cup of coffee in this place, mate?" asked Jones.

"I don't work here," he replied. "I'm a paediatrician, actually. Just on a day-visit."

"I wouldn't want you looking after my children," drawled Donaldson.

In there with the medical textbooks was a small white box labelled *midazolam.*

The doctor snapped the briefcase shut. "It's an all-purpose sedative. There are many medical uses."

"What was all *that* about?" said Jackson when they were inside.

"Midazolam is the drug they use in the US for lethal injections," said Donaldson. "It was in the news recently – a British company got in the shit for supplying it to the State of Arkansas for executions."

Jackson laughed. "Sometimes it's best not to know, boss!"

Shortly afterwards a fourth blacked-out estate car arrived, also swallowed up by the fort. Inside was Johansen, nabbed at last from her Tower Hamlets redoubt.

So now they had the full set.

Harkness was escorted from the car into the open air. Seagulls cawed and he could hear waves, though muted by stonework. He'd last been in Fort Monckton during the eighties for his training and assumed this was the central courtyard. After a bit of beeping and fussing he was led into a building and along a corridor where the carpets smelled rubbery. He was patted down and led into a room; the click and sudden silence told him this was somewhere deeply secure. His handcuffs were removed, then the hood. As he'd suspected, it was an interrogation cell. And sitting opposite him was Aled Wilson.

*

Sonia Dynes, a cleaner, kissed her husband on the cheek and set off for Fort Monckton. She crossed from Portsmouth to Gosport on the ferry, thinking as always that the tower they'd built on her side of the estuary belonged in Dubai, not southern England. On dry land again she set off through the Trinity Green council estate.

Someone grabbed her from behind and she was dragged behind a garage.

Naturally, Dynes' first thought was rape – but the attacker was a woman of her age and build. *She* pulled a knife and briskly cut the cleaner's throat.

Dynes jerked violently, convulsed and expired. *She* stripped the victim to her underwear and put on her clothes – but the day's butchery wasn't done. For now the Russian assassin produced a hacksaw and sawed off Sonia Dynes' right hand at the wrist, the grind of steel on bone filling the small space behind the garage. She used a pair of garden secateurs to snip through the last band of flesh and baby wipes to clean the appendage of excess blood before placing it in an ice box. Her preparations complete, she stepped out from behind the garage and made for the fort.

90

"I knew it," said Harkness. "It was blatantly obvious."

"Well done for giving me the slip in Brazzaville," said Wilson.

"So how many of our problems were caused by you lot?"

"The incident in arrivals. The problems with internal flights. The helicopter company was on-side too, as you rightly suspected. Your vice chancellor didn't come cheap, but he had his price. Unfortunately we reckoned without your sheer, pig-headed determination. Plus the chutzpah of your young Jedi." Wilson sighed. "We were trying to *protect* you, Randolph. We were trying to keep you safe. You've put us in an extremely difficult situation."

"What do you mean by that?"

"Our colleagues across the pond are putting a lot of pressure on our officers to exercise Class Seven powers under the Intelligence Services Act." He would not meet the prisoner's eyes. "At their most extreme."

Harkness knew the clause.

He shall not be so liable if the act is one which is authorised to be done by virtue of an authorisation given by the Secretary of State.

Legalese for a licence to kill.

"Don't look so appalled," said Wilson. "It's not as if you don't have the blood of a few men on your hands."

Harkness looked downward. "That was unintentional. And we were in a war."

"As we are now. And by the way, the Soviets weren't bombing teenage girls at pop concerts."

Harkness appreciated that this was part of the interrogation. They were going in hard and strong, kicking down the front door of his psyche and wrecking the place. His soul had been laid bare during his own Developed Vetting, which was an opportunity for agents to reveal their innermost demons to MI6 and thus protect themselves from blackmail. And Harkness's was the guilt.

For Elizabeth. For the technician accidentally killed when they had blown those radar domes sky-high. And for the driver of the plutonium delivery whose life had been ended by sweet Aibek Abdulov, when he'd panicked aged nineteen.

During the last thirty years these three deaths had intertwined themselves in his subconscious, like snarling Celtic dragons entangled about the hilt of a dagger. Why had he never taken another partner? Some part of him felt he did not *deserve* to be happy.

"I'd rather not get psychological," he said. "If it's all the same to you."

Wilson did not appreciate the quip. "If I were you I'd start being cooperative, because that will be a factor in your favour. As it will in Ross's."

Harkness's kneecap jerked spasmodically beneath the table. McCartney was his salvation.

"For Christ's sake speak plainly," said Harkness. "It's not like these walls have ears. You are saying that if we won't cooperate you'll kill us. Correct?"

Wilson leaned inward and lowered his voice. "Very well, let me be absolutely clear. If you don't tell me everything I ask, you and Ross are to be buried at sea the day after tomorrow. As will Anita Johansen… and that demented MP you've been cavorting with."

"Thank you." Harkness's pupils were pin-pricks of rage, but he seemed strangely comforted by the admission. "But what's the point? You know it all anyway. That Brian Finer was investigating the Neanderthal extinction and stumbled upon their lack of New Brain. That this gave you a gateway into the human psyche that allowed you to manipulate public opinion like nothing else before or since. In what, 1980?"

"'79," said Wilson.

The younger man didn't realise he was being reeled in.

"Evidently you shared it with the Yanks. El Salvador, Panama, the Falklands, Iraqs one and two, Somalia, Libya, the never-ending Afghan nightmare – every military action we've been involved in since, our rulers were having their justifications crafted for them."

Wilson nodded. "And if Finer had come along five years earlier the Americans could have continued in Vietnam."

"Only in 1998 the Russians got wind of it – from Richard Wakeford, who I assume is one of yours."

"Wakeford?" breathed Wilson.

"He's proved a very effective double-agent for them, evaded MI5 all these years. But then he messed with Gloria. Not somebody I'd recommend making an enemy of."

"She's a force of nature," admitted Wilson.

"So they grabbed Finer, the progenitor of it all and the master-craftsman. Which is why with everything going on in the world you're so desperate to have him back. He's in the building right now, isn't he?"

Wilson blanched.

"And since the days of Thatcher and Brezhnev, East and West alike have been petrified of someone else following Finer's line of enquiry, through ancient genocides to New Brain. Because it would lead to your de-fanging. Even Christodoulou's work was – how can I put this? – uncomfortably close."

"Nicely summarised," said Wilson.

"So what could I possibly tell you that you don't already know?"

"We need your source in Whitehall," said Wilson. "How you and Hastings seem to know everything. Give up the source and I will endorse a lifelong detention instead of… that other thing."

"You know as well as I do that Sir Hugh Alexander was thrown over a waterfall the day before yesterday," snapped Harkness.

"I refer to *his* source. There's no way Sir Hugh could have known about the rescue attempt – nor the Christodoulou report or all the rest."

"I don't actually know." Harkness clapped his hands together. "Didn't want to ask. Isn't that what you lot call 'sterile corridors'?"

"We'll see about that," said Wilson. "Section Seven is a rather *permissive* bit of legislation, after all. Crafted with all the guile and ruthlessness of the finest lawyers of the United Kingdom."

Harkness closed his eyes, and in that instant he saw not Elizabeth but Olivié. It was the precise moment he *forgave himself*. He saw that, while things had often turned out badly, he'd always meant the best. And that was the important thing, wasn't it? He was a good man. So he came to another resolution. If he got out of this, he would go back and find her. It would be reckless returning to a place so close to his Russian enemies. But if he had learned one thing from McCartney it was this: just sometimes, reckless is good.

"Penny for your thoughts," said Wilson.

"I'll admit it," said Harkness. "Some bad things happened in Central Asia all those years ago, and I was the catalyst. But at least we were fighting for *democracy*, or so we thought. And you? You're corrupting it. You're thieving the demos of free choice."

A golden thread led from Magna Carta to the Glorious Revolution of 1688, on through the Great Reform Act and universal suffrage to 1940, the Finest Hour. *This* is what Harkness had joined MI6 to protect. Democracy and freedom.

"As a matter of fact, it's never been used for party political advantage," said Wilson. "Only matters of national security. By and large, British Prime Ministers are an honourable breed. Not one has broken the covenant."

"Even if that's true, what if we got a tyrant?"

Wilson made no reply.

"And so we come to the child." Harkness shook his head. "My god, I've seen some wickedness over the last few weeks. But incarcerating a boy for the purpose of psychological experiments? That's Josef Mengele levels."

"We have treated him well," said Wilson.

"What happens when he grows up?"

Something in Wilson's lack of reply disturbed Harkness.

"My god, you're going to get rid of him, aren't you? Now that the heat is on…"

Wilson stood up. "Of course not. That's enough for today, I think."

"Sat down and worked it all out, have you? Thought it would be prudent and clever to eliminate every trace? New Brain decided killing children is a good idea?"

That which makes us human makes us monsters.

"I'm a patriot, Randolph," said Wilson. "Once you were, too."

Harkness was taken to another room, where – to his surprise – McCartney awaited. There were sofas, a hot drinks machine and copies of *Top Gear* magazine and *Country Living* on the coffee table. McCartney had a black eye; his grin was resolute.

"You didn't tell them anything, I hope?" asked Harkness.

"Yup. I told them to fuck right off."

He couldn't help but laugh. "Good lad. They are listening to us now, by the way. That's why we've been put back together. They actually think we'll talk to each other and tell them what they want to know."

"Like we'd be that dumb." McCartney addressed a wall. "Guys, New Brain is fully engaged..."

91

His Lordship Richard Wakeford was one of the more convivial of MI6's far-flung band of associates to occasionally visit the facility, so the guards were unsurprised to see him making conversation with a humble cleaner. On production of passes they were waved straight through the first two sets of steel doors and on to identification checks in the guardhouse. Wakeford placed his hand on a scanner, which read the bone structure within and signalled assent. *She* did likewise, although more alert security guards would have spotted that the right hand looked greyer than the left. Wakeford took a phone call and she fiddled with her shoelaces until a senior manager emerged from within the fort.

"Hello, Rajinder," she said brightly.

"Hello, how are you?" replied the senior manager's Old Brain.

An armed guard watched this exchange. Wakeford's iris was scanned and he stepped through the security gates – but the cleaner's eye was not recognised.

"It's fine," said the guard, overriding the gate to let them in.

Her hand had scanned without a glitch, and she was evidently familiar to Wakeford and Rajinder Singh.

The ruse had been carefully planned. Wakeford had obtained photographs of all permanent staff, which they memorised – and what sort of manager when hailed by a cleaner will confess to not remembering them? In that split second judgement between security and losing face, Singh's decision had been automatic. New Brain was not deployed to check.

Staring out at the raiders from the suite above the gatehouse was Dr Andrew Starling, in attendance for the grand interrogation. Even from behind the Chief of MI6 recognised Wakeford, whose establishment connections the agency had first found a use for in the mid-eighties. Starling frowned. What was *Wakeford* doing here? He phoned security who disclosed that the cleaner's iris scan had malfunctioned; then someone found a speck of blood on the hand-reader.

Wakeford and the assassin were in the west wing when the alarms went off. There were running boots behind them, shouts of, "Stop exactly where you are!"

She and Wakeford spun on the spot and opened fire with silenced Berettas in a single ferocious fusillade until all four guards sprawled dead in the corridor. Then they broke into a run.

*

Donaldson and his men had located a bar in the west wing, decorated with mementoes from various Secret Operations Executive ventures over the years. They were abstemiously drinking coffee when the alarm went off.

"Bloody hell, what now?" said Jones.

A head poked around the door. "You three are the Increment guys, right?"

"That's right," said Donaldson. "What's going on?"

"We're under attack. Don't know if it's terrorists or what."

"Can you arm us?" asked Jackson.

"Obviously I can't just hand over firearms," said the man. "There are procedures. But we've got two guys you could keep an eye on while we're all hands on deck."

Two minutes later the three commandos were peering through a one-way window at Randolph Harkness and Ross McCartney. Both gallery and cell were soundproofed, the gunfire and alarms lost to them. But the voices of the prisoners were in high quality.

"I found something else out," Harkness was saying. "The child. The little boy they've been carrying out their sick experiments on…"

"Oi oi," muttered Jones. "What's this then?"

"They're going to kill him, Ross. They're cutting their losses – rubbing out any trace of what they've been doing here."

Donaldson's eyes widened. "What the hell?"

"Do you get the feeling we've been working for the wrong side, Staff?" said Jackson.

"Midalozam," said Donaldson. "He was a fucking paediatrician, for fuck's sake."

The Welshman stood. "Well, this I will say. I didn't join the forces to stand for the killing of children."

"What shall we do?" asked Jackson.

Captain Donaldson looked suddenly weary, a man tired of death and deadly decisions.

"Staff?"

Donaldson stood up. He sighed. Then he smiled and flexed his knuckles.

"I'm resigning my commission," he said.

*

The cell door opened to reveal three men with a distinctly military bearing.

"Who are you?" said McCartney.

Faint gunshots could be heard.

"What's going on?" shouted Harkness.

"I haven't got the foggiest who you are, but we are getting you out of here," replied Jones. "And we're finding that kid they want to do in and all."

So they followed the sounds of the carnage.

There were four bodies at the end of the corridor and the SBS team snatched up their machine pistols. Then they advanced towards the fighting. Past a gymnasium, a photographic studio; a small museum with obsolete surveillance equipment on display. They rounded the corner as *she* put a bullet in the head of the last of the defenders, who'd made their stand at the laboratories. Wakeford had been shot in the arm and his hair dangled wildly.

There was no ceremony, no flourish, no pithy remark; neither Lord Wakeford nor his assassin had time to turn. It was simply a *stamp–stamp, stamp–stamp*, and they fell. His lordship whimpered as he lay upon the floor; *her* citrine eyes juddered in their sockets. As Jackson and Jones lowered their sights for the *coup de grâce* Harkness recognised the woman from Itanga.

Stamp–stamp.

And that was it.

Donaldson led the way into the laboratory, its floor littered with brightly coloured puzzles and building blocks. The child cowered against a wall.

When Harkness stepped into the room he moaned.

He was transfixed.

The ginger hair and the bulky head; the short but powerful limbs. The eyes – huge and brown and blinking – and the brow-ridge already becoming prominent. Harkness sank to his knees and sighed, for there could be no doubt. He was looking at an infant Neanderthal.

92

Britain and America had been trying to breed one for decades. But with recent advances in genetic technology the task had become child's play, and the political will was there.

1. A DNA sample was extracted from a bone belonging to the first specimen of the species to be discovered, from the Neander Valley in Western Germany.

2. The DNA was cut into random chunks with restriction enzymes, and then sequenced using the Sanger sequencing method.

3. Markov chain analysis was used to put the DNA back together in the correct order.

4. The full genome was compared to that of *Homo sapiens*, looking for Single Nucleotide Polymorphisms.

5. Site directed mutagenesis was used to change the sites where human and Neanderthal DNA differs in a human cell, and the Neanderthal version inserted.

6. That genome was inserted into a human oocyte, which was implanted in a surrogate mother. A European with a larger than average amount of Neanderthal DNA was chosen as the host; prehistoric human-Neanderthal breeding in Eurasia meant the oocyte would be most likely to take.

7. Nature took its course.

All in all, the guilty scientists remarked to one another when the baby was born, it would have been infinitely harder to have gained a mainstream ethics approval than accomplishing the technicalities.

Still on his knees, Harkness opened his arms. The little boy – he guessed five or six years old – took two steps forward. Then certainty formed in those blinking brown eyes, an instinctive trust – Old Brain – and the infant ran to Harkness.

And to his astonishment, he spoke.

A high-pitched voice, just as he'd always hypothesised: "Hello, man. Hello, man."

Harkness wrapped his arms around the child.

"Come on, boyo, we oughtn't to hang around," said Jones.

They fled the laboratory and exited the west wing through a fire escape. Now they were standing on Fort Monckton's private stretch of pebbled beach, wire fences protruding out into the waves on both sides. There was a boathouse.

"Got to be something there with a bit of oomph," shouted Jackson.

They dashed into the long, low building and found three speed-boats pointing out at the Isle of Wight. Jones and Jackson shot the engines of the nearest two while Donaldson retrieved a key from a box on the wall.

"Does anyone know how to pilot one of these things?" shouted Harkness.

"We're the fucking SBS, mate," said Donaldson.

Thirty seconds later they were streaking across the harbour and out to sea. The child shrank into the prow and Harkness held him by the wrist in case he dived from the boat. He took in this new world with eyes built for hunting, those gargantuan orbs filled with bewilderment.

"What now?" McCartney roared into the spray.

"Now?" shouted Harkness. "Now we call my contacts on *The Guardian* and *The Times*. Now we bring down the Prime Minister and the US president and the whole edifice of MI6. Now we lift the blind-fold from 140 million Russians and the Anglo-Saxon world."

"But we still don't have enough evidence, surely?" shouted McCartney.

But Harkness was smiling, and one hand slipped inside his shirt to reappear with a square of black the size of two hotel matchboxes.

"The recorder," breathed McCartney.

"They patted me down but never found it," he said. "Wilson confesses everything, incriminates the Prime Minister and the White House. The facility's on camera, our rescue, the lot. And it's all been beamed to my phone, which is currently down a chimney in Bloomsbury. We've got them, Ross, we've bloody got them. When we put this out there we can change history."

In that moment of euphoria, Harkness made out very clearly the form of Wilson on the beach. Why was he so still? No sooner had Harkness's Old Brain provided the answer – he was taking aim – than Wilson fired. Harkness heard a crack as the sniper's bullet passed his cheek. He wanted to destroy the evidence. But McCartney had seen it too and made an Old Brain decision to dive between the infant and the gunman. He was shot through the jugular notch.

At once Jones took evasive action, zigzagging aggressively as they moved from the gunman's range. The perfect circle at the base of McCartney's neck was mirrored by his mouth. He was breathing through the bullet-hole.

"No," said Harkness. "Please not that."

Then the lifeblood erupted from the wound in a sudden torrential rush. Harkness did his best to staunch the bleeding and cradled McCartney in his lap. But his friend merely stared into the sun.

*

He was thinking of the places they had seen. The savannahs of the Congo, shimmering silver in the night; the Pamirs in all their majesty, capped by snowy white. The wild woods of Eastern Europe, a single wolf fleeing through the mist. And finally the Forest People, with whom this raging soul had briefly felt at peace. McCartney's fingers fluttered as he reached for his collarbone, and when Harkness understood he lifted his friend's hand so that he could touch the Forest one last time.

"Randolph?" His voice was strangely windy.

"What is it?"

"Thank you."

Harkness clasped his hand as the boat bashed and smashed along the surf. Still McCartney stared into the sun as it became fractals and then a blur; finally he could see no more, and he closed his eyes. He had gone to join the Forest.

> *hero*
>> 1. *a person who is admired for their courage, sacrifice or noble qualities.*

93

The next few weeks were among the most dramatic in the history of journalism. First the British government fell, and then the US president; the Russian ruler hung on though badly weakened. But soon the long inexorable ebbing away of his support began, as though a spell had been broken. A brainwashing was washed away.

From a safe-house owned by *The Times*, Harkness oversaw it all. After the initial earth-shattering revelation, the material was open-sourced to every UK national newspaper, the BBC, the Centre for Investigative Journalism, *Le Monde*, *The New York Times*, Global Witness and *The Washington Post*. This was WikiLeaks writ large: there was too much material for one organisation to handle. Thousands of political speeches had to be scoured for appeals to Old Brain, conflicts and political controversies ranging from the inconsequential to the cataclysmic re-examined. Media organisations raced to find psychologists who could test Finer's paradigm, and all of them found it was bulletproof. A world awoke, and Harkness's faith in the goodness of humanity was restored.

The lawyers did good business, too – and not just those who dealt in libel. For several individuals, new consideration had to be given to the charge of war crimes. It was decided that MI6 would not be shut down, as it was needed in the ongoing fight against terrorism – but an inquiry was launched into how transparency could be married to the demands of the Secret World. No such gentle evolution in the US, where the vice president's first act as he stepped into the White House was to close the CIA and temporarily hand espionage duties to the Intelligence Branch of the FBI.

Like the aftershocks of an earthquake, a wave of academic inquiry rippled after the journalistic. Everything had to be reassessed: myth, language, culture and evolution; our place in history, who we are.

Dr Anita Johansen was at the forefront of this wave. Like Harkness, she was now protected by layers of gatekeepers: literary agents and publicists handling the interview bids pouring in from around the world. The advance for her book on the origins of myth would finally be negotiated at £200,000. Harkness had already received an offer five times that, though he spent these weeks in a fog of grief for McCartney.

Mirza was arrested and charged with that most exotic of crimes, treason. His trial would be an amusing side-note to the affair. Jasper, the getaway driver at Fort Monckton, was never seen again. David Motion also got away with it and was able to hoard his taxpayer's gold for his dotage. And Finer disappeared, too. Harkness's best guess was that the latter had been given a new identity and told to enjoy his freedom. After all, his chicanery *no longer worked*.

It is true that many cognitive illusions still fool people even when they have been made aware of them – think of the Müller-Lyer illusion. But all those who'd been inoculated would notice an appeal to Old Brain some of the time, and that could shift opinion by a crucial few points. Moreover, with the press on high alert no politician would dare to resort to it. The final Sapient Paradox: New Brain made us human and New Brain made us beasts. Yet it was New Brain that could, just possibly, lift our species to a higher plane.

Dr Sakiko Tsuda never lived to see the crimes she'd stumbled upon be exposed, but Nowak also took comfort from his wife's legacy. She was a woman who had reshaped the world, even if she never quite found the traces of that first language.

*

After two months, Harkness felt safe enough to return to Bristol. He and Percy were dropped off by taxi at the bottom of Blackboy Hill in Clifton and he turned on to his street. Harkness would replay what happened next countless times, always unsure whether he knew what was going to happen before it actually did.

An odd thing, premonition. Brian Finer would have you believe it's a trick of the subconscious and associative memory. A good example is the firefighter who had the premonition a burning building was about to fall through and evacuated his team moments before the roof collapsed. Finer thought that the subconscious had recognised signals of impending disaster that the conscious mind was unaware of. It was Old Brain. In any case, Harkness had the premonition he would see Olivié Lefebvre before he did.

And there she was.

She ran towards him with that smile he had thought of often, but at the last moment she slowed. They held each other by the elbows for a moment and then, at last, they kissed.

"How did you know where to find me?" he asked.

"A rosarian."

I live in a city called Bristol just off an exceedingly steep street called Blackboy Hill. I also grow roses...

She pointed to his bedraggled garden. "But they have, how I think you might say, 'seen better days'. Shall we go inside?"

They heaved aside the mountain of unopened post that had built up on his doorstep and Percy bounded through each room. Harkness made tea, and then Olivié explained how she had realised that she loved him and had to re-join the world. And when she encountered television and newspapers it was to learn he was famous.

She'd called *The Guardian*, *The Times*, Bristol University, tried everything; but amidst the deluge of enquiries, her communications had not got through to him. They had all put her down as one of the many nutters bombarding Harkness with requests. Neither were his neighbours passing on messages: conspiracy theorists from around the world had descended on their little corner of Clifton. So she had come to Bristol and merely sat on his wall each day until he came home. Harkness made more tea and they sat long into the night, planning their lives together.

Throughout all this, the child was hidden – smuggled to a safe-house in north Wales with Captain Donaldson. Were the truth of what Britain had created to be known, the story would reach still more frenzied proportions. The child would not have a moment of peace from infancy to adulthood; hunter would become the hunted.

Donaldson couldn't raise him, however. He was too much of a free spirit, and intended to start a luxury yacht holiday company in the West Indies. And so it was decided. Once things had calmed down, Harkness would look after him. An adoption, to use a better word.

This was done under the radar: so extraordinary was the case that any dealings with social services would surely leak to the press. But as Harkness predicted, those in the British Security Services who knew of the child breathed not a word of it. Outrage at what they had brought into being would have taken the scandal into another stratosphere. So an unsaid agreement was hit upon by Harkness and the people who had once stalked him. *Let's leave one another alone.* And when it was safe Harkness simply brought the child home to Bristol, where it was assumed by the neighbours there was some genetic condition that meant he was not quite like other children. Which was, of course, exactly the case.

EPILOGUE

Six months later. A late summer's day. Randolph Harkness and Olivié Lefebvre were lying on a rug in a park, watching their son clatter about with that curious loping run Harkness had already come to love. The kid would never get used to Percy, his forefathers vanishing many millennia before the dog's domestication in Siberia. But they would have to muddle through as best they could until the bassett hound died of old age. Harkness, whose character was animated principally by loyalty, had been adamant on this point: the dog stays.

His son's language was one of nouns and verbs, lacking syntax or grammar. But he *was* intelligent, he could work things out; after all, his forebears had fashioned spears. He did indeed lack what you might call a New Brain, but Harkness hoped his son could just about manage in society one day. He could see him becoming a landscape gardener, for – ironic though it was – a child whose ancestors were hunters had a deep fascination with plants (although it was noted at the crèche that he had a voracious appetite for chicken and was none too keen on his vegetables).

All that was if they stayed in the UK. But perhaps the modern world was too mad and complex for this most special of children. If they returned to the Wakhan Valley then Harkness could walk and write and have the semblance of a normal life again, and Olivié would be at home. He had only to figure out how to get the youngster there without a passport. But nothing really *c'est impossible*, as Harkness had once told a friend. After all, look what had happened to him. He had something he thought he would never possess. A family.

Summer had come late in his life, Harkness reflected as he lay in that park, fingers intertwined with Olivié's and blades of grass twitching in the heat. But when it had come at last, the sun had shone more brightly than he could have dared to imagine. They let Ross play for a while longer and then took him home, walking hand in hand with the last Neanderthal.

AUTHOR'S NOTE AND ACKNOWLEDGEMENTS

It is another human paradox that the study of human origins – which encompasses an expanse of time so vast as to defy proper comprehension – is one of the fastest moving fields of science. During the writing of this book, new genetic evidence pushed the extinction of the Neanderthals back numerous millennia, and the oldest anatomically modern *Homo sapiens* skeleton yet found – he lived in about 300,000 BC– was discovered in Morocco. Not only did this set the date of our species' emergence back by a whopping 100,000 years, it also rewrote the very story of human evolution. Rather than beginning in the relatively small 'cradle' of Kenya and Ethiopia, a 'pan-African' evolution is now favoured; until recent decades, most anthropologists believed we evolved in Asia. All this means that any fiction about human origins is necessarily based on a mere snapshot of the research as it stands at any particular time. The facts as related in this book will therefore almost certainly go out of date as new discoveries are made; however, I have endeavoured to imbue the text with the best available knowledge at the time of writing.

Readers of psychology will have recognised that Old Brain and New Brain are based on the System I/System II paradigm of the leading psychologist Daniel Kahneman, whose work was a major inspiration for this book. Finer's puzzles are based on Kahneman's, as are the following turns of phrase, which I could not improve on (unsurprisingly, as his is a Nobel Prize winning brain): *'Blind to the obvious and blind to our own blindness.' 'Cognitive illusions.' 'Machine for jumping to conclusions.' 'Stranger within you.' 'Mere exposure effect.' 'Answering the wrong question.' 'Bad is stronger than good.'* (The character of Finer is of course in no way based on Mr Kahneman, whom I have not had the privilege of meeting, and any misunderstandings of his work are my own failings.)

As previously stated, all scientific studies and Ice Age sculptures I refer to are genuine, though I have taken liberties with the rock carvings atop Saimaluu Tash. Many of the skeletons referred to are real, too, and it should be obvious which; however, if Google cannot satisfy any curiosity, feel free to tweet me (@eddavey1) with your queries. *Tik* was indeed inferred as being present in the human mother tongue by the great historical linguist and classifier of African languages, Joseph Greenberg (whose theories, if rather beautiful, remain highly controversial). Patin's research on the precipitous drop in numbers of prehistoric Forest People can be found as an open access study online. 'The Sapient Paradox' was a term coined by the archaeologist Colin Renfrew to describe the oddity of the fact that our species appears to have achieved modern intelligence many, many millennia before the first vestiges of agriculture or civilisation appear.

Further thanks are due. Professor Fiona Jordan, an anthropologist and expert in cultural phylogenetics at the University of Bristol, kindly showed me around 'Harkness's' home department. Joseph Fisher, an expert in computer security, advised me on the hacking chapters. Ian Mann, an author and leading authority on social engineering, once again shared his expertise willingly. I found the novel *Fieldwork* by Mischa Berlinski very instructive on the realities of anthropological work in the field. Colin Turnbull's *The Forest People* was a great help in furnishing the details of Ba Aka culture that I was unable to research on my own trip to Congo-Brazzaville. 'Completely dead' and 'Dead forever' were his. When it came to undocumented Forest People languages, I had to use neighbouring tongues as the source material and get creative. Other writers whose work I found extremely useful include Chris Stringer of the Natural History Museum, Ian Tattersall, Yuval Noah Harari, Francis Fukuyama, Jared Diamond and of course, Charles Darwin, who was quite astonishingly prescient in so many of his speculations about human origins. Again, any errors are my own. A spell working for the Royal National Institute of Blind People some years ago gave me a small insight into what it must be like to lose one's sight as an adult. Belated thanks are also due to the novelist Robert Dinsdale, whose terrific advice on character arcs I have called upon repeatedly through three thrillers now in print.

I am very grateful to my travel buddies Josh Bramall, Joss Plant, Nicky Owen, Jack Davey and Jonathan Davey for accompanying me into the lands described in this book. I cannot in all good conscience recommend Congo-Brazzaville as a tourist destination, although it was a beautiful country whose population were warm and welcoming. We also drove more than 1,400 miles through Central Asia so that you don't have to – although both Kyrgyzstan and Tajikistan were both fantastic, if occasionally trying, destinations. Thanks to the Ministry of Defence for not having me arrested while I was snooping about Fort Monckton. Holyhead Marine is of course a perfectly respectable company which was included simply to add a dash of veracity, in the same way as I have Harkness driving a BMW or Hastings frequenting Gordon's Wine Bar.

This was a particularly tough project, and I'm extremely grateful for the support of my indomitable agent Robin Wade and my parents Robin and Faith Davey, who are excellent proofreaders! Henry Freeman provided valuable feedback on the manuscript, too, while Tim Howe and Tom Stirzaker both gave plentiful advice on science and biology. Thanks to Jim for injecting some of your wit and wisdom into the character of Ross McCartney. Well, your wit, anyway. Benjamin Rhys Davies, another old friend who contributed his knowledge of party politics and Parliament to the novel, tragically died during the writing of the book. He was a wit beyond compare with a razor intellect (and a controversialist to make Gloria Hastings blush). You will be missed, mate.

Gesche Ipsen's contribution to the manuscript while she was my editor at Duckworth cannot be overstated, and Deborah Blake has been a brilliant copy-editor of all three of my novels. I'm grateful as well to Matt Casbourne, who has guided this fine old publishing house with an expert hand on the tiller. Fellow Duckworth author Tarn Richardson has been a great sounding board, too. But most of all, thank you to my wife, Anna. You are all a bloke could possibly ask for and I couldn't have done it without you.

ABOUT THE AUTHOR

E.M. Davey is a thirty-six-year-old journalist specialising in undercover investigative journalism. During eight years at the BBC he worked on investigations for programmes such as *Newsnight* and the national *News at Six* and went undercover for *Panorama*. He is currently an investigative reporter at Global Witness, working to expose corruption, environmental crime and human rights abuses around the world. When not working he enjoys travel to far-flung and occasionally dangerous spots to inspire his fiction, and just for the heck of it. He has visited more than fifty countries; to research this book he journeyed through the Congo and along Tajikistan's porous border with Afghanistan. History has been his lifelong passion. This is his third thriller.

@EdDavey1
www.emdavey.com